Praise for *Th*

"Outlandish and highly entertain   *nan*

"*The Last Jew Standing* is a terrific detective story, smart, dark, and acidly funny. A wonderful read!"   —Kevin Baker, author of *Striver's Row*

"In his trademark neat, almost noir prose, Simon perfectly conveys the dilemmas facing a perpetual outsider determined to do the right thing. His hero is subtly drawn, his problems plausible and his colleagues are smart renderings. A graceful thriller."   —*Kirkus Reviews*

"*The Last Jew Standing* is a great rollicking yarn about good guys and bad guys in many splendid shades of gray. It is also a brilliant exploration of the complex ties of family and the price we pay for love, and for loyalty. This is a crime story that transcends any bounds of genre. Michael Simon is a literary force to be reckoned with."

—Thomas Kelly, author of *Empire Rising*

"Fast, furious and anarchic!"   —*Booklist*

"*The Last Jew Standing* is one of the few crime novels of the past decade by a relatively new writer that I've felt is a 'must-read.' Gritty, dirty and violent, *The Last Jew Standing* brings to life characters I don't think I will ever forget. Some are heartbreakingly sad. Some are shockingly selfish and violent and others wander through life improvising with the creativity of the desperate. Michael Simon is a masterful teller of tales that made me care. I've already purchased his other two books and I will consume them immediately and hope for more. Don't miss this author who may remind you of James Ellroy or George V. Higgins or even Don Winslow, but is uniquely his very arrestable self." —Stuart M. Kaminsky

A PENGUIN MYSTERY

THE LAST JEW STANDING

Michael Simon, former actor, playwright, and Texas probation officer, is the author of the Dan Reles thrillers *Dirty Sally*, *Body Scissors*, and *Little Faith*. He has taught at Brooklyn College and New York University. He lives in New York City.

Michael Simon

The Last Jew Standing

A Novel

PENGUIN BOOKS

PENGUIN BOOKS

Published by the Penguin Group

Penguin Group (USA) Inc., 375 Hudson Street, New York, New York 10014, U.S.A.

Penguin Group (Canada), 90 Eglinton Avenue East, Suite 700, Toronto,
Ontario, Canada M4P 2Y3 (a division of Pearson Penguin Canada Inc.)

Penguin Books Ltd, 80 Strand, London WC2R 0RL, England

Penguin Ireland, 25 St Stephen's Green, Dublin 2, Ireland (a division of Penguin Books Ltd)

Penguin Group (Australia), 250 Camberwell Road, Camberwell,
Victoria 3124, Australia (a division of Pearson Australia Group Pty Ltd)

Penguin Books India Pvt Ltd, 11 Community Centre, Panchsheel Park, New Delhi – 110 017, India

Penguin Group (NZ), 67 Apollo Drive, Rosedale, North Shore 0632,
New Zealand (a division of Pearson New Zealand Ltd)

Penguin Books (South Africa) (Pty) Ltd, 24 Sturdee Avenue,
Rosebank, Johannesburg 2196, South Africa

Penguin Books Ltd, Registered Offices:
80 Strand, London WC2R 0RL, England

First published in the United States of America by Viking Penguin,
a member of Penguin Group (USA) Inc. 2007
Published in Penguin Books 2008

10   9   8   7   6   5   4   3   2   1

PUBLISHER'S NOTE
This is a work of fiction. Names, characters, places, and incidents are either the product
of the author's imagination or are used fictitiously, and any resemblance to actual persons,
living or dead, business establishments, events, or locales is entirely coincidental.

Excerpt from *Hand Book of the New York State Reformatory at Elmira* courtesy
of the New York State Department of Correctional Services.

THE LIBRARY OF CONGRESS HAS CATALOGED THE HARDCOVER EDITION AS FOLLOWS:
Simon, Michael, 1963–
The last Jew standing : a novel / Michael Simon.
p. cm.
ISBN 978-0-670-06324-6 (hc.)
ISBN 978-0-14-311431-4 (pbk.)
1. Reles, Dan (Fictitious character)—Fiction.   2. Police—Texas—Austin—Fiction.
3. Austin (Tex.) —Fiction.   4. Fathers and sons—Fiction.   5. Jewish men—Fiction.   6. Jewish fiction.
I. Title.
PS3619.I5625L37 2007
813'.6—dc22 2007006662

Printed in the United States of America
Set in Minion   Designed by Francesca Belanger

To Calvin Chin

It was considered that schooling in letters was an essential factor in reformative work in that it aided in preventing the inmates from degenerating in mental power, during confinement; and aside from this, was of great value because it aided them to take a more elevated station in life, upon their release.

—Fred C. Allen, *Hand Book of the New York State Reformatory at Elmira*, 1916

The Last Jew Standing

Pax Berelman met with a regrettable incident involving a hotel room in Elmira, New York, a piece of exhaust pipe and his trachea. Whether it was an accident or a suicide or a simple misassessment of the laws of biology is a total crapshoot, owing to Pax's rumored general dizziness and his habits regarding hallucinogenic drugs. He was known to be a garbagehead, that is, someone who will get high using anything he can get his hands on—grass, meth, cleaning products—but while his chemical habits may have contributed indirectly to his early death, they had little to do with the exhaust pipe itself. Investigators at the site considered but dismissed theories that he may have been employing said pipe to create a more direct route for intoxicants to travel to his stomach or lungs. Moreover, his drug use proved unrelated to the loss of his vehicle, a jet-black Buick LeSabre with racing trim, to the hands of a driver not known to him, barreling down Highway 15 in a southerly direction toward the Pennsylvania border. The loss of the vehicle in question occurred several days subsequent to Pax's demise and was therefore unlikely to create the heartbreak which might cause him to fall or thrust himself upon the rusty eighteen-inch fragment of exhaust pipe, now lodged longitudinally in his gullet.

What makes this a subject of further inquiry is how Pax's unfortunate accident resulted in a chain of occurrences leading to me, four days later and two thousand miles away, pinned in the front seat of my cool blue Chevy Caprice, which faced north on the six-lane Congress Avenue Bridge in Austin, Texas, after midnight as a big black Lincoln rammed into its driver's-side door. The blow thrust my Caprice sideways and tore its tires as my vehicle skidded on its rims, up the curb and onto the walkway, while Mora, who had been standing by the passenger door, ran for cover. As I tried to break loose, the Lincoln backed up in a screeching curve across the six lanes, pulled forward and then backed up hard, again pummeling my driver's side. It crushed the door inward as far as the steering wheel and rammed my Chevy against the guardrail, barricading the passenger door shut and me inside. I was struggling to roll down the passenger window and jump when the Lincoln burned rubber and rolled ass-first, hitting the Chevy a third time, now demolishing the driver's side and pushing it up into the air so the two-foot guardrail, instead of protecting me from a fall, served as the fulcrum I'd be tipped over when the Lincoln made the inevitable final strike and knocked me over the rail, trapped between the battered doors, toppling into the cold, dark water below.

One could argue that this development was only part of the inevitable cascade of events set off days earlier by Pax Berelman's untimely death, or even decades earlier with my family's first involvement in certain circles. But considering the issues at hand, the story really began when it walked in on my otherwise-manageable life just two nights before.

The first thump jarred me from the most peaceful sleep I'd had in months. The second made me open my eyes, blink, scan the unfamiliar room in the light from the clock radio and zero in on the bedroom door. I pinned the third thump as the sound of Josh's small hand. The red digits on the clock told me it wasn't 11:30 P.M. yet, on our first night in the new house. We'd been asleep less than an hour.

Rachel groaned, "Oh, God."

"I'll get it."

"Good luck."

I slipped my shorts on and opened the door. Josh stood on the carpet in his dinosaur pajamas, rubbing his nose and eyes. "Mommy?" Standing just over three and a half feet, Josh bore the same brown hair his mother did (a shade or two lighter than mine), to go with his mother's low forehead and dark blue eyes, turned up slightly at the outer corners. His nose hadn't yet developed in bulk but measured Mediterranean length, just what my nose looked like before puberty and multiple breaks gave it its "character." Josh's prominent proboscis seemed to be a dominant trait, inherited from his one Jewish grandparent.

I closed the door behind me. "She's asleep. What's up?"

I'd told him he could call me Dad, or just Dan. So far, he hadn't used either.

"I want Mommy," he said.

"You'll outgrow it."

The door opened on Rachel in a black silk robe which, like Rachel, had seen better days. "It's okay," she said without commitment, and reached down to hoist him up with a groan. As he clamped his limbs around her, she managed to pull a Bic lighter and a pack of Marlboro Light 100s from her robe's pocket and light one, completing the maneuver one-handed before she'd taken three full steps toward the living room, all the while dodging the cardboard boxes positioned around the floor.

"Ow! God damn it!" she yelled. She untangled his hand from the hair at the nape of her neck.

"I'm sorry, Mommy. I'm sorry, Mommy."

"It's okay," she said, eyes on me and trying to reverse the sudden Jekyll-and-Hyde change, the type I'd asked her to avoid in front of Josh. "It's okay. It's Mommy's fault."

Josh had turned four in August, and in spite of the recent development of a regular income, a full refrigerator and a house to live in, he hadn't loosed his grip on his mother any. If anything he tightened it in the face of a new threat, another man. That the man was his father, so people said, was of no interest to Josh.

Rachel had vanished from my life almost five years before, while she was pregnant with Josh. Their life without me involved a series of unsuccessful jobs and living conditions that worsened from apartments to furnished rooms to crack hotels as her savings dwindled. More often than not, the Rachel that Josh saw was drunk or passed out. For him there were nights alone in soiled diapers, while Rachel was out drinking or unconscious at his side, oblivious to his cries. Once, after she brought the boy back to Austin, I found him screwing the cap onto her wine bottle and putting it in the fridge. Once I yelled "NO!" as he reached for the flame on the stove. He shrieked and covered his head, anticipating a blow.

Rachel had returned to me, drunk, when Josh was three and a half, with the idea of dumping him on my doorstep and going off on her own to drink herself to death in peace. But then she told me her deepest, darkest secret, the worst thing she ever did. When she found out that I loved her anyway, she decided to stay. She remained with me for the following eight months. On the couch.

Josh understood that she'd dumped him, and he didn't take it well. When she came back, he resolved never to let her go.

Meanwhile I got promoted to lieutenant, which let me delegate authority, stay off the street and come home at five, a situation unprecedented in my lifetime on the Austin Police Department. I'd never wanted to be a cop, never wanted to be on Homicide. Now they'd put me in charge. But I knew that my work made Rachel nervous. I cut a deal with her: if there's danger, a bad situation, a standoff, I send someone else. I have a family now.

I even offered to retire. If she said the word I'd hand in my badge, but she had to say the word. At eighteen years of service, I could leave with a chunk of my pension, though it would mean a financial setback. Rachel wasn't bringing anything in, and I sensed she didn't want us to lose the income.

She resolved to keep a lid on her drinking, this resolution meeting with periodic and partial success. "I'm not like I was," she said once. "I haven't touched cocaine this whole time." She meant since she started drinking again. She might have been telling the truth. On the other hand, she had a tendency to wake up and not remember what she'd done the night before. Or, for all I knew, who she'd done it with.

Rachel might stick to wine in the house, only two glasses in an evening, but I could tell it hurt. She was way past the point where a glass or two of chardonnay would take the edge off. One Friday she greeted me at home with the announcement that she was "going off."

"What do you mean?"

"I need a few days to myself." She had her coat on already. I didn't see an overnight bag.

She added, "I need money." I stared, until she said, "Now."

The once-turned-up corners of Rachel's big blue eyes had sagged under the weight of childbirth and drinking. In spite of the puffiness, the muscles in her face grew taut, like she couldn't quite breathe. She needed air fast.

I gave her two hundred I kept in my sock drawer. She drove off in the used Subaru wagon I'd bought her.

I spent that weekend distracting Josh as best I could, promising him she'd come home soon, she was only going away on a break.

"Why?".

Good question, kid. And why did I give her the two hundred? Because she would have gone anyway. If I *let* her go, if I gave her expense money, she would come back. I hoped.

She was gone until Monday afternoon. When she made her way through the front door, I let Josh hug her once. Then I suggested he let Mommy take care of herself. She spent two hours in the bathroom and a day in bed. I never asked where she'd been.

This became her pattern every month or so. She'd be gone for days at a stretch. Eventually I learned to see the warning signs: agitation, short temper. The sudden personality changes that made Josh, and now me, increasingly nervous. After a while she'd come back "sick," lie in bed, apologize at length and remind us why we loved her. She'd tell Josh stories and sing to him. She'd take us out to the park or to the movies. She'd clean the house, make elaborate dinners and aerobicize like a fiend "to sweat out the toxins." This last item improved her mood, briefly. I couldn't deny that it had a positive effect on her appearance. What had been sagging was now rising and growing firm again, including her cheeks. Her high, wide-set cheekbones emerged. Her lips looked full again, instead of just chapped and withered. She brushed out her chestnut brown hair. She stood taller, slouched less. She began to look the way she did before, like a movie star, if a weary one. I felt bad for appreciating the change.

What Josh couldn't see was the other Rachel, the one I met twelve years before, when she was twenty-five and tall and graceful, with long, smooth legs and full, round breasts and thick hair combed back from her tanned face. Beautiful like a model. Strong, dynamic. She worked as a real-estate broker, making money in a depressed market. Stepping out of her independence and her feminism for five minutes now and again to serve dinner to her husband, Joey, and his partner, me, because she thought playing house was funny. Flirting with me in plain view of her husband in the months before his death, forbidden love with Oedipal undertones. He was my mentor, after all, my father figure, so what did that make her? My heart did the samba whenever she looked at me. I thought she was playing games. Then I found out she wasn't.

After the smoke cleared from Joey's death, I realized I had a chance with her. It was passion that brought us together. She touched my hand and I felt it in my toes. We had a good time together, a historical moment but a brief one.

It was my fault that she started drinking again. She'd kept a lid on it for ten years by then. She had a good pattern going, working hard, exercising and staying busy. And I screwed that up, with the crazy life I brought her into, the dangers and the threats I couldn't keep away from our home.

Suppose you were in love. And the person you loved was beautiful and brilliant. She had a fire in her heart, a passion for living—you could feel it when you were near her. Then suppose she was in a car accident and it screwed up her body and her outlook. It even seemed to put out her fire. You wouldn't just leave her by the side of the road, would you? Especially if, when the car accident happened, you were the one driving.

I was pretty sure she loved me. She'd put up with a lot from me in the past. I'd tough it out for her.

The new house where Rachel now consoled Josh was the first home I'd ever owned. I made a good salary and had plenty in the bank I'd stashed away during my single years. I was a good bet for a mortgage. Because of her real-estate background, Rachel knew just what to put on the forms. On paper we looked like Ward and June Cleaver, less a marriage license and a roll of foreskin. As the movers hauled in the furniture, mixing our musty, dusty cardboard-box smell with the chemical new-carpet smell, I noticed Rachel take her one suitcase into the master bedroom and leave it there, a welcome development after her chaste months on the sofa. I didn't say anything then, or later when she unpacked her clothes into the dresser, or later still when she killed the light and slipped into my bed for the first time in nearly five years, as if she'd done the same thing every night for the last decade. She slid close, and I put my arms around her. Then she kissed me. Then she kissed me like she meant it.

We were in our first real clinch when it crossed my mind that she was doing this out of gratitude, or worse, obligation.

"You don't have to," I said.

"Shh."

It was one beautiful dream later that Josh slapped the bedroom door and woke us up.

Now she hauled Josh's forty pounds all around the dark house, weaving between boxes and flipping lights on as she went. "No monsters," she said. "Nothing." I followed her through the hall, the living room, the dining room, the kitchen. She turned, and we locked eyes. I'd known her first as a beautiful, young, sober career woman. Now she was a drinking mother, thrust into middle age and domesticity. Maybe she was embarrassed. But we understood each other.

Something scampered across the roof. Josh gasped.

"Shh. Shhh," she said. "It's only a squirrel." She smoked and hummed a tune in a minor key. It sounded like a gloomy lullaby, until I started to recognize it as "My Funny Valentine." I knew a little about Rachel's childhood, enough to make me wonder if she'd ever heard an actual lullaby. As a cop I spent a generation working on the front lines of domestic violence—battery, murder and rape—and if there were worse parents than Rachel's, I hadn't met them yet. Rachel's skills as a mother weren't much, but she put her own mother to shame. Soon she started making up a song.

> "Joshuaaaa . . . and Mommy. And Daddy.
> In a big new house.
> Joshuaaaa and Daddy. And Mommy.
> Love to whine and gr . . ."

She shifted to just humming.

Rachel could boast French parentage. I imagined her folks as a beautiful young couple in a 1960s French film, or a black-and-white print of a man and woman kissing on a Paris street. Rachel had no such romantic notions about them. Her father was an émigré, a professor, and pathologically charismatic. He bore the surname Gagnon, which Rachel dropped as soon as she could, taking her mother's maiden name, Renier, pronounced "Ruh-NEER" in central Texas. Her last name became Velez when she married Joey in her early twenties, then Renier again when his untimely demise preempted their divorce. Joey was my mentor on Homicide. A legend. Everyone who'd worked in the department in the Joey days still addressed Rachel as "Mrs. Velez," even when she answered the phone in the house she shared with me. *It's Dispatch, Mrs. V. Is Lieutenant Reles at home?* (Reles, rhymes with "trellis.") Mrs. V, widow of a hero cop, a martyr, his crimes and excesses washed away in death. That she was sleeping with Joey's protégé once played in HQ gossip like a soap opera; time fatigued the story into the ordinary, a flaw in the wallpaper. That Rachel and I had a son together was starting to put a dent in her status as Joey's widow, and that seven years had passed since 1988 when he died meant there were more people in HQ every day who didn't know me as Joey's pupil, Rachel as his wife. The scandal became a footnote, and Joey's identity shrank to a photo on the lobby wall.

"Why you sleep in there?" Josh asked, fatigue allowing for lapses in his grammar.

She took a drag on her Marlboro. "That's what mommies and daddies do," she said, then let out smoke. "They sleep in the big bed, in their own room."

"Why?"

Silence. Then, "Because they smell funny and it keeps children awake."

Josh considered that carefully and didn't argue.

We'd been in the new place less than eight hours and Rachel had already fought with a neighbor. He stood his stereo speakers in his windows and broadcast Christmas carols as an unsolicited gift to the neighborhood. She pounded on his door and told him that she was Jewish (a lie) and that she found the music personally offensive. But in the interest of healthy relations "between our people and yours," she asked if he wanted to make a donation to the Jewish Defense League.

"We need guns and ammunition to protect our homes," she claimed.

"In . . ." He hesitated. "In Israel?"

"Oh, no. Here in Texas!"

He didn't donate any money, but he killed the music, closed the windows, locked them and pulled the curtains.

It was December of 1995. Chip giant Intel was dwarfing Austin's Motorola and Advanced Micro Devices. American troops had landed on the ground in Bosnia for some very good reason or other. They were digging in to spend Christmas there. And the president reached toward the last year of his first term, when reelection becomes the sole motivator.

I wandered into a room in the back of the house that seemed like a den, now a doorless repository for boxes and unplaced furniture. Out the window, between the two houses behind us and across the street, there stood another house, lit up like a movie marquee. Christmas lights ran along the gutters, framed the windows and coiled around the tree in the front yard, next to the sled shackled to four full-size reindeer and weighed down by the fat man himself. Red plastic script on the roof read SEASON'S GREET-INGS. Electric candles burned in each window.

"Guys?"

Rachel, still holding Josh, followed my voice into the den. We stood silent by the window.

Josh gaped at the spectacle of the glowing house. Occasionally, in panic states like this, he could get distracted, his attention drawn by a balloon or a puppy or some Christmas lights, and the constant threat of his mother's departure would slip his mind. Then he'd settle in and remember, his face reverting to its standard fear and remorse. Fear had become his most constant companion, more constant than his mother ever was. Fear of her mood swings, of her disappearances, of the monsters that would come and get him in her absence. I wanted to tell him it would go away. Or that you should only be afraid of real things, like getting fired or running out of money or people shooting at you. But in truth I wasn't afraid of any of those things, not at that minute, and neither was he. What scared him was that his mother had tried to leave him once, and she could leave again.

For all Josh's tears and night terrors, the sight of him always filled me with hope. I'd watched him grow, maybe just an inch or two over the eight months since we met. His face had slimmed and taken shape. He'd become less of a baby and more of a child. And I held firmly to the belief that he didn't have to spend the rest of his life the way he was now. I'd also lived my childhood years in misery, from age ten on up. I spent my teens and beyond wondering what I'd done to make my mother leave me, what was so wrong with me that she couldn't stay, couldn't even call. I wanted a different life for Josh.

I knew one thing for sure: we were better off together, the three of us, than we were apart. Rachel and Josh needed someone to look out for them. And while I'd managed to go to work and pay the bills when I was single, I needed someone to care whether I came home or not. I decided right then, standing with them in a den we'd never use, staring at someone else's happy home, that I'd *make* our home stable and I'd make it happy, if I needed to do it by force.

I just couldn't remember what a happy home felt like.

"We should spruce this place up," I said. "Lights, trees, the works." Josh brightened at the idea. "Get a nice big Christmas tree. Spray that snow stuff on the windows."

"I hate that shit," Rachel said with venom. Josh seemed to wilt. "My parents used to do that. Making everything look good and acting happy for the guests."

"We won't have any guests," I said. "And we can be as miserable as we want."

We let the idea hang in the air. Personally I hated Christmas and Hanukkah both. Two cultures agreeing to spend money they couldn't spare on crap nobody needed. But we were entitled. I had a job, a good income, a nice house, a wife—sort of—and a kid. Soon we'd have toys on the floor, food in the fridge, a calendar in the kitchen with all our family activities. A real home, like none of us ever had before. If only I could keep things on an even keel.

And it was just then that Josh let out a rising, whooping scream as a ghostly white figure appeared in the window before us.

Rachel took two leaping strides backward. I said, "Wait a minute," and flung the window open, letting in a rush of cold air as I zeroed in on the small, white-haired man standing in the darkness, backlit by a thousand Christmas lights. His head was shorter than mine from crown to chin, almost abbreviated, like the head of a jockey. His Roman nose was distorted by one too many punches, never quite set right, and a faded scar ran across it, making him an object of possible terror to children. His face showed disappointment, maybe pity. I remembered looking up at the same expression from where I lay on the canvas of a boxing ring when I was eleven. I had to blink.

It had been twenty years since I'd set eyes on him, nearly fifteen since his last postcard. Time had changed him into a small old man. But here he was popping up from my memory to real life. And no more or less a stranger than he ever was.

"I scared him," the old man said. The *r* in "scared" was absent.

I said, "Josh, there's nothing to be afraid of," but I wasn't quite sure. "This is your grandfather."

My father measured five foot six during his brief boxing career, half a foot shorter than me, but he seemed smaller now as he walked stiff-kneed through the carpeted house like he was casing it for a robbery. I followed him just as a precaution.

"Nice, nice," he said, stepping into each room and pacing its perimeter. "What's this, an extra bedroom?"

I stood in the archway, trapping him. "It's a den," I said. "It's for *work*." My father's career arc historically involved doing a variety of tasks for cash, but little that the average shopkeeper or laborer would describe as "work." Some of these tasks made use of his skills as a boxer, but in an unfair playing field (two against one, four against one). A few jobs involved taking some poor slob for a drive, one he wouldn't return from. As a kid I resented not being able to answer the question "What does your father do?" I'd respond with painful silence, until the teacher or the friend's parent who asked it dropped the subject and never brought it up—or looked at me—again. There wasn't even a fake answer for that question, a feasible lie or euphemism like "He freelances" or "He's in consulting."

In grammar school I had to write an essay about what my father did. The kids in my neighborhood weren't writing about fathers who were doctors or professors or bank managers. Their fathers were mechanics, janitors and short-order cooks. Their mothers were waitresses and maids, jobs that probably gave the kids great shame to write about. But they seemed like good jobs to me, legitimate and respectable. My father worked at a gym, drove a little and visited shopkeepers on business I was not quite too young to understand. And the week of the writing assignment, he was jailed on a weapons charge. I wrote that he drove a truck.

Standing in the den, Pop avoided my eyes until the limited options led him to stare out the back window we'd seen him through just earlier. Twenty years and we still didn't have anything to say to each other.

"How'd you find me?" I asked.

A silence. Then, out of nowhere, "Who was that kid you fought in the ring the first time?"

"What? What are you talking about?"

"You know. The one who flattened you."

"What . . . Why?"

"No reason."

Some months after my mother left, I turned eleven. For lack of another idea of what to do with me, Pop dragged me along to the Mafia-owned gym where he spent his days and many of his nights. One day he got the idea of putting me in the ring with a larger kid, a blubbery, ass-faced monster who flattened my nose with his first punch, resulting in my nose's first break and my landing on the canvas and staring up at Pop, his own mangled face tinged with shame and disgust. I became a better boxer in the following months and years, with no help from my father.

"Ferber," I said, seeing his bulbous cheeks as if they were right there in front of me. "His name was Ferber."

"You sure?"

Like the boxers of his generation, Pop had no notion of taking a broken nose to a doctor. Some gym character they called "Doc" set mine with his hands, and he set it wrong. I would forever look like a battered boxer. "Yes," I said. "I remember. Why?"

He only shrugged.

"Where ya been?" I asked.

"What do you mean?"

"The last postcard I got from you was, what, 1981? Almost fifteen years. Where ya been? Prison?"

He dropped his jaw as far as it would go. He was trying to look offended. He said, "I am . . . shocked—"

I cut him off. "Oh, Christ, you were in prison."

I headed into the kitchen. Josh was sitting at the table watching Rachel at the stove as she stirred oatmeal and sipped wine. The midnight oatmeal was something she did once in a while to get him back to sleep. I was grateful she didn't give him wine. I walked over to Josh and spoke softly to him. "That's Grandpa," I said. "You dry?" I checked his overnights.

Josh waved his hands. "Shh. Shhh!" I looked up and saw Pop in the archway, squinting at Josh.

"He's still in diapers?"

Josh blushed and hid his face in his hands.

"Only at night," I said. "How about you?"

Rachel sipped and stirred. She caught Pop's eye, which would have been a fine time for one of them to say something, or for me to tell them a little about each other.

Rachel, this is my father, Ben Reles. He met my slumming mother in Elmira, and by the time she realized how low he ranked in the mob, she was already married to him and pregnant. He treated me like an intruder in his home, my mother's new love. She babied me until he went off to prison when I was eight, to do a jolt for one of the big boys, and she kept babying me for those two more years. The day of his release, she called a cab, kissed me goodbye, and disappeared from my life. He came home from the Joint to find his wife gone and his strange kid still there. He raised me, but we didn't know or like each other very well.

Pop, this is Rachel. She used to be married to my best friend, but he croaked. We shacked up, things went bad, really bad, and she took off without telling me she was pregnant. She's been back for a while with our son, who doesn't really know me. Sound familiar? Oh, and she can drink either of us under the table, God bless her!

Pop grinned at Rachel. "You didn't offer me a drink."

"Are we having a party?" she said.

"Why not?"

She didn't return his good spirit and she didn't get him a glass. For a first meeting between my wife and my father, it wasn't a hit. But, as it turned out, we had bigger problems.

Pop looked to me in appeal, and whatever he saw caused him to twist his mouth and head out of the kitchen. Rachel dumped Josh's oatmeal into a bowl and served it to him, joining him at the table with her glass. It was nurturing, Rachel style. I wanted to kiss her but I wasn't sure it would be welcome.

I found Pop in the den. In spite of his stiff movements, Pop still struck me as fast, wiry and athletic, like the scrappy little boxer he once was. But his boxer's stoop had continued curving and I was sure he'd lost at least two inches in height. He seemed to be constantly testing his reflexes. His eyes darted from one window to the other to the ceiling, then back to the door where I stood.

"Went by your old place," Pop said. "You know you're in the phone book?"

"I am? Fuck." Then I said, "So why didn't you call first? You know, instead of showing up like a ghost and scaring the shit out of my son."

He reached into an open box and plucked out a picture frame. It held my mother's glamour shot, one she had taken in the early fifties, not long before they met. Her hair was bundled up on top of her head, her eyebrows tweezed to delicate arcs, and she flashed a warm, knowing smile into the camera, less a come-on than an inside joke, something just between her and the viewer. Just you and I. People who saw the photo always guessed she was a movie star, only they couldn't remember which one. Most people guessed Audrey Hepburn.

"You still have this," he commented.

I took it away from him and didn't explain myself.

He shifted. "When you gonna get some curtains? Place looks like a fishbowl."

"You need money. Is that it?"

"No, I'm flush."

"Then what are you doing here?"

"We were just driving. That's all I thought about at first. Where were we going? I could go down the East Coast, but to what? Georgia? Miami

Beach? Jeez, now I think of it, I could've blended in there. What's one more old Yid?"

I could tell by then that he was on the lam again. Most people don't drive cross-country looking for a place they can "blend in." He went on.

"Anyway, I wasn't thinking, I was tired. The second day I'm wiped out. Driving through Tennessee. Snuffy Smith country. I'm driving this long stretch of highway, I can see the mountains in the distance. Five hours later I'm still driving, the same mountains, and they haven't changed. I decided I needed to go someplace, a carrot on the end of a stick. I lived here longer than anywhere. So I decided to come here."

There was no point in telling him he'd have been better off starting over with a new ID, in some town where he didn't know anybody. He'd figured that out by now. I said, "Hey, try something. Say hi to your grandson. Tell him you're pleased to meet him. Tell him he's a big boy, he's gonna grow up to be a giant."

"You're spoiling him, I can tell."

No comment.

He said, "Come outside."

I pulled on some clothes and led him out back. The temperature had dropped to about forty, as cold as most Austin nights get, even in late December.

"You weren't my first choice," he said. In the Christmas-lit night, his face took on an unreal glow appropriate to someone you haven't seen in a decade or two. "I tried everybody. Donny, Bobby." Old friends from his Austin days, a cab dispatcher and a bartender who took bets. "Everybody's gone or dead or in the Joint. I figured I'd find *some*body."

I wondered if that meant he'd dropped on my doorstep just because I didn't qualify as somebody. I'd only ever gleaned details of my father's travels. I knew he'd spent his childhood in the Bronx, some chunk of his early adulthood in Elmira (including part of that behind bars) and several years in Austin, leaving some time after I came back from the army and entered college, a veteran at twenty. Since then he'd called a thousand hotels his home, in cities all over the country, wherever it looked like the pickings were good. A casual tip was enough to get him to move from Kansas City to Chicago, chasing a name and a dubious business proposition.

It had been maybe fifty years since he left the Bronx, and he couldn't go back to Elmira. He and I had left Elmira suddenly in 1968 when I was fifteen, under circumstances that suggested he'd never be safe going back. If he was going to find anyone who'd help him in a pinch, give him a few bucks or a place to hole up, I could see why he'd choose Austin. But he didn't choose it because of me.

"You remember Ida?" he asked.

"The barmaid."

Ida was someone my father dated when I was at Austin High. I remembered her as a mousy little woman with sweet, sad eyes and a hairstyle that looked as if it had been concocted by her mother with the help of some scissors and a soup bowl. Like most women Pop dated, she tried to win me over as a son, as hard as she tried to turn him into a husband. But Pop wasn't in the market for a wife and I wasn't looking for a mother. I'd seen Ida once or twice through the years. The last time she was serving pancakes, warming stomachs, at a breakfast place on Barton Springs Road. She always had a sad smile for me.

"Waitress, yeah. Somebody said she's still here, but I couldn't find her."

"I saw her at Holiday House."

"No shit."

"Maybe . . . I don't know, ten years ago?"

"Oh. Well, maybe it's best, considering."

"Considering what?"

He led me around the side of the house, where he'd parked his car, a silver four-door Oldsmobile Cutlass. It was a recent model, in good shape, not as big as the older models but with cushy light blue velour interior and power windows and locks. It leaned in the direction of a luxury vehicle. A used car, but not so used that Pop could have afforded it legitimately. I noticed it had Pennsylvania license plates.

A girl sat in the car, asleep, with her white-blond hair mashed against the passenger window. My neighbor's floodlights hit the windshield at an angle, and the sun visor laid a shadow across her eyes. Her chin was on the small side, giving her cheeks a rounded, pouty aspect in spite of high cheekbones. She was wrapped in a yellow plastic raincoat, a kid's raincoat.

I turned to Pop. "Is she legal?"

Pop said, "Let's go for a bite."

I considered the few late-night eateries available in the area and told him to meet me at the Denny's up on Burnet. I wanted my car with me so I could leave when the conversation turned bad. And I wanted him to have his car so he wouldn't need me to chauffeur him around. I went inside again. Rachel had put Josh back to bed, sheer exhaustion winning out over his thousand fears. I told her I was meeting Pop for a snack, a curve she seemed to take with boozy resolution. Then she turned and muttered, "First night in the house."

I said, "I'll be back soon," but she didn't respond.

If I knew what would result from Pop's introduction of the girl, what he was bringing into my world, I would have told him to get in his car and keep going. I'd have offered him gas money. Maybe I wouldn't have prevented what followed, but at least it would have happened somewhere else. Not in my home.

The house Rachel and I bought stood in stylish Hyde Park near my old place, a few blocks south of the new Koenig Lane overpass. I liked it because it was in the middle of town, the streets were numbered and the avenues were lettered, giving me a sense of order. I hopped into my blue Chevy Caprice, a car issued me by the department, identical but for the color to the Caprice my partner Joey had died in. This spooked me when I first saw it. Now I took it as par for the course, Joey's ghost peeking up and saying hello. I headed west on Forty-fifth Street, then north up Burnet.

When I got to Denny's, Pop and the girl were standing in the parking lot. I pulled up near them. The girl had a cloth tote bag over her shoulder, and she clutched it close to her side with her elbow while holding a cigarette close to her lips. The other arm wrapped around her waist.

She had dark, deep-set eyes, disproportionately large for her Slavic features: the sharp nose, the stark, high cheekbones, the unearthly white-blond hair cut straight just below the shoulders. What made all this spookier was pale white skin, smooth and delicate like an eggshell, a china doll. The clips on her yellow raincoat hung open, exposing a ragged sweater and floral skirt, and she wore sneakers of the quality you'd find in a supermarket. Sleeping, she looked like a ten-year-old. With her eyes open, she was probably about twenty. A jaded twenty.

Pop said, "This is Irina." The *r* had a Russian trill to it.

By way of greeting, Irina eyed me with suspicion.

When I was a kid in Elmira, one of my friends had a black cat that got pregnant before she was full-grown. The kittens came out okay, but the cat's torso stopped growing after that, though her legs reached full size. People would look at her twice, trying to figure out what was wrong. This is what I thought of when I saw Irina.

I turned to Pop, his breath barely making clouds in the cold night air. He stood near her but not too near, one shoulder oddly positioned higher than the other, eyeing me like he was waiting for a judgment, like a kid waiting to get smacked or, in his industry, a functionary waiting to get shot.

He gestured to the restaurant. "We could do better than this."

"When I was a kid, you used to say, 'Food is food.' "

He shrugged. "People change." He opened my passenger door and flipped the seat forward to let Irina in the back. Then he slid in next to me.

We headed south, through the middle of town. Irina lit a cigarette.

Finally I said, "So, Irina. What do you do?"

Pop groaned.

She blew out smoke. "In Russia I was waitress."

"Uh-huh. What about here?"

Silence, drag on her cigarette. "Here I am prostitute."

Long silence. In the rearview mirror, I saw Irina smoke with desperation; her fingers shook as she raised the cigarette to her lips. She would sit still for minutes, staring and filling the car with smoke, then suddenly turn her head and look behind her. We rolled past downtown on Lamar, toward the river. Then across the bridge and into South Austin, over to Congress and down to the Magnolia Café, all-night haunt of hippies, vegetarians, near vegetarians, dopers, insomniacs, cabdrivers and cops.

We entered unnoticed and sat ourselves in a padded vinyl booth. They ordered burgers, and I got eggs, which seemed more suited to a late-night snack, but I didn't know where Pop and Irina had been or what kind of appetite they'd worked up. The waitress, like the rest of the staff, wore some combination of tattoos, dreadlocks and piercings. I think the house rule was that you had to have two of the three. A trifecta would get you the manager's job. They'd carved a hole in the kitchen wall and turned it into a breakfast counter, though I never saw anyone eat there. Pop and Irina sat across from me, and I wondered about the nature of their connection. Mostly they looked beat. Irina reached for a cigarette.

"You can't smoke in here," I said.

Her eyes bulged. She scoped the room, saw no other smokers to prove me wrong, then slapped the cigarette pack on the table.

Pop looked around. Community bulletin board. Art on the walls. Diverse crowd. "This your place?" he asked.

My father came from a world where the last place you were likely to find a guy was at his home. You asked around until someone told you where he drank, shot pool, got laid or boxed. You could tell that a guy was at his place by the way he walked in. Was this my place?

"Yeah," I said. "Pretty much. No one gives me shit for being a cop." A passing waitress suddenly slowed her pace.

"Yeah," he said, "what's that about?"

"I'm a cop."

"I heard. Why?"

I knew from the postcards Pop sent me between the mid-seventies when he left Austin, and '81 when the postcards trailed off, that he heard I'd become a cop, like he heard I'd gotten married to my college sweetheart. Who told him these things was something I never learned.

"Who'd you hear it from?"

He shrugged and started a new conversation. "Is that the same wife from before? I heard you got married around '77."

"No."

"What happened to the old one?"

If I wasn't getting any straight answers, I sure wasn't giving any. I said, "You sleep on the road?"

"We took turns."

Eventually the burgers showed, and Pop and Irina laid into them. I picked at my eggs. "So," I said to Irina, "what brings you here?"

That I addressed the question to her and not both of them registered loud and clear: He didn't need an explanation. She did.

Pop defended her. "She's Russian. She could be your cousin."

"No, she's too young."

Irina said, "I don' need your help."

Pop said, "It's okay."

I said, "No, seriously. I *like* you bringing hookers to my house. I don't know why you haven't done it sooner."

"She was looking for work," he said. "They kidnapped her."

"And you rescued her? You?"

I sensed people at other tables shifting to hear us better. I lowered my voice. "I haven't heard from you in fifteen fuckin' years," I said. "Not a postcard."

"What are you, a baby?"

"Seriously. Fifteen years. And now this."

Irina said, "I am 'this'?"

I stared at Pop until he looked away. "All right," he said. He leaned forward and spoke in a strained whisper. "Kansas City, '81. I got six to ten. I did a nickel, got out in '86."

"Jesus. For what?"

"It's complicated." I stared him down until he said, "It was a deal. Two doctors, a house, some papers. Anyway, they caught me in the house, alone."

"So . . . what? Burglary?"

He closed his eyes and tightened his mouth. He was ashamed. He nodded.

If he'd been caught and tried for larceny, fraud, money laundering, it wouldn't have insulted his dignity. But six to ten for burglary, that was beneath him. What was worse, he was probably the mark in someone else's game.

He said, "I didn't want to write while I was inside. You would know where I was."

"What about after you got out?"

"I felt bad for not calling."

"So you didn't call."

He shrugged. It made sense.

I said, "What about now?"

"We left in a hurry. We didn't know where we were going."

"Pennsylvania plates."

"What?"

"Your car."

"Oh," he said, returning to his burger. He swallowed, and something seemed to get stuck in his chest. He struggled with it a moment, then showed some relief and took another bite. "Yeah. That's not my car."

"Whose is it?"

He leaned toward Irina. "The guy who . . ."

I finished his thought. "The guy who Irina works for." No argument. He chomped on his home fries. "You stole a car," I said. "From a pimp."

Irina said something in Russian, a sentence's worth. Pop nodded.

I said, "Do you speak Russian now?"

He bounced his head side to side. "Couple of words. From the old neighborhood."

"What did she say?"

He ate one more mouthful of potato. "What was I gonna do?" he said. "Call the cops? They'd bust her for prostitution, then throw her back to him."

I looked back at Irina. Small nod. That's just what they'd have done. That's just what they'd do in Russia, too, and though we didn't like to see it that way, that's what we'd do in Austin. Like most cops, I had mixed feelings about prostitutes, but not about pimps. Prostitutes committed a crime that had no victim. Pimps roped in vulnerable young women and made money off their misery. Pimps were nearly impossible to catch. They made me angry, and righteous. And they gave me a feeling of moral superiority that I really liked.

"Mostly I been in Vegas," he said, through a mouthful of burger and potato, in response to the question I was probably thinking about asking.

"Is that so?"

"Legal gambling. Legal prostitution. It's a cash city. I first got there, I dressed up in a golf outfit like an old retiree. Hit the casinos. 'Here, have some quarters, try out the slots. Have some chips, try the blackjack table.' I'd play pissant, nickel and dime, till they got bored watching me, go on to the next place with leftover money in my pocket. Kept it up longer than you'd think. I started driving a cab. Soon the hotels are paying me to bring fares from the airport. I got deals with a couple of hookers to bring 'em customers. Everybody's tossing cash around like it doesn't count till tax time."

"Perfect place for you," I said.

"Well, yeah."

"So why'd you leave?"

His expression flattened, like the question was out of line, like I'd cheated at the game.

The check came before he bothered trying to answer. I paid it while Pop and Irina used the bathroom. Then we headed out to the parking lot under the cold, dark sky and the glow of the neons.

I let out a breath. "Okay. Where'd you park the Olds? We have to go get it."

"Can't get it," he said. "We ditched it."

"What do you mean?"

"Parked it, wiped it down. Ditched it."

I scanned the lot as it dawned on me. "You're telling me I just helped you dump a stolen car."

"Borrowed. We borrowed it."

We piled back into my Caprice and I headed up Burnet again toward Denny's. Pop said, "There's no point. It's ridiculous."

I wasn't even sure by then why I was taking him back to the car. He'd only ditch it again. But at least I wouldn't have helped him ditch it.

"You made me accessory," I said. "Now I have to either lie for you or bust you."

"You're serious."

"I'm a cop."

"Whose side are you on?"

"I'm not gonna help you steal a fuckin' car!"

"When you were a kid you used to help me."

No argument there. When I was a kid, I helped him unload stolen TVs and sofas off a truck. I even played lookout while he slipped through the occasional unlocked window. And once I helped him move a truck full of hot plumbing fixtures. Any of this could have landed him back in stir and me in juvie. He should have been the one to keep me from doing that stuff. But there was no telling him that.

Now I was finally pulling my life together, my family's life. And here was my father showing up and dragging us all down. Now he wanted favors. And he wouldn't believe I was really a cop until I arrested him, a development I hoped to avoid.

As we approached Denny's again, Pop said, "Turn left." I went off onto a side street. He said, "Um. Wait. Right?" I went right. "No, go back." We doubled back, then made another circle. I could keep this up as long as he could. Finally we saw an elementary school and, next to it, a stretch of greenery—a children's playground, a soccer field and a baseball diamond with a chain-link backstop. "Over there." Across the park, maybe two hundred feet away, parked in front of the houses along the field, sat the car, gleaming silver, with a shadowed figure standing by it.

"Who's that?" I asked.

"How do I know?"

To get to the car we'd have to circle the school or make a left onto Northcross Drive, wait for the light, and another left back to the park. Or drive across the field. The shadowed figure opened the car door and got in.

"He's stealing it," Pop said in a near monotone. "Holy shit. He's stealing our car."

I got out of the Chevy and strolled across the grass. Pop hissed, "Wait a second. Wait a second!" I ignored him, approached the baseball diamond as Pop climbed out of my car. I had plenty of time while the thief hotwired the Cutlass. I just wanted to scare him off, deal with the car some other way. Maybe legally, if my father hadn't ruled that out.

Suddenly the engine started and the lights went on. I sprinted for the street, Pop a hundred feet behind me. I reached the pavement and stood in the car's path. I could see the driver jolt at the sight of me in his headlights. He slapped the Cutlass into gear and screeched forward, closing in and weaving. I faked right then leaped left onto the grass. He turned hard, passed me, jumped the far curb and rolled into the backstop. I headed toward him, waving my arms. He ground gears, found reverse and floored it, heading for a driveway and missing it, instead crashing his rear bumper into a Range Rover. I could make out that he was a youngish guy, probably Caucasian with long, dark hair. I flashed my badge, yelling, "Police!"

If he heard me, he didn't change his tune. This time he found forward and pulled out of the Range Rover, heading toward me in the street. I jumped aside and he roared down the block, weaving.

I walked back across the playing field. Pop, winded, met me halfway. I stared him down and kept walking, then got back into my car. Pop got in beside me, Irina still in back. "He hot-wired it pretty fast," I said. No comment. "You left the key."

"I left the key. Now it's his problem."

"Tell me something," I said. "What the hell were you doing in Pennsylvania?" It crossed my mind that my home town of Elmira, New York, stood only a couple of miles from the Pennsylvania border. In a pinch you could walk it. In a real pinch, you could run. "Wait a minute," I said. "Were you in New York?"

"What are you worried about?" he said, now angry. "What's with the gloom? Jesus!"

Something ratcheted my spine tight as I made the realization. He wouldn't tell me where he'd been. There was only one town in America where he had no good reason to go and plenty of reasons to avoid.

"Holy shit," I said. "You were in Elmira."

Sitting in my Chevy in the cool night, parked a few blocks from the playing field, I waited for Pop to explain what the hell he was doing in Elmira, the town we'd left when I was fifteen, fleeing for our lives. He stonewalled, grumbling in the passenger seat. I counted to thirty, then put the car in gear and headed up to the Greyhound station by Highland Mall. When we got there, I said, "Here we are."

"It's closed."

"It'll be open in a few hours."

He waited a moment. Then, with no fanfare, he got out and tipped the seat forward for Irina. She climbed out with her raincoat and bag and, somehow, her dignity. Pop slammed the door and zipped up his jacket, and they took positions by the bus station entrance, gazing off in opposite directions. I pulled away.

I got to the other end of the vast parking lot before I realized I wasn't going anywhere. To leave I'd have to follow the driveway out to Airport Boulevard and keep going, leaving my father to spend the night in a parking lot outside a bus station, while he was in two different kinds of trouble, maybe more. He'd gotten himself into all that trouble, sure. But I couldn't just leave him there.

When I drove up to the bus station again, Pop and Irina hadn't moved, maintaining a stoic stance like they were posing for a painting. I opened the door, and they climbed in, registering neither surprise nor gratitude. I shouldn't have expected either.

It was nearly 2:00 A.M. when we reached my house. I got them settled into the den. I gave them all the spare blankets we had, figuring they could make a comfortable pallet on the carpet. Or two separate pallets. I didn't stay to find out. I almost made it into bed, back to Rachel, when the phone rang.

"Hello."

"*Lieutenant Reles, this is Dispatch. We have a sort of situation. Who's next in line?*" The Homicide Squad took turns as the murders came in, with me, the man in charge, keeping track of the lineup. Usually I gave two or three names in advance to Dispatch, but I'd lost track and another case had come in earlier that day, taking their last name.

"Where is it?" I asked.

"*Well, it's headed to HQ, to the auto shop. It's, um . . . It's a silver Oldsmobile Cutlass.*"

I felt a wave of suspicion, which I located about the area of the den. I scoped Pop crossing the hall toward the bathroom. He saw me.

"What?" he said.

"I'm headed in," I told the operator, still staring at Pop. "I'll take a look myself." I clicked off.

"What?" he repeated.

Less than an hour had elapsed since we watched the Cutlass get stolen. A patrol must have seen the driver weaving, with a smashed tail end, and pulled him over.

"Put your shoes on," I told my father, and then gave him a statement he'd surely heard before, if he hadn't said it himself. "We're going for a drive."

I parked inside the dark garage behind HQ. Pop rode shotgun with Irina in the back again. She'd insisted on coming along. I said, "Wait here."

"Why?" Pop asked.

"Okay, don't." I got out and slammed the door, leaving them. I went down the back stairs, through security and into the APD auto shop—half car-repair operation, half crime lab. A steel column rising from the cement floor hoisted a fake Yellow Cab we used for undercover operations.

In a far corner, a guy behind a welder's mask raised his searing flame to the side panel of a very nice new Lexus, searching for hidden goodies. Somewhere a drill squealed.

The night boss, whose name I couldn't remember—Kahn or Kane or maybe Smith—limped over and shook my hand. "Merry Christmas."

"What do you have?"

He flipped through the pages on his clipboard and plucked out a report.

"Haven't towed it in yet," Kahn said. "It fits with a leave-the-scene up on Silvercrest, near Northcross Mall. The driver's in Central Booking."

"Lieutenant Reles?" A patrolman I knew, a guy named Scotto, entered from the hall. "They said you'd be here. I'm the arresting officer."

Scotto explained that he'd pulled the car over at a light, going down Lamar Boulevard. He'd noticed the damage and missing taillight. The driver couldn't produce registration or an insurance card, but he had two joints in his wallet, a mild intoxication being the necessary prerequisite to a world-class stupid action. The driver first said the car had been lent to him by a friend, but he couldn't name the friend. Finally he admitted he'd found the car with two loose wires jutting out from under the dash. He twisted them together and the lights came on. It wasn't until later that he realized someone else had hot-wired the car and dumped it. He tried to frame the evening as a joyride rather than grand theft. It was more than that.

"The car was stolen all right," Scotto said. "But not in Austin. I called the PD in Mansfield, Pennsylvania, where the car is registered. The owners reported it stolen there three days ago, and the Mansfield PD told me the FBI took the case."

"Why?"

"No answer. But they gave me this number." He handed me a scrap of paper. "I called, and they said they'd only discuss it with you."

"Why me?"

He shrugged and handed me an interoffice envelope. "They faxed these."

I took the envelope and went back to the parking garage where Pop and Irina stood waiting by my car. I led them inside, past security and into the elevator. Then I hit the button and the doors closed.

Pop hissed, "What's going on? What's going on?"

"Don't you wanna see where I work?"

The doors opened and I led them down the hall toward my office. Halvorsen, a tall, slim, Chicago-bred Nordic under my supervision, walked out of the squad room. Seeing his CO there after midnight, he lifted his prominent chin by way of greeting me. It was the most I got out of much of my team. I nodded. Halvorsen spotted Pop, then looked at me, then Pop again.

"Hey," he began.

"Later, Halvorsen," I said as I taxied Pop and Irina into my tiny, windowless office and closed the door. There was barely standing room for the three of us. The scrap of paper in my hand had a phone number with a western New York State area code and the words "FBI Elmira." I held it up for Pop.

"Talk," I said.

"What do I know?"

"Why's the FBI after a stolen car?"

"Interstate commerce?"

"Try again."

"Maybe it belonged to the president."

When my old boss had this office, he kept a bottle of scotch in the drawer for just such occasions.

I said, "Siddown."

There were two guest chairs and one behind the desk. They sat. I dialed, on the unlikely chance someone would be in the office after midnight. That someone answered on the second ring.

"FBI."

I introduced myself, explained the Cutlass situation. He said he was Special Agent Hayden. While he spoke, I sat behind my desk and opened the envelope.

"The Olds Cutlass was stolen three nights ago from the Corwins of Mansfield, Pa. But that doesn't warrant a federal case. Funny thing is, the very next morning, two blocks away, the Mansfield police found another car, a jet-black

Buick LeSabre. No one would have noticed the Buick, except that it was parked in front of someone's house and they called the cops to complain. Well, the cops traced the registration to a Paul Berelman living in Elmira, and when they couldn't get Berelman by phone, they called the Elmira cops. The Elmira cops knew where Berelman was. On a slab in the morgue. They'd found him a few days earlier in his hotel room in Elmira, ready to pop."

A dead body begins to swell after about three days. After a couple of weeks, give or take, it'll burst. You don't want to be there when that happens.

He went on. *"The Elmira cops wanted to take care of it themselves but Mansfield insisted on calling the FBI, since it was interstate."*

I pulled the faxed pages out of the envelope, grainy photos of Berelman's driver's license, of the LeSabre, of Berelman's bloated little body, curled up on the hotel bed like a fetus.

Hayden said, *"His skin was mostly red by the time they found him. He was asphyxiated, an eighteen-inch length of exhaust pipe jammed down his throat."*

I surveyed my father. Was he capable of killing a guy, like that? I didn't think so. But I wouldn't swear to it. I'd have to find out before I gave anyone else a crack at him.

Hayden continued. *"Naturally, when you guys called Mansfield, they let us know. We have no fingerprints and no guarantees, but we're of the belief that whoever dumped the black LeSabre also boosted the silver Cutlass. Can you lead us to him?"*

"Let me get back to you," I said. I hung up and looked at Pop. Small. Old. Brittle. I wanted him to tell me that he hadn't killed Berelman, that Berelman wasn't Irina's pimp. That it was all a series of unlikely coincidences. I could see him shifting under my stare. I showed him the faxed photo of the LeSabre. He shrugged. I showed it to Irina, and she shrugged too. Only she did it better.

Shrugging was, I began to consider, something that Russians did best. Eyelids at half-mast, staring at you or just through you, one shoulder raised slightly along with the opposite eyebrow, then back to normal. The reaction of someone who had seen governments rise and fall with no positive change and no hope of same. A shrug that says, *I don't care, and why should I? You think I'm a murderer? So what? Cigarettes cause cancer? Big deal.*

I passed them the driver's license and the death photo. Pop turned white. Irina clamped a hand over her mouth and bolted for the door.

Clenching the fax pages, I followed her into the hall, Pop on my heels. I shouted, "On the right!" and she pushed into the bathroom. I stood in the barren hall. I wasn't going to give her a chance to escape.

"What am I supposed to do now?" I hissed. "Charge the car thief for murder?"

"Let him go," Pop said, then heard his voice echo and dropped to a whisper. "He boosted a car. Who's gonna press charges? Berelman?"

I leaned close to Pop and whispered. "You stole the Cutlass from Mansfield, Pennsylvania. From a family named Corwin. You didn't leave the key. You hot-wired it."

He turned away, annoyed, but he didn't deny it.

I said, "Did you *know* the Corwins?"

"No."

"Two blocks away someone dropped Berelman's LeSabre. Was that you?"

He refused to meet my eyes. In a court of law it wouldn't stand up as a confession. But we weren't in a court of law.

I could see it. Berelman was the pimp. He terrorized Irina. Pop discovered her, took mercy in a rare moment of conscience. There was a struggle, two old Jews fighting over a beautiful young woman. Pop, a veteran boxer, won. Maybe.

I whispered, "You killed Berelman."

"No!" Pop snapped out the word before I finished saying Berelman's name. "No," he said again, quieter.

The beauty of it was that Pop was standing by me in the shadowless hall of the police department. If he wasn't oblivious to possible murder charges, his tone said that he was more worried about how murdering Berelman would make him look than he was about a possible lethal injection. He didn't understand that after nearly twenty years in law enforcement, I was serious about my job.

I spotted Halvorsen's tall shadow in the squad room doorway.

When Irina came out of the bathroom, wiping her mouth with a paper towel and watching the floor, she looked paler than her customary eggshell white and about two pounds thinner. I escorted her into the briefing room, a small conference room with a projection screen. She took a seat, and Pop tried to follow. I stood in his way.

"I need to talk to her. Privately."

He took the affront in the jaw, but a look in my eyes told him I meant business.

I said, "You want to help? Stay here and make sure no one listens in. You want to make a break for it? Be my guest. Please. But I'm talking to Irina first."

He took a step back and turned away. I closed the door, set the fax pages on the long conference table and told her she could smoke. I found her a half-empty coffee cup and placed it in front of her as I sat down. She drew cigarettes and a lighter from the pocket of her raincoat and lit up fast, hands shaking. I asked, "Who was Berelman to you?" She didn't answer right away. "Was he your pimp?" Nothing. I leaned back. We weren't going anywhere for a while.

After a long silence, she said, "I come from Siberia. Yakutsk. Is very bad now. No work. Even in Moscow is bad. Mafia runs everything. My mother is sick. Is no money for doctor. I answer, in newspaper, what you call . . ."

"An ad."

"Ad. Adver*tise*ment. Hiring women. Waitresses, dancers, singers. Three hundred dollars a month, it say. A woman, Katya, tell us pack, meet her at train. I am thinking, is bad. I should not go. Getting on train, I am thinking, do not go. But there is no work. No money, my mother need doctor. I am hungry, even. Owe money . . . everywhere. I cannot go back without money. So I go. We get train to . . . Istanbul. Is worse. I know something is terrible going to happen. Only now I have no ticket home. We know we are working illegal, we lie to customs. She take us to parking lot, is ten of us. Now we are wondering, where we going? She say not worry, go with man. She say we have no visas. We do not go, will be arrest. He give her money." She smoked, holding the cigarette in rigid, shaking fingers.

"We take truck. Is no windows. Cannot see where we go. Hotel. In hotel—terrible hotel—they take me alone to room. I am think is like doctor office, you wait. Only no doctor. Two men come in and two women. The women, they hold me. The men, they tear off my . . . blouse, pull my skirt up. I scream. I think someone will hear, someone will . . . save me. I am afraid. Shamed. They all seeing me naked. I try pull away. I think I will kick, I will bite. But I am afraid . . . make it worse. Whole time I think this terrible thing is happen, also think it will not happen, cannot happen. Nothing this terrible can happen. They are holding me down, my legs . . . spread, I am screaming. And he does it."

She didn't cry, but tears welled in her eyes.

"Is bright light in my eyes. Is two women holding me down, man on top of me. Pain . . . I cannot tell you. It burns and it hurts, first in my private. It screams. I feel it, like a fire, up to my . . . to my neck. My whole body, it hurts. I beg him to stop. And then he makes noise, he is finish. I still hurt, burn. My private, it pounds, the pain. I am bleeding, crying. And now other man, is his turn."

I turned away. She doused her cigarette and lit a new one.

"All this time I am waiting for someone to help me. A woman, the women, why can't they see? How you could do that to other person? Person like your mother, your sister. Can't you see, someone could do this to you?

"They tell me I have to work, is nowhere to run. Soon I am working, fifteen men a day. And the man, Ari, he beat me always, every day."

"Did you go to the police?"

She almost smiled. "Police come. We fuck them for free. Once I follow them, I run from the house, my legs hurt, I can barely move. I wave, try to make them see me. I know I will be beat if they don't stop and save me. I am . . . I cannot get my breath. They see me, stop. I beg them to help me. They bring me back to house."

"Christ. How long were you there?"

"No calendar. Two months? Ari, the . . . pimp, he say I am no longer work. I am *special*. I rest, two weeks. Bruises heal. I am . . . I do not . . . hurt . . . so much. He say I am sold. An auction. Another truck. Soon I am in Belgium. I get . . . sick." She gestured to her lower abdomen. "No doctor. They say I have new job, I am going to America. First, Canada. I am quiet in customs. I do not want to be deport. By now I do not trust police. So I go to Canada. From there Buffalo. Is where I meet the *makher*."

I asked, "The *makher*?"

I knew the word was Yiddish, not Russian. The *kh* sound doesn't exist in English and sounds to the unaccustomed ear like you're trying to bring up something from the back of your throat. Irina had no trouble with it.

I hadn't taken Irina for Jewish. My grandparents' generation of Eastern European Jews grew up speaking Yiddish, and it showed in their body rhythms and their humor. But later generations grew up speaking Russian. It showed in their staid posture, their fatalism and, of course, their shrugs. Communism had versed them in not giving a shit.

"What is in English?" she asked. "The boss. Big man. He take me to his home. I think I am in America, I will be free." She shook her head. "He is the worst."

"Berelman?" I asked. He was small and skinny, the fax said, like a jockey. An old jockey. But if she said he was capable of a high level of malice, I'd believe her. Napoleon was short, too. So was Hitler.

She started to tremble. I could see sweat on her lip. I said, "That's all right." I stood. "We can find you a safe place to stay until all this is straightened out."

Irina answered an ad and wound up getting sold into prostitution. But someone figured out that her appearance, a hard angel, would have enough appeal that she could be auctioned off like a virgin, provided they gave her wounds a chance to heal. And the highest bidder was the *makher*.

She looked at me, then shook her head. I couldn't blame her for not trusting me. I'd grown up around lots of cops and lots of hoods, and I couldn't say I trusted one group more than the other.

She said, "I go with my friend."

Her story won my sympathy, or I would have asked more questions. I should have asked more questions.

I left Pop and Irina in my office. In Central Booking I asked for the car thief, ID'd as an unpronounceable Alfred Drzymoa. Aguinaldo, a uniformed young woman working the desk, led me personally into the first bank of cells. The suspect sat locked in a cell by himself, behind a steel door painted baby blue to match the concrete walls and give a cheery aspect to a windowless eight-foot cinder-block cube. I peeked through his feeding vent. Black windbreaker, army-green pants, hair longish but not for style. More likely he couldn't afford a haircut. He sat tapping his feet, punching his thighs, then jumped up, paced the possible four steps in each direction and back, slapped on the walls and moaned.

I wanted to have them open the door so I could talk to him. But I was afraid he'd recognize me from the baseball field, which would add a complication I didn't need.

"What did they book him for?"

"It's incomplete," she said. "Scotto said he had to talk to you."

I rolled it around. Finally I said, "Check him for priors, warrants. Then book him for unauthorized use, third." The DA's office would make a final decision on this, but that would be influenced by my assessment, and also by the fact that the car door was open when he found it and the car had already been hot-wired. Unauthorized use of a vehicle in the third degree is a misdemeanor. It almost implies that he took his father's car without asking.

Aguinaldo looked over her notes. Like the rest of the world, she wanted someone to think that her ideas were important. "What about grand theft?"

I couldn't explain it. Grand theft was a felony. I wanted this guy's wrist slapped and out of the system as fast as possible.

I stammered, "Just . . . just . . . unauthorized third, all right? We're charging him with unauthorized third."

She shifted her look at me, and I left the cell bank.

As I walked toward my office, Halvorsen stuck his head out of the squad room and snapped my name in his Chicago pinch. "Reles."

"Lieutenant."

"Hah?"

I said, "Call me Lieutenant. I'm your CO."

"Uh, yeah. That old guy, he sure looks like you."

"No. Really?"

"Yeah," he said, "only smaller."

Halvorsen, like me, was an immigrant to Texas. He even came from a city. You'd think that would make him an outsider to department culture, and he'd be stuck on the fringe with me. Except he wasn't a New Yorker, and he wasn't a Jew. And he was blond. I'd been in Texas since I was fifteen but I was still an immigrant.

In polite Texas society, people kept their mouths shut about their racism, at least in front of the races they loathed. They might call me a Christ-killer behind my back, but never to my face. The police department was different. Gateway to the big city of Austin for some backwoods crackers and Klansmen, the department met and surpassed its quotas for racism, expressed in muttered comments or the occasional act of sabotage. It made my own situation worse that I had a known alliance with James Torbett, the head of Internal Affairs, the office that polices the police. Torbett didn't like me personally but he'd stuck by me. He was widely hated for his position, and for his African descent. There were those who thought I got a free ride for being his pal.

Beyond that, I made plenty of enemies on my own. I had a history of unbridled angry outbursts and a tendency to say what I thought, when wisdom and Texas etiquette would have suggested a more roundabout approach. And Halvorsen had his own reasons for hating me, which had nothing to do with religion.

"You need something, Halvorsen?"

"Same busted nose and everything. This have anything to do with that Cutlass they found?"

I fought back a couple of suggestions regarding his mother and said, "What are you working on?"

"Rabbit case."

While searching for lunch, a homeless Dumpster diver discovered a woman's severed head in a bag, along with a dead rabbit. Halvorsen was trying to identify the woman.

I said, "You need any help?"

He said, "Yeah. How about a full squad?"

A full-squad case meant top priority, high profile. It was a chance for the officer in charge to make points with the department and the press. I didn't like Halvorsen. I was suspicious of him. I knew he wanted my job, which was understandable. But I wasn't sure how much harm he was willing to do me in order to get it. The problem this presented was that you can't transfer a guy off your squad, or refuse him the help he needs, just because you don't like him or think he wants your job. It looks like reprisal. Halvorsen hadn't harmed me, yet.

I said, "Full-squad *briefing*. Tomorrow. Ten A.M. No. Eleven. Then we'll see."

I headed back into my office. Pop jumped up when the door opened.

I held up the photo of Berelman, dead, and said, "The truth. Now."

He gave me a long, cold stare that was supposed to make me ashamed. He was my father. Not much of a father, but he'd kept me off the street. Well, he hadn't really. He gave me a place to sleep at the end of the night. And here I was questioning him for murder. My eyes drifted back to the photo of Berelman, dead on the hotel-room floor, on his side, knees curled up to his chest.

Berelman's effects, the faxed report said, amounted to about eighty-six dollars in cash—his death wasn't about money—a driver's license with an Elmira address and a hotel key. Room 416 at the Allerton Hotel.

I remembered the Allerton as a decayed residential flop on Water Street along the river in downtown Elmira. Even when I was a kid, the Allerton bore little of the charm people said it held for visitors in the twenties when it went up, when it was stylish for single folks to live in hotels, along with those visiting and those passing through. I remembered a large, comfortable lobby gone to seed, furnished with wing chairs and sofas bearing the threat of lice. There were classier places then, like the clubs at the Mark Twain Hotel where cigarette girls walked among the guests, where people met for a drink before dinner. At the Allerton, men met to pay off bets, make deals, go off to the track or to the bars, or up to a room for an hour with one of the girls who worked the lobby or the adjacent streets. The inhabitants were people with no furniture of their own, no serious financial resources and, often, no change of clothes. Gamblers, drunks, dope fiends, whores and plain out-of-work losers. I always worried that Pop and I would end up there.

Pop and Irina sat in my guest chairs while I leaned against the edge of the desk, tossing questions. "When's the last time you saw Berelman alive?"

Pop said, "Never. I never saw him before."

"Alive or dead?"

"Neither!"

"But you knew who he was."

No answer.

"Okay," I said. "You knew who he was. How did you know?"

No answer.

As a kid I'd seen my father lose his temper. He could yell at the phone company for cutting off our service. He could holler at me, even hit me, for fucking up in school. But the more I thought about it, the more I knew that the violence he committed professionally was just business. Killing a guy in obvious anger, killing the guy brutally—that wasn't my father.

The problem was, in a court of law in Texas, he wouldn't be found innocent on the grounds of my character testimony. "Your Honor, my father may be a habitual criminal, a thief and a mob extortion collector, he may even have taken part in several mob hits, but one thing he ain't is temperamental." My second problem was that if Pop didn't kill Berelman, someone else did. And whatever Pop and Irina knew, they weren't talking.

I asked him how long he was back in Elmira.

He shrugged. "A week?"

"Can you prove it?"

"Can I *prove* it?"

"In case you go to court."

He mulled that over. "Yeah, I guess so."

"What brought you back?"

"Mmm. I got bored. Things aren't popping in Vegas like a few years ago."

"Bullshit."

He looked away, a Mafia evasion, like he was stalling until his lawyer showed.

I said, "You weren't scared to go back?"

"Those guys are all dead and gone. Nobody gives a shit about me anymore."

I turned to Irina. Her eyes darted away. "When's the last time you saw Berelman?"

She considered the question with more care than a prosecutor would allow. "I don' know. Ten days, maybe?"

"What happened?"

She looked to Pop for help.

I repeated the question, louder. *"What happened?!"*

Her shoulders jumped. She said, "He was . . . cruel . . . to me."

"Berelman?"

"The *makher.*"

"So Berelman wasn't the *makher*?"

She looked to Pop.

"Hey!" I said. "Eyes on me."

She said, "Your father, he bring me things. Food. Medicine. Women's things."

"That's swell. How long did this go on for?

Pop said, "A week."

"Shut up," I said. "Just her."

"A week," she said.

"Great. You met her the day you came to town?"

He was evading. "Around there."

"How? How did you meet?" No answer. "Singles bar? Whorehouse?" Nothing. I turned to Irina. "And you don't know who killed Berelman?"

She looked away. Then a feeble, "No."

Pop said, "All right, leave her alone."

"No," I said, "and cut out this white-knight shit. I want to believe that you didn't kill Berelman. Hell, I'd even buy that you didn't know it was his car you rode out of town. But I'm supposed to believe that you drifted back to Elmira a week ago for no reason after almost thirty years, met Irina and decided to drive her to Texas? Not a chance."

He stared up at me, his jaw jutting. If I was his son, why wasn't I respecting his privacy? If I was a cop, why should he talk to me?

I said, "All right, fine. Let's go." I led them out of the office.

If he thought I was about to book him, he didn't run. Downstairs in the lobby, the desk sergeant gave a sidelong glance at my father and me leading a slightly green Irina through the reception area and out into the cold air. I walked them back around to my car in the enclosed lot.

"Tell me something," I said, the chill clearing my head as we walked.

Neither Pop nor Irina as much as looked at me. They were pleading the Fifth. But they were human, and, as such, they really wanted to talk. Humans are like that.

"Berelman wasn't the pimp at all, was he?" No answer. "There was a third party," I said, "the guy who killed Berelman."

Irina almost missed a step, like she'd hit a bump in the road. She didn't say anything, though. It was the first time anyone had mentioned a third party.

Of course. Pop hadn't killed Berelman. Pop wasn't shoving a pipe down anyone's throat, not at his angriest.

But he was involved, and that involvement could land him behind bars. At his age a two-year sentence could mean dying in prison.

I kept talking, now watching Pop. "This other guy, the *makher,* he's the one you're afraid of. Not Berelman. The *makher,* the guy who killed Berelman, he's why you ran away. He's why you're here."

The first time I saw a dead body, I was a kid in Elmira. My friend Steven Wilcoff and I had stolen a pack of cigarettes and we went into the trees by the river just east of town to smoke them. Drawn by the suspicious buzzing of flies, we followed the noise until we saw it. He was lying on his side among the weeds, face staring at us with a naked embarrassment I'd never seen on an adult. I couldn't tell you how tall he was, whether he had a mustache or not. But I knew fast that he was dead, and that his death hadn't happened in any normal way. No one just lay down by the river and died. Steve and I stood where we were, and something shifted inside me, something to do with this man and his unfortunate death and how I was being changed just by seeing it. Also, I'd picked up a few details in my father's company. I knew there was such a thing as people going to prison for being in the wrong place. I knew people got killed for seeing the wrong thing.

Steve lit a cigarette, took a drag, coughed and passed it to me. We had a whole pack. We each could have had our own cigarette. But we passed that one back and forth, dragging and coughing until it was gone. Steve flicked it toward the water and missed. It lay smouldering on the rocks. Later I told my father about the body. He stared off in silence for a moment, then asked if anyone saw us. I asked if I should call the police and he said he'd take care of it, but I never saw him make that call. It took me years to figure that, since Pop traveled in the circles where people got killed and dumped by the river—or more often, *in* the river—he might have worked for the men who left that body. Or he knew them. Either way, he wasn't innocent enough to call the cops. And still, years later, I couldn't look at a dead body without feeling in some way associated with the guilt of making it dead.

Now, the same guilt had me trying to protect my father, tucking him away where I was sure no one would find him. The Austin Hotel on South Congress was established in 1938, and unlike most small businesses, had avoided both bankruptcy and corporate ownership since then. In the style of its era, it consisted of a small reception building close to the street, with a neon light and a pay phone on the front wall, and a cluster of tiny bungalows tucked with varying degrees of obscurity into the cedar and palm trees. Pop insisted they take the bungalow by the road, allowing him a chance to see anyone coming and also to duck out the back if necessary. I checked in for the two of them so the clerk wouldn't know he had an old Jewish boxer and a young Russian hooker, in case anyone came looking for them. I gave the name Ford (it came to me in the parking lot) and planted them in the room, its entrance tucked between the bungalows. Pop told Irina to settle in, and he came outside with me. We stood leaning against the shingles on the hidden side of the little house, staring into the trees. Here he was, a man who should have been enjoying retirement on a golf course. Instead he was hiding out from some crazy pimp in a moldy hotel. He had nothing to show for his career. No money, no house, no pension, not even a safe place to sleep. And he couldn't meet my eyes because he didn't want my pity. We were both embarrassed.

He offered me a cigarette and lit both. I don't smoke, but since that time on the river in Elmira with Steve Wilcoff and the corpse, I usually take a cigarette when someone offers me one. I figure offering it is his way of saying something. Taking it is my way of listening.

"Do we have to do this?" he asked.

"It's this or take your chances on the road. You must be tired." I added, "There's always protective custody."

"Okay!" he blurted, as if fighting off an attack. Then, quieter, "Okay."

"It's just a holding cell. It's not so bad."

His hands seemed palsied as he waved off the idea. "Ever been in one?" I said, "Just for a minute."

"Try it for a night. And sleep with one eye open. You know it's bad in the Joint with the lifers and the psychos. But you see the same guys in county jail and the holding tanks. I'm little, I was always little. Back when, some of those big guys would look at me like I was gonna roll over. I had to fight with all I had. Sometimes two guys tryin' to hold me down, I knew I was gonna get my ass kicked, I had to fight so hard they'd know it wasn't worth it. Maybe they'd lose an eye or a ball. Make 'em back off and go fuck with somebody else. Now I'm old. I can't defend myself like I did." He scowled at the ground.

I knew that Pop did short time more than once, and I knew about that two-year stint in Elmira. I didn't know what it was like for him, or what he went through in prison, in the interest of taking the sentence for his boss and, he thought, investing in his family's future. I opted not to ask.

Instead I said, "What do you think about Irina?"

"She won't testify. You see her? She shakes. She just wants to be left alone."

"Not gonna be so easy."

"There's rules," he said.

"Fuck that. Are you kidding? 'There's rules'? Is this some kind of honor thing?"

No response. I asked him flat out who the *makher* was, just to give me a name, but he wouldn't. I asked again, cajoled, threatened. I was wasting my breath. If I wanted anything from him, even a straight answer, I'd have to stop acting like a cop.

My father had a unique understanding of right and wrong, a code of ethics that he followed religiously, in spite of its apparent flexibility and adaptability to different situations. Stealing isn't wrong if they have something and you don't. Ratting out another guy is unacceptable under any circumstances, even if he killed someone, which is wrong but what are ya gonna do?

My father's situational ethics always rankled me, the second-greatest factor in my anger toward him. The first was a little more involved.

I could never shake the idea that it was his fault my mother left and that we had to flee Elmira in the middle of the night, me grabbing my jeans and my mother's photo as we ran for the car and never looked back, so I could grow up motherless in a strange world, a perpetual outsider. It wasn't like

I lost her once and got over it. I was a kid, and I felt her absence every day. No mother to clean my bloody noses or heat up soup when I came in from the cold. By my teens there was no mother to make me good, to push me into medical school, to make me marry a nice girl from the neighborhood. The neighborhood became Austin and no nice girl would have me, a Jewish hoodlum from New York. I settled for not-so-nice girls, a decision I have yet to regret, even in the case of Rachel. But even as an adult I felt the hurt whenever I thought about the loss of my mother and the loss of my home. And for all this I blamed him.

I couldn't explain all that. I zipped up my bomber jacket against the cold and tried to figure how I was going to keep my father out of prison and, if someone *was* after him, how I was going to keep him alive. I pointed a thumb at the door. "What's up with you and her?"

"Oh, no, it's not like that."

"You're not in love with her?"

"No. A little." He turned away, took a drag on his Camel and squinted into the wind. "Not so much anymore. You know. When you're old, everything gets stiff except what's supposed to."

It was the first personal thing he'd ever said to me, and I wished he hadn't.

I said, "So why?"

He breathed in deep. "I had a heart attack."

"What?!"

"A year ago."

"What— Why didn't you call me?"

"What are you, a doctor? I'm coming back to my hotel one night and I feel a little sick, cold maybe, and all of a sudden this sharp pain in my chest, pain like you wouldn't believe. I'm on the floor, I don't even remember falling. I can't get to the phone. I kick and drag myself over to the door and I reach up and open it and fall on the floor again. Someone comes along and sees me, figures I'm not just drunk and calls 911. Two days later I'm lying in a hospital bed thinking of all the shitty things I did, the shakedowns and beatings and the—" He stopped, cornered by his words. I guessed he was about to say, "The kills."

"They made you do it," I said.

"Tell God that. So I'm laying in the hospital with tubes in my arm and my ass hanging out of this stupid hospital gown, and I'm going down the list. I try to think of something good I did. And I can't think of a fucking thing."

"So . . . Irina."

He looked off. "I tell you one thing, though. Some of these tough guys, they're worse when they're old. A tough guy sometimes, his whole identity is his prick. Once he can't do it anymore, he gets mean, crazy. His woman, she hides a world of secrets, and not because she's being nice. She's shit scared." He shook his head. "I was a boxer. I wanted to be known for my fists. And you don't see *me* hitting a woman."

I waited. Still no answer to how he came to running off with Irina in a dead man's car. "So . . ."

With a wink he said, "I steal another guy's girl. I figure fifty-fifty I'm gonna wind up dead anyway. But I saw her, I saw the look in her eyes. Christ, she was *broken*, like a little kid. Like . . ." He glanced at me and stopped talking. I wondered if he was remembering me as a boy.

"Anyway," he said, "she needed help. I saw the chance." It sounded a little too generous for my father, considering that helping her got him into life-threatening danger. But I let it go. "I always wanted to die in bed," he said. He took another long drag, held it and blew it out in a stream. "I shoulda waited in bed."

I remembered to take a drag on my cigarette. He hadn't answered half of my questions and I was tired of asking them. But I still had a big one. "I always wanted to ask you," I said. "What happened that night?"

His gaze froze. He knew I'd ask one day, about the night we fled Elmira. He stalled. "What night?"

"Listen," I said. "Maybe you have some great reason for not telling me how you met this girl, how you came to drive off in a dead man's car, who's after you. But this business of us leaving Elmira, that changed my whole life. I deserve to know."

He blew out smoke, rubbed his forehead and nodded.

I t was so different then. You can't imagine."

So says my father as he leans on the shingled wall of the bungalow at the Austin Hotel. Inside the tiny cottage, his charge, Irina, is washing herself with tiny hotel soap and trying to figure out how to sleep with one eye open. Pop is stalling with his answer to my question, to why we ran from Elmira, using the cigarette to help him think, rolling his eyes upward toward the past. He goes on, spewing more words in a few minutes than I've heard from him in my whole life before.

"I didn't want to be in the business. I wanted to be a boxer. Same as you. I was smaller, though, and wiry. Fast. I'd fight some guy. . . . He'd ground his feet to throw a power punch, and by the time he launched it I'd be on the other side of him popping him in the ear.

"But it's the Bronx and it's 1950. Joe Louis just retired. Marciano was still coming up. And Jake LaMotta. You shoulda seen him. I saw him once get pissed off and punch a wall. The wall shook. I mean *shook*.

"I was never gonna be those guys 'cause I was so little. But there was Willie Pep. Will o' the Wisp. Fifty-three wins in a row—in a row!—and he takes the featherweight title in '42. Youngest titleist in forty years. A hundred and twenty-six pounds, just like me. What the hell. Everybody wants to be the next Marciano or whoever. I'm just trying to make a fuckin' buck, make a name for myself, and I can't even do that. And I have a wife and two kids, your big brother and sister. Half brother and sister. Jesus. Dolores, my first wife—you never met her—she's bitching at me, how I should knock this shit off and get a real job. I think about it now, I feel bad for her. She's scraping by and I'm training all the time, coming home bloody from a fight with maybe fifty bucks in my pocket, and that's supposed to last her till God knows when. But then all I could think was, I wanted to box, this is what I do, and why won't she back me up? She crabs at me whenever I walk in the door, and it gets harder and harder to walk in the door. I come home later, and when I get a chance—you know what I'm saying, if I get another offer—well, I don't come home at all. Tough on your brother and sister, I guess, but they hardly even knew me. They were babies. Who's this guy who comes in and fights with Mommy?

"You should look them up," Pop says.

I say, "*You* should look them up." This he meets with a grimace, a bad taste in his mouth, a shrug from his face rather than his shoulders. He shakes off the idea and moves on.

"I got this tip. This guy—jeez, I can't remember his name—says Elmira is smaller, he can set me up for a couple of fights, hundred-dollar, two-hundred-dollar purses. In those days a working shmoe pulls in maybe forty-five, fifty bucks a week. I figure I'll go, make a name for myself, come back to New York famous, the bad-ass from Elmira. So I go to Elmira."

Pop knows I'm here. But he only glances at me once in a while, to make sure I understand. Then he goes back to the past.

"This guy—Epstein, that's it—he covers my travel, gets me a room, and I'm training full-time at the gym. I feel like something good is happening, finally. I'm building momentum. I get up and I train, nothing else. Don't have to haul crates all fuckin' day just for a few hours at the gym at night. And there's a fight, a four-round opener, Lou Meile from Buffalo. No one's even watching. You shoulda seen me. One-two-three! I pop him in the ears. I knock him like a speed bag. I jab his nose so many times it looks like a rotten apple. Everyone says, 'What? What's going on?' They're still buying hot dogs, finding their chairs. I know I can finish him, but I want people to see it. I give him a belt in the chest, he's so busy trying to cover his face. He stumbles backward, gets his balance. Now everyone has a chance to look at us. He comes back with a right hook. It rolls off me, mostly. I figure, what the fuck? I won't feel it till tomorrow. And I start pummeling his ribs. He clocks me once, in the side of my head, 'cause I wasn't watching. Dumb. But I back up, shake it off, and go in for the kill.

One-two, right-left, and he's spitting blood, and I go after his ribs again, right-left-right, and I ground myself and throw everything into a power punch. It takes forever, and I'm sure he's gonna stop me, or see it coming and dodge, but I land it and I hear *craaaccckk!* He grabs his ribs and backs up, crying almost, and he waves at the ref. Which is worse than getting knocked out because he looks like a chicken. 'No more, I can't take it.' And I'm winner by TKO."

Pop shows me his right hand.

"Look at this," he says. His little finger is twisted inward from the point of one outsize knuckle. I know it well, like I know all his scars, details I stared at as a kid when I studied my father and tried to grow up to become him. "That busted pinkie," he said. "I didn't know it till I peeled my gloves off. I don't know how long I had it, if it was the final punch or not. I tried to set it, but it came out funny. Never got right. Still, it never stopped me fighting.

"I'm the big star that night. Not really. I was just the opener. But I get invited to a nightclub after, the Morocco, over at the Mark Twain Hotel. There's broads and a jazz band. Cigarette girls, camera girls. 'May I take your picture, sir?' Guys asking if that was me in the opener and slapping me on the back. First time I tasted champagne.

"Next day at the gym I go to—what'd I say his name was? Epstein—I go to Epstein for my purse, a hundred bucks. At this point I ain't got a nickel to rub against a dime. And he tells me it's gone, he spent it on gym fees and the trainer and my room and board, plus I still owe him five C's for what's left over. Man, you could hear my face drop. I figured I was in the clear, and now this. I tell him I'm bailing out, and he says I'm on contract, plus I owe him money. It wouldn't be good for my health to try and walk away. I didn't get it at first, I'm still a little green then. Finally I see he's connected, I'm out of luck. Then, to show what a good sport he is, he lends me forty bucks—*lends* me—and I send twenty back to Dolores. Around then I find out she took the kids and moved in with my mother. *My* mother. Least she coulda done was move in with *her* mother."

Pop shook his head at the injustice.

"This goes on for maybe five more fights. I'm six-and-oh, flat as a matzo, and by now I owe Epstein a thousand bucks. Even if I was making fifty a week at a regular job, how long does it take to raise a G-note? And I'm not taking anything home. But I'm getting a reputation. And Epstein hangs this nickname on me, Kid Twist after Abe Reles. You heard this. I knew Abe Reles was a crazy gangster. But I didn't follow gangsters, I followed fighters. So I didn't know what everyone else knew, that Abe Reles got tossed out of a hotel window in Coney Island in '41 while he was waiting to testify against the mob. So there I was with a rat name and a rat nickname, and everyone knows it but me. By the time I figure it out, it's too late. And by then Epstein sold my contract to Ike Zelig. So now I owe a G-note to Ike Zelig. Terrific.

"The big night comes, I'm at the Drill Hall in Elmira by the cop station. You remember that place. It's like a barn. It's got that peak ceiling, the balcony with two aisles. The place is mobbed. Everyone's there—the mugs from the foundries, dairymen and bakers, plus every cop, every boxer and hood. And not just from Elmira. Big boys from Buffalo and Syracuse. I figure now's my chance.

"First round I'm bouncing around on my toes, come up to him like I don't mean any harm. I pop him, one-two-three in the head. Not so hard, just fast. He blinks like he wasn't expecting it. And he comes back, he's not gonna hand me the fight. He comes back mad, which is stupid. But I see it, and I'm wary. He goes for my chin and misses, mostly, and then gets my ribs while I'm after his face. I'm not thinking. He gets one good shot in my ribs, and I feel it, and I'm thinking, I'm faster than this guy. That's what I've got. So I take a breath and go in, and pop-pop-pop in his face, his ears. He grabs me in a clinch and I don't break out of it, I step back with my feet and pound him in the guts. And when he breaks loose, I let out one solid *whap!* to his eye. I feel it land and then slide, and the bell rings. I get to my corner and look across, and I see I ripped his eyebrow right open."

Pop is actually smiling. He can see the crowd.

"Oh, man!" he says, bouncing on the balls of his feet. "The crowd is *screaming*. You know, it's that kind of moment, when they can tell they're seeing something good, that the main event is gonna be a letdown after this. And I'm in my corner, and I see the big boys in their suits talking, someone's running around, something is changing. I get it now. They were changing their bets.

"Mortellaro, that's the guy, he's in his corner. There's blood pouring down his face, they're trying to pinch it shut, but, you know, once a guy's eye is cut, the fight's pretty much over. And I can see it. Two minutes from now, they'll announce me the winner, and there'll be a big roar, and I jump up and there's champagne and broads, finally the payoff for all those years of eating shit. I can see my career about to happen. My life.

"And they come to me before the bell and tell me I go down this round."

The air went out of Pop. He'd told me this story a hundred times in a hundred ways. But each time he felt the pain again.

"I swear to Christ," he said, "I could've cried. I'm busting my ass for years, running around with nothing in my pockets but dust, and all I get out of it is I'm up to my ears in hock to the mob. I get one big chance, and they tell me to take a fall. I'm nothing. I'm the guy who sets it up for them to win the money on Mortellaro. It looked like I was winning, so they doubled the bets against me. That's what happened between rounds.

"And I went down. What else was I gonna do? Mortellaro comes in with his bleeding eye and his left hook I could see a mile away. I go down, and they throw beer bottles at me.

"I had a couple of fights after that, but no one took them seriously. And soon I'm driving cars for the big boys, making pickups, sometimes breaking fingers. And worse. I hate it like poison. I got cash in my pocket, the boys are paid off. But all I can think is, I'm racking up more debt."

It was just then that Irina said something from inside the room. I couldn't tell if it was English or Russian, but Pop, her caretaker, said, "Just a second," and headed inside.

I told him I was gonna make a phone call.

I fished out some change from my car and started dumping it into the pay phone outside the hotel office. I thought about calling Rachel to check in, but she'd be asleep. I dialed some numbers and finally got the police department in Elmira, New York. I identified myself and asked who was in charge of Vice.

"*Hmmm, let's see. Tonight, I guess that would be . . . Sergeant Lowry. He just came in. Hold please.*"

I stood near the sidewalk, looking northward at the Congress Avenue

Bridge and straight up the road where it dead-ended at the capitol building. Hidden spotlights lit the building's pink sandstone dome like day.

Another minute. Then, "*Lowry.*"

"This is Lieutenant Dan Reles, Austin Police Department."

"*Lieutenant . . . Austin, Texas?*" he asked, verifying which Austin I meant.

"Yeah, Austin, Texas. I got a problem here. Ever hear of a Paul Berelman, lived in Elmira?"

"*Pax.*"

"What's that?"

"*Goes by Pax Berelman. Went. Little guy, bald, skinny, right? Looks like a jockey.*"

"That's him."

"*Deadbeat. Loser. Small-time dealer. Got him on possession seventh degree, petty theft, like that. We found him in a hotel room last week.*"

"Not a pimp?"

Lowry laughed. "*Berelman couldn't scrape up the cash for a hand job from a wino.*"

I pegged Lowry's accent as native Elmira—a left-twisting version of any New York accent you'd hear in a movie—with undertones of second-generation Irish cop. He was a baritone, but he could go tenor to sing "Danny Boy."

"Know who he worked for?"

"*No, why? Oh, right. Suspect.*"

Yes. Suspect.

"*The feds took this one from us.*"

I buddied up to him. "Fuck that," I said. "Guy's in a hotel room with an exhaust pipe down his throat. What do feds know about that shit? We know who the real cops are."

He thought for a moment. "*Let me call you back.*"

"I'll call you. Ten minutes?"

"*Five. How do you spell your name again?*"

I gave it to him, then stood at the phone. Pop's and Irina's shadows moved around behind their window shade. I wondered what he could be helping her with. I looked north, up Congress Avenue, at the glowing capitol. Around the capitol grounds, the older downtown buildings with their texture and character were now outnumbered by the modern big-city variety of steel and endless panels of glass, tinted and unopenable, a sign of things to come.

I called Lowry back. *"Hey, Tex,"* he said, sounding sluggish. *"I've got a few things on Berelman stretching back to 1980, but no boss. A few known associates."*

I waited for more, didn't hear it and said, "Can you read them to me?"

One full second of dead air. *"It's a big file."*

"You're the Vice guy, right?"

"See, Reles, you could call back tomorrow and I could pull some stuff together for you if I have time. We have lots of names. I can't read it all to you, and I can't Xerox it and send it. You can come look at it anytime you want. Search to your heart's content."

His last sentence washed in irony and contempt. Not his kind of syntax.

I told him I was glad for his help and gave him my office number.

"One last thing," I said. "Ever hear of a guy called the *makher*?"

"Can't say I have," Lowry said, and I realized everything he'd said was probably a lie short of his name, and maybe even that. Why should an Elmira cop help a Texas cop? But I couldn't figure the sudden shift in his attitude.

"Tell ya one thing about Berelman," he added. *"A year ago he's working for the crematorium up on Lake Street. He's supposed to wheel the body into the oven, then brush it with this goop, makes it burn faster. Well, he's supposed to brush it on both sides, you know? And he's lazy or he forgets or whatever. He just paints the top. Gets out, turns on the heat. A few minutes later he's supposed to peek into this heavy glass window, make sure the body's burning right. Well, see, the stiff is only greased on top, so the top is burning faster than the bottom. Berelman looks in the window just in time to see the dead guy sit straight up."* Lowry laughed. *"Berelman screams, runs out in the street and gets pounded by a minivan. He's in the hospital six months."* Lowry laughed again. *"If you ask me, Berelman winds up with a pipe down his gullet, I say he fell on it."*

❖ ❖ ❖

Someone had killed Pax Berelman. My father, in spite of being positioned to take the blame, knew who it was, and he wouldn't tell me for anything. The mug's code of honor. If I could pin the murder on the killer—I figured him for Irina's pimp—and get him arrested in Elmira, then my father was off the hook.

But the Elmira cops would be no help. And Pop pissed off this guy by taking his girl. We knew what pimps were capable of when they were pissed off.

I saw the bungalow door open and Pop emerging. I joined him between the tiny buildings.

"Hey," he said. "These two Jews are in front of a firing squad. The captain asks if they want a blindfold. One of them says, 'No. I want to look my assassins square in the eye.' Other one turns to him and says, 'Meyer, please! Don't make trouble!' "

Pop watched for my response and I realized he'd just told me a joke. He'd never done this before. He shrugged.

"Back in '43," he said, "soon as I was old enough, I joined up. Army sent me to Japan. I'd've done anything to fight the Nazis. What do I care from the Japs? After the war we heard about the Jews who died in the camps. We knew that something was up before, but we didn't know how much, how many. Then the numbers came in. Thousands, they said, then ten thousand, then hundreds of thousands. By the time it hit a million, we knew the world was over. Different. We'd never be the same, none of us. I could see them. It hurt, but I could see them walking into the gas chambers. And I kept thinking, Why didn't they stand up? Where was their grit? What kept them from fighting back? What could they lose? I'll tell you what. Meyer, please! Don't make trouble! They were afraid of making trouble. I figured I wasn't that. I wasn't some sheep, marching to the slaughter. So when the time came, boxing was over for me, the boys wanted me, I sucked it up. I worked for them. I wouldn't be the one to get pushed around. But I got it wrong. I wasn't some tough Jew standing up to the Nazis. I was the guy in the firing squad. I was the guy at Nuremberg who said he was following orders. Took me years to figure that out.

"By then Dolores, my first wife, filed for divorce, and I'm sending everything I can. I was making decent money then, for me anyway. I couldn't walk away from it. Not like they woulda let me.

"One night we're all at the club. I wear a suit and I hang around with the big boys. I'm with them, but I'm not one of them. I bring the car around, I go out for ice. Go out on a job. Whatever. And your mother walks in."

Pop's eyes lit up at the memory.

"Christ, I'll never forget it. All these goombahs in their oversize suits, alligator shoes, looking like gorillas at a bar mitzvah. And she's wearing this cocktail dress, blue silk, goes down just to her knees, with ripples like a movie curtain. She has a fur stole, and pearls on her neck. Hair twisted up on her head. Tall. And classy. My feet take off on their own. Remember, I'm still pretty fast. If I thought about it, I woulda known she was out of my class. But there I was, standing by her and asking where she's from and what brings her here and can I get her a drink. She's got some friend with her, some other broad who disappears, and soon we're at a table and I'm cracking jokes and she's laughing and having a good time. And I take her back to her hotel room, she's staying there at the Mark Twain, very innocent. Leave her at the door. I don't even try to kiss her goodnight.

"She leaves the next day, but she comes back and I show her around. This goes on a few weeks, I figure I'm doing great. And one night we're at a table at the club, the Morocco again. Bottle of champagne shows up in an ice bucket, waiter says it's from that gentleman. Sam Zelig, Ike's brother, is waving at us and smiling. We knock off the champagne and Sam comes over to our table and says hello, real nice, and shakes her hand and tells her how great I am. I figure she makes me look good to the boss, the boss makes me look good to her. I'm on top of the world. And he slips me the key to his suite. I say, 'No, no.' He walks away. But she went back to the suite that night with me.

"Not long after that, we were married. That's when it went wrong. She comes back to my apartment, and she realizes it's a dump, one crappy bedroom, stains in the kitchen sink. I tell her it's just temporary, I didn't need anything fancy when I was single. But you can tell she's disappointed. She thought I was one of the big boys. She didn't realize I was just the runner, maybe the muscle. On a good day, I was the mascot. So *she* sucked it up, made the best of it for a while. And by then she was pregnant.

"I don't have to tell you what happened next. You came along. Not like I wasn't proud. I see you in the cradle, I see My Son, I feel like a million bucks. I had a son already, but he doesn't know me. Now I'm proud. But she hardly looked at me after that, only at you. Eight years of this. Meanwhile I start hating my job more. I hate the guys I work for. *Hate.* Like I'm looking at one of the boys one day, and I'm thinking, he's not some cool, well-dressed ladies' man. He's a thug whore-chaser, in stolen clothes. He shakes down money from people who worked hard for it. And if they don't pay out, he breaks their legs. I break their legs. For landing in the wrong guy's path.

"You know, they call you up, 'We need you tonight, meet us in ten minutes at the hotel,' or whatever. You never know—am I the muscle tonight, or the mark? But you go anyway, you have to go, or they'll come get you and kill you. They'll find you if you run. Doesn't matter where you go. Fly to Rio, hide out on a mountain in Tibet. Spend your whole life waiting, but you know they'll get you sooner or later. You'll turn a corner, step out of the can, and there they'll be. There was this one guy, boss called him up, guy figured he was screwed, he hit the road. He was on the run maybe three years. Worse than hiding from the cops. They said he stayed up all night, hid out in hotels in the daytime, hardly slept. He knew they'd get him. After three years of this shit, he jumps off a bridge. We hear this story, we figure when they call you, it's easier if you just go. Maybe they just need your muscle. But the longer they have to wait, the worse it is. And if you make 'em look for you, it's not like they're just gonna put you out painlessly. They're gonna make you pay.

"One night I go out on a call like this, 'We need you, meet us.' This guy, call him Joe. I worked with him. They said he was skimming. He's the mark, not me. Wind was blowin' a different way, it woulda been me. We put him in the trunk, took him out on Sing Sing Road, out by the airport. Airport's only there since '45, so figure not too much civilian travel by then, mostly military, commercial, a few passenger flights. They say, 'Disappear.' You figure he's getting off easy. They just want him out of the way, maybe they think it's easier to make him walk away than it is to dump the body. Guy says, 'You can't do this to me! My father ran speakeasies with Meyer Lansky,' or he was in the Hundred and Forty-fourth Cavalry Unit with General Custer or whatever. Can't do this to me. Was he wrong! You wouldn't believe they would tie someone to a car and drag him, but they did. A couple of miles later, the guy is *screaming*. His face is gone. His ass is gone. He begs them, 'Please, God, please kill me!' They shoot him in the leg. Then the balls. Then the gut. Finally in the heart. Then we had to pick him up and dump him. We figured it was a warning, to us as much as anyone. Don't step out of line. Don't even think it. They'll make you beg for death.

"Hey, those two miles the guy was dragging? Guess who was driving."

It sounded like a joke, but he looked away after he said it.

"One time, way before I was around—I heard the story—they tied up another guy, a rival, tied him to a chair. Cut him up, cut his cheek out, poked a hole in his lung and tossed him out a third-story window, still tied to the chair. Cops come around, ask him, 'Who did this to you?' He can hardly breathe to talk. He says, 'Fuck you,' and he dies.

"Heard that story from a cop. It was supposed to be about how tough the guy on the chair was, he'd still cover for the guy that killed him. Bullshit. Guy's facing down death, I say the one thing he's afraid of is pissing off the boys.

"By '68 your mother's gone, what, five years already? You're in high school, businesses are getting shaky. Since the war, really, things are slipping, but it's worse by '68. I'd come to collect, and they didn't have it. I'd take what they had. They'd show me the till, the books. I felt bad. The boys lean on me, and I have to do something, break a thumb or smash a window, but all that costs money. Can't get blood from a stone. Tell the boys that. They look at me like it's my fault, maybe I'm going easy, maybe *I'm* skimming. One night I'm about to drive them somewhere, in this monster Cadillac. They yank a bag over my head, kidney-punch me, take my keys and toss me in the trunk. Long ride, I'm wondering what I'm lookin' at, what's in store, and they let me out on Sing Sing Road. I see a plane taking off, a little one. My car is there. They say beat it. Disappear. On the road or under it.

"Some other guy woulda stood up for his rights. Not me. They gave me my keys, and I came home for you. Maybe they would have given us till sunup. Maybe we could have packed. I wasn't taking the chance.

"I thought I got you out of trouble, once and for all. Now look at you. You're in the same fuckin' game, you're just on a different team. You could have been a doctor or something. I kept you from that. I taught you that this was the only game in town. And now I come out of the bushes and I stick you back in the middle of it, deeper and deeper. And I stick your son in it, too."

. . . God did tempt Abraham, and said unto him . . . Take now thy son, thine only son Isaac, whom thou lovest, and get thee into the land of Moriah; and offer him there . . .

—Genesis 22:1–2

Somewhere in my father's whole story, I was sure he was finally going to tell me about the fight that mangled his nose, making the bone look like two roads that didn't quite meet, but he didn't. I knew what ended the story, though, after we got to Austin: I finished high school and left for the army. I came back for college. He hit the road, drifted away on his continued adventures. I married my college sweetheart, got rejected by the FBI and joined the force in '77. Pop told me bits of his life in postcards, which I stopped getting about 1981. My first wife, Amy, left me. I got a new partner and fell in love with *his* wife. That was Rachel. We had a son.

I had a lot to lose.

I'd slipped back into the house and into bed without waking Rachel, but she shifted to accommodate my bulk and settled in close to me as I lay on my side and wrapped my arm around her waist. I must have fallen asleep before I took two breaths.

By the time I woke up, the room was light, and either we hadn't shifted or we'd rolled back to the same position. The work I did, the world I saw, didn't give me much faith in God but I thanked him anyway for the beautiful woman in my bed and the fact that my job allowed me to stride into the office at ten or eleven, looking self-important, as if I were popping in between meetings with the president rather than stashing my gangster father in a vintage hotel and then sneaking a few extra minutes of warmth with my boozy bride.

Rachel seemed to know me well enough to know when I'd opened my eyes, even with her back to me. She said, "Where's your father?"

"At a hotel."

She lay still a moment, then pulled my arm tighter around her belly. Then she said, "Why isn't he here?"

I lifted my head to try a look at her face, to see what she was thinking. "What difference does it make?" I asked.

"It doesn't."

I dropped my head onto the pillow. "There's no room for them here."

"Plenty of room."

I listened for signs of Joshua's movement—the TV, the bathroom— but didn't hear any. His first day in the new house, his first night in the new room.

I said, "You didn't seem too happy about his visit."

A pause and then, "He's your father."

"That's what my mother said."

She rotated a quarter turn toward me and shifted away, now lying on her back and staring at the ceiling. I could smell last night's white wine seeping out of her pores, but she seemed clearheaded.

"Josh should know him," she said at last.

"Why?"

She turned to me. "What do you have against your father?"

"Nothing," I said, but it sounded feeble.

I wondered how long we could stay like this, even in the discomfort of early morning and awkward conversations about something I didn't want to think about, before hunger, bathroom needs and child rearing made us jump up. We had so few quiet, sober moments together. I missed her so often. It was times like this that reminded me why I stuck it out with her.

She spoke toward the ceiling. "Everyone loved my father. He was smart. And handsome. Cultured. My parents had dinner guests all the time, little parties. They played card games and word games. You could see him seducing the wives, and even the husbands in a way, though I don't think he ever slept with them. We lived in a pretty house, and there was always food in the refrigerator. I had nice clothes."

So, I thought, Rachel's father was the opposite of mine.

She went on. "And he used to come into my room at night."

I knew this already. I knew how it had destroyed her life then, for years since and maybe even now. But I'd never heard her come out and say it before.

She rolled her head toward me. "Your father isn't so bad."

By the time I showered, shaved, dressed (adding now the necktie that allowed me to mingle in the ranks of the administration) and got Josh out of bed, Rachel had made it to the kitchen. I fixed breakfast for the three of us and left the dishes. Rachel promised to take care of them, but I expected they'd be waiting for me when I got home for dinner. I didn't mind. I had bigger problems to deal with and so did she.

It was past nine thirty when I headed downtown, to South Congress and the Austin Hotel, pulled in to the driveway in front of the bungalow, knocked and felt the pounding pain in my stomach and the realization that I'd been gone an hour too long.

The bungalow door opened without resistance. Unmade bed. Dresser. Sink. No signs of struggle. Bathroom undisturbed. They'd left voluntarily, or with their hands up.

But that wasn't what had happened. No one knew where they were besides me.

I went into the main office, the building marked RECEPTION. The morning clerk was on duty, a guy of about sixty in a worn plaid shirt, long gray hair and a look of general hopelessness I'd seen around town a lot. I asked him what time the couple in the front bungalow had checked out. He said they hadn't. I paid for the room and asked if he had any way of looking up what phone calls they'd made or received. He said he didn't know. I thought of asking him if he saw the world as one massive waiting room for death, but I knew his answer.

For everything I'd said to my father, it must have finally gotten through that I was serious about being a cop. And if I was, that meant my loyalty to the department was greater than my loyalty to him, an issue that doesn't even come up in families where no one is a career criminal. Pop didn't trust me not to turn him in. He was wise not to. But it made me sad.

Sorry I didn't help you more, Pop, I thought. Stay one step ahead of the law and two steps ahead of the bad guys. Go with God.

I radioed Central Booking and had them set up Alfred Drzymoa, the car thief, in a glass interview room, the same one where he'd see his lawyer.

I was wearing a leather jacket when I witnessed him stealing my father's stolen car. I showed up at Central Booking in a blazer, locked up my weapon and tightened my tie. Central Booking had a copy of the arrest report for the judge who would see Alfred later that morning. There was also a tech report, explaining the damage to the car and the absence of any fingerprints besides Alfred's. Pop had wiped the car clean, and he knew how.

Alfred sat, nervous, in his jailhouse-green coveralls. I asked him about the night before, asked him again, asked him a third time. The details didn't vary. He left work, went for a few drinks, got stoned. He was wandering home when he spotted the car, wires jutting out from under the steering wheel. The third time he mentioned this, I said, "You just happened to notice?"

"The car door was open."

"Open?"

"It caught my eye. You know, you see a car door open, the light is on. But not this time. So I looked. And I saw the wires."

If I didn't know who'd left the car, I would have wondered. But Pop left the door open in hopes that someone would steal the car. He probably figured he was just passing the burden, passing a hot potato. It wasn't brilliant, but he wasn't Meyer Lansky.

I asked Alfred about his week. He was at work all day, the last four days, at a car wash on Airport Boulevard. His time sheet would prove that. He had ATM receipts and witnesses, he assured me, who would place him in town for each of those nights. The judge wouldn't wonder if he'd been the one to steal the car from Pennsylvania.

Then he started volunteering information, which is what you normally hope for.

"My girlfriend broke up with me. I hate my job. Every minute of it. So I come out of work and I go out drinking. What difference does it make, right? So I get out of the bar—I'm flat broke—and I realize I didn't save enough for the bus. I have to walk five miles now. And I'm fuckin' wrecked. I'm wandering up the side streets. And I see this car.

"I swear I wasn't gonna steal it. I just saw the door open, and that made me notice the wires. And all I could think was, 'I borrow the car and I can drive home. I'll be in bed in five minutes.' It's just there like a hot pizza. You don't think about it. You just eat it. I start it up and this guy comes at me and all I can think is to get away from him. If I was on my feet, I woulda run."

He didn't recognize me, I thought. Until just the moment I said good-bye and got up to go. Then he gave me a long, hard look, and I wondered if he'd make the connection, that the cop who interviewed him saw him steal the car in the first place.

I made it to the briefing room just before eleven as the detectives wandered in for Halvorsen's full-squad briefing. It was months since I got rotated back onto Homicide and since the night when—for reasons only a few of us knew—I got put in charge of it. (TV cameras had pinned me as a whistle-blower. The administration needed some good press, fast, and thought it would improve their reputation if the whistle-blower got promoted instead of fired.) The good old boys on the squad still saw me as an intruder, a Yankee Jew who'd somehow bought his way into leadership, 'cause you know about Jews and their money. My presence could inspire a suspicious nod or an outright dirty look, obedience but never respect. The one exception was Sergeant Cate Mora, the squad's first woman.

Standing about five-six with dark skin, Native American cheekbones, thick black hair cut just to her shoulders and a tight, powerful body, Mora had earned rank through hard work and resourcefulness. She'd made a few mistakes in her career, and I was one of them. We were both drunk at the time and lonely, in love, but not with each other. And it was only a day after that that they made me her supervisor and we agreed to forget the whole thing ever happened. From this I knew that she could keep a secret. Mora was there in the briefing room, along with Halvorsen, who stood as close to her as he could, almost swaggering in place. I reminded myself that it was none of my business.

Also present was Fuentes, who preceded my return to the squad by a year or two. He was loyal to the department, not to me. LaMorte, a chubby little toady, spent a lot of time trying to impress me without success. And

Jeff Czerniak, a retread on the squad, like me. A few years younger, dumber, and dubiously indebted to me. I brought him back to Homicide after I helped screw up his status on another squad. All around, I could have done worse.

Halvorsen killed the lights and LaMorte turned on the slide projector, flashing a white square on the screen. Halvorsen said, "Call yesterday from the 7-Eleven at Guadalupe and MLK Drive. A transient by the name of Dennis Ayres was Dumpster diving, fished out a taco and climbed out to eat it. He said he noticed there was ketchup on it, the ketchup was congealed, and then he realized it was blood. The clerk called 911."

The screen flashed a slide of the store and the Dumpster. Halvorsen went on, reciting through the side of his mouth like he didn't mean it.

"Patrol Officer Ricardo Cruz cordoned off the area. Cruz offered the transient ten bucks to climb back in, and the transient fished out a human arm in a plastic garbage bag. Homicide was alerted. I took the call and brought Sergeant LaMorte. We donned regulation coveralls and climbed into the Dumpster."

LaMorte chimed in. "I . . . I climbed into the Dumpster."

LaMorte was trying to earn points, to make sure everyone knew what he'd done, that he'd climbed in while Halvorsen stood by. This lowered LaMorte's status. People made no attempt to hide their smirks. Halvorsen had dragged him along just to make him do the shit work.

"Duly noted," I said. "Go on, Halvorsen."

"Other bags we pulled out contained her head, her arms and a dead rabbit. We figure she was knocked up."

I was pretty sure they didn't use rabbits anymore to test for pregnancy, but I said, "Halvorsen, last time you knocked up some underage girl, did you do your own rabbit test?"

Chuckles all around. Halvorsen first cocked half a smile at the implication regarding his sex life. Then he realized he was being insulted.

He found his spot in his notes. "We located her clothes. Maternity clothes."

"Ah."

He said, "We figure she was pregnant, she told her boyfriend and he killed her."

Mora said, "How long was she pregnant before she told her boyfriend? I mean, by the time she had maternity clothes, he would have figured it out."

Halvorsen wasn't stupid, but if I was any judge of character, *he* wouldn't stick around long enough to see anyone in maternity clothes. The whole issue threw him.

Fuentes said, "Maybe he hadn't seen her for a while."

Next slide: Autopsy table. Detached arms. Fingertips cut up to avoid fingerprinting. Next slide: Head. Blood. Blue-black skin, like a full-face bruise. Wide eyes.

"Anything else?" I asked. Nothing from Halvorsen. I opened it up. "Any ideas?" Blank looks. I stared at the slide.

Finally I said, "Talk to the medical examiner and the police photographer. Clean up the face. Take a picture of it. Put it on a background. Make it . . . make it look like an ID photo."

A few mouths hung open. I couldn't tell if people were impressed by my inventiveness or disgusted by how jaded the idea was.

I said, "Put it on the news. 'Who is she? Who is this mystery woman?' And leave out the part about her being pregnant. Leave out the part about her being dead. Let someone tell you what's special about her." I got up to leave.

Halvorsen said, "What about my full squad?"

"You can have LaMorte," I said, which sounded like an insult to both of them. "Everybody else get back to whatever you were working on." I walked down the hall. Halvorsen was behind me. The others followed Halvorsen as he spoke, then faded back toward the squad room, but not so far as to miss the fight.

"No suspect," he said. "Unidentified victim. If it was your case, you'd have the whole department on it."

"Mm-hm." A phone rang in the squad room.

"It seems to me—" He poked me once on the shoulder, which prompted me, foolishly, to spin around and knock his wrist out of the way.

"I don't give a fuck how it seems to you. You have your orders."

Mora stuck her head out the squad-room door. "FBI," she told me. "For you."

"I'll take it in my office." I turned away, leaving Halvorsen in the hall, looking stupid in front of his peers, the exact action I would take if I were trying to make an enemy.

I sat in my box of an office, lifted the receiver and hit the blinking light. "Dan Reles."

"*Dan, it's Taylor Hayden, Elmira, FBI. You find anything for us? We were talking about the auto thief.*"

"Yeah," I said, stalling. "The . . . um, the guy," I tried to pronounce Drzymoa's name. "We have him in booking, waiting to see the judge. He stole the car from somewhere in town here. We're pretty sure he never left Austin."

"*How do you know?*"

"We haven't verified yet, but there are time sheets from work. ATM receipts. He could have flown up, but—"

"*No direct flights from Austin to Elmira. He'd have to change planes at least once. And he'd have to drive the Oldsmobile back, which would take maybe thirty-six hours.*"

"Right."

"*Which means someone stole the car here and ditched it there.*"

"Um. Right."

"*Did you question him about the original thief? Maybe they're working together.*"

I was afraid I'd sound negligent. Had I questioned him?

"I talked to him. He said the car was hot-wired when he found it. He twisted the wires and went for a joyride. He's telling the truth, I'm pretty sure."

"*Which opens up the question of who drove a stolen car from Mansfield to Austin.*"

Pause. "Right."

"*Well, I tell you,*" he said, blissfully taking off in a different direction. "*The first car, the Buick, belonged to Berelman, who the locals found at the Allerton Hotel in Elmira. Hell of a spot,*" he said. "*Stinks of urine and crack smoke. Or maybe freebase, who can tell? It's a twenty-eight-day place.*"

"Come again?"

He explained, "*Social Services moves them in, leaves them for twenty-eight days and transfers them out. So they do in the hotel whatever they would do on the street. But Berelman wasn't there through Social Services. He checked in on his own. And one night, maybe a week or so ago, he choked on the exhaust pipe. Maybe he tried to swallow it, or maybe someone went into a psychotic rage and rammed it down his throat. So I took the exhaust pipe and showed it around, went to a muffler shop and had the guy match it to the car it was from. Dead end, because it was just a rusted piece of pipe. We finally found the rest of it sitting in the hotel parking lot. Whoever killed Berelman must have gone to the Allerton looking for him, then found the pipe in the parking lot and picked it up on impulse and brought it inside.*"

"And no one witnessed any of this?"

"*Fair question. I knocked on every door. There seemed to be an epidemic of amnesia and temporary blindness. Even the clerk said he didn't see anyone unusual enter or leave the building that night, which is possible. If their usual is crackheads, hookers and pimps, there might not be much that would qualify as 'unusual.' Or the clerk could have been distracted, or stoned. But the building had other points of entry, so whoever came and went could have bypassed the lobby altogether.*"

I asked, "Was he a pimp?"

"*Interesting question,*" Hayden commented. "*What made you ask that?*"

What made me ask that? I said, "Who knows? Little guy goes into the business, sells women, sells drugs. Steps on someone else's toes, doesn't even know it, winds up dead in a hotel."

"*Compelling theory,*" he said. "*I'll follow up on it.*"

"Great." A pause made me think he was done and the call was over. "Well, thanks."

"*No problem. Oh, by the way, Reles. Where are you from?*"

Bingo. He was onto me. I tried to rewind the tape and figure out if I'd committed any crime of omission. "Elmira, New York," I said, mustering up something that sounded like pride.

"*Why didn't you tell me before?*"

I took a moment. "I thought you knew." Then, "You did, didn't you?"

"*Well, yes.*"

"All right, then."

"*So someone took a car from your old home town and drove it cross-country to your new one.*"

"No, someone took a car from Elmira and drove it to Mansfield. You still haven't proven that was the same someone who came to Austin."

At this point I wasn't sure if I was covering for Pop or for myself. And if I was really helping my case or committing further acts of accessory after the fact. And I still didn't know what "the fact" was. Had Pop killed Berelman? Had he helped?

I took small comfort in the fact that my reticence could pass for a typical lack of cooperation between city cops and feds.

Hayden chuckled. "*Good enough, Reles. You'll let us know if you find out anything.*"

"Sure."

"*Of course you will.*"

"Same to you. Keep me posted." As I hung up, I saw Halvorsen standing just outside my door.

It was midday, cool and bright. I hadn't accepted the fact that driving around town was no longer the head-clearing activity it had been five or ten years earlier. Housing developments erupted at what were once the edges of town, strip malls grew on every corner and we counted enough roads to move about half the cars that pumped smoke into our air. Popping into a store meant waiting in a line, and a drive meant gridlock.

As I fought traffic through town, I thought about my father taking off from the hotel. He came to Austin, dopey with sleep deprivation. He couldn't find any of his old friends, and if he had, he wouldn't have come to me. I interrogated him, scared him into running from the hotel in the middle of the night for fear I'd send a patrol or two to lock him up. He was out of my life again, probably for good. Better for everybody.

And at the same time, I thought, who should he go to? When he's on the run, when he has no place to go? Was my job so important that I should turn my own father away?

I found myself pulling in to the parking lot at the Department of Public Safety, proprietor of the finest crime lab in the state, executor of DNA tests and recorder of drivers' licenses. Badged past the guards, asked for directions, then down the hall and up the elevator, to a single pine door marked DEAD RECORDS. Inside, behind a counter, one clerk, a thirtyish white male with no distinguishing marks besides a receding hairline and an air of twitching desperation, sat at a computer terminal typing information from a tower of files to his left. Steel file cabinets and cardboard boxes, all packed with files, crowded the rest of the room.

I raised my badge. "Is this where I'd look up old drivers' licenses?"

He turned to me, eyes wide, cheeks and jaw limp. This was not the job he went to college for.

"You can if you want to," he said.

Computers are wonderful. They allow access to mountains of information at the touch of a key. But someone has to enter that information. I'd found him.

DPS had been issuing drivers' licenses since well before the advent of microchips or even photocopy machines. The records proved spotty, ill kept and inconsistent. I moved boxes, sifted through files and, in about an hour, found my father.

Benjamin Reles, born March 15, 1925, Bronx, New York. Texas driver's license issued November 11, 1968. Previous license, Elmira, New York, and a license number. Height, weight, hair color. License canceled May 27, 1975.

"Hey," I said to the clerk, showing him the documents, four cards clipped together. "How do you know where someone moved to?"

"I *don't* know. And I don't care." He didn't stop typing or raise his eyes from the document on top of his pile.

I sorted through Pop's cards: a document about his Elmira license, a stub from his Austin license, a cancellation card, then a stub with another name, James R. Flynn, born July 18, 1927. It was the same as Pop's Austin license stub, with a reference to the guy's old license, this one also in Elmira. I showed it to the clerk.

"What's this?"

No answer.

I got in the clerk's face. "Hey."

He swung his arm and spun toward me, his cheeks suddenly red. "I have a thousand of these to type in today. You know what I get to do when I get home? I get to try to forget that I'm coming in tomorrow to type in a thousand more. All I can look forward to is someday in twenty years I'll finish and they'll move me on to something else or fire me. That's it! That's it!"

I looked around the room. Even at a thousand a day, he was in for the duration. I was suddenly grateful for my job. It was hard, dangerous and potentially deadly. But every day was different.

"You should put a radio in here."

"What?" he asked.

"If you had some music, it wouldn't be so bad."

He looked around the room and reevaluated it. "Huh. Okay." Then he took the cards from me. He plucked out Flynn's.

"It's just a license transfer," he said. "Elmira to Austin."

"Why's it with my father's? The dates don't match." Flynn had made the southwesterly trek in '75, seven years after Pop and me. Flynn would know more about Elmira than I did.

The clerk said, "This shouldn't even be here, unless he left town. They've had a hundred clerks in here in five years. They keep coming up with new ways to organize the system. Probably someone thought the transfers would be grouped by city of origin."

"So this guy might still be in town?" I asked.

The clerk squinted at the card, changed screens on the computer and typed in the license number. It came up.

"Valid. 2016 Fortune Drive, Austin."

I thanked him, found my car and headed down Lamar.

The years had taken their toll on Flynn's house and on Mrs. Flynn, who answered the door wearing a colorless housedress and an expression that matched. Most people answer the door with the vague hope it might be good news. Not Mrs. Flynn.

I asked her if I could see Mr. Flynn. Without asking who I was, she said, "Elks Lodge," and shut the door.

I checked the phone book I kept in my car. The nearest Elks Lodge was on Dawson, just a few blocks away. I headed over.

Beyond the stone front of the Elks Lodge, past the entry area, I found a vast, darkened barroom. There were a dozen or more unoccupied tables, also dartboards, pinball machines, an old jukebox and neon beer signs providing most of the light, supplemented by a smattering of Christmas lights here and there and a full-size lit-up fir tree, which fit in strangely well with the neons. A blackboard listed the lunch offerings, meat loaf or chicken pot pie, both at humble prices. Two old men sat, separately, at a bar that turned two corners. A heavy guy a few years older than I was gave me the once-over from behind the bar. "Where'd you serve?" he asked.

"Frankfurt," I said when I realized he wasn't talking about food. "MPs—'71 to '73."

"So you weren't There."

We were talking about 1971, and "There" meant Vietnam. Having been There would have bought me a particular badge of veteran's honor, along with a bitching case of post-traumatic stress disorder. In that room it also would have bought me points for being a grunt in a war waged by politicians, a hero deserving of a hero's welcome he never received. And somehow it would have entered me in a club of vets who hated, more even than the rich politicians who sent them to the jungle, the war protesters who objected.

"No, man. I wasn't There."

He nodded. He hadn't been There either, or he wouldn't have talked that way about it. "Beer?"

"Coffee. I'm looking for Jim Flynn."

I followed the bartender's eyes to the old man at the near corner of the bar, perched on a stool and sagging around it in every direction. The stools had padded back panels which allowed longer periods of sitting. Old Jim wore an Elks cap with a few gold pins on it, something to do with the military. He wore a button-down shirt and a green nylon jacket, with tan polyester pants. The bulk of his gut sat below his belt. Fluid filled his eyelids, upper and lower, and blood vessels stained his nose and cheeks. He sipped beer, smoked and munched salted peanuts. If he was waiting for a heart attack or a stroke, he wouldn't wait long.

Jim Flynn raised his chins. He'd been warming that barstool for years, and I was probably the first person who ever came asking for him. I walked over.

"Can I join you?" He didn't object, so I sat on the next stool. My coffee clopped down before me. I sipped. It was cold. His beer was nearly empty. "Buy you a drink?"

Jim looked to the bartender, who gave him a fresh beer. I slapped a fiver on the bar. It disappeared. Soon four singles and two dimes appeared in its place. I left them.

"You're from Elmira?" I asked.

He raised an overgrown eyebrow. That was one too many unexplained bits of information for me to have on him. He didn't answer, but he didn't deny it.

I said, "Do you know a guy named Ben Reles?"

"Why would I?" he asked.

"That's funny," I said. "That's different from saying, 'No, I don't know him. Why do you ask?'"

He said, "Who wants to know?" and I fought back a smile.

My father was a gangster, the real thing, even if he had no influence. His colleagues were thieves and killers. So people might think that my father and his associates talked real gangster talk, whatever that was. The truth was, they learned to talk from the movies, like everybody else.

"I'm Dan Reles," I said, and it sounded less like boasting than like confessing. "I'm his son."

His old red eyes lit up, and he chuckled. "Marty!" he yelled to the bartender. "Get the lad a drink. I knew his father!"

Soon we were at a table, digging into the house special Elks Club meat loaf with a side of Jameson Irish whiskey, in the glow of the jukebox. Rosemary Clooney rhapsodized on Cape Cod, and Jim Flynn went off on Elmira.

"Wait till you see what my daughter sent me," he said, and pulled from his jacket a pack of vintage hand-painted postcards. I wiped my hands and took them, flipping through watercolor scenes of my home town. The old city hall, the stores on Water Street along the river, the long-gone carousel at Eldridge Park. Stare at those postcards a while and you'd expect to see Little Lord Fauntleroy in his round ribboned hat, skipping home from violin lessons on buckle shoes. Here Mark Twain and his family summered in the 1870s and '80s. Here Twain wrote *The Adventures of Huckleberry Finn*, inspired, I'm sure, by kids playing in the unpredictable currents of the Chemung River. Here he penned *A Connecticut Yankee in King Arthur's Court*, the ultimate fish-out-of-water story. I think of it often.

Elmira reared Hal Roach, creator of the Little Rascals and their integrated classroom. And two boxers, one Red Mekos, the other Art Sykes, who fought Joe Louis and almost beat him until he didn't. In Elmira, rumor had it, gangster Buggsy Goldstein hid out to avoid testifying against Louis "Lepke" Buchalter of Murder Incorporated. It was said Lepke himself hid out there to avoid prosecution by zealous district attorney Tom Dewey, Lepke's dark-suited, fedora-wearing flunkies drawing the stares of suspicious locals and awestruck kids as they hauled groceries up dirt roads. Nearby in Apalachin (pronounced "Apple-akkin" by the residents and "Apple-achin" by the state police), a few miles east on Route 17, the heads of the New York mob met in the late fifties. They were spotted by a state trooper suspicious of the preponderance of fancy cars, instigating a raid and a bunch of obese, well-dressed men waddling into the woods in their alligator shoes and silk socks, only to huff back hours later, exhausted, their exposure causing FBI boss J. Edgar Hoover to acknowledge, at long last, the existence of organized crime.

And mostly, Elmira had the prison, as vast and imposing as a castle. Famous criminals from as far as New York City spent time there, apprenticed and got their training, including my father's namesake, Abe Reles, called Kid Twist for his hands-on killing technique. During the Civil War and after, the prison was a camp for Confederate prisoners, a third of whom died of disease during their stay. The drinking water was drawn from a spot downstream of the toilet facilities. Inmates dubbed the place Hellmira.

Paint pretty postcards, talk about famous sons all you like, but the town lived and always will live in the shadow of the prison. You can't miss it. It's the big house on the hill.

Among the painted cards was a black-and-white photo, circa 1950, of the prosperous downtown shopping district on a sunny day, mothers in pretty dresses, leading children from Iszard's Department Store to Thom McAn's for shoes. The photo lied, like photos do, by making everyone look unworried. But it showed a town I remembered.

Flynn and I gazed into the photo. He said, "I don't know if you remember the town back then, in the fifties and sixties."

"Sure I do," I said.

"Stores everywhere. Department stores, jewelers. Furriers. Dairies, men's shoes, photographers, butchers, bakers. Anything you need."

I remembered that. Water Street made up the heart of downtown—shops, restaurants, department stores. Families could spend a Friday evening, especially near the holidays, shopping, bumping into friends, stopping for a bite or a drink and shopping some more. We must have done this as a family, my parents and I, when I was little, but I couldn't remember. I could remember doing it just with my mother.

He said, "The flood comes and now look at it."

"What flood?"

"In '72," he said. "You should read up on it. Houses wiped away, flipped over. The river came up, breached a twenty-foot floodwall. Ripped up the Walnut Street Bridge. Knocked out most of the foundries—the steel, the fire-engine factory. And the dairies. Cows don't swim so good. The whole downtown under six feet of water. Nixon called it the greatest national disaster in the nation's history. We were doing terrific before that. Everybody was working. The foundries were smoking, people made money, spent it at the stores. Everyone was happy. Flood killed us. We got federal money to rebuild. City spent it on that crazy park on Water Street. You can't shop in a park! Corning got money, and they rebuilt their downtown district. Now Corning is rich and we're in the toilet."

He showed me one of the postcards bearing a map of the town. What struck me was that it had the same layout as Austin. About two-thirds of the town sat north of the river, which ran east-west. When I came to Austin at fifteen, I must have figured that all towns were laid out this way.

"Well," he said, "the recession hit. The foundries that were still there closed, one by one. The typewriter factory went last. No jobs, no money to spend, so the stores started closing, even the big ones. And the movie houses. Then there was the Mob."

"The Mob?"

He squinted at me. "You remember a place called Kareem's Big Store, on Zoar?"

Sure I remembered it. It was a stone's throw from my high school, South Side, on the lesser end of town. A white house with a big painted sign on the roof, a Pepsi logo in the window. On the left as you went in, the comics rack. Superman, the Flash, Green Lantern and all those Marvel guys operating on the edge of the law, the renegade heroes. On the right, the soda fountain. Five spinning stools. Two immersion blenders for malteds, a display with every conceivable kind of candy, red hots and jawbreakers and Turkish Taffy. In the back of the store, model airplanes and cars. The place was kid heaven, specifically for the neglected kids who had a few ill-gotten bucks in their pockets and no mother to bitch them out for filling up on junk before dinner.

Flynn said, "Your father used to go in and empty the cash register. Kareem, the poor bastard, counted his profits in pennies. If there wasn't enough, your father would break bottles, frighten Kareem's wife."

I tried to imagine my father doing that, and it took less effort than I'd have hoped. He hated the work, but he did it. Maybe he broke bottles so he wouldn't have to break bones. "I'm sorry," I said. "That's terrible."

He nodded, eyes on me. "I worked for Coleman's Dairy," he said. "Little place. I'd start early, finish around three, stop at Kareem's, sit at the counter with a cup of coffee and a daily paper. I remember you," he said, with something other than fondness. "You used to swagger in with your gang, tear the comic books and steal the penny candy. Scare off the little kids who came in for their ice-cream cones."

"We never scared off the little kids." I wanted to believe that I never did that, at least not deliberately. But our presence could have had that effect. It was supposed to. I did remember walking in like I owned the place, the same way I walked into my high-school classes and anywhere else. It was a strut I learned at the gym. The guys I learned it from had probably picked it up in prison. It was a good ploy for pretending you had something.

Flynn said, "Why do you think that old Arab put up with you? He had a shotgun under the counter. But he knew whose kid you were."

"I'm sorry," I said. "That's not who I am now."

"What do I care who you are now? Your mob friends killed that town. We were sick, but they killed us."

"That's crazy."

"Ask your father. Maybe we could have grown back. Who knows? But the shakedowns, they never stopped. There was no money coming in, and they kept sending someone for their share. Soon there was nothing. And then they'd torch the stores for the insurance money."

It didn't seem right. If there was a flood and a recession, it wasn't like the mob killed the town. Or did I just argue the point to defend my father? "Was it the same for everybody?"

"Most of us. The small ones. The chain stores left because there was no business. But the local owners, they all paid. After a while it was easier to close down and let the fires take the store than to stay and struggle. There's nothing now. No one left to rob."

It was about time for me to pay up and split. I threw a twenty on the table, enough for both our meals and a 90 percent tip. I stood and made to go, and something stopped me.

"Just one thing," I said. "What brought you down here?"

"Looking for work," he said.

"Yeah, but why here?"

"I heard there was work down here. Someone said there was jobs, the town was growing. So I came."

"Did you know my father was here?"

"Here in Austin?"

Flynn got to Austin in '75, right around the time Pop left. "How well did you know my father?"

"We'd drink in the same places, back in Elmira. Small town. I knew everybody."

"Tell me . . . tell me something. You stayed in touch with people in Elmira?"

"My daughter married the city records keeper. I go back every Christmas."

It was a long shot. "Did you ever hear of a guy called the *makher*?"

Flynn pursed his lips and eyeballed me like I was fucking with him. "What do you take me for? You know anyone in Elmira who *doesn't* know Sam Zelig?"

One promising night, word got to my father in the ring that he was to take a dive in the next round. Mortellaro was supposed to get Pop with his famous left hook.

"His famous left hook blows dogs," Pop said in one version of the story. "Doesn't matter. Ike says so."

Ike Zelig. Who owned my father's contract. Who owned my father.

In the months after my first fight, when I was eleven—the fight that gave my nose its character—I built up my skills. I was sparring no-contact with a bigger kid one day when one of the bosses came in. Flashy suit, gold rings around his heavy fingers. He spotted me and mocked my showing in the ring the day of my broken nose. He went on to mock my father's performance in the ring the night of his dive, years earlier. He topped it off by calling me a motherless chump. The bigger kid laughed with him. I flew into a blind rage and pounded the bigger kid bloody, didn't stop hammering at him when he went down, not until they pulled me off him. The gangster stuffed a fiver into my glove and said I was a tough Jew. That was Sam Zelig.

It was the first time I experienced the blind rage that would plague me most of my life, and with it the shame that went with being ditched by my mother. On top of all that, there was Sam Zelig making fun of me, calling my father a loser for taking a dive they made him take, calling me motherless after mob life drove my mother away. And I couldn't even take a straight shot at him. But in my mind every punch I threw at that kid cracked Sam Zelig's rotten teeth.

Four years later, in 1968, my father did something to piss off the Zeligs, and we fled Elmira in the middle of the night. Which is how I got to Austin.

Yes, I know Sam Zelig.

Pax Berelman was a nobody, a loser. He must have worked for Zelig, done errands for him the way my father had. The jet-black Buick seemed more like something a mob boss would own and have registered under someone else's name than it did a car owned by a two-bit lackey who lived in a welfare hotel and burned bodies at the crematorium.

But if Zelig killed Berelman, why didn't he do it on the road somewhere, somewhere with fewer witnesses, instead of in a hotel? Maybe he did it impulsively. Maybe he wanted people to know how dangerous he still was.

Maybe it was about Irina.

And here I was two thousand miles away after all these years, getting dragged back into Elmira's muck. Sam Zelig would have to be past seventy, but he was still alive. And kicking.

If Sam Zelig was still operating after forty years in crime, he'd lived to see the passing of the RICO Act. Under that act, the federal government could prosecute criminals for racketeering, rather than just for their many individual crimes. The FBI would have a file on Sam Z.

But there was no calling the FBI without telling them what I knew about Pop, how he was a sure bet for the guy who dumped Pax Berelman's Buick in Pennsylvania and stole the Cutlass for the trip to Austin. And there was no convincing them that Pop had dumped the Buick without knowing Berelman was dead. We knew who we were dealing with.

I made it back to the office in the thick of the afternoon, flipped through my notes and dialed a long shot.

"*Elmira Police.*"

"Lieutenant Reles, Austin Police, for Sergeant Lowry."

I held on. A few minutes later, I heard, "*Lowry.*"

"Lowry, this is Reles in Austin."

"*Hey, there, Reles. Any luck with that—what was his name?—Berelman?*" He was screwing with me already.

"A little. I know he worked for a guy named Sam Zelig." I knew no such thing, but I suspected. "Know anything about him?"

"*Can't say I do.*"

Right. Never heard of a mob boss operating in his shrinking town for nearly half a century. "Okay," I said, "why don't you put me in touch with whoever's in charge of Organized Crime."

"*We don't have that here.*"

Funniest words in the English language. J. Edgar Hoover used that line for decades and never failed to get a laugh.

"You're sure about that."

"*Tell you something about vice in this town, Reles,*" he said, and I kept expecting him to address me as "me boy." He started slow and built momentum as he spoke. "*The guys who used to run it are dead. The couple of wops who are still around, holy shit, so fuckin' stupid. We got this tape from Buffalo, one of 'em introduces this guy, 'He's a friend of ours.' You know. He's a made man. But this one wop says, 'How could he be a friend of ours? I never fuckin' met him!'*" Lowry laughs, a bellow. "*They had to explain to him what 'a friend of ours' means. He never saw the movies. They learned all this from the movies. Well, this one boss in Buffalo, you know, the big one. Pitaro or whatever. He makes more money from his pizza place than he does from his operations.*" Again he laughs. "*Changing times.*"

I asked him about the Jews.

Lowry said, "*The Jews were more sophisticated. Not so much leg breaking. More like a clique. A couple of guys working together. Two guys, five guys. They'd invest in property, back each other's enterprises. This one guy buys a Frank Lloyd Wright house up by the war widows' home. Stained glass, copper pipes. Well, you can't ransack it, it's historical. Right? So he sells it to five or six companies. They strip the house. Everything. The stained glass, the grandfather clock. Copper piping alone is worth a million. Then they rent it out as a toxic waste dump. Someone from the city figures out what's up, the neighbors are getting sick, kids' hair is falling out. They try to find the owner. The house is now owned by fifteen offshore companies. Can't find any of them, by then the value is gone, the city is robbed, and there's no one to take the blame for cleaning up the waste. You ask Hymie, the guy who bought the house in the first place, he says*"—and here Lowry put on what he figured for a

Jewish accent—" *'What do I know from toxic waste? I buy the house, I sell the house.' That's your Jew mobster.''*

I knew Lowry wasn't smart enough to make up the story about the house. But I knew there was more than one story.

If you drove west along Water Street, past the downtown areas, past the now-abandoned businesses, the jewelers and furriers and restaurants, you'd get to a more posh area called West Elmira. The houses didn't look too big. They just had more levels, more windows and gables. They gave a sense that their size was normal, that every house should have three flights and eighteen rooms. In south Elmira where I grew up, a house like that would have been broken up into apartments, and that was before the flood.

Anyway, if you drove far enough, you'd see a synagogue, a low brick building with no ornamentation. Drive another block, and on the same side of the same street you'd see another synagogue.

Figure one of the synagogues is more Orthodox, or more Reform. Or someone in the community got pissed off and built a rival temple down the block, allowing the tiny community of rich Jews in West Elmira to take sides, forever. For whatever reason, they couldn't build one *shul* big enough for their needs.

Story: Jewish guy gets stuck alone on a desert island. They find him a year later, he's built *two* synagogues. They ask him why he needed two.

He points to one of them. "That's the one I don't go to."

There are different kinds of Jews. There are different kinds of Jewish criminals.

"Listen," I said to Lowry. "I got a comfortable chair here, my phone works. I can spend the rest of the day and tomorrow calling every official in Elmira, telling them you never heard of Sam Zelig. Or you can put me in touch with someone who can help me."

"Look," he blurted, *"I don't know what this place was like when you were here . . ."* And I remembered I hadn't told him where I was from. Someone had. The FBI?

He took a breath. *"I'll call you back."*

Before I hung up, I noticed Halvorsen in the doorway again. "What?" I inquired.

"You wanna come in here a minute?"

In the squad room, the phones were ringing. Halvorsen's desk was piled with pink message slips. LaMorte added one to the pile and took another call. Mora was trying to do a phone interview on a cold case, but her phone kept ringing, too. "Could you hold, please?" she said. Click. "Homicide. Just a minute." She reached for the message pad, scribbled something and handed it to LaMorte.

I stepped back into the hall, Halvorsen following.

"This is just from the midday news." They'd passed the photo of the murdered woman to the TV stations. "It takes two of us just to take the messages. How are we supposed to—"

"All right," I said. "What do you know?"

"The rabbit and the woman, smooth, neat cuts, from the same knife. If the phones would stop ringing, or if I could put one man on the phone full-time, then one to chase the names. If someone says, 'I think that's Jane Smith.' We call Jane. If we can't find her, we run her name by DPS, ask for her picture."

"Tell me why you need the whole squad."

"You'd do it for Mora."

It was a great argument, because it factored in the stupidity and childishness of most official decision making, including mine. Of course I'd do it for Mora, because I liked her and because we had a past together. And I wouldn't do it for Halvorsen because I hated him and he was after my job. But I couldn't lay it out that way, especially if he might file a grievance.

"Fine," I said, and his head almost popped open in triumph. "But show me some results. Fast."

My phone was ringing when I got back to my office. "*Yeah, Reles, it's Lowry. I got someone to talk to you about Sam Zelig.*"

"Great. Who is it?"

"*Ike Zelig.*"

Ike Zelig. Sam's big brother. Lowry wouldn't even talk to me about Sam, but with his back against the wall, he'd give me Ike's home phone.

"Why would Ike talk to me?"

"*He's sort of a captive audience. He likes to talk. Don't say I never gave you nothing.*"

It turned out Ike Zelig was doing ten to twenty for murder, in Elmira prison. This, apparently, helped him avoid federal prosecution and kept him in a state facility close to home. I called the number at the prison, waited, got transferred, waited, was told to call back in an hour. The last of the afternoon slipped by. I called Rachel at home, and she didn't answer. I hoped she'd taken Josh shopping or something equally safe. I checked the machine for messages and left one of my own. I made a few other calls and tried the prison again. Finally the guards at the New York State Correctional Facility at Elmira put me on with one of the specters of my childhood, owner of the gym, fixer of fights, the great and powerful Ike Zelig. He was eating something.

"*Delicious,*" he said, still chewing. His voice was weak and breathless, wheezy, but had an undertone of threat. "*I'm not allowed intoxicants or porn. They don't want me getting a hard-on. In solitary. Hah! I weigh three-fifty. I haven't seen my dick in years. So I have people bring me food. You know I keep kosher here.*"

"No, I didn't know."

"*The kosher food is better. Rabbi says—we got a rabbi comes in twice a month—he says there's seventy guys on the kosher diet. Me and maybe one other are real sheenies. But I converted to Muslim for Eid al-Adha. It's a feast day.*" He let out a weak cough. It sounded like his mouth was still full, but that could be blamed on fat cheeks or a bloated tongue. Most interviews you wonder if someone will talk. Other times you wonder if you can even squeeze in a question. He went on. "*It commemorates Ibrahim's willingness to sacrifice his son. But to the Arabs he was supposed to sacrifice Ishmael the raghead, not Ike the kike.*" He paused. "*Two brothers, right? One of 'em gets sacrificed. The Jews say it's Isaac, and the Arabs say it's Ishmael. Everybody wants to be the sacrifice.*"

He puffed out some short breaths. Maybe he was laughing. "*I'm Isaac,*" he said.

"*Anyway, God lets Ibrahim off the hook at the last minute, and he sacrifices a ram instead. So we eat ram, or cow. I converted for a fuckin' steak dinner.*"

He laughed so hard he coughed, brought up some phlegm and spat it somewhere. "*You should see those bastards eat. But the warden got clued in. Now you can only convert twice a year. It's hard. The Muslim holidays move*" *around, the Jewish holidays move around. I gotta time it right, be a Jew again by Passover. Fuck Yom Kippur! Who invented a holiday where you can't eat?"*

From far away, *"Shut the fuck up in there!"*

Ike said, *"You shut up, cocksucker."* Something about his voice kept the guard from talking back. Then he said, *"You a cop? They said you were a cop."*

I said, "Yeah, in Texas. Does your brother send you food?"

The sound came from him like thunder. *"Don't mention that bastard to me!"* Something about him made me jolt even though he was two thousand miles away, behind bars and at a weight that didn't make fast movement a likelihood.

He went on. *"If it wasn't for me, he'd be selling used clothes to niggers. I made that fuck!"* He settled down to muttering. *"Son of a bitch. Bastard fuck. Like to see him in here. Shoulda fuckin' killed him when I had the chance."*

"Why didn't you?"

He groaned with what must have been the shifting of his tonnage. He asked, *"Ever hear of Arnold Rothstein?"*

"Sure."

"There was a man. The first Jewish boss. The first real crime boss. Before that, Monk Eastman and those assholes, just street kids. Rothstein was the one who made it big, made the industry what it is. What it was. Organized. Classy. He didn't grow up on the streets. Rich man's son. Management material. He knew how to dress. Everyone who came after him was a knockoff. You see mob guys in silk suits, fancy dago shoes, diamond stickpins. They're all trying to be Rothstein, they don't even know it. But they don't have what he had. Like dressing up a gorilla. Doll him up, he's still a fuckin' gorilla. Rothstein, he was the genuine article. But he died young, and I'm still alive. How do you figure?"

I could never figure a mobster living beyond forty, least not one the size of a walrus. To be nice I said, "You're smarter than him?"

"Thank you. No. He trusted too many people. I didn't trust nobody. Not even my piece-of-shit brother. You know he did some time now and then. We all did. He was the only one came out happier than he went in. I don't mean

he was happy to get out. It was like the Joint made him happier. Stronger. Meaner."

"What did he do?" It was hard to keep the conversation on Sam.

Ike wheezed. *"It was drugs that did us in,"* he said. *"Before drugs you could do anything. Booze, broads, gambling. Insurance. But you can't buy a judge on a drug charge. Why? The public won't let you. They'll put up with a lot of shit. But not that."*

"What happened?"

"We stayed out of it. And in come the niggers and the chinks and the wops, the dumb ones. They bring the heat down on everybody. After the flood I figured, shit, we been on the way down since Apalachin. Take the money and run. Guys who want real money go to L.A., Vegas. But Sammy won't budge. He's in construction. Okay, construction. I could go to Florida, but I have to stay here to keep him from getting whacked. The old guys are all gone. Now it's the kids—Russians, Jamaicans. They don't know the rules. You can't even call it the mob. Bikers and shitkickers, fuckin' Aryan skinhead Nazi shits! I'd tear 'em apart with my bare hands!" He built to such a frenzied peak that I wondered if another few minutes of talk would set me up to hear his overdue final coronary. He caught his breath and went on. *"Dopeheads with their meth labs. Crap. So Sam's getting into this new shit—"*

"What kind of shit?"

A silence. I interrupted his thought.

"Don't worry about it," he said. *"I've had enough of this."* He wasn't speaking directly into the receiver.

"Ike, wait, please."

" 'Ike'?" he roared. *"I'm your buddy? I'm Ike Fucking Zelig. Who the fuck are you?"*

"I'm Dan Reles. You used to own my father's boxing contract."

Another silence and then a breath. It could have been the contented sigh of something that had just eaten a child.

"Ben Reles. He married that pretty cooze—"

"My mother, yeah."

"Ri-ight," he said, in two syllables. *"Thanks for calling. Fuckin' guards got me all shaky."*

Ike went on. *"So Sam keeps bringing the heat on, and all they can find on either of us for sure is me on an old extortion rap."*

"They said you were in for murder."

"Ah, we cut a deal. So I could stay here instead of going to the Fed."

It didn't make any sense. Take a murder rap to live out his life in a state facility, just to dodge a RICO prosecution and dying in the Fed? Someone was lying, but I didn't care. "You ever work with a guy named Pax Berelman?"

No answer. *"I been in for two years. What do I know?"*

Another lie. It was a cinch he hadn't heard of Irina, or that I'd get the same answer anyway.

"Pax Berelman," I said again. "Little guy. Looked like a jockey."

"Doesn't ring a bell."

"You see my father lately?"

"Your father? Not for years."

I realized that he still had the mobster's aversion to answering direct questions, but he was stuck in the Joint and he liked to talk. I tried to think of something that would launch another monologue. I took a chance on pissing him off, even if it might make him hang up, and asked, "Do you think Sam's crazy?"

He breathed hard, and I could hear his chair squeal in pain as he settled back. *"He's rough on girls. Always was. And dogs. I gotta tell you, he was the meanest fuck I ever saw."* It sounded like admiration, even affection, as he outlined his brother's exploits. *"He could kill someone with a piece of wire, a shovel, an ice pick. Well, anyone could do that. He'd squeeze the life out of a guy with one hand, gouge an eyeball out with his thumb. Sam once jammed a pen in a guy's eye so far it killed the guy. A ballpoint! I saw him slash a guy's throat with a fuckin' credit card. Clip a guy's throat cables with a wire cutter. Once he stuck a meathook in a guy's head. No, his ear, like a fish. Stuck it all the way into his brain, twisted it around, put chains on it and dumped him in the river, still breathing. And don't let him near your balls!"* He laughed again, finally wheezing for air.

"Was he beaten?" I asked. "I mean, as a kid."

"We were all beaten!" he yelled suddenly. *"Liberal bullshit. Tell ya some-*

thing. Our father would come home drunk. He blew his pay. And he'd tell us we had to go out and make ten dollars. That was a lot of money then. We're maybe thirteen, fourteen years old. He didn't care how we got it, but we couldn't come home until we had it. This happens maybe five times. One day we're out, we roll drunks, shake down kids, old ladies. Pull together maybe fifteen, sixteen bucks. I came up with the ideas, but Sam was mean. He could do anything. And I'm thinking, *Why are we handing this over?* We go home and wait for Pop. He comes in drunk. We knock him over the head, throw him down the fuckin' stairs. Falls over the landing, crashes straight down on his skull. Crack.

"Tell you a story. Before this, we had this big Doberman named Max. We got the food for him ourselves, so Ma let him stay. Sam paid this whore on the street to blow him, blow the dog, just to make her cry. Anyway, one day my sister comes home with this little gray kitten. Cute thing. Climbs into the dog's food dish to eat something. Great big food dish, little cat. Max, that's the dog, he comes up. Cat looks at Max, curious, not scared. Max looks at the cat. Sniffs it. Then he opens his mouth, puts it over the cat's head and bites it right off. My sister screams. I tell you, even I hollered, and by then I'd seen a guy croak. Sam, he laughs. Thinks it's the greatest thing he's ever seen.

"I know he cut up a cat after that. First that one, that was already dead. But then a different one. Some cat from the street. My mother caught him at it. Christ, she beat him bloody, then prayed for him. If I were her, I would have left God out of it. Keep it in the family. Once she prayed and then held his hand on the stove. But Sam was her baby. Me, I could chase whores all night and she wouldn't lose any sleep. Sam . . . after my father left, she made Sam come in and kiss her goodnight. It was crazy."

"The cats," I reminded him.

"Yeah, cats, dogs, birds. Girls, later. Used to be he'd just smack 'em around. Everyone does that. But he liked it. After a while . . ." He was going to add to that, but he didn't.

"You want an explanation?" he said. "His mother didn't love him enough? Bullshit. He's a sick fuck, that's your explanation. And that's not the half of it."

◆ ◆ ◆

The last light in the sky had slipped away by the time I pulled up in front of my new house. The house was dark, too, and Rachel's Subaru wasn't there. I hoped they'd gone out for dinner, Rachel and Josh, and left me a note.

I was holding onto this thought as I slammed my car door shut and walked up the path, when I sensed someone rushing across the lawn toward me, a hulking figure in the dark. I turned and saw another one, a matching giant, taller than me and broader. I didn't stop to check facial features. It would have been a great time to draw my .38, shoot one, whip around and shoot the other. But that takes time, to see the threat, evaluate the threat and choose action, then to draw the weapon, aim and fire, aim and fire again. All this time they were running for me, from only a few feet away. So by the time I realized I wouldn't make it to the house, then reached for my suddenly evasive weapon, one of them tackled me, and we both hit the ground hard.

I struggled—force of habit—as they lifted me and slammed me against their car, a four-by-four, my arms splayed crucifixion-style. The men both rose well over six feet, fat but powerful. Maybe in their mid-thirties. A smaller third man appeared, about the same age, dark-haired and thin, dressed sporty in a black leather blazer. He said, "What's this?" and pulled the .38 from my belt holster. "Well?"

"Family heirloom," I said. I didn't know if he'd caught my response, but he dumped my bullets onto the pavement, clicked the cylinder back in place, tested the weapon's weight and whacked me across the face with it. Then he put it back in my holster and spoke to his goons.

"Throw him in the back." His voice sounded nasal and raspy at the same time and gave him the aspect of a high-strung rat.

I didn't see another soul standing out on the street. It wasn't past dinnertime. People would still be circulating. But if they were, if they saw the tumult from their windows, they were savvy enough not to interfere. Flip side, it would have been helpful if someone had thought to call the cops.

For my part, I could have screamed for help. But that, or even slipping a glance in the direction of my house, might have tipped them to look inside. I couldn't swear the house was empty, and I didn't want Rachel and Josh to be part of this.

The two giants started moving me toward the four-by-four's rear hatch. I could see from the red on my jacket that my cheek was bleeding, a realization that might scare someone who hadn't grown up in a boxing ring. I pretended I was all wiped out, half unconscious from the masterly blow to my face and not likely to be a problem. I dropped at the knees and let them carry me, dragging my feet across the pavement while I grasped for the brilliant idea that would get me out of there. The boss headed for the driver's seat.

There were two rows of seats in the vehicle, plus storage space in back for me. In a moment they'd tie me down or knock me out, to make sure I didn't escape.

Any idiot can tell you that the chances of surviving an involuntary ride are slim. Give a guy your car, your money, your Rolex, the deed to the farm. But don't get in the car with him. No matter what it takes.

One of the big guys wrestled with the back-door latch. I figured that was as good a chance as I was going to get. I punched the other one in the throat, hard enough to knock him down, but not kill him. He writhed on the concrete, choking for air. The guy with the keys spun around. I popped him in the eye. He lost his balance, but his left shot out and caught me in the jaw. I rolled with it and cracked him twice on the side of the head and ran. But I was too slow.

This time they knocked me down and kicked the shit out of me. I could see that the little guy was doing most of the kicking. In the ribs, in the gut. One in the kidney that made me want to cry. And one serious one in the head. If I was standing, it would have knocked me down again. I managed to get out of that with my eyes and balls intact, but everything else hurt. I had no fight left in me when they tossed me in the back.

The car seemed to swirl as I lay twisted on its floor like a battered dog. Some talk from the front seats.

"You figure why?"

The rat said, "Beats the fuck outta me."

"Hey," I said. "You guys work in town?"

"Shaddup."

I tried to sit up but my gravity went haywire and my head dropped again. From all the turns, there was no guessing where we were going. Think. Who could these guys be?

I asked if I was under arrest. They laughed.

"Yeah, you're under arrest all right."

Not cops. Of course not. And not Texans. Christ, I'd heard that accent before, but where? I was so dopey I was almost dreaming.

I should have known right away, but I was half dead. Western New York. Elmira. Oh, Pop. What did you do?

I must have sounded drunk, but I tried again. "I know you're not feds." They didn't bite.

We turned onto gravel, rode another fifty feet or so and stopped. I needed more power than my brain was putting out.

The back door opened. They reached in and hoisted me to my feet. The ground dipped. I tipped my head in a direction that might have been forward and puked up Elks Club meat loaf.

They cursed, but they didn't hit my addled head again. I'd get my balance back if I got the chance. Suddenly I realized how cold I was. And with the abrupt emptying of my stomach, I felt even weaker.

Two of them took my arms, and the smaller one took my legs, carrying me facedown in case I heaved again. A door creaked open, and we headed into darkness, someone shining a flashlight. I got from the echoes of their footsteps and the wind that we were someplace large, like a warehouse. I smelled sawdust and oil, motor oil. I tried to focus my eyes, but all I could see was a floor—part concrete, part wood—moving under me.

"Here," the rat said. They dropped me, and I curled inward like a caterpillar. I struggled to sit up.

Suddenly there was light, a hundred-watt bulb, suitable for blinding someone already near blind. I had to blink a few times before I saw that it shone from the cage of a yellow drop light, the kind with a hook, a handle and a cord leading into the darkness. I pushed myself up to a sitting position on the dusty floor and tried to see where I was.

I thought I knew the town pretty well, but not so well to guess where a barren factory would be, or a warehouse with no wares inside. One of hundreds of empty buildings that could fall down in the night without anyone missing them. I could tell that the ceiling was high, because the light didn't reach it. Seeing how the light didn't reach the walls either, I couldn't quite gauge the room's size. What I did see in the light of the single bulb was a piece of machinery, mounted on wheels, attached to the same extension cord that led to the bulb. Painted yellow. Cylindrical like a cement mixer. I'd seen one before. A wood chipper.

The beauty of a wood chipper is that you can feed a whole tree into it, and with little effort it'll reduce the tree to pulp. My face would put up even less resistance.

"This is a chipper," the rat said, missing the final *r*. He threw a switch, and the machine revved, roared, then screamed. Just then the two goons yanked me to my feet and showed me the feed. I could see a whirl of sharp edges moving at blurring speed. The rat tossed a chunk of wood he'd found into the feed. With a slight raising of pitch, the chipper bounced it around, ground the wood in its teeth and spat kindling out the other side.

The rat flipped the switch again, and the machine softened to a less-painful screech, then slowed nearly to stopping.

He said, "I see two options. We feed ya in headfirst. You'd see where you was going, the blades close in on your face, your eyes. It would scare the fuck out of ya, but you'd be dead pretty fast. Heh-heh. Option two is we shove ya in feetfirst. This saves your face, so to speak. But you'd be alive for a long time. Maybe you'd be lucky, pass out from the pain before, say, we mulched you up to your knees. Maybe not. How much of a guy can you cut off before you kill him? His feet? His knees? His balls? I figure if you cut a guy off at the waist, you kill him. Now we'll know for sure."

I felt my jaw tightening. "What . . . do you want?"

"The other thing is," he said, "if you change your mind, give us what we want, you still have time. Maybe you lose your feet. So what? Lots of people don't have feet. Maybe you lose your legs, but you can still fuck."

Then they threw the switch again, and the engine roared.

I scanned their faces. They'd done this before. They weren't bluffing. I yelled, "What do you *want*?!"

They flipped the switch, and the engine slowed. The two huge guys shoved my face close to the chipper's open end. I pushed back, but I was no match for them. I could see a whirring kaleidoscope of saw blades. They didn't look very accommodating, even moving at half speed.

"Where's the girl?"

The question "What girl?" would have cost me my face, so I asked, "The Russian?"

That was the one.

"I left her and my father at a hotel on South Congress, the Austin Hotel, the one with the little bungalows. I went back for them this morning, and they were gone. No note, no nothing."

There was a silence, some signal I didn't see, and they hoisted me up. One had me around the chest, the other holding my feet. They were going to feed me in headfirst.

Show me a man who says he'd never sell out his father, and I'll show you a man who's never been held face-first over a wood chipper.

I told them everything. About my father and the car, and Irina. About Pax Berelman and Sam Zelig. About my phone calls with the feds. I wasn't holding much back. I didn't know what they'd do next, how they'd use this information against me, or against Pop. But I was out of options.

The rat thought it over. Then he said, softly, "Bullshit." He flipped the switch and the chipper cooked up to a squeal.

"I'm a cop!" I yelled over the engine. I reached for my badge but didn't get it. "I know Lowry. I know the mayor."

I looked inside the chamber, guessing how long I'd suffer before my heart gave out. And what they'd do to my father afterward. Or, if they didn't find him, what they'd do to Rachel and Josh.

There were three men. Two were huge, and I was weak and dizzy. But the third man, the rat, was dealing with the dials. And one of the apes had just been punched in the throat. That meant one man was holding me up, around the chest, and the weaker one, the one I'd punched, had my legs. And if I had any strength in reserve, this might be my last chance to use it.

I reached over my shoulder and found the ear of the guy who had me around the chest. I yanked hard.

He fell back screaming, and my head hit the floor.

I was starting to lose consciousness when I felt the heat and smelled the smoke, and the shriek of the machine reverberated against my sore skull as I realized that the room was on fire.

As dawn was breaking, the two angels hurried Lot. "Get moving!" they said. ". . . You don't want to be swept away because of the city's sin."

—Genesis 19:15

There's smoke everywhere. I'm staggering down a hall. I kick open a door, and there's my mother. She's weak, but beautiful. Younger than I am now. I try to save her, but my legs won't move. She says something.

"You never came back."

I say, "I was here. You left."

But it's not my mother. It's Rachel. I left her alone. And the smoke is thicker and I try to suck in air and my throat burns and I wake up.

The room really is full of smoke, and I can see the flames in a doorway a few feet away. I smell oil. The place is soaked. I've only been out a few seconds. I try to get up but the floor dips and I fall.

Knocked down in the ring, and the count is six.

I crawl. I'm coughing, spitting. I can't find the exit. I feel the heat behind me.

Seven.

The smoke gets thicker. There's no air to breathe. My throat burns when I try to inhale. I crawl away from the heat, the fire that comes through a back door and spreads along the floor by one wall. I still can't find the exit. I can't see.

Eight.

My eyes burn. I blink, but I can't see any better with them open than closed. My skin is hot.

Nine.

I am fucked.

Two hands grab me by the back of my jacket and drag me along the floor. The smoke is lessened, there is no smoke, it's cooler.

It's cold. I'm sitting in the dirt. Someone puts something in my hand, and I drop it. He gives it to me again, raises it to my mouth. Water. I suck water from the bottle. It rolls down my burning throat. I spit, cough painfully. Then I drink. I can breathe. I'm cold.

I'm alive.

I was in the passenger seat of someone's car. The window was open, thirty-five-degree wind whipping through. I was cold, but not burning. I didn't know who he was or where we were going. I didn't care. I was alive.

I needed to get home, make sure Rachel and Josh were okay.

Out of the car, I was able to stand on my own and take a few uncertain steps. I was dizzy, but I could walk. He got me inside, into an elevator. He pushed open a door.

"Clean yourself up."

I was in a bathroom. I blinked under the light over the mirror. I was dizzy from the blows to my head. There was soot on my face, and blood, from when they pistol-whipped me. I'd looked worse. Sawdust and dirt coated my hands. My right was caked with blood also. I washed it off. No wound. Not my blood. Someone else's.

Outside the bathroom he led me through another door, a big bright room, then a small office. Soon I was sitting in a comfortable leather chair opposite his desk. Some guy with rubber gloves was standing over me. He wiped my face, said something about the wound on my left cheek, patched it with small bandages. I closed my eyes. When I opened them, the guy with the gloves was gone. I saw a window behind the man opposite me. Dark. It was still night. To my right was a wall of shelves, holding stacked papers, bottled chemicals, machines that printed out something on rolls of paper. Everything I'd seen in any office and much of what I'd seen in a crime lab, plus a few items I didn't recognize.

He sat behind the desk. Asian. Tall. White shirt with narrow blue stripes, which meant I could see. Gold necktie. Late thirties. I blinked and focused. He had a bronze coin the size of a silver dollar, and he was rolling it over his fingers. It seemed to move under its own power, over the fingers of one hand, one finger at a time, then the other hand, then under the fingers and peeking up between them. He didn't glance at me but said, "There are eyedrops on the desk."

I found them and wet my eyes. They burned at first, then settled.

I cleared my throat. My first words in my extended life: "You don't mind if I name my kid after you."

He said, "It's Chu. C-H-U. Watch this." He held up the coin in his right hand, placed it in his left palm with a flourish, then closed his left hand. He snapped his right fingers, opened his left hand, and the coin was gone. I pointed to the right. He opened it. No coin.

I said, "My house. My family."

"They're fine. I have someone watching them."

"Where are we?"

"Federal Building."

"There was blood on my hand. I remember reaching for some guy's ear."

"I saw him running. I didn't get a good look. I say you tore his ear, but you didn't tear it off."

He spoke in clipped sentences, with absolute clarity, military and scientific precision in each phrase, like checking off points on an outline. The only hint of an accent was a slight blurring of the final *r*, but not the way anyone in New York blurred it. I guessed he'd been to business school. Harvard Business School.

"He'll go to a hospital," I said. "We can catch him there."

"We can, but we won't. Where's the coin?"

I couldn't guess. He reached into his shirt pocket, plucked out the coin.

He did the same trick again, held up the coin, placed it in his left, made a fist, waved, snapped. This time he opened both hands. No coin.

"Let's see your badge," he said.

I pulled it out and opened it for him. The coin dropped from the leather protector and clanked onto his desk. He caught it on the bounce.

"Bullshit," I said. "You had two coins. You put one in my wallet while I was out cold."

"Of course it's bullshit," he deadpanned. "It's all bullshit. But for a split second, you believed that the coin had magically transported into your back pocket. A moment later you knew you were being bullshitted, but your eyes lit up anyway. Because just maybe it was true. Look."

He rolled the coin over his fingers again. This time when it hit the end of his hand, it popped into the air, two feet up, and he caught it with the other hand, letting it continue its caterpillar roll across those fingers.

"The French drop is a very simple technique. I can't explain it to you because the Society of American Magicians would make me disappear. But let's say I have the coin in my left. I pass it over my right. Is it still in my left, or did I drop it into my right?"

The conversation was harder for me than it should have been. I said, "What's with the vaudeville act?"

"And now you're jaded. I can work with that, too. There is no vaudeville, or we wouldn't be having this conversation. My father pushed me into law school, but the law doesn't interest me."

"What does?"

"Deception." I was looking at his left hand when he opened his right and displayed the coin, then began rolling it again. "There are three principles in every illusion. Mechanics: I move the coin from one place to another. Maybe I do this through telepathy. Maybe not. Misdirection: while I'm doing the mechanics, I have you looking somewhere else, thinking about something else. You're watching the wrong hand. You're watching the lovely assistant's ass when you should be watching the magician. And showmanship, the third element: the lights, the costumes, all the stories and jokes and lies he tells that make the trick seem incidental."

"Who the hell are you?" I asked. "And why am I here?"

He planted the coin solidly in his left palm again and closed it. When he opened his hand, a business card popped out, jumping into the air. He caught it and passed it over to me. It bore the gold-leaf crest of the Federal Bureau of Investigation. Alexander P. Chu, Special Agent.

"Nice," I said. "I have one that says I'm a bikini inspector."

He pulled out a billfold and flipped it open, displaying the gold shield of the FBI, with its depiction of blindfolded Justice and her scale and the words "Department of Justice."

"We met last spring at the Convention Center," he said, "when you pulled that stunt in front of the cameras."

I had arrested a dirty cop in front of the news cameras and promised the press he'd be prosecuted. The press made it happen.

He said, "I shook your hand."

"Everyone shook my hand that day," I said. Except Chief Cronin, who didn't like me much.

Chu said, "I've been getting calls from the Elmira office. They said you were less than generous in your interviews."

I coughed. "I never saw a badge. He could have been anybody."

"You're feeling better. Your bullshit level is rising," he said. Then, "I was watching your house."

"You could have saved me a beating."

"I didn't arrest you for withholding information regarding your father's actions or for interfering with a federal investigation. I didn't arrest you for aiding and abetting. And I didn't figure they'd kill you, at least not until they got you wherever they were going. By then it was too late to call for backup. I was hoping they'd lead me to someone, but I couldn't keep following them, not if I wanted to save you."

"Who were they?"

"You know who they were."

Thugs from Elmira. Sent by the *makher*, Sam Zelig. After the girl.

He opened his top drawer and pulled out a slim file, which he tossed in front of me. It bore the name Dan Reles.

"Is this my file?"

"No. Your real file would be much bigger."

"Seriously?"

No answer. His party trick.

Inside the folder was my college yearbook photo. (I'd spent two years in the army as an MP before college, and even with my hair 1977-long, I looked like a narc.) Also my academic transcript and my FBI application. With that, my fingerprints and rap sheet, all minor juvenile offenses and most before I left Elmira.

There was an area just east of downtown Elmira known as the Bowery. With a concentration of sleazy bars, hookers and other corollary industries, it was a favored playground for cops and hoodlums alike, in their interactions and crossovers. A young tough caught in the Bowery committing a lesser offense—vandalism, assault, "mouthing off"—might not get arrested. Instead a cop, or two cops, would kick the shit out of him and leave him in an alley. Today, this strikes me as a violation of everything the police stand for. But back when I was fifteen and it happened to me (just a few months before my emigration), I didn't even take offense. It was no more unjust than the rest of life. And it beat spending the night in a cell.

I didn't have to look far into the file to see the names Ben Reles and Sam Zelig and a rubber stamp marking me REJECTED.

Chu said, "Public agencies are full of mob functionaries. Police, sanitation department. Good benefits."

"You think I work for Zelig?" No answer. "Then why did he do this to me?"

"You pissed him off."

Public agencies *are* full of mob functionaries, at least in cities with a mob presence. And if Chu believed I was one of them, nothing about my pedigree would convince him otherwise.

My head was clearing up. Chu didn't know what the men had said to me, what they wanted. It seemed like a bad time to lie, but I didn't want to give him everything I had. I didn't want to tell him what they were after, not yet.

I said, "You knew that Zelig's men were in town. How?"

He pointed to his card and squinted. "We have ears everywhere." He broke into a grin. "Seriously, we only got a tip he left Elmira in a hurry. Our agent there, Hayden, he was the one you spoke to. He put it together that Zelig was headed here. My question is, how did he even get the idea to come here?"

I thought hard, and he must have heard the click in my brain.

"Whatcha got, Reles?"

"Lowry," I said. "The Elmira police. Only person I spoke to there."

He said, "Sergeant Lowry. Friend of yours?"

The realization of my stupidity dawned painfully. "Lowry works for Zelig."

"I won't say no."

We were back in Chu's car, a very nice black Chrysler sedan with gray leatherette seats and a simulated wood-grain dash. There was a screen of some kind on the dash and a laptop computer sitting folded between the bucket seats. We headed down MoPac toward the middle of town. I delicately touched the bandages on my face. My ribs ached, my head swam and I kept fighting off moments of dizziness and nausea. I told Chu all the specs of my father's situation: Berelman's car, Berelman's body in an Elmira hotel and Irina. Chu seemed open to the possibility that my father hadn't killed Berelman.

"You should probably see a doctor," he suggested.

I shook my head. I was patched. I was fine. I said, "Your Elmira guy had an exhaust pipe. I think Zelig shoved it down Pax Berelman's throat."

"Uh-huh."

"Who else is crazy enough to kill a guy like that?"

"So?"

I said, "Arrest Sam Zelig."

"Arrest him! Good God, why didn't I think of that? Here I am busting my ass on a racketeering investigation. I could just *arrest* him!"

My skin itched. I cracked the window. Cold wind whistled in.

Chu spoke over the wind. "Sam Zelig is under constant surveillance, all the law will allow. We're using every tool at our disposal from wiretaps to tax laws. We spend decades on a case like this. Sometimes we're lucky and we get a few convictions. And a year later they come back stronger than before, or they're replaced by someone worse and smarter. And meaner. They invent new crimes with new technology. And they have advantages in the physical laws of the universe."

"How do you figure?"

"Entropy. The universe falls toward disorder rather than order. It's easier to destroy a civilization than to build one, or to maintain it. Zelig and his like are still killing people and abducting girls and dealing drugs to children." He watched the road as he spoke through his teeth. "And renegade city cops withhold valuable evidence to protect their dirty friends. You've done damage."

I said, "I didn't start that fire." No response. It dawned on me. "You started it."

"No. Nooooooo. Setting fire to an abandoned building? That would be arson. No, I followed you and your buddies. There wasn't much chance I could take out three of them by myself. No time for backup. It was lucky that fire broke out just when it did."

"Yeah," I said. "Lucky, like someone got a traffic flare from his trunk and tossed it in the back way at just the right moment."

"Something like that. Misdirection. Showmanship."

He turned off MoPac at Forty-fifth Street and rolled into my neighborhood.

"Where are we going?" I asked.

"You're going home."

"What about my father?"

He took a deep breath. "Sam Zelig has an open file stretching back for decades. We follow it in Elmira and at the Buffalo field office. In the span of years this file has been open, agents have joined the Bureau, enjoyed long and prosperous careers and retired. For the last few decades, Zelig has been facing prosecution for racketeering, not just for his individual crimes, many and varied though they are. And yet every time we get close to a RICO prosecution, a key witness disappears or someone steps forward and takes responsibility for a key predicate act, and the case falls apart. And these stooges, these men who will take a sentence for him, they've been doing that since before the RICO Act. In 1961 he dodged a term for aggravated assault when a man took the blame for that crime. What was his name again? Reles, that's it. Ben Reles."

He went on.

"And all these years, we're investigating Zelig for organized crimes like extortion and random violence like assault. But never rape. The women he associated with, they never ever stepped forward. In Zelig's file we have pictures of him with girls, many pictures. In nightclubs, with martinis. Some of them look happy. Sometimes Sam is all smiles and the girl is looking down, to the side, away. She's miserable. This is not a nice man to women."

As we approached my house, I saw another black sedan parked in front, another fed keeping an eye on the place.

"What's going on?"

Chu said, "While I was busy with you, my colleague got a hunch and decided to take a look in your house. He peeked in the windows—you have no curtains—and your son was asleep in front of the TV. But your girlfriend was nowhere to be found."

"You said she was okay."

"Did I? What we're wondering is, did your girlfriend go out and leave him? Is this just a case of criminal neglect? Or did Zelig's boys catch her before they got you? Keep the sucker busy while the lady vanishes from the glass case. Mechanics, misdirection, showmanship."

nside, Josh was sleeping, snoring gently on the couch. I ran through the house. No one else present, no signs of an intrusion. I hoped to God this was just one of Rachel's fuckups. I left her a note, packed a few things in a suitcase—overnights for Josh and myself—and woke Josh.

"Where's Mommy?" he asked, eyes barely open.

"She stepped out. We're going for a sleepover."

He didn't resist as I wrapped him in a blanket and picked him up like a Persian rug, kicked the suitcase outside and locked the door behind me. Chu grabbed the suitcase and followed me to my car. He had dismissed the other agent, who drove off into the dark.

"Where are you going?"

"Haven't decided yet. You want to follow me? Or you want to help me find Rachel?"

"Say thank you," he said.

I loaded Josh into the back seat and the suitcase along with him. "What?"

"Saved your life, put a guard on your house to protect your son when you were kidnapped."

"Thanks. Hey, next time save me before they put my face in the wood chipper."

He said, "I did."

We probably had more to talk about, but he didn't say anything as I climbed in the driver's side, started the engine and left him in my rearview mirror. I knew I was too dizzy to drive, but I rolled the window down, blinked and grabbed the microphone.

"Homicide one to Central, K."

Delay, static. Then, *"Go ahead, Reles."*

"Send a patrol to my house to stand guard until Mrs. Velez gets there. I'll explain later. And get me Jim Torbett at home."

In half an hour, I was standing inside the living room of Lieutenant James Torbett's home, talking with Torbett. His wife Nan, an attractive black woman in her early forties, looking something less than surprised to see me bring a fresh crisis into her stable home at eleven at night, set up Josh in an extra bedroom.

I knew that I could trust Torbett, even if he didn't trust me. And I knew that his doors were made of steel. Being a Texas cop and black, he was used to protecting himself and his own. Whoever might be coming after Pop wouldn't get to Josh, at least not here. Now I just had to find Rachel.

Torbett insisted I stay a moment and that we sit at the heavy oaken table in his dining room, a shadowy, somber room worthy of a family with an old fortune rather than one living on a city salary. I explained as little as I could. That a Russian girl had escaped from her pimp, that my father had helped her, that the pimp would be looking for my father and he'd be looking for him at my home. I left out the business of Pop stealing two cars, one owned by a dead man. This omission could be considered a felony.

Torbett sat at the head of the table, judgelike, and weighed the evidence carefully. He breathed in deep through his nose. "Leaves out the question of when you decided I was a fool."

"What . . . ?"

"Reles, everyone knows your father is a gangster. That's why you couldn't get into the FBI, that's why you work for us. So why don't you tell me what you're not telling me, like why your face is bleeding and why you smell like a gas fire, and when I'm satisfied that your father isn't trafficking prostitutes, then I'll help."

He passed me some napkins, and I blotted the blood dripping from my bandaged cheek. Torbett had a few years on me. He'd been raised in segregated Austin, which meant he came up in a world where it was the police department's job to keep black people in the part of town that had no pavement and no electricity. I never learned why he joined the force. Against all odds he became the department's first black detective, which didn't please people in certain corners. Now he was our first African American head of Internal Affairs, a target known to tempt the more corrupt elements of the force. Torbett was a perfect fit for IA. He accepted the fact that people hated him, so he had no problem calling them in for questioning on the most minor of infractions. Given sufficient proof, he'd have no trouble having someone fired or even prosecuted, even me. All things considered, it amazed me that he was still alive.

We'd served together on Homicide years earlier, and I knew him to be a straight arrow, uncompromising and uncorruptible, if such a thing existed. He'd stuck by me more than anyone who didn't like me ever had before. He was the most honest and the most reliable person I knew. I needed to take advantage of that.

I told him about my father's old bosses, the Zeligs, how they chased us out of Elmira. I told him how Pop hit the road when I was in college, saw the world, then went back to Elmira last week, for reasons still unknown. I told him that Pop had shown up in Austin last night, at my house, with the girl.

"This have anything to do with that stolen Oldsmobile?"

I tried not to look surprised that he was so far ahead of me. I shouldn't have been. In spite of all the cops who wouldn't give a straight answer to anyone in Internal Affairs, somehow Torbett always seemed to know what was going on. There was a paper trail attached to almost everything, and he'd learned how to follow the trail. He'd keep on following it, whether I liked it or not. You had to hand it to Torbett. On his off shift, at home and asleep, nothing happened in the department that got past him.

"Yeah, I was getting to that," I said feebly, and then I ran out of air. There was no way to tell the story without confessing to at least one of my father's many crimes. I took a breath. "My father left Elmira in a hurry again. I believe he used the Olds without the owner's consent—"

"He stole the Olds."

"He stole the Olds to get away from Elmira."

"And he dumped a black Buick LeSabre that belonged to a murdered man."

I didn't answer. I didn't breathe. Then, finally, I said, "Yeah. Probably. I don't know for sure."

"Reles—"

"I'm telling you, Torbett, if you saw the pictures of the victim—"

"I did."

"Then you'd know that's not my father's doing. Sam Zelig is a crazy sadist. If my father helped in any way, if he even agreed to dump the body, he did it because it's what he had to do to live. And he saved this girl!"

"Reles, you know I won't make that decision."

A miniature grandfather clock ticked on the wall.

Torbett meant that he wouldn't decide something only a judge should decide. He would arrest my father if he had charges against him. Why shouldn't he? And he'd let the judge, or the jury, decide my father's fate.

"Listen," I said. "The guy who knocked the girl around. Sam Zelig. I think he might be in Austin."

Torbett said, "You think. You don't know?"

"He wants the girl. That's why his guys did this to me. It's a good chance he'd kill my father if he found him, but they didn't ask about my father. They asked about the girl."

"What do you suggest?"

"We can't bust Zelig. There's no charge. I have circumstantial evidence and a couple of witnesses that make him a key suspect in the murder of Pax Berelman."

"The witnesses would be your father and his girl."

"Well, yeah."

"So . . ."

"I don't know if he wants to sell Irina back into prostitution or just keep her for himself. Whatever it is, he's got at least three guys down here. I don't know if he's with them or not. But no direct flights from Elmira to Austin, and he got down here on a day's notice. With backup. For what?"

"We can bring your father and the girl in."

I thought of Pop and Irina being told they were being locked in a jail cell for their own safety. "Yeah. No. Not even if we could find them."

"*If* we could find them?"

I explained how Pop and Irina took off sometime before 9:30 A.M. They had no car that I knew about, but it might not be a waste of time to look for cars that had been stolen near their hotel around that time. Then I got another wave of vertigo and had to grab the table to keep from falling over.

Torbett sighed, then led me down the hall and opened a door onto what looked like a small hotel room. A double bed, centered between matching night tables with matching lamps. A crisp bedspread. A chair. No hint that the room was used anytime recently, except maybe to change the sheets. The Torbetts' guest room.

"Nothing to do tonight, Reles," he mumbled. "Best get some sleep."

I wanted to argue. I had to find Rachel, make sure she was okay, make sure she was just off on another binge. And I had to find Pop and Irina before Zelig did.

But I'd taken blows to the head, stared into the mouth of a wood chipper and lost consciousness in a fire. I still stank like burning oil from as near-death an experience as I hoped I'd ever have. And now I had to hold onto the doorframe to keep from falling over. It was a big day.

I fell onto the soft, scented sheets, the kind I hadn't felt since childhood. The bed dipped once and I grabbed it to keep from falling off. Then, before I got a chance to close my eyes, I was out.

I wouldn't rest long.

Suddenly the door swept open and light poured in from the hall, and I thought I saw Nan Torbett retreat in a robe. I climbed to my feet, wavered and found my balance. I felt like I'd had a bad boxing match the night before. My head pounded, my cheek throbbed, my ribs ached from the kicking and my balance kept going haywire. I still had my pants and shoes on, so I made it out to the living room. The light hurt my eyes and the sound of Rachel's voice shook my skull.

"Mizzuz Reles," Torbett was saying in a voice designed to project calmness. I didn't correct his mistake. The Torbetts were religious. I figured they'd be more excited about protecting my hard-drinking wife than my hard-drinking girlfriend. "Please lower your voice."

Torbett's proximity kept Rachel from moving farther into the house, but she held her ground just inside the front door. She had on the worn brown raincoat that had become her armor for confronting the world, rain or shine. She'd been drinking for hours, though not for days. I'd seen her worse. But not in public.

"Where's my baby?" she demanded. "You're keeping me from my baby."

"He's asleep," I said, with what was supposed to be finality. I wanted the words to resound in Torbett's dark, civilized living room, over his dark carpet and his varnished end tables and the painted portrait of his wife, and make Rachel act like an adult.

Rachel spotted my battered face and clapped her hand over her mouth, tears suddenly appearing in her eyes. She ran to me and tried to touch my face, surveying the damage. "What happened? What happened?"

"Okay," I said, holding her waist but dodging her hands. "Relax."

A door opened and Jule Torbett, about six, appeared wide-eyed at the spectacle of Rachel's performance.

Nan said, "Go to sleep, baby, it's all right." Jule didn't move, and Nan escorted her back into her room and closed the door behind them. Rachel would be the subject, there, of a parent-child "talk."

The most remarkable element of Rachel's appearance was how little she behaved like herself. The Rachel of her sober years, or even hungover Rachel, moved with a quiet dignity. This Rachel shifted with remarkable speed from one personality to another. First the irate mother. Now the devoted girlfriend. Sober, she'd seen me beat up worse than this and not even blinked as she tossed me the first-aid kit.

Another click and she became the concerned mother again. She said, "Where's my baby?"

Torbett stood behind her and, I could see the subtle shake of his head. She had no business seeing Josh, not like this. I'd fought tougher people than Rachel. I'd faced down death, even in the last few hours. But I couldn't tell her that she wasn't allowed to see her son.

"Will you be good?" I asked.

"I'm sorry. I'm sorry. . . ."

"Will you be good? Or are you just gonna be a nasty drunk shooting your mouth off?"

She lowered her head, contrite for however long that would last. I stepped down the hall ahead of her and opened the door to where Josh slept. I gave her the "shh" signal, but she breezed right by.

She sat at the edge of the bed. Josh woke. "Mommy?"

She got close to him. I couldn't hear what she said—probably nothing—but soon he was crying. And then she gathered him up to her stinking raincoat and held him close. I noticed Torbett standing by me.

Somehow, soon, Josh had cried himself back to sleep. Rachel tucked the covers around him, pulled herself vertical and tiptoed out of the room. Then, with no great effort, I managed to get her to settle with me into the guest room. As she undressed, she muttered, "You had no right."

"You left him alone!" I blurted. It was a fluke that Zelig's men didn't go into the house and take him. "You left him alone, and you went out!"

Her eyes were tearing. "You left *me* alone!"

"You're a grown-up!"

At that she settled back to the sad drunk she often became late in the evening. She cried, sitting in her slip and mangled pantyhose. I was about to go over and comfort her. Then I thought of her with Josh, and something stopped me. I thought, Go ahead and cry.

"I'm sorry," she said, digging in her impossibly deep pocketbook for a tissue. "I'm sorry."

"All right."

"I'm sorry. You hate me."

"No, I just . . . I just want you to take care of our son when I'm not around."

"I had to get out. I had to."

We'd talked about this before. She was claustrophobic, she said. Sometimes she couldn't breathe. It would come up on her all of a sudden, and she had to get out. But she never seemed to wind up running around in an open field. She was never on the shore of a lake or even in our own back yard. She always wound up at a bar. It didn't escape me that men went to bars also. And that many of them would be looking for an easy mark, a sad and beautiful woman with a past she wanted to drown out of her memory.

I slipped off my smokey clothes and killed the light, and we climbed into the unfamiliar bed. I didn't remember turning my back to her, but I must have, because she reached her arm around and squeezed me close, which was fine. Then she splayed her fingers against my chest, which was fine also. A moment later she had her hand over my stomach. I wrapped my own free hand around it, squeezed it, and let it go with what seemed like a final goodnight. Then she slipped her hand into my boxers. I reached in, gently took her by the wrist and guided her hand back to my belly.

"Why?" she said softly. She nuzzled my neck.

"You know. Lips that touch liquor."

Her hand made a sweeping motion down my chest and in the direction of my shorts again. I grabbed her fingers, kissed them and rolled toward her.

"I'm tired," I said, though it had never stopped me before, and she knew as much. So I added, "You've been drinking."

I couldn't spell this out at the time, but it would have been like taking advantage of someone who didn't know better. On her side, maybe she wanted to give me sex to make up for the drinking, and I didn't want that.

And somewhere inside the car accident that Rachel had become was the thoughtful, brilliant woman I loved. I didn't want anyone else.

She touched my face near my new makeshift stitches. "I'm not drunk," she insisted.

I didn't respond, and the reality must have hit her, because she rolled away and pulled her knees up. She was mad and hurt, but also embarrassed. She was drunk, and everyone knew it. This embarrassment would follow her into the clarity of the next day. Sadly, it would have no effect when her body wanted to drink again.

She didn't fight me as I slid one arm under her neck and the other around her waist and pulled her close. But she was a million miles away.

The next morning, by the time I got up, showered, carefully shaved, rebandaged my cheek, dressed and made it to the kitchen, Rachel was up and showered and wearing something clean she'd borrowed from Nan. My headache settled into a steady throb, and the dizziness dropped by half. My ribs felt worse than they had the night before, but I could move.

Nan Torbett proved to be an unusually good sport, I thought, about the kind of life her husband led and the curves it kept throwing her. A few of these curves had something to do with me, but I wouldn't flatter myself that they all did. It was a crappy life, being married to a cop, with the crazy schedule, the midnight calls that had him jumping out of bed and out of the house, the late nights where he just might never come home. And yet there was Nan fully dressed at seven-thirty in the morning in slacks and a sweater, looking like a million bucks, with a breakfast spread on the kitchen table (the Torbetts had a kitchen table *and* a dining-room table) that made it seem like she'd been planning for this sleepover all month. Eggs and biscuits and French toast, and fresh coffee that seemed to draw Rachel like a vampire to blood. When the coffeepot got passed away from her, she looked worried until it came back. And she didn't meet anyone's eyes. The stark contrast between the two women made me wonder what Torbett could have done to make Nan so happy.

I managed to wash down a few biscuits but was feeling too bruised and battered for much more. To the unschooled observer, Rachel and I might have been suffering the same ailment. Josh and Jule discovered the hilarity inherent in putting a tablespoon in your mouth and pressing your cheek out of shape with it. They were making slurping sounds and laughing, and Rachel said, "Josh, don't play with your food," as if it were his behavior, and not her own, that embarrassed her.

"I'm not!" he declared without even losing his smile. There was no food in his mouth. And it was a rare independent thought.

Nan said, "It's okay," and I realized how unaccustomed we were to seeing Josh have fun.

I tried to make myself useful by clearing the table, but Nan shooed us out of the kitchen. Josh and Jule went off to play something and I took Rachel into the guest room. I gave her a quick rundown on the situation and the danger of going back to our house. I asked her to stay put until I got things settled, which might take a few days. She flinched at the thought of behaving herself that long, but she'd humiliated herself last night and bowed to the idea as if it were a reasonable punishment. I said goodbye to Josh and headed out for my car. Torbett followed me. We stood on his lush green lawn, looking up and down the street.

"What are you gonna do?" he asked.

"Find my father. Find Zelig, if he's here."

Torbett just nodded and looked away. Finally he said, "It's none of my business. . . ."

He was thinking about my family. If it was none of his business yesterday, it was in his lap right now, while my kid was wetting his extra bed and my girlfriend was sniffing around his liquor cabinet.

"Knock yourself out," I said.

"Last night when your wife woke your son up." He had my attention. "She said something to him, and he started to cry. Then she comforted him. But he didn't need comforting. He was asleep. He was fine until she woke him up."

Sometimes you come home after a vacation and your house smells funny. You think it must be the closed windows, the mustiness, the inactivity that makes it smell that way. The truth is, it always smelled that way. You didn't notice because you live with that stink every day. And all it took to make you smell it was some time away, smelling clean air for a change.

But a stranger smells it in a second.

I could see it now. Rachel woke Josh, said something, maybe something low-key, but something that made him cry. Maybe she told him she was glad he was okay. Maybe she told him how worried she'd been or how much she loved him. She could have told him the sky was blue, and if she said it in a certain way, he would get a whiff of something that scared the shit out of him. And he cried, and then she could comfort him. But holding Josh, she looked less like a mother and more like a little girl squeezing a teddy bear. He didn't need the comforting. She did.

I didn't know what to do with the information. It was too late to trade Rachel in for a newer model. But I thanked Torbett just the same and promised to be in touch, as I headed to HQ.

My father had taken a hike over twenty-four hours earlier, with his Russian girlfriend in tow, with a sadistic killer's hired muscle after him. I called Dispatch and put out a BOLO on the bunch of them, Be On the Look Out for two big scary goons and a weaselly little goon, trying to kill a scrappy old Jew over a skinny blond hooker. I went to the APD auto shop and asked if they'd learned anything new from the stolen Cutlass. I called the cops in Mansfield, Pennsylvania, and asked the same, about Pax Berelman's Buick.

I hit the squad room and discovered it in high activity. Halvorsen made good use of the squad on the rabbit case, the female whose limbs were found in the Dumpster along with maternity clothes and a dead rabbit. They sent what they had to every police department in Texas. It wasn't that you couldn't leave Texas if you were on the run, but we were right in the middle of the state and you could drive five hours in any direction without hitting a state border. For that reason also, many people never thought to break free to the wilds of Louisiana or Arkansas or New Mexico, even with the cops at their heels. Texas was their world.

There had been scores of phone calls responding to the woman's picture on TV. Halvorsen eliminated the craziest ones (references to space aliens and cloning). He had Czerniak and LaMorte check as many by phone as they could. Fuentes ran details between the lab and Records. And

Halvorsen personally went out on the most suspicious calls, in the company of his colleague Cate Mora. None of my business yesterday and none of my business today.

I could have taken half, or even all of the squad away from him to help me find Pop. For that matter, since Halvorsen was the only one of them who had actually seen my father, he would have been the most useful. But for all I knew, Pop and Irina had hopped a bus for Laredo. Interstate 35 cut through Austin and San Antonio, and it made a straight run for the border. They could be, at this minute, wading across the Rio Grande against the flow of northbound human traffic. If Zelig tracked down Pop and his hooker in Mexico, Texarkana or anyplace else outside of Austin, there wasn't much I could do about it, legally or otherwise.

The other reason I left the squad out of my search while I could was that I'd held back information at a few key moments, incidents that had already been described as withholding evidence, interfering with an investigation and other cheery possibilities. This kind of thing might not worry a guy who had friends on every level but could put someone like me in a serious pinch. I didn't want to draw any more attention to the case or to my father than I had to, until I had to. I didn't want to give Halvorsen or anyone else something they could use against me. So I went on my own. If there was any nagging doubt in the back of my head, I stayed busy enough to ignore it.

I phoned the FBI and asked them to send a recent photo of Zelig. They had a good one, with Sam Z in a white suit, a blue nylon shirt with a big collar and gold chains in his chest hair. There was, as always, a girl in the picture. This one looked young, maybe mid-twenties, young enough to be his granddaughter, and happy. They'd just met.

They couldn't find a recent mug shot for my father on file, so they sent me his driver's license photo. For Irina they had nothing, not even a green card. I didn't know her last name, and I couldn't be sure of her first. I sat down with a police artist and we worked out something that seemed to capture the specifics of her face but not the essence of it. A charcoal pencil couldn't capture the unearthly blondness of her hair, the porcelain skin or the cold, dark eyes. I wasn't even sure a camera would get it.

But I sent these pictures out to every police department in the state anyway, and I made copies for the patrols to take at the beginning of the next shift at 3:00 P.M., at the bottom of their stacks of photos and lists of the day's new requirements and prohibitions. I drove pictures to security at the airport, and to the train station and the bus station, and to every car-rental place I could find. I dropped them at a local TV station and was told they'd just done a story like that—the story on the rabbit case—and they weren't interested. Then I drove a few miles down Congress, stopping at every bar or cheap hotel that looked like it would make my vagabond fa-ther feel welcome. That was a waste. Pop wouldn't stay in the area if he thought the cops were after him. Not if he had a choice. But I didn't have many options. I left my card everywhere, telling clerks and bartenders to tip my father, if they saw him, that I'd be at the Magnolia Café that after-noon. He'd feel safer there than at HQ. Then I made the same trek up Air-port Boulevard and back down Lamar.

My head pounded and my ribs ached. Nan's biscuits were all I'd eaten since the previous night's dinner, which Zelig's ex-cons had kicked out of me anyway, and it was past 2:00 P.M. when I drove back up Congress until I found, by its twenty-four-hour neon-lit window, Magnolia Café.

I barely had my eyes open when I staggered in, dropped into a blue vinyl booth and ordered fried eggs, toast, home fries and coffee. A Leonard Cohen song played over the speakers, something about waiting for a mira-cle. The midday sun shone through the plate-glass windows, too brightly for my tastes, and I covered my eyes to rest and think. Rachel was safe as long as she stayed put. Josh was safe. No way Zelig's men could have found Pop at the hotel. No way. They couldn't have left Elmira until I called Lowry, and they wouldn't have known where to find Pop once they got here. And if somehow they did find him, there would have been signs of a struggle. Unless he went quietly.

I sat crumpled in the booth, palms over my eyes, considering options, until my plate clanked down on the table and I opened my eyes and saw that I was facing Sam Zelig.

When Rachel left me five years before, she was pregnant, a detail she'd neglected to share with me, along with neglecting to say goodbye. She returned with our son, Josh, about four years later. I'd spent the eight months since I met Josh trying to convince him not to be afraid of things that weren't real—monsters, ghosts, boogeymen. It didn't seem wise to replace these things in his mind with legitimate sources of fear. No, the boogeyman doesn't want to kill you, but watch out for men who want to get you alone in the park. Watch out for creepy teachers, and scoutmasters, and big dogs. And while you're at it, watch out for your mother when she's on a bender.

Because my own childhood didn't go to hell until I was ten, I would never embrace fear as a way of life, the way Josh had. His life sucked from the beginning, filling him with abstract fears. I didn't believe in anything I couldn't see.

But by my teens I'd seen plenty. I knew that there were tough guys and there were victims, and it didn't take much thought to decide which I wanted to be. Like my father, though, I deluded myself that I was tough. Pop walked into the candy store and emptied the register because he worked for Zelig. I didn't realize it then, but I strutted into the same store like I owned it, for the same reason. I wasn't tough. I was just in Zelig's orbit, like everyone else.

I hated Sam Z when I was a kid, for the way he spoke about my father and for calling me motherless. I couldn't take a swing because he'd have killed me, and I'm not being figurative. Still, somehow all the loathing and fear added up to respect. It was like the fame someone gets for being a serial killer or a real-estate pirate. He didn't deserve it, but there it was.

If Sam didn't see me jolt, he'd have been blind, and he wasn't blind. He sat taller than I did, still broad and powerful like in the old days, silver hair slicked back over a hypertrophic skull. His face wore a tan, a dark one, in spite of wintering in the mountains of western New York State, and he'd tanned enough through the years to leather his skin. Cancer would get him eventually, but I couldn't wait for that. Cavernous dark eyes gave the impression of someone with a soul. A fire burned in those eyes, and his temples shifted as he ground his teeth. He wore a gold silk shirt open at the collar, gray chest hair, gold chains and a blazer of tight plaid. A gangster who'd kept up with the changes in fashion well into the 1970s. His massive left hand rested on the table, not far from my eggs. On his thick, hairy fingers, four fat gold rings, one monogram and three jewels for maximum damage should you feel his fist across your face. It would crack your jaw and take your cheek along for the ride. Next to the hand, my business card. He'd picked it up at one of the bars or hotels, looking for Pop same as I was. His right hand—likely also bearing four rings—he hid under the table. I didn't have to guess he had a gun trained on me.

There's memory and there's reality. Some people, when you see them again, seem smaller than you remember them. Less impressive, less vivid. Zelig was bigger. And, as the look in his cold eyes told me, meaner. Some people hold a gun on you to get information or money, but the last thing they want to do is kill you. Zelig would kill you without blinking. If he had regrets, it would be that he didn't do it more slowly. The gun would ruin the experience for him. There was no point in reaching for my weapon. It was tucked into my waist holster, and the bullets, I remembered, were lying on the pavement outside my front door.

I didn't believe he'd kill me right then in front of a roomful of witnesses. But anyone who has stared down a sociopath wielding a loaded gun knows not to take anything for granted.

"Food good here?" he asked.

"Try it." I pushed the plate toward him. "I come for the atmosphere."

"I ate on the plane." He pushed it back with his free hand. *"Ess, tatele. Es."* Something you'd say to a little boy to get him to eat.

"I'm not hungry."

He smiled. "Just eat the eggs." It wasn't a request. I cut into the eggs.

He said, "My doctor tells me to lay off the cholesterol. Says it's bad for me. Fuck that. I eat steak and eggs for breakfast every day. Look at me." He pounded his chest. "Strong as an ox."

"Funny thing," he went on, his gravelly words falling heavily over the table. "I call your old man in, goodness of my own heart. I'm generous that way. I forget old grudges. Call him in to do some work for me, pay him a decent wage. Bastard takes off with my girl."

I shrugged. You wouldn't think that would inspire his anger, but his eyes burned.

He said, "What the fuck does that mean?"

I said, "Love is blind."

He laughed and sipped my coffee, a gesture of expanding his territory. "You don't mind?" I didn't figure it was worth fighting over. He said, "My family came to this country in 1840. Rich German Jews. Seligman. Not your Russian rags-and-patches crowd. They lost it all in the crash of 1919. I worked my way up from nothing. From *nothing*!"

I knew this to be bullshit. The Zeligmans, with a Z, came over at the turn of the century like the rest of my father's Bronx neighborhood. And Sam Zelig would have been a hired killer if he hadn't ridden the coattails of his enterprising big brother. But I'm always glad to listen to people's lies. They tell you who the person is. Sam, for example, wanted both status for coming from money and street cred for working his way up. He hadn't done either.

He went on. "Meyer Lansky, Bugsy Siegel, all the *makhers*." Sam's heroes, the Jewish kings of crime. "All dead. My own brother, God bless him, rotting in prison. Their sons went to school to be doctors and lawyers. Got out of the Life. I'm the last *makher*," he declared. "The last of the old bosses, the last Jew standing."

When Irina first told me about someone she called the *makher*, I figured it was her word for him. I realized now that it was Zelig's name for himself. He felt it put him with a higher class of tough guys, admirable, enviable. Leaders of the community.

I ate, keeping my eyes on him. He hadn't come to kill me. Not yet.

"I never had a son," he said. I could see the regret in his eyes, and something else I couldn't pinpoint. He went on, suddenly high-spirited. "Look at me," he said. "Seventy-two years old. Still fuck around. Different broad every night. Still got all my hair." His eyes burned as he added, "And all my teeth." He bared his massive yellowed teeth, tight gums curling away from them to give each tooth an air of dangerous independence.

I remembered this same man mocking me when I was a kid, and me pummeling the bigger kid I was sparring with. And in my mind, how every punch cracked Sam Zelig's rotten teeth. And there they were again.

Then, suddenly furious, Sam said, "And your father, that piece of SHIT!" It felt like the floor rumbled when he yelled that last word, like he let loose the power he'd been holding back all that time. The rest of the patrons froze. A crazy man ranting in his booth. He went on. "That jailbird, who couldn't get out of bed without getting busted! He thinks there are no RULES?"

My father's longest time behind bars, until recent years, was the deuce he pulled for Zelig, the one that lost me my mother, and by extension, my childhood. That Zelig should blame my father for that, should call Pop a jailbird for what Zelig made him do, set me off. I didn't say anything but he must have seen it in my eyes.

He zoned in on me. His scowl gave way to a grin, and he cackled. "I remember you," he said. "That skinny little fuck. You got your nose cracked at the gym, went down like a sandbag." He laughed hard.

His eyes lit with a new idea. "Hey! Like a week later, I was riding you about it, and you went apeshit, beat the crap out of that mick kid, Lowry. That was you?"

I said, "Lowry?"

"Sure. Big kid. He's a cop now, of course."

"In Elmira?" I asked.

"Yeah, in Elmira. Twice your reach, and you pounded his face in." He laughed harder. "They had to drag you off." He laughed so hard he coughed up phlegm, grabbed my napkin and spit into it.

I was a kid, and I beat up another kid because I couldn't do it to Zelig. The kid, who'd been standing there laughing along with Zelig at my expense, got decked by someone half his size, publicly humiliated as I had been. That bigger kid was Lowry. I'd made a lifelong enemy in him. And thirty years later, when I called him at the Elmira Police Department, he recognized my name. Why not? He remembered the kid who made him look stupid, just like I remembered Zelig. He remembered my name and passed it back to his good buddy Sam Z.

As the waitress went by, Sam said, "Sweetheart, bring me another cup of coffee, will ya?"

"Don't call me sweetheart," she said, and before she could step away, Sam's hand shot out and grabbed her upper arm, his fingers circling it with room to spare. She'd have a bruise. The girl let out a cry.

I jumped up. "Hey, hey . . ."

Sam turned his glare to me. "Who's in charge?"

"You're hurting her."

"Who's in charge?"

Customers shifted around, and I turned to see the manager and the cook approach from the kitchen. "Hold it!" I said to them. Then to the young woman, "Miss, bring my friend his coffee. Don't keep him waiting."

Satisfied, Sam let her go and she rushed to the kitchen. I gave a warning look to the manager and sat down. I needed to finish the meeting and get Sam out of the restaurant with a minimum of disruption. Customers began signaling for their checks.

"Tell you something about your father," he said. "We were kids together. We grew up on the same block. He tell you that? Of course, there were a hundred kids on that block. Not like we were pals. But I knew him.

"His old man, I don't know what he did besides leaving. Hit the road, after the crash. Lots of 'em did. Your grandmother hauled in laundry or whatever. I used to see her. Nice piece, too, like your mom. But she's got a few kids and there ain't enough to go around. Lots of them back then—no food, they get thrown out of the apartment, you see them sitting on their furniture on the sidewalk, crying. Heh. Funny.

"Your father, musta been nine years old, goes out and gets a job, delivering for a kosher butcher across the street. Rest of us are hanging out on the corner, playing stickball, rolling drunks. He's got this bike. The back of it is a regular bike with a seat and a back wheel and pedals. The front is a big metal box like a steamer trunk with two little wheels, one on either side. And he pedals this thing all over Fordham and delivers to the sheenies in the neighborhood. He's hauling fifty pounds of meat, he's gotta stand on the pedals, use his whole weight just to move the thing. And I see this happen once, he comes up in my building and he delivers to the woman next door, and I see her pay him and give him something extra. Who knows? A dime, a nickel. Ike is with me and I get an idea, and he says wait. So we wait.

"One day there's a hurricane. Hundred-mile-an-hour winds. We're hanging out in the alley, watching the storm. And there's your old man on his bike, trying to keep it on the sidewalk, wind blowing him all over the place, water in his eyes. He's little, too, for nine. And this big wind comes, I swear to Christ, picks him up in the air, turns him around and puts him down across the street going the other way. We practically pissed ourselves. No one saw it but us, but I swear to you that's just the way it happened.

"You know the butcher shop was right across from our alley. So we're watching two hours later—we're soaked ourselves by now, but so what—when your father comes back and parks his bike. He's finished his route, I can tell he's cleaned up, big tips, 'cause his pockets are bulging out and he's got this huge grin on his face. So we call him. We're a couple of years older, so he listens. 'Benny! Come on over!'

" 'Not now,' he says. 'I gotta go in.'

" 'We gotta show you something. It'll only take a minute.'

"And like a dope, he comes over. Ikey swings this club, hits him in the face—broke his nose right then—and I punch him in the balls, and he's down in the mud, crying. We take the money, all of it. And"—Zelig had to stop to laugh—"and he's begging us, 'It's not mine! I have to give it to Mr. Scheinbaum!'

Zelig laughed, wiping tears from his eyes. "Naturally, your father didn't keep that job. Guess what we got out of him. Eighty-seven bucks! You know what that was back then? But we told him, you know, if he ratted on us, we'd kill his mother. After that he ran errands for us, followed us around with the bandage over his nose. 'Hey, guys. What's up, guys?' Funny."

I felt my skin cooking with rage. Keeping my voice to a low rumble, I said, "Why are you telling me this?"

His eyes zeroed in on me.

"You think I'm a bad guy. I used to pay your father to run errands. I was the one who brought him to Elmira, set up his fight career!"

I knew that someone had drafted him out there to fight when he was struggling in New York City. My father had mentioned a guy named Epstein. "I thought Epstein brought him out. You and Ike bought the contract."

He looked away, made a raspberry sound. "Epstein was our guy. We brought him out, trained him, set him up. He won six fights, got the odds up, then lost one."

"What do you mean, you got the odds up? Those first six fights. They were fixes?"

He howled at that. "They were all fixes. You think your old man beat anyone for real?"

He almost cried, he was laughing so hard. Then he wound down and caught his breath. His smile slipped away, and he became very thoughtful. An angry rabbi. "Consider this," he said. "You hand over Irina, I cut your old man loose. He pays me a thousand a day for lost income. That makes it, what, five grand? Plus the vigorish. Five percent a day, compounded. I don't even fuck him up too bad, how's that? Though I should, for appearances. And her, too. I thought about the girl running off, your father taking off with her. I couldn't figure why. It hurt me, after all my generosity. Help her into the country, give her a nice place to stay. And now I gotta follow them. Can't have people take off with my girls. It looks bad, very bad."

It seemed more personal than that but I didn't say as much. Zelig had no income from Irina because he kept her for himself. There was an urgency about him, like he'd been interrupted in mid-coitus, like my father had literally pulled the girl out from under him and he needed her back. I knew by now that Zelig didn't have my father and Irina. But he came to Austin for them. He was after them.

I said, "You know I don't have him. You got my business card. I was asking around for him, same as you."

Sam pinned me with a look. "Find him."

"Here's what I get," I said, trying to lighten the moment, very matter-of-fact, like we were solving a math problem. "You hired my father out of the goodness of your heart—"

"Absolutely."

"And brought him back to Elmira. Maybe had him drive around a little."

Here he grew suspicious.

I said, "And the car he's driving is owned, on paper, by a little schmuck named Berelman. And Berelman turns up dead in his room at the Allerton."

Zelig showed his teeth. "You don't say."

I jumped over the obvious issue of homicide and said, "So my question is, why Pop? Why a guy who blew town twenty-seven years before? Why him and why now?"

He took a deep breath and looked over the restaurant, as if he was going to enjoy telling the story. The remaining diners had settled back into their meals with only an occasional glance in his direction.

"Like you said, he took off, when, '68? He didn't know anything between '68 and now, so it didn't matter if they questioned him. Plus which, he was reliable. Loyal. Like a dog."

He leaned back and enjoyed a loud, pumping guffaw. I smiled to encourage him, but I could taste my bile.

I sat up straight. "Sam," I said, and saw him back up at the affront. "I'm a cop. I can't just hand over the girl because you want her."

Sam snapped to furious attention. "Don't play that police shit with me, cocksucker. I got cops on my payroll. I *eat* cops." I believed the part about his payroll. In Zelig's world, cops were a manageable problem. I could see him thinking I'd be the same. Then he snarled, "You think I won't blow your fuckin' head off right now?" The restaurant stopped dead for a moment—all the hushed conversations, all the eating sounds, all the movement. Someone in the booth behind me must have heard, because Sam peered over my shoulder. "You need something?! You wanna come over here?" Sam threatened. I didn't have to glance behind me to guess that the person's lunch had just become very interesting.

I tried to play cool, but his bizarre mood swings and death threats started to make me edgy. I said, "Kill me and you'll never get the girl."

Suddenly soft-spoken again, he said, "You'll never live to find out." He looked around. "Maybe I'll get the waitress instead. Blow her tits off.

Heh-heh. Or how about those two chicks in the booth?" He moved one leg out from under the table.

"All right," I said, palms forward.

"Get outta my way," he said. "I'm gonna spit."

"All right!"

He grinned again, settling back. A few people resumed eating, but the rest beat a path for the cash register. He said, "You know what that line's from?"

I knew it was from a gangster movie. "*Public Enemy*?"

"*Scarface*. Paul Muni. There was a tough Jew." He changed ideas like the click of a camera. "You won't bring in the cops. Your old man's a jailbird." Then he flashed on an image. "I remember your mother, too. Nice tits. What she was doing with your old man, I never figured out."

"Yeah, yeah, thanks."

He said, "I'm a humble man, Officer. I'm practically retired." Then another shift. "The future isn't racetracks and shakedowns. It's Internet gambling and mobile phones. Maybe I'm dumb, maybe I'm just some dumb-ass kike from the Bronx. Maybe I don't know about shit like that. But if I don't, I can hire some guys who do."

Whatever hints anyone had given me about the old mob's weakness were bogus. Sam might die tomorrow, but you could have said that about him fifty years ago. He was as dangerous old as he was young. Maybe worse.

He'd forgotten the coffee he ordered—the waitress never returned—and he sipped mine again, though it must have been cold. Then he went on. "I don't get everything I want." He leaned forward. "I don't like to lose what I have." He paused. "You wouldn't like that either. To lose what you have? Your wife? Your son?"

Boom. He knew one too many things. He slid out of the booth and stood, automatic at his side.

"Midnight. The girl. And the money. Call it five thousand. I'll let you know where. Don't disappoint me." He bent over toward me. "And if you get the idea of following me, I'll make you regret it. Stay where you are." Then he leaned close to my ear and whispered. "Bring me my girl and I'll let your son grow up."

Human trafficking. Blackmail. And he was walking away.

I sat as he walked out behind me and out the door. I could see him cross the parking lot and disappear behind the shrubs to the lot next door. I dropped money on the table, waited a few minutes and stood.

Two shots rang out, and the plate-glass window shattered.

I shouted, "Get down!"

Suddenly people were screaming, running for shelter, crying, checking each other for damage. I climbed through the crowd and ran out the door, but his gambit had worked. By the time I got outside, he was gone.

This would have been a fine time for the FBI to come out of the woodwork, catch Zelig and pay for my lunch. And if the idea of calling Chu just then popped into my head, it popped right back out for reasons that never would have stood up to analysis. You don't ask the feds to bail you out.

On the plus side, now I knew that Zelig was in town. And I had an excuse to arrest him. He'd fired a gun inside city limits, destroyed property, endangered recklessly. On the minus side, I had a deadline I couldn't keep. You don't just hand over an innocent to a criminal, no matter what he says. At the same time, Zelig was threatening Rachel and Josh. They were safe with Torbett, but I didn't take his threat lightly. He wanted Irina, by midnight. I had until then to catch him or set something up.

I didn't know where Pop and Irina were hiding. At least Zelig didn't have them. It would have been reverse logic to think Pop and Irina were still in Austin just because Zelig was looking for them here. He was looking here because I'd tipped him off they were here, when I spoke to Lowry in Elmira. So I was still part of Zelig's vast machine, the system that told him where anyone in his influence was at any moment. If Pop hit the road, the search could last weeks, even years. But if Pop was still in Austin, I had only a few hours. And I had to stay ahead of Zelig.

I called Dispatch for a crew to take reports at the restaurant, soothe and counsel the traumatized and find Zelig's two bullets. Then I headed back to HQ. I went into the auto shop and mentioned that I'd seen a four-by-four but I didn't know the model. They gave me a book to flip through. The vehicle Zelig's men tossed me into looked like a Jeep Cherokee of recent vintage. I headed up to my office, reloaded my weapon and spent an hour calling around, trying to find a place in town that rented out Jeep Cherokees, but no one had them or anything that looked like them. I would have made note of the license plate, but I was too busy trying not to die. I tried airport security. They couldn't find Zelig on the flight manifests of planes into Austin in the last thirty-six hours, at least not under his own name. They'd keep an eye out for him, but there was no guarantee. One old Semite among thousands of Christmas travelers. And for all I knew, he was traveling by helicopter.

I called Torbett's house. His wife answered. *"Jim's at the office. Josh is playing with Jule. Your wife is asleep."*

I heard the two kids giggling.

"I'm sorry about this," I said. "We're not exactly friends. . . ."

She cut in fast. *"They're fine,"* she said. *"They're fine. Take care of your business."*

I thanked her again and headed down to Internal Affairs to see Torbett.

"How's your wife?" he asked as I stood opposite his desk.

"She's been better." He knew what I was up against with her, so instead I told him about Pop's disappearance and Zelig's arrival, how I'd put out a BOLO on all of them, how I hadn't tracked Zelig's four-by-four or found the plane he'd flown in on. I knew he hadn't traveled alone. He had at least three men with him.

I noticed a stack of copies of Zelig's photo on Torbett's desk, which was impressive since I hadn't given him one. Then I noticed a stack of photos of my father.

"We're giving them to the news," he said, "and I'm hoping the incident at Magnolia Café makes them want to run it. You know we'll have to arrest your father if we find him."

"We . . . he didn't kill Berelman."

He pressed his fingertips together. "I don't know that. And he stole that car."

"Berelman's? He could've borrowed it."

"Reles," he warned me, "you understand if you hide a felony, that's a felony, too."

"Of course," I said. "Sure I do." That sounded ridiculous so I said, "You could have told me you were running my case without me."

"You could have told me what you knew about your father's actions. I can take this case out from under you. I can waste my time investigating you for withholding information, and you know what I'll find. Or we can work together."

"You could always trust me to run my squad."

"You gave up that right when you lied to me about your father's involvement. Do you know what kind of risk I'm taking by pretending that didn't happen?"

I thought it over, nodded, surrendered. No one else would have given me the option.

I headed up to my office, grabbed more copies of Pop's and Zelig's photos and Irina's sketch, and took them to the squad room.

Mora was sorting messages, along with Halvorsen. Fuentes scanned mug shots. LaMorte and Czerniak talked on the phone. They all looked up. I waited until LaMorte and Czerniak finished up their calls. I dropped the pictures in three stacks on the nearest desk. Natural curiosity drew all eyes to the pictures.

"Take a look at these, people," I announced. "We're trying to find three individuals. The first is Sam Zelig, a New York State crime figure. He shot up the window of Magnolia Café this afternoon. He is armed and dangerous and probably accompanied by a group of at least three men, also armed and dangerous."

Czerniak gawked at Irina's picture. "Who's the chick?" Then turned to Mora. "The lady. Sorry."

I said, "She's why he's here. She goes by Irina. We don't have a last name. And she's in the company of subject number three." I made sure everyone had the third picture and tried to be cool when I said, "Ben Reles."

I heard a shift in the room, but I'd be hard-pressed to say where it came from. Halvorsen broke the silence first. "The old guy I saw ya with?"

"That's right."

"Your old man?"

I grabbed onto my most professional tone. "Zelig is here chasing the other two. He wouldn't stop at killing Reles—my father—or anyone else who got in his way. He has a long history of violent behavior. We don't know if my father and Irina are still in town."

Fuentes asked a legitimate question. "Um . . . your father and the girl. Are they wanted for anything?"

I took a breath. "If you see my father, take him into custody, whether he wants it or not. You're not authorized to use force."

Halvorsen said, "Unless he does."

"He won't."

Halvorsen went on. "You wouldn't hide anything from us, would you, Reles?"

I shot him a look. "After all we been through together?"

Mora broke in. "If it's interstate, shouldn't that be the FBI?"

"You wanna hand this over to the FBI?"

None of us ever wanted to hand anything to the FBI. I didn't even want the squad in on my business, but I couldn't find Pop on my own. If they tossed him in the lockup, Zelig's men could get at him there. But that would take time. If Pop was on the street, Zelig could kill him on sight. I gritted my teeth and told them where we might find my father, based on his habits and his professional involvements.

I explained that my father was a frequenter of the lower class of nightspots, and not just bars. Illegal bookie joints, gambling houses, prize-fights if he could find them. His friends were people who worked nights, who were open to unusual business propositions or who might propose them: cabdrivers and bartenders and dubious security guards. Small-time entrepreneurs whose projects made only a nod to legality.

What I didn't quite explain was that my father was less likely to work a steady job, legal or otherwise, than he was to engage in some such deal. He once rented an abandoned gas station which he used to fence unfenceable goods, in this case a dozen or so stolen coffins. He never got rich, never had more than a few bucks in his pocket, but he'd seldom done more than a short term in a county jail. As criminals went, he was neither brilliant nor stupid. Tonight he wouldn't be in these places looking to place a bet, but maybe to work a deal. Who would hide him? Who would get him out of town or arm him to the teeth?

I pointed out that Zelig knew my father well enough to know where he might hide and would be looking in the same places. The trick would be to spot Zelig before he spotted you.

On the strength of that threat, I decided to send the squad out in pairs. I started assigning sectors of the city according to the department's grid. Mora and Czerniak would take East Austin—Charlie Sector. Charlie Sector was separated from Central Austin by the highway and by a calculated decision of the city planning commission in the 1920s to keep low-income housing, as well as social services, well east of the interstate so that Austin would remain segregated, even after segregation was prohibited by federal statute. Isolated by geography and economics, Charlie had long been the target of a particularly coldhearted breed of opportunism. It was rife with bars, liquor stores and gun shops, as well as loan sharks, drug dealers and pimps, making it the land of the dubious low-cost "deal." The dubious high-cost deals would happen at the capitol, but you wouldn't find my father there.

Halvorsen cut in. "What about the rabbit case?"

"Priorities," I said. "You can stay on that. I need the rest of the squad."

"For what?"

The wise answer would have been that Zelig posed an immediate threat to the town. He'd proven as much by shooting out that window. And I would have said that if I were thinking straight. But Zelig had threatened Rachel and Josh, and I knew that my father was running for his life. In spite of all Pop had done to get himself into that situation, I was finally in a position where I could help him.

I also knew that any claims of my compromised authority on the subject, the likelihood that I was hiding something for my father's benefit, were true. So when Halvorsen pinned me on this obvious fact, I shot back with, "This is my squad, and I give the orders. Go find your fucking rabbit killer."

The fact that Halvorsen stood a few inches taller than me didn't make it easier on him. He had to physically look down at my eyes while I insulted him in front of his peers.

I gave the rest of the town to Fuentes and LaMorte, saving the immediate areas of South Austin for myself.

Mora and Czerniak headed east, Fuentes and LaMorte started central and worked their way north, and Halvorsen fumed and planned in the squad room. I drove farther south than I had before and worked the shoe leather again—check-cashing places, bars, pawnshops, hotels, cab dispatchers. Have you seen my daddy? Have you seen Zelig looking for him?

Zelig didn't know the area. I figured that for an advantage. But the mob was known for employing out-of-town talent, men who could show up in a place, case a situation, maybe kill a guy and be back on the train before the cops found the corpse. I'd laid eyes on Zelig already, and the unfamiliar territory didn't seem to make him tread cautiously or politely. He posed an immediate threat, in any town.

I retraced a few of my steps. I remembered a cab company where Pop's friend Donny had worked years ago, and I went by the office. Nobody knew who Donny was. All the taverns Pop once frequented were gone, including the one where Bobby had worked. Pop had told me earlier that he couldn't find any of his friends, not Donny or Bobby.

Then I remembered Ida, the good-hearted barmaid who deserved better than the casual treatment she got from Pop and the scowls she got from me. She'd be Pop's age, or nearly. He mentioned that someone had said she was still in Austin.

And someone had told him, years earlier, that I'd become a cop. Was that her? Had he stayed in touch with her after he left town?

I got out at a pay phone, called information and came up empty. I called Social Security and identified myself, asking, "Can you give me a Social for Ida . . ." and realized I couldn't remember her last name.

Minor. Meyer. Meinard. Menard?

"Ida Menard. She lives in Austin. Born maybe 1928."

Some wait and they gave it to me. I called the IRS and got a phone number and an address off South First. The phone number was a dud. The address, too. "No, we been here ten years. Don't know who was here before." Then I thought of Holiday House on Barton Springs Road, the breakfast place where I'd last seen her working ten years earlier. I headed there. The old manager blinked when I mentioned her name. He remembered her, sure.

"What's wrong?" I asked.

"Little guy came looking for her before. My age."

The manager had told Pop how he remembered Ida, loved her, then gave Pop her home address. She left to get married, the manager said, seven years back. Pop was glad to hear it.

I explained that that was my father.

The manager said, "I didn't think nothing of it till you came in."

I showed him my badge and he gave me the address. The house was in the same neighborhood, on Mary Street. I floored it there with the lights flashing.

With faded green paint chipping off the front shutters, the house stood smaller than the others on the block and had probably preceded them. I could imagine it alone on a stretch of prairie. But I could tell that the place was much loved, the lawn trimmed, the flowers watered. Pickup truck in the driveway. The home my father could not or would not give her. I knocked, then tried the doorknob, unlocked. I walked in.

On the right, the kitchen. I could see the sink and pantry and a Formica table with fake wood grain. On the left, the living room. Slouching black chairs, TV on wheeled table. Upright piano with a yellowed folio: *Albert's Piano for Adults*. Toppled lamps and photographs. And two bodies on the rug.

One was Ida's.

I drew my .38 and prowled the house. Nothing but a single bathroom and a bedroom the homeowners would never use again. Windows closed. The killer left through the door. Back in the living room, I surveyed Ida and the guy she'd taken as husband. Her head lay back on his chest as if they were relaxing on a picnic blanket. The old man was heavy and florid. He wore loose green pants, a pajama top and slippers. There'd been a fight, and he'd gotten the worst of it, eyes blackened, cheek swollen. But there were no gunshot wounds, no strangulation marks, no broken neck. What there was was a screwdriver embedded up to its grip in its ear canal. It was only when I got close enough to check him for warmth that I noticed Ida was still breathing.

Tiny and shriveled from a career of serving beer and slinging hash to ungrateful slobs like my father and me, she'd finally made a home with her Romeo. And here she lay, breathing in shallow sips. Eyes wide but moving. I knelt over her.

"Ida?"

She wore a light housecoat. I could see some blood, but not as much as a bullet would set loose. She stared, terrified. I put myself in her sight lines.

"Ida?"

Her eyes met mine, stopped there and softened in recognition, even comfort. She knew me. I was a friend.

Then she died.

◆ ◆ ◆

The doors weren't forced, so I guessed Ida and her husband had allowed the intruders in or responded to a threat. From the positioning of the bodies, I suspected that the killer had attacked the old man, beaten him and probably killed him before turning his attention to Ida. I twisted her around and looked her over the way I'd seen a medical examiner do. A thick stripe of a bruise, like a man's arm, stretched across her tiny mangled back. It seemed like he'd held her close, squeezed her until she screamed and couldn't scream, until she ran out of breath or her spine cracked. He was trying to get information from her, to torture it out of her, something she didn't have or wouldn't give. If he killed the husband first, maybe that was his mistake. She had nothing left to live for.

I found hair clutched in her tight fists. Silver hair. A big tough guy with silver hair. Sam Zelig.

Before I got to the phone, two patrols pulled up in front of the house. I greeted them at the front door, wondering how they knew to get there before I'd called for them.

One of them said, "How'd you get here so fast?"

I said, "What do you mean?"

He led me back to his car, radioed Dispatch and asked them to play the tape. It went like this.

"911 operator. Where's the emergency?"

"Please help us. I'm at 2106 Mary Street." Ida.

"What is the nature of the emergency?"

Long pause. Then, "There's a man trying to get into our house." She sounded alarmed but not panicked.

"Does he pose a threat?"

Another long pause. Then a near monotone, "Oh, my God. It's Ben Reles." Then she dropped the phone into the cradle.

We hadn't missed Zelig by long. Less than twenty minutes had passed since he'd fed those lines to Ida. No one would remember Ida for her acting. Pop posed no threat to her, only a nuisance. Fifty-fifty she was still in love with him, and that's why he thought he could count on her. I knew that she would never call the cops on him, not even if she was mad. But the department didn't know that. The tape put official suspicion on Pop, adding two more murders to Berelman's, the one he was already a suspect for.

I would bet money that the silver hair was Zelig's, which would mean he'd questioned her and killed her himself, tasks he could easily have farmed out. That he used a hands-on approach meant he took a personal interest in the search, a mistake his smarter, more rational brother would never make. What I couldn't figure was how Zelig found Ida. Had he found Pop's address book? Followed him?

The last was unlikely. If Zelig tracked Pop to Ida's house, he'd have grabbed Pop, rather than waiting for him to leave and questioning Ida on his whereabouts.

Maybe Ida gave my father up before she died. Maybe Zelig had him now.

At the house I processed Ida and her husband, their deaths part of an ongoing investigation. The silver hair in Ida's hand would be tested as DNA evidence, but the testing would take weeks at best. I phoned Dispatch and had them tell the patrols and everyone else who had Zelig's picture that he was now wanted for two local murders and was armed and dangerous. By the time that was done, the sun had gone down and I was hungry again, and it would have been a good time to go back to Torbett's and check on Rachel and Josh, but if I checked on them by phone I could save some time and keep moving. I picked up Ida's living-room phone and dialed. Torbett answered on the first ring.

"*Yes.*"

"It's Reles. How are they?"

I heard him move and close a door. "*Your wife wants to go home and get her things. That's what she says, but her hands are shaking. And your son isn't much better.*"

I gave Torbett the rundown on the murder of Ida Menard and her husband.

"*I heard the tape,*" he said. Of course he'd heard it.

"It's a setup," I told him. "Ida was my father's friend."

"*Friend?*"

"Okay, they were ex-lovers, but they were on good terms. That double homicide isn't my father's style."

"*That may be so—*" he said, and I cut him off.

"I know, I know. It won't stand up in court. There was silver hair in her fist. Zelig's color, not my father's. DNA tests will prove that. Eight to five the lab'll match his Brylcreem. How long can you watch Rachel and Josh?"

"*Don't worry about that.*" I'd found Torbett's soft spot. He'd bust me if I stepped out of line, strip me of my rank and, if necessary, my freedom. But he'd watch out for my family like they were his own. "*You want to talk to her?*"

"Can I?"

In a minute I heard Rachel's voice. "*I need to leave here.*"

"You can't go home. It's dangerous. Not even for a minute."

"*I need my things.*"

I knew what she needed.

"Can you have some wine?" I asked. Wrong question.

"*I'm not a baby. I don't need you to tell me what to have!*"

"I'm sorry. This is a bad time."

"*It's always a bad time.*"

"You know that's not true." No answer. There were two things she couldn't handle. One was being humiliated. The other was not having a drink. I didn't know much about it, but Rachel had gone out drinking the night before and planned to do the same thing again. The disruptions had thrown off her delicate balance of daily wine rationing and monthly binges. She was suffering a hangover and the watchful eye of the Torbetts. She needed a real drink, which meant a lot of real drinks, which meant she couldn't have people around. Not me, not Josh and certainly not strangers.

"Listen," I said. "If you could just hold it together for a little while. You can go crazy when I get back, whatever you want."

"*I'm not that bad,*" she said, adding a weak chuckle.

"I know. Just . . . whatever you do, just stay away from the house. Can you promise me that?"

Silence. Then, *"He misses you."*

"He . . ." It took me a moment to figure out she meant Josh. "Seriously?"

She hung up, and I dialed my new home number. I punched the code into the machine and heard the tape rewind. Then I heard Pop's voice on the tape.

"Meet me," he said. *"At your place."*

At first I thought he meant my house. Then I remembered what he said when I brought him to Magnolia Café two nights before. "Is this your place?" My answering machine wasn't so sophisticated as to tell me what time someone had called. Pop had neglected to suggest a meeting time, on the reasonable concern that someone might be listening in. So he might have been waiting at Magnolia for hours, or I might wait for hours if I got there first.

I drove down Congress to Magnolia. I pulled past the boarded front window into the back of the lot, close to the trees. I didn't see Pop or anyone. I stepped out of the car in the dark, thinking about Pop, Zelig, Zelig's threat to Rachel and Josh and the possibility that Pop's message was a setup, the same way Ida's 911 call had been. In the momentary distraction, I felt a hand on my shoulder. Instinct kicked in and I swung my right, pivoting my full weight with the punch and walloping my father in the ear.

He went down hard on the gravel, clutching the side of his head. "Oh! Fuck!" He checked his hand for blood. "How long you been waitin' to do that?"

I tried to help him up. "You all right?"

"Jesus! Shit! Don't touch me. Oh, God, my head! Fuckin' shoot me. It'll be easier on both of us."

When I was a kid, my father said I was a crappy fighter. Later, when I became a good one, he never said a word about it. Not when I started winning, not as I worked my way up through the ranks of the Golden Gloves. Complaining about how hard I'd hit him was the closest my father ever gave me to a compliment. It was difficult not to smile.

"What's the matter with you?" he said. "You're so fuckin' moody!"

"You want to raise me, you should've done it when I was a kid. Why'd you put your hand on my shoulder?" He'd never done that before, not ever. "Why didn't you just say, 'Hello'?"

"I'll remember for next time. Shit."

"Where you been?"

"Took another hotel. In the morning we tried to get a bus. They had our pictures on the wall."

He wavered on his feet. I asked if he needed to eat.

"Not here, not here," he said. "Get in. Drive." He followed the car around to the passenger door. "Fuck."

I headed down South Congress, checking the mirrors. I was pretty sure we were alone.

"Why didn't you tell me you were in trouble with Sam Zelig?"

His head jolted like he'd been hit again. "Wha—?" Then, "How . . . who told you . . ."

"Tell me something," I said. "How long were you back in Elmira?"

"I don't know. A week?"

"He told you to come back?"

Pop shifted, sighed and said, "He said if I didn't come, he'd find me. He just needed me to do some driving, keep an eye on things." I wasn't sure, but I thought my father looked proud.

"And you weren't worried?"

"Sure I was worried. What was I gonna do? Let him come for me? I closed out my business, tried to collect on a few nickel-dime bets people owed me. You know me. Everything I got fits in one suitcase with space left over." I knew this. He owned a comb, a toothbrush, some foot powder and a change or two of clothes. Everything was clean, but nothing was extra. His pockets would have been filled like Berelman's, with pawn tickets, betting tickets, IOUs and some amount of cash, small or large depending on how things were going lately. But that was all. If he had to get out of town in a hurry, leaving his suitcase behind wouldn't be a major setback.

"I came into Elmira at night," he said. "Cold, so fuckin' cold. I forgot how cold it got there in the winter. Wind whistling down these streets. I figured I had the night to find out what I was up against, what Sam was into, what my chances were. Then I could meet him in the morning. If I waited longer than that, he'd find out I'd been in town a whole day without coming by, and he'd be mad. So I hit the bars, looking for old friends. Place was like a morgue. There was this flood—"

"I heard."

"Yeah?" He noticed my bruised face. "Hey, what happened to you?"

"I fell."

"Uh-huh. Anyway, all I found out was Ike, Sam's big brother, is in the Joint, and it looks like he's in for the long haul. This worries me, because, you know, Ike was the grown-up. He was what kept Sam from going apeshit. See, Ike knows you can't just go around doing whatever you want. Sam knows that, too, but not when he gets pissed. Then he forgets.

"Anyway, I show up, and Sam's all friendly, gets me a brandy, sit down, put your feet up. We're talking over old times. He needs someone to fill in, drive him around, take care of some things. Same as before, only I'm a little higher because all the old guys are gone."

"Where'd they go?"

He said, "Gee, I didn't think to ask." Then he blurted, "They're dead! What do you think? They're dead or in the Joint."

"All right. Did you meet Berelman?"

"I met Irina. I knew there was another guy before me. That's who I was replacing. Took me a few days to figure that out. But Irina, I kept seeing her, those big eyes. She always looked like she was at a funeral. Maybe she was. Anyway, this one night Zelig sends me to the garage. He's got a car, a black Buick, and he wants me to drive it to the foundry, the one where they made the fire trucks, and bring the girl."

"What for?"

"How do I know? Take the girl, drop her off. I guess he was tired of her, I don't know. Maybe he sold her off. But she gets in the back with her yellow raincoat and her little bag, and he watches us drive off. And I drive for a while, and she says, 'You know where you're taking me?' and I say to some friends. And she says, 'You are taking me to die.' I say no, no, it's nothing like that. Because if I was taking her to die, there would be a bunch of us. But she says we're gonna go to the foundry, and they'll fire two shots, one into her and one into me. And that's when I think, The foundry? That's not where you drop a girl with another pimp. That's where you take someone out of action. Maybe she saw something, she knows something, maybe

Sam thinks *I* know something. He's only had me back for a week. I'm better to him dead than I am alive."

Streetlights rolled over us. The stores spread out as we reached the outer stretches of South Austin. Houses sparkled for Christmas. "What happened?"

He said, "Well, you know, I always figured when they called me, when it was my time, I'd just go. Beats running around looking in the rearview, sleeping with one eye open. And then the time comes, and I just can't do it. Something kicked in. Try hitting yourself in the head with a hammer. You can't. And I'm driving south toward the river, and I'm supposed to turn east toward the foundries, and the time comes, and I turn west and head out of town.

"Now I look back, I don't know why I listened to her. Maybe she was full of shit. I didn't have too much time to think about it. But I don't think so. Everything she said, the pieces fit. She told me that he killed the girl who came before her."

"What girl?"

"I never found out her name. And Berelman, that's when she told me his name. The guy who came before me. Berelman must have said something about it or mouthed off to Zelig about whatever. And one day Berelman's gone. Berelman was a dopehead, too, a garbagehead, Irina said. He got busted, he was pending trial, he told her that before he disappeared. He said Zelig was afraid they'd get him to flip, tell all about Zelig in exchange for leniency."

"Why'd he tell the girl all this?"

"Maybe he was high. Maybe he was in love with her. Who knows? Anyway, what if she was full of shit? She played a dirty trick on me by getting me to run away with her. Can you blame her?" He stopped for a moment. "I played a dirty trick on you by showing up here. I didn't think about it. We'd been driving for a day and a half. Took turns at the wheel so we could sleep a little. If I was calm, if my head was clear, I never would've come here. I never would've dropped this on you." Then he said, "I'm sorry."

Those last two words were so out of character that I wasn't sure I'd heard him right. We drove along in silence. "Tell me something about him," I said.

"Like what?"

"Anything."

He thought for a moment. "You didn't know him in the old days. Christ, he was a powerhouse. Huge, strong. Ike was the brains, but he couldn't build what he did without Sam. Slots, jukeboxes, pinball, the numbers. Shylocking. All because of Sam. Fists like sledgehammers, he had. You remember all the rings he wore? Tear a guy's face up. He didn't need them. When he was a kid, they said he got jumped by two guys, cracked their fuckin' heads together. Cracked! He only kept muscle around to save himself sweat. And mean. I've seen him yank a guy's arm out of his shoulder. He's still big today. Shit, he's my age, and even *you* wouldn't mix it up with him. But it's in his eyes. The party's over and everyone left but him. The last *makher*. We're not so different, Sam and me. You mellow with age."

Pop had, but I wasn't so sure about Sam. "You ever find Ida?" I asked. I knew he'd tracked her from Holiday House, and unless I missed my guess, visited her while she was still alive.

"No," he said. "Why?"

I didn't bother to tell him he was lying. I took a breath, then said, "Zelig did."

"What do you mean?"

"He's here. I saw him. He found Ida."

Long silence. Then he figured it out. "No. No." I could see him drop his head into his hands. "Please. No, please." It was the closest I'd seen him get to crying. Or praying.

"Listen," I said. "Did you ever mention her to Zelig? Can you remember that?"

"Oh, Jesus. I don't know. Maybe."

"When?"

"A week ago or so. Right when I got there. We were at his house, having a few drinks, shooting the shit. Take me there. Take me there."

I did an illegal U-turn and headed to Ida's. "Zelig asked you about Ida?"

"I don't remember," he muttered. "We had a few drinks."

"How many drinks?"

"You know, we had some drinks. Talked about the old days."

"Do you remember everything you said?"

He brought both fists up to his forehead. "Fuck. No. I don't know what the fuck I said. I got drunk. I woke up in the same easy chair the next morning."

It didn't take much to figure that Zelig had gotten Pop drunk and pumped him for information that might be of later use. Maybe he did this with a specific goal in mind. Or maybe it was just something he did, the same way the FBI put together a file on each of its employees. Even the probation department questioned every new probationer about his friends and family, so they'd know where to look once he absconded. Maybe Sam didn't know at the time exactly how he was going to make use of my father. He just gathered information he might need later.

Pop could talk when he wanted to. I learned that the night before. He'd told Zelig that he'd lived in Austin, that his son was still there, that he'd had friends named Donny and Bobby and an ex-girlfriend named Ida Menard. Maybe he even knew her married name. He probably gave Zelig the rundown on half a dozen other cities he'd lived in. But I called Lowry from Austin, and Lowry tipped Zelig that we were here. So it took both our efforts, my father's and mine, to set Zelig loose on my town.

I noticed then how much bigger I was than Pop, taller and wider. I realized that, in the ring, I'd pretty likely kill him. But half of that was the age difference. If we were both twenty-five, size difference aside, I wouldn't put money down. Small but fast, like he said. Now he looked small and beaten. Suddenly he was showing his age. He noticed me looking at him. "What?" he asked.

"Is there something else about why we left Elmira, something you didn't tell me?"

He said, "Get me to Ida's."

"Tell me first."

"Bullshit. Ida's first. Then I'll talk."

We reached Ida's, and the house was barren, save for a few huddling neighbors and some crime-scene tape we slipped under. I opened the front door, and Pop went in.

The crew had removed the bodies along with whatever hair, nails and other fragments that might tell a story. They'd dusted for prints, so we could now touch the surfaces to our hearts' content. Pop stood just inside the doorway, eyeing the blood on the rug. His face crumpled. He'd brought this on Ida. Then he shook off the notion and paced the house, walked the kitchen and living room, went into the bathroom and the bedroom, opened a window and stuck his head out, closed it and came back in with his head down. He opened a cabinet in Ida's living room, the mirrored inside displaying a humble but diverse selection of liquor.

"How'd you know about that?" I said.

"Same cabinet. She had it . . . at the old place."

He poured himself a scotch from a pint bottle shaped like a flask. The bottle took away some of the class that Ida's liquor cabinet was striving for, but she didn't need it now.

When he finished the drink, Pop slipped the pint bottle into his jacket pocket and we headed back to my car. We drove off with the windows cracked. The air was cool and clear, the traffic a bit heavy, but we had no place to go, no place safe.

I asked him if he knew a cop named Lowry.

"That's it," he said. "The one I asked you about. Irish punk. You boxed him when you were a kid. He beat the shit out of you."

"That was Ferber. I beat the shit out of Lowry."

"Ohhh," he said. "That explains it."

"What?"

"Lowry busting my ass the whole week I'm in Elmira, following me around, pulling me over."

"Lowry works for Zelig," I said, as the feds had told me.

"Why'd he fuck with me?"

"Who knows?" I said. "Spite?"

Pop thought about it for a while. I sneaked a look at his hunched profile. The scotch had softened him. Finally he said, "I wasn't there that day, the day you leveled that kid, Lowry I guess it was. But I heard about it. They razzed me about the day you went down in the ring. Then you flattened Lowry, and everything changed. Sam started talking about what a tough Jew you were. And I got scared."

"Why?"

He shook his head. "You grew. Christ, you looked bigger every day. You were fourteen when you passed me. And eat? You ate like a fuckin' horse. You worked out like you had a fire under your ass. I saw you ask the other guys about fighting. I felt bad I couldn't teach you myself. I was a lousy teacher."

I said, "You weren't so bad," but we both knew I was lying.

He went on. "You moved like a little guy. You could duck and weave, but you could punch with all your weight. Only you fell for the piss-off trick."

"The what?"

"You know. Guy pisses you off, calls your mother a whore. You go nuts trying to take him down. You're not thinking, you open yourself up. It's okay when you're a kid, the lower ranks. You're fighting street kids who can't box at all. But you would've lost to smarter boxers. And you hung out with that fucking gang."

All this was true. Fighting in the ring, I was fearless and reckless. But my Elmira gang and I were posers, a parody of a gang, more prone to acts of vandalism and beer theft than to any major conflict. Eight or nine guys made up the unit, with a few girls attached, and me emerging eventually as the leader. This development occurred one day when we were hanging around outside at a pool hall. A mob goon came out to shoo us away, recognized me from the gym, said, "Oh. Hey," and went back in, sealing my status with my peers. That's all that moment meant to me. But someone was watching.

"Sam had his eye on you. He said you were good because you weren't afraid of getting hit. I think he had an eye on you on the street, too."

"Who?"

"I never found out. Lowry maybe? Sam said you had 'leadership potential.' I said you didn't, that you were weak, you cried at night. He said bullshit, that you were cut out for the Life."

I drove in silence, up and down the residential streets.

"It was my fault," he said. "I should've kept you away from the gangs. But look who my friends were. What was I gonna say? Find better friends?" He took another drink from the bottle. "Your mother would've."

"Would've what?"

"Kept you in line. Made you come home at night. Pushed you to go to medical school, law school, some Jew thing. I wasn't any good at that."

"Something I don't get," I said. "When we left Elmira . . . why did they just let you go?"

"They *told* me to go. I fucked up enough, and they told me to beat it."

"Why? Why didn't they just kill you?"

" 'Cause they didn't!" he yelled. "What difference does it make? You wanna give 'em another chance?"

I abandoned that line of questioning. "What do you know about Berelman?"

"What I said, that he worked for Sam. I never met him."

"You think anybody else could have killed him like that?"

Pop shook his head. "Anybody else would have just shot him."

Still not ready to drop anchor, I found a drive-thru burger place, and we ate while I drove. There were a few gaps in Pop's story, a few connections I didn't quite get. I asked him about my half-brother and -sister, his kids from his first wife, Dolores. He looked away. I asked if he ever saw them after the divorce.

"No."

"Why not?"

"What do you care?" Then, quietly, "They had a mother. All you had was me."

I mulled it over. I kept thinking how, when I was a kid, Pop didn't talk much, apart from yelling about whatever pissed him off. I didn't even remember him calling me by name. I only knew he was talking to me if there was no one else in the room. Now he was a fast-talking deal maker, a *kibitzer,* with an angle to work and a story to tell, and he didn't mind telling it. I said, "You never talked to me like this before. Before this week. When I was a kid, I hardly remember you stringing twenty-five words together."

He shifted around and finally tossed out an explanation that seemed obvious to him. "You were a kid!"

After a while I asked where Irina was.

He said, "She's safe."

"What?"

"Don't worry about it."

"Are you kidding me? I'm keeping the whole department off your ass. You're looking at three counts of homicide. You won't give me a straight answer?"

"You can't tell them what you don't know."

"Great," I said. "In the meantime your good buddy Zelig wants his pet Russian back, with five days' rental plus interest. If she's been with him too long, she knows too much to go free. So everyone who gets between her and him dies, and that includes Rachel and Josh. He wants her by midnight, and nobody seems to know where he is or what he's driving around in. So maybe you have some brilliant fucking idea about how we stop this seventy-year-old killing machine, because we've got about two hours to get ready."

The corners of his mouth rode up. "Sure," Pop said. "We give him the girl."

At around 10:00 P.M. in the cramped Communications division at HQ, Lieutenant Jake Lund, with his horn-rimmed glasses and prematurely gray, steel-wool hair, sat with his weird tech buddies in front of a row of control panels, an antiquated radar system, what I thought was an oscilloscope, various receivers and a glass map of Austin. Jake's skull bore visible forceps marks from his birth, his first unsuccessful attempt to avoid the world. Pried out into the open, he retreated when he could, his consciousness masked with sugar and long hours of television until computers came around. We'd served together on Homicide for years, though he hated the street and tended to stay in the office, communicating by telephone and the budding Internet. He was so far ahead of the curve in terms of computers that the police brass, the "Fifth Floor," drafted him as head of Information Technology, promoted him to lieutenant and stationed him in the administrative offices for easy access. He had a staff of four civilians, one of whom, a programmer named Lynn, he had married. He worked in a windowless office from which he seldom emerged. He was happier than he'd ever been.

Zelig had turned a corner when he killed Ida and her husband. If the DNA matched, we had him for a double homicide. Whatever he wanted Irina for didn't matter. Now he was a fugitive. But I wasn't going to tell him that.

Sergeant Luis Fuentes watched Jake and his men. Sergeant Catarina Mora sat with a mirror, wiping pale pancake makeup on her dark skin. She'd already strapped herself into a bulletproof vest. Over that she wore a light summer dress similar to the one Irina had been wearing, along with cheap sneakers. She topped this off with a raincoat and a thin blond wig she'd scrounged from the closets of Narcotics and Street Response. Pop watched her with undisguised delight.

We were keeping Pop under supervision rather than under arrest. No one present believed he was responsible for any of the deaths involved, but we needed his insights, the way you might protect a mob informant until he helped you catch the big guys. When the smoke cleared, Pop would still be facing charges for auto theft and maybe more.

I'd sent Czerniak and LaMorte home. We were only looking for one subject, and he was headed straight for us.

I got FBI Agent Chu on the phone, trying to figure out exactly how Zelig and his stooges traveled to Austin, in hopes of tracking them down. *"I've been on with the field office in Buffalo,"* he said. *"We know he used fake names, more than one. He probably used multiple credit cards to charge the separate flights—"*

"Can he get multiple credit cards?"

"He can get anything. We're talking to people in Elmira who could have supplied them. We're hoping he runs out of cards or slips up and uses one twice. Then we jump on him."

I got off the phone as Mora checked her wig in a mirror, but not the way a girl does. No ladylike attention to detail, no primping. All business. She turned to me. "Well?"

She looked like Irina if you were far away and didn't distinguish shapes very well. All they had in common was they were both women. Mora was wider in the shoulders, and anyone who couldn't tell her from the frail and battered Irina, didn't care. Zelig cared.

Mora tied a kerchief over her hair and knotted it under her chin. The raincoat didn't match Irina's, but it would hide her shape. I told her about Zelig's holding Irina captive, raping and torturing her, and asked how good a shot she was.

Mora said, "At fifty feet I can clip one of his balls and save the other for court."

Pop said, "My kinda woman."

I put on my bulletproof vest, too, just for good measure. The new ones were awkward, reaching down to the upper thigh, but thin and light. I never trusted them, and I hoped not to find out just how good they were.

We arranged to intercept any calls that went to my office or my home and forward them to HQ. Jake Lund and his buddies manipulated knobs in front of their glass map. My house was clearly marked on the map, though we guessed Zelig would call there rather than show up. That my phone number was brand-new and also unlisted wouldn't slow him down. Then we settled in and waited.

And waited.

I was about to call Torbett's house at 11:45 P.M. to check on Rachel and Josh when the phone rang. I picked it up.

"Yeah."

"Get in your car. Turn the radio to channel six. Go west on Eighth Street." He had a police radio. He could have gotten one anywhere. He knew where we were.

"Okay," I said.

"Bring the girl. No one else. I'll be watching."

Jake and the boys signaled each other, turned knobs, pointed. Jake signaled me to stretch out the conversation.

I said, "You know I can't just give her to you."

"Fine," Zelig said. *"Don't."*

"Wait, wait. I can bring you together. So you can talk."

He said, *"You get the idea of bringing anyone else into this, I'll make you suffer."* He hung up. I watched Jake and his friends. A moment passed before they shook their heads.

"Nope. Sorry."

Mora and I went down to my car in the darkened lot attached to APD, scanning the shadows for an intruder. We headed out to Eighth Street and drove west.

Mora said, "What did that mean, 'I'll make you suffer'? He had something in mind?"

"Rachel," I said. "Josh. He was telling me he'd kill them."

Mora said, "Are you sure you want to do this?"

"What should I do?" I said. "Give him what he wants and hope for the best?"

Zelig's threat meant that we *had* to catch him. Or he'd make things much worse than they already were. I turned the radio to channel six and grabbed the mike.

"Sam?"

Nothing. I could see headlights in my rearview, several pairs, but I couldn't make out one vehicle.

The radio crackled, and I heard Zelig's voice say, *"Go right at the light."*

That startled me. I was hoping we'd spot him first. I turned right and headed north on Rio Grande, until he said, *"Go right at the light,"* again. I turned right at Martin Luther King Drive and rode along the southern border of the university.

I checked my rearview mirror. It was dark and the traffic was thin, but I couldn't see anyone following me. What Zelig didn't know was that in another unmarked car my good buddy Jake Lund rode shotgun while Sergeant Luis Fuentes from my squad drove, listening to channel six and waiting for clues to find us. For good measure we had a hand radio Mora kept low. There were other technologies for this sort of thing, but that would have taken more time than we had. Fuentes could handle a car and a gun. Between him and Jake, I had one devoted, high-functioning cop. I was afraid to bring more, adding to the chances of Zelig's spotting them.

I stayed on MLK until I approached Interstate 35. Zelig said, *"Turn right."*

"At the highway?"

Zelig went nuts. *"Shut up, you cocksucking fuck!"* he screamed. *"Shut up. Shut the fuck up!"*

I turned right and headed down the frontage road. Jake would know I was on I-35 and could guess which way I was going.

I continued down the frontage road, stopping at every light and checking the mirrors until I reached Oltorf.

"Turn right," he said.

"Olt—" I stopped short. "Okay." I released the mike and said, "Right on Oltorf," loud enough for the hand radio to pick it up.

Sam said, *"Baby?"* I figured he wasn't talking to me. *"Is she there?"*

I headed right on Oltorf, stalling. Jake and Fuentes would be at least five minutes behind, and even then they'd have to play it cool.

"She's here," I said.

"Put her on."

Mora grabbed the microphone and spat into it, *"Zhopu lizhi mnye, yevreichik."* She let go of the button. Zelig howled.

Pop had coached Mora on this one, a Russian sentence he'd learned in the old days. The radio took out the highs and lows, and one woman's voice sounded pretty much like another's. The words meant, literally, "Lick my ass, little Jew." Zelig might have missed the specifics but he got the gist. I heard him laugh.

It was a calculated risk. She was insulting him, but Zelig liked that. It turned him on in a way that was both sexual and violent. Her assertiveness gave him something to beat down.

He settled down and said, *"Reles, go right and go slow."*

I said, "Right up Congress," then headed up Congress, praying we would get the jump on him.

By the time I passed the point where Barton Springs Road forked into Congress Avenue heading north, it was well past midnight and the traffic was nearly gone, effects of cold weather on a pre-holiday night. I headed onto the bridge, and Mora said, "Check behind you." I looked in the rearview. Someone was setting up orange traffic barricades to block access to the Congress Avenue bridge. I couldn't see him well, but he was smaller than Zelig and his hair wasn't silver. It might have been the guy who'd held me captive, the skinny one. Zelig wasn't alone.

Mora spoke into the radio in her lap. We would have been better advised using a code, but we hadn't come up with one. "Congress bridge. Come south."

I slowed to a crawl in the right lane as I passed over the midpoint of the bridge, twenty feet directly above the river called Town Lake. Headlights faced me from the same lane. The barricades blocked the bridge from the north also. I stopped the car.

Mora kept her head bowed. Staring into the beams, I read her Zelig's license number, a Texas plate, and she wrote it down. The car was a big-ass Lincoln, dark blue or black. My Chevy Caprice had some weight, but not as much as that. Fuentes would be driving a Toyota four-door. Zelig could see Mora's wig and kerchief. He could see that she had a face, but not what it looked like. I squinted through his headlights. I could see Zelig in the passenger seat. I could see one of his big goons driving and that the goon's ear was bandaged, the ear I tore trying to save myself from the wood chipper.

"*Kill the lights,*" he said through the radio. I checked behind and ahead for Jake and Fuentes and didn't see them. The guy who'd moved the traffic barricades was gone.

Mora didn't lift her head when she said, "Just give me one shot."

"Ain't up to me," I said, and killed the headlights. By now he could see us bright as day. If Mora looked up long enough to shoot, he might see her face and fire first.

"*Here's the deal,*" he said. "*You give me my girl and I let your father live.*"

I said, "You don't have my father. We have him."

Zelig laughed at that. He'd have my father if he wanted him.

"*Okay,*" he said. "*Send her out.*"

Zelig would have to be nuts to think I'd just hand Irina over. Or so frantic about having her that he *couldn't* think. Why?

Mora said, "What are the chances of him having a bulletproof windshield?"

I said, "Slim, but he's sheltered by the dash, while you're wide open."

"Buy me some time," she said. "I'm thinking."

"He can see you in the lamps. We have maybe five seconds before he figures out he got the wrong girl."

"*Reles?*"

I spoke into the mike. "I can't just hand her to you."

He barked, "*Why not?!*"

"This isn't like buying a car. I can arrange a sit-down or something." Come on, Fuentes.

"*People buy people every day,*" he said. "*Everybody's a slave.*"

"But not you."

"*No, not me.*"

Mora opened the door. I said, "Sit down."

"*Now you're talking.*"

She had an automatic at her side, a SIG P230 with a plastic grip. Sam sat less than fifty feet away. If she could raise her hand and make the shot before he got a look at her, she was fine. If she couldn't she was dead.

"Now send her over."

"Come and get her," I said. "She wants to know she's safe."

There was nothing protecting her but the car door, and it would be only seconds before Zelig's eyes picked out her facial features as not matching a woman he'd been torturing for a while.

I dropped my head so he couldn't read my lips. I hissed, "Mora, now!"

Maybe the car door was in her way. She had to raise her arm above it to make the shot, and by then it was too late. As I looked up, I saw Fuentes's Camry barreling through the orange traffic barricades and racing toward Zelig. Zelig's driver heard the Camry, put the Lincoln in reverse and floored it. Mora fired and hit his radiator.

Zelig's driver pulled enough to the right to hit the Camry at an angle. His rear bumper bashed in the Camry's grille and sent it spinning. Then he shifted gears and headed for us.

"Run!" I shouted and Mora tore out for the north shore, shooting at Zelig's passenger window and missing the driver's head, then diving for cover as they peeled out toward my car, the Lincoln's eight cylinders roaring and me trying to get the Caprice in gear until I gave up and moved toward my passenger door as Zelig's Lincoln rammed into my driver's side, bashing in the door as far as the steering wheel and trapping my left foot against the steering column as the car slid sideways onto the curb, probably tearing the tires, and me trying to yank my foot loose as they pulled back in a big circle across the six lanes, straightened out, then came barreling toward me again, trunk first, demolition derby style. I slid my foot out of my shoe just as the Lincoln smashed into my Caprice again, this time pounding it sideways against the steel railing, all that protected me from the cold, rushing water below. The driver's door was too mangled for me to open its window. The passenger door was butted shut by the rail, so I tried to work its window down. It went an inch and stopped and I squeezed my fingers in and tried to break the pane in or out and I heard the Lincoln's engine roaring louder again as it closed in on me and I yanked my fingers loose—and *CRASH!* The car crunched, the steering column jutted up toward the roof, the vehicle folded and tipped up on the fulcrum of the steel rail, and I thought one more shot like that and I'm headed for a watery grave and I can't open the doors and I'm backed against the crushed-in driver's side kicking at the passenger window and shots are firing from somewhere—Mora? Fuentes?—and I can see the dark water of the river, and I'm wondering how much time I have left when all of a sudden I hear someone shouting, singing, like kids in the street.

"Saaaaaaammmyy! Sammy Zeligman!"

Pop.

It should have crossed my mind that Pop would insist on coming along with Jake and Fuentes, and that they would find no compelling reason to protect him by leaving him behind.

The Lincoln revved, but it didn't move. Pop had gotten out of the battered Camry. I could see Jake and Fuentes hiding behind it. They'd been shooting, but it wasn't stopping Zelig any. And now Pop was singing, some kids' song.

> "Ikh heys Sammy Zeligman
> Shtam ikh fun New York.
> Khasene hobn mit der mamen vel ikh
> In der kumendiker vokh."

My Yiddish was never much, but I was pretty sure the song had old Sammy marrying his mother next week.

Sammy Zeligman fell for the piss-off trick.

I'd never know if it was the accusation regarding his mother, or regarding his excessive affection for her, something Ike had hinted about. Maybe it was just being reminded that he was no more than another immigrants' kid from the street. But there was Pop standing up to Zelig for the first time, stepping out of line the way little flunkies like Ben Reles don't do, and there was Zelig's Lincoln rolling away from my car and heading straight for Pop. Pop stood in the headlights until Zelig's car almost reached him. Then he feinted to the right. Zelig turned toward him, and Pop jumped to the left. Zelig missed him.

Fuentes fired shots at the Lincoln. Zelig's driver backed toward them fast, sitting low in his seat, and they jumped as he rammed the Camry.

I picked up again with wrestling the window when I heard a screech of tires, a single gunshot and a thud, and I looked up and saw my father in midair, then landing hard on the pavement. Pop.

I spotted Zelig in the Lincoln in front of Pop and we locked eyes and he laughed, and the driver gunned the engine when I realized that I still had my .38 and could shoot through the windows, and I pulled my fingers free as the Lincoln crashed into my driver's side again hard, and there was no more room to give, nothing left to crunch as my Caprice tipped over the railing and fell twenty feet, rolling over sideways before hitting the water hard and sinking fast, with the doors smashed into place and me stuck inside.

So they took up Jonah, and cast him forth into the sea. And the sea ceased from its raging.

—Jonah 1:15

My Caprice sank straight down into Town Lake and hit the sandy bottom, water pouring in through the inch I'd managed to open the window and seeping up from the cracked floor. I could see all this only by the tiny bit of lamppost light that hit the water and wormed through the current. I'd made it into what was left of the passenger seat, fifty-degree water rising past my single shoe and my socks. The cold water made me gulp air as it reached my waist, and I yanked my .38 loose, realizing that if I succeeded in opening the window, I'd face the water rushing against me. If it filled the car before I could get out, I'd have trouble firing the gun or bashing it against the window.

The water reached my chest. I tried to pull my knees up, but there was no room. Gritting my teeth against the chill, I dipped my head back into the water to protect my ears, and fired into the cracked windshield.

The bullet poked one tiny hole, enough for a fountain of water to hit my face. They'd made the windshield to be shatterproof. Thanks, Chevrolet.

I bashed the butt of the .38 into the window. The glass cracked and the water rose to reach my face. The gun slipped from my hands, and I realized I had about two more seconds of air to breathe.

When people drown, I remembered, they hold their breath as long as they can. Then desperation makes them try to suck in a lungful of air. But there is no air, so it's water that they suck into their lungs. Do that while trapped in your car at the bottom of a cold, dark river and you have yourself one dismal, claustrophobic, painful way to die.

I breathed in and out four times, reaching my mouth toward the car's roof. On the fourth breath, I went under. I tried to open my eyes, but there was nothing to see. I felt around for the .38, couldn't find it and finally righted myself, bashing the windshield with my hand, the water forcing my movements into slow motion. I located the bullet hole with my fingers, thinking, Now I die. Now my wife is alone. My son grows up without a father but instead with nightmares of a drowning death.

I needed more air. I let out a few bubbles, knowing that once my lungs emptied, I'd have maybe a second before I gasped for more. Then the windshield caved in. I reached through the opening and felt a hand, a small hand. I struggled to release my legs from under the dash. The hand led me over the dashboard, through the windshield, swimming up as my lungs compressed and I couldn't hold it any longer, blowing out the tiny bit of air I had left slowly, like whistling, as we swam up toward the light and popped out to the cold night air, Cate Mora treading water by my side, me sucking the air in deep and coughing, wheezing, freezing, breathing hard.

Once Jake and Fuentes "helped us" climb ashore ("Hey, thanks. Those last few steps onto the mud are always the hardest. You guys get your shoes wet?"), Jake took Fuentes's car and circled the area until he spotted the guy who set up the barricades on the north end of the Congress Avenue Bridge. Turned out to be some homeless slob who did it for ten bucks that Zelig promised and never paid.

I'd survived two attempts on my life in twenty-four hours, a trial by fire and one by water. I took heart in the fact that the fire wasn't Zelig's fault and his men never quite pushed my head into the wood chipper. They might have been bluffing. I suspected that Zelig didn't even mean to kill me when he pushed my car into the river, just to show me who was boss. But if the water killed me, he wouldn't lose sleep over it.

In the commotion Zelig had taken Pop. I'd lost my father, and with him, Irina. No one but Pop knew where she was, and Pop was out of my hands. Shaken by my close brush with eternity and the sudden awareness that my father, if he was alive, was now a captive of a man who could easily and gladly kill him, I limped through the mud in my wet socks and single shoe, waiting for the other shoe to drop.

We piled into what was left of Fuentes's Camry, shivered all the way to my new house, took in the mail and opened the liquor. It was around 1:00 A.M. Jake and Fuentes sat in my curtainless living room. Jake had found a soda, and Fuentes was drinking my good scotch, a privilege he hadn't exactly earned. Mora got the first shower for saving my life. It was Mora who found a brick near the bridge, realized she'd never be able to swim with it, hauled it to the point on the bridge where I'd been knocked off, and jumped. She said she missed the car and had to fight the current as she walked the few feet back upstream, nearly blind, along the river's floor. By this time Zelig had skidded away. Fuentes and Jake stared, amazed and dry, at the spot where Mora had hit the water. Fuentes was a good cop, and Jake had stuck by me through thick and thin. But Mora jumped off a fucking bridge for me.

Because Zelig had blocked northbound traffic, there was no one heading north on Congress but him and his driver when they tore into the dark in the mangled Lincoln with Pop bleeding in the back seat. By the time patrols finally spotted the Lincoln an hour later, it was abandoned on West Fourth Street, barely a mile away.

When Mora finished her shower, she opened the door a crack and called to me. I passed her a dry shirt and pants of mine (she wouldn't wear any of Rachel's "girl clothes") and a half tumbler of scotch. On the bed, Rachel had left some blouses I hadn't noticed before. I realized I was shaking harder now than when I climbed out of the river, soaking wet in the December night air. Even in the hot shower, I was shaking like a pile driver. I thought I'd break something. Maybe it was the cold river. Maybe it was nearly drowning like a trapped dog, and now it was catching up with me. Maybe I'd just lost my balls.

I dressed in the bedroom in the warmest stuff I had, heavy cotton pants and a jersey and a wool sweater. I dumped the wet clothes and vest and my remaining shoe in the kitchen, emptying my pockets of a soaking wallet, a badge holder and a handcuff case. I towel-dried these items and stuffed them into the pockets of a dry baseball jacket I'd be using later. I braced myself, walked into the living room like a lieutenant and joined the crew. I grabbed a scotch, hoping it would ease the shaking or at least give me a cover. Mora was putting down the cordless phone.

"What do we know?" I said.

Mora said, "Your father didn't turn up at any of the hospitals."

Fuentes said, "We know where Zelig ditched the car and that your father wasn't in it. We don't know if someone picked him up or if he stole another car. If he did, odds are no one will miss it till morning."

I said, "What about my father? What shape was he in?"

Jake and Fuentes looked at each other.

Fuentes said, "The first time, your father dodged the car. The second time he didn't."

I nodded.

Fuentes went on. "I don't know how hard the car hit him, but the pavement got him bad."

My jaw stiffened. "Was he breathing?"

"Yeah. I think so," Fuentes said. "He shouldn't have been moved. We fired a few rounds. Zelig was firing back at us, and the driver opened the far door, I guess to haul your father in. I didn't want to shoot. I was afraid I'd hit your old man."

My father wouldn't have been a match for Zelig on his best day. Now he was hurt and couldn't fight anyway. And even if he wasn't hurt, no one had to tell me his chances of surviving a kidnapping.

I said, "Fuentes, get ahold of Auto Theft and Traffic and see if you can find out what he's driving." He reached for the phone. "Better if you go in person. Drop Mora at home."

"Bullshit," she said.

I said, "No, you're off the hook for tonight."

"I don't wanna be off the hook."

"Jake, get your buddies over here and keep a trap-and-trace on my phone."

Jake said, "Do I have to stay?"

I stared at him as my jaw shuddered and seized. "Are you kidding me?"

"Well," he said, "it's late. You know. I'm married now."

"Yeah," I said, "go. Stay warm. Get some sleep."

"I'll stay," Mora said.

I said, "I'll call you when I need you." She took me at my word and left with Fuentes. Jake stayed behind with his soda, standing by the couch.

I said, "What?"

"Your father lifted my gun."

"What?!"

"We were sitting in the back seat. We shouldn't have brought him. And he falls over me like he's passing out, and I help him sit up, and then he's out the door and I realize he's lifted my gun. He was just singing to get the guy's attention. When the car got close to him the second time, he aimed. They gunned the engine, and he fired. He didn't hit anybody. And the car hit him."

"Jesus."

Jake went on. "Fuentes promised to keep his mouth shut, but if anyone finds out I let your father lift my weapon . . ."

"I get it.

"It's not like I don't look out for you."

"I know you do."

"I'm not on your squad anymore. You don't even outrank me."

"Jake . . ."

"No, man, it's like . . . you could call me when you don't need something."

All I could think was, Why? Maybe it had something to do with my not having many people I'd term friends. I wasn't quite sure what friends did when they weren't working. Instead what I said was, "He took my father. He threatened my family."

"You know, it's always something. You call me up, I'm supposed to drop everything. And now you're pissed off because I didn't jump in the river after you."

"I can't talk about this now—"

"When's the last time you did something for *me*?"

I searched my memory. "You never asked for anything."

"Think about it."

He put the soda on an end table and walked to the door. Then he turned.

"For what it's worth," he said, "when your father fired that shot, the Lincoln was coming straight for him. He didn't try to dodge it the second time."

"What to you mean?"

"He stood in the Lincoln's path because he knew that's where he'd get the best shot. Even if he hit Zelig, the car would have flattened him. It was the car that dodged, not your father. Get it? Your father went on a suicide mission for you."

Jake headed out without another word.

Somewhere in a stolen car or an abandoned house or a hotel room, my father was bleeding. He'd risked his life for me. No, not risked. Offered. It was luck that he wasn't dead. Somewhere he needed a doctor, maybe surgery, and the clock was ticking. Zelig was torturing him to find out where the girl was. Pop wouldn't tell him, I knew that now. And I wasn't much of a friend to Jake Lund, but that was too fucking bad, which was what I was thinking when the phone rang and I grabbed it as I heard, from the street, the soft but unmistakable *choop* of a silencer and the front window cracking above my head.

must have dropped the phone as I jumped for the light switch, killing the living room light as I rolled onto the floor and reached for my .38, which was at that moment oxidizing in a compressed Chevy Caprice at the floor of Town Lake. Now I was unarmed in a house with no curtains at night. Anyone could see in, but I couldn't see out.

A tiny voice chanted from the cordless, now on the rug a foot from my head.

"Daneel Reles-eh. Daneel Reles-eh."

Zelig.

I grabbed the phone.

"Got your attention," Zelig said.

"This is Texas," I said, grasping. "You don't own the judges."

"Come and get me, copper." It was something out of a James Cagney movie. I couldn't tell if he was kidding or not.

"Where's my father?" Dumb. Never give away your first concern.

I stayed low on the floor, snaking toward the bedroom. I suddenly wished I hadn't let Jake leave. Maybe he hadn't gotten far. He could be crouched behind a bush, ready to get a good shot at Zelig. If he had his gun.

Zelig shouted, *"Where's my girl? The real one!"*

He knew that Mora wasn't Irina. Probably the sharpshooting tipped him off. I slithered into the bedroom, found the lockbox I'd already placed under my bed, fumbled for my keys, dropped them, finally opened the box and drew out the Browning BDM I kept there. I kept a similar one locked in my car, no use to me now. The Browning carried ten rounds. Most shoot-outs are over in three or four shots, win or lose, so the .38 was enough for most occasions. But you never know.

I said, "The whole town is looking for you. How long can you dodge us?"

"I been dodging cops for forty years. And some tough bastards, too."

The truth, he was more ready for this than I was. After surviving a shoot-out with four cops, he'd have been smart to lie low. But he wasn't about being smart.

He'd come to Austin to get the girl. Why? What could she offer that no one else could? And in the meantime he'd killed two innocent old people and kidnapped a third. He was tough and relentless and crazy. He wanted what he wanted, and he wouldn't leave until he got it. And maybe we had more men and more artillery, but it was our town and we had more to lose. A half million potential victims. What was worse, he didn't experience fear. The threat of violence or arrest meant nothing to him.

Maybe he thought we'd hand Irina over, but he wasn't surprised when we didn't. And while I was fighting my way out of a sunken Chevy, he was planning his next move. He was way ahead of me. I had to end that.

I said, "Even if we had her, even if we gave her to you, you'd never get out of town alive. You can't go home. The feds are waiting for you." I peeked through the side window. Dark street. No one.

"I want what's MINE!"

The glass shattered over my head. I covered my eyes as the gunshot echoed and the glass tinkled to the bedroom carpet.

I tried another angle. "You don't want her now. She's ruined. You think you'll have any fun with her now?"

"I decide when it's over," he said, and then, *"A woman deserves a jab once in a while. Besides, she gets something out of it, too."*

It seemed like a logical leap between subjects, but not for him. "What? What does she get?"

His voice registered the obviousness of the answer. *"She gets sex."*

I didn't know how to answer that. All the research on rapists says they see rape as violence, punishment, which was half of what Zelig was saying.

But he also saw it as sex. That he could flip back and forth made him scarier.

His voice sounded refrigerator-cool when he said, *"How far you gonna go, boychik?"*

I slid toward the back of the house. "What do you mean?"

"To save a whore? What's she worth?"

I left the kitchen light burning, slipped the Browning into my belt and covered the receiver with my thumb so he wouldn't hear me when I reached up to open the back door and crawl outside. He didn't spot me, or at least he didn't shoot, as I crept to the edge of the house and peeked around the corner.

"I'll give you the five thousand you asked. *Ten* thousand!"

"I'm beyond money now," he said.

Static rocked the connection. *"What's she WORTH? How many man-hours? How many tax dollars? How many dead people?"*

I spotted a hulking, shadowed figure moving against the brick house across the street. I drew the Browning.

"Is she worth your old man? Your kid?" The connection clicked once and was gone. I dropped the cordless in the grass and waited to make sure I had the right guy, aiming. Then I saw his arm clear the wall, pointing to my house. I tightened my aim.

He pivoted toward me. I dove for the ground, firing *BANG BANG BANG* as I flew. Two shots went over my head, chipping my neighbor's shingles.

He went down.

I ran low across the street, zigzagging to make sure he didn't have a clean target in case he wasn't quite dead. I shouldn't have worried.

The brick house lit up. Someone opened the front door. I shouted, "Call 911! Get an ambulance!"

In the shrubbery next to the house, I found him face up. Not Zelig, not nearly. It was one of the thugs, the two big guys who tried to feed me into the wood chipper. It wasn't the one with the torn ear.

There was so much blood I couldn't find the wound at first. He was pumping it out. I took his weapon and frisked him.

"How many more?" I asked him. He wrinkled his brow, wincing from the pain. He could hear the question but didn't get it. I looked up and down the block, ran with my gun drawn, hoping to see any of them hiding beside the neighboring houses before they spotted me. Then I made it back to the gunman.

I said, "Zelig flew you down here?" Tiny nod. "How many more came with him? Two? Three?"

His head moved a fraction of an inch to one side and rolled back on its own. He didn't seem to know, or he wasn't talking. I tried one more question.

"Where did he stash my father?"

I heard him wheezing. I dropped his gun and ripped his shirt open. He had a bloody hole in his shoulder. I'd missed his heart and lungs.

"Where's my father?" I said.

He opened his mouth and choked out, "I'm . . . sorry."

I bunched his shirt over the wound and put his hand on it. "Hold it just like that."

Nothing on his person led me to Zelig, not even a phone number. A credit card and a New York State driver's license named him Craig Saffer, information I'd pass on to Agent Chu. The weapon was a long-barreled Ruger automatic with a silencer and a mounted scope, the modern spin on a target pistol. He fired at my living-room window while I was standing in plain view. If he wanted me dead, I'd be dead.

I took the Ruger, stuck the Browning in my belt, grabbed the cordless from the grass and headed into my house again, locking the back door behind me, for all the good it would do. I checked each room, every closet and the underside of each bed for intruders, then killed the lights and squinted out the windows into the night. I could see well enough by the Christmas lights shining in the windows and would make a slightly harder target that way, if someone else was out there and really wanted me dead. I was in the kitchen when the phone rang again. I let the machine pick it up. *Beep.*

"*Daneel! We got cut off or something. Anyway, I want you to check your mail.*"

The mail sat on the kitchen table where I'd dropped it earlier.

"*Are you listening? Pick it up. I left you something special.*"

I grabbed the envelopes and held them up to the window, reading by the light of a neighbor's electric snowman. Coupons. Long-distance bill. Insurance company. Credit-card offer.

Blank envelope. They'd been to the house. They'd dropped it off.

I tore the envelope open.

Zelig went on. "*You have these things around the house, you don't think about them, and one day they're twenty, thirty years old, and you say, 'Hey! That's nostalgia! That might mean something to someone.'* "

I pulled from the envelope a photograph, maybe three by four inches with a white border. From the lurid color, I figured late 1960s. The FBI told me Zelig's file had a bunch of photos like this, with Zelig over the years in nightclubs and fancy restaurants, toasting with martinis and showing off his women. Sometimes the women smiled. Sometimes, like this time, the woman's eyes were downcast, in spite of or because of Sam Z holding her hand. Miserable and trapped, the same broken look I'd seen on Irina. And Zelig was as big and strong as ever, like he was when I last saw him in '68, with just a little silver in his slicked black hair. And the woman, in the style of the time, had her dark hair trimmed short on the sides and puffed up on top, with pale lipstick and fake eyelashes and a sparkling cocktail dress. And though the picture would have been taken maybe five years after I last saw her, there was no hiding the fact that the woman Zelig was making miserable in that picture was my mother.

"*I fucked your mother,*" he said. "*Now I'm gonna fuck your town.*"

My gut seized, and before I had a chance to react, the room went black.

Since we hadn't hung the curtains in my house yet, and since all the neighboring houses had been lit up like day with Christmas regalia, it didn't take me long to figure out that the power outage didn't limit itself to the Reles home. The block was dark. And I had a safe guess that the lights going out while I was on the line with Zelig at one-thirty in the morning, wasn't a coincidence.

Thousands of Austinites wouldn't learn of the blackout until they woke late in the morning feeling unusually well-rested. But once it gets past one or two in the morning, the only ones who aren't asleep are the people who want to be—the night shift of cabdrivers and waitresses and cops—and the ones who should be. These would include drunks and junkies and whoremongers, along with the purveyors of their chosen fare, the bartenders and dealers, pimps and whores. Among them you'd also find the small deal makers, *kibitzers* like my father, and the big boys, the movers and shakers like Zelig, who think in strokes too bold to consider a single human life here or there.

Enough of these people were awake when the power died that I couldn't get an outside line for ten minutes, even after lighting matches one after another as I dug from a cardboard box in the den, the one phone that had nothing attached to it—no answering machine or cordless base—the phone that would work without an electrical outlet. Every number I dialed rang busy until I got through to a cab company. I ordered a cab, then called two more cab companies and ordered two more cabs. I called HQ and got busy signals again. Then I called Torbett's to make sure

Rachel and Josh were okay. I couldn't get through, but I kept trying until thirty minutes later when the first cab showed up. I slipped the Browning into a dry shoulder holster I never used, zipped on my baseball jacket over my wool sweater, pocketed an extra round and Saffer's Ruger and went outside. The ambulance had shown by then, and the medics were working on the gunman, watched by a cluster of neighbors who glared at me as I approached. I told the medics who I was and climbed into the cab, wondering how many people were hopping into the backs of cabs just now, as heavily armed as I was. It sped me from the dark neighborhood and the suspicious eyes of my new neighbors.

My father had told me varying versions of why we left Elmira. But each time there was something he left out. If Pop wanted to leave to save me from a life of crime, that meant that the Zelig brothers wanted me. And they already had Pop. Mob bosses rarely let one employee go, let alone two. So maybe he finessed the situation, fucked up just enough to get exiled but not so much as to get killed. Maybe. But my father wasn't known for his finesse.

By 1968, five years had passed since I last laid eyes on my mother, since she went away. I slipped the photo out of my jacket pocket. My mother in false eyelashes and pink lipstick, still beautiful but no longer in the bloom of youth, and not a trace of a smile. Maybe Zelig was the end of a five-year party, one that began the day she left my home, saying, "I'm leaving your father. I'm not leaving you." She'd left in a cab like this one. She wouldn't have taken it far. To the bus station? The airport? Across town? I flipped the picture. On the back was printed, EL MOROCCO, MARK TWAIN HOTEL. If she'd been around Elmira those five years, I would have seen her. Even if she was dodging me, even if she was hanging out in fancy nightclubs and hotels. She must have left town and come back. Maybe that photo was taken after Pop and I left.

Maybe she'd been back, briefly, while I was there. Her being back had something to do with our leaving. And she didn't swing by to say hello.

Zelig could have tracked her down and brought her back, seduced her back, dragged her back. Instead of the wife of a flunky, she'd be the wife of the boss. Or his girlfriend. Maybe she was drawn by the vision of shiny objects, gold and diamonds. And Zelig needed my father out of the way.

Or maybe Pop didn't want me to see my mother in the arms of his boss. Would he give it that much thought? Wouldn't he be more distraught over seeing that vision himself?

For whatever reason, Zelig had forced him out or let him go, and I wondered what had happened to my mother. She'd been Sam Zelig's pet for some length of time, his toy and his punching bag. I knew I'd do whatever I could to track him down, use all the resources the law would allow.

And then I'd kill him.

My taxi turned off the highway and got stuck in traffic two blocks north of HQ on the I-35 frontage road. The traffic lights in the area hung dark and useless, and there was nothing to prevent intersection collisions except politeness, a substance I knew to be in limited supply under the circumstances. I paid, hopped out of the cab and ran zigzagging between cars. I saw two fender benders, both mid-intersection, both involving drivers now on their feet and arguing fault. If they could walk, they didn't need me. TV news vans, topped with complex antennas and satellite dishes, packed the road in front of HQ. I weaved between them, and by the time some reporter spotted me and shouted my name, I broke past the crowd and dashed up the brick steps of HQ.

At the reception desk, flashlights, candles and a gas-powered lamp lit a frenzy of human activity. Injuries, complaints. Patrols running in and out. Two harried officers at the desk, a man and a woman. He left to relay messages. She fielded complaints, tried the phone, hit buttons, listened and hung up, surrendering. I pushed to the head of the line, waving my sopping-wet badge, but it didn't keep people from cursing at me.

"What's going on?"

"What's going on?!" the desk sergeant said. Her hair was tied back in a ponytail, and I could see the stress of the last hour wearing her down. "Half the city is dark. Our emergency generator is broken. We can't get any of the cars on the radio, and they can't get us. We have two phones working in the whole building, here and Dispatch. We get calls but we can't send anyone out. We try to wake up guys to come in on their off shift, but their phones are all plugged in through answering machines and they don't pick up. Two rapes phoned in in the last hour, and all we could do was send a fire department ambulance. Why don't they just send her flowers?"

"Is Torbett around?"

"Fifth Floor. Everyone important is on the Fifth Floor."

"Lieutenant Reles?"

I turned to see a press card—*Austin American-Statesman*—and a reporter, thin and bespectacled, scholarly, in clothes he'd grabbed from the floor when the phone call came.

"This isn't the time," I said.

He smiled. "It's exactly the time, *Lieutenant*." He leaned on the word, to remind me that part of the job of administration is to talk to the press. "Is this the worst blackout in the city's history?"

"That the best you can do?"

"No, I was just warming you up."

I said, "Public Information will be out with a statement." I guessed this to be true.

He said, "They've given us a statement. They said they didn't know anything."

"I just got here." I turned to go. He grabbed my arm and offered me his business card.

"Hold on to this," he said. "You might need it."

I took it and walked away. "Uh-huh."

"Seriously."

I made it to Ballistics, the office operating by candlelight, to drop off the gunman's long-barreled Ruger. Ballistics had analyzed the two bullets Zelig fired through the window at Magnolia Café, and I told them to hold on to the information. In Dispatch I muscled in on one of the two working phones and called Chu at the FBI, left a message about the big gunman with the ID naming him Saffer. I stumbled past the elevators and the last of the light from the lobby, realizing that APD headquarters was as likely a place as any to get stabbed in the dark, and found the door to the stairs. In the pitch-black stairwell, I hugged the wall and measured my steps up the four flights to Administration, then pushed into their carpeted lobby. I followed the muffled-speech noise and the dim light to the conference room and stepped inside.

Chief Cronin, his shining skull rimmed with once-blond hair now a forever-lightening gray, his jowls sagging as far as his Adam's apple, stood in his street clothes, a rumpled shirt and slacks, before a small crowd of officers, all jarred out of bed, all on edge and twitchy. The three assistant chiefs stood among the officers, along with a handful of commanders and lieutenants, including Torbett and me. The ones they couldn't get by phone they'd probably sent patrols for, or taxis. The room was too small, cramped and quiet for me to whisper to Torbett.

As far as the press was concerned, Ron Oliphant was the most prominent of the three assistant chiefs. A thickset man in his fifties, he was the highest-ranking African American in the department's history. He'd been hired, like Cronin, like the two white assistant chiefs, from out of state. Given that fact, no one in Austin had served with him, no one knew details of his career as a cop, and many suspected he was a born administrator. The other two assistant chiefs, Macaffee and Bueller, fit the same mold. But Oliphant had been hired in the face of well-publicized accusations of departmental racism. Cronin named him the department's liaison to the African American community, the NAACP and other community organizations, and he functioned as the black face of the department or, as some suggested, the black face with the creamy white middle.

A uniformed sergeant read off a sheet. "Two rapes reported in the first hour. We have a preliminary report on the first. Marsha Gorman leaving Deep Eddy Pub as the lights went out, approached by two men and raped in the parking lot. Plain view of the front entrance, if not for the blackout."

"Was she white?" Cronin asked, and I could hear a collective gasp as heads swung toward him. It was like asking whether or not the rape was important. "What?" he said. "The papers will ask."

Cronin looked to Oliphant, who nodded thoughtfully.

The sergeant hesitated but went on reading. "Baker Sector is completely dark, along with Charlie Sector all the way up to Highway 290."

Someone muttered, "Shit." Baker included the downtown area, the university and Hyde Park, my neighborhood. Charlie Sector was rough by the light of day. A blackout there meant chaos.

"North of Baker and Charlie seems to be okay. South of the river is dark down to about Ben White Boulevard. We have word of a thunderstorm over Hays County."

Cronin tried out a conclusion. "So it's their fault." No one agreed, but it was a neat idea.

The sergeant said, "It's possible," but I thought I heard a question mark at the end of that statement. "If it overloaded in Hays County, sure, it could have affected all of us." It didn't take much to figure out that the guy wasn't an electrician. They were a long way from figuring out what had caused the blackout. I didn't know what caused it, but I knew who.

Cronin said, "Anything else?"

The sergeant stalled a moment, then said, "City of Austin Utility says they're trying to locate the source of the problem but they can't yet give us a time frame."

Cronin said, "On finding it or on fixing it?"

"Either."

"What else?"

"Reports of looting in four department stores." There was a shift in the room. Traffic problems, even a rape or two by jaded standards, could be described as standard fare for a rough city night. But looting meant general frenzy. Looting meant anarchy. And we couldn't have that.

Cronin said, "What about the governor's office?"

A woman in uniform, also a sergeant, said, "The governor's out of town. So's the lieutenant governor. We can't reach either of them."

Someone said, "Who's next?"

Oliphant suggested, "The mayor?"

Cronin said, "Do you want to trust this to the *mayor*?"

The sergeant pointed out that the mayor had been contacted. He was visiting the family estate in Laredo for the holidays. He issued a statement and made it clear that he was planning on staying right where he was.

I said, "Where's DPS and the sheriff's office?"

Cronin snarled. "They're out on the street with no radios like us. Keep up, Reles!"

A patrol rushed in and handed something to the first sergeant. They exchanged whispers.

Someone I couldn't see said, "Call the National Guard?"

Cronin said, "You think I want to look like an idiot?!"

Torbett said, "Sir. You might look worse if you don't." Torbett knew how to make "sir" sound like an insult.

Cronin looked like he was going to tear Torbett's head off. The female sergeant said, "Sir, there's a message from the governor's office, but it's unofficial, and they wouldn't say whether it came from the governor or not."

"What is it?" Cronin demanded.

The sergeant measured out the words, " 'Use . . . Your . . . Discretion.' "

Cronin stopped dead. His eyes didn't move, and I could guess he stopped breathing as he took in that information, gave the matter three seconds of serious thought and said, "All right. Here it is. All nonessential personnel are to hit the streets in teams of two, using any available vehicle. Wear vests and sidearms. Batons. Stun guns if you can find them. Check with Dispatch to see which sectors are the darkest. Spread out evenly over the dark areas."

The room quieted, and I had a sense we'd all stopped breathing. We were witnessing the absolute worst decision we'd ever seen.

Cronin added, "That includes administrative personnel."

The assistant chiefs, the administrators, fat and out of shape and long off the streets if they'd ever been there, gaped at each other.

"You mean . . . us?"

"Create a presence," Cronin said. "No arrests." And he left the room.

Torbett and I followed a flashlight beacon and the crowd of administrators as they huffed down four flights and headed for the equipment dock for vests and nightsticks and stun guns. Torbett never turned to me to ask where I'd been since I last visited my hungover wife at his house.

I pulled him aside. "How's Rachel? How's Josh?"

"They're fine."

"I couldn't get through."

"They're fine!"

"We're not really gonna do this."

Torbett said, "You know what an order is, Reles?"

"Zelig took my father."

He stopped walking. "When? Where?"

"Congress Avenue. Hit him with a car and took him. Jake's having Communications put a tap on my phone—"

Torbett said, "Communications is out of action."

When I thought about it, I wasn't sure Jake was going to do anything more for me anyway. "We don't know where Zelig is or what he's driving," I said. "He had a gunman shooting up my house. I shot the guy. He's at Brackenridge. I don't think he was trying to kill me, just send a message."

Torbett scanned my face in the shadowed hall. "Reles," he said with a wave that seemed to encompass the administrators suiting up, HQ, the entire city. "Any chance your mobster did all this?"

I knew in my gut that Zelig had caused the blackout. But now there was more involved: looting, rape and probably random murder. Had he planned it this way?

"Maybe," I said. "Yeah. I'm pretty sure."

Torbett nodded. "Get a vest."

The tasers were all gone when we got to the front of the line, but we left HQ in vests, with nightsticks and hand radios that would work as soon as the main transmitter came back on. We headed out by way of the garage. It was the first time I'd seen the city so dark. I looked up to see so many stars it looked like it was snowing. Torbett's car was parked among a dozen or so unmarked vehicles. "Get in," he said.

We headed west along First Street. As we passed through the darkened downtown, lit only by the stars and the headlights, we stopped at an intersection where two teenagers merrily guided traffic. They should have been at home if they had one. My trained impulse was to say something, but what was I going to do? Stop them for upholding the law? They waved us on, and Torbett nodded at them as we passed.

"Your wife went out," he said.

"What?!"

"Around eight-thirty. Your son was asleep, and Nan was in the bedroom when she heard the front door slam. By the time she made it to the front window, your wife's car was gone."

"Is she—"

"She's okay. She's back. She went into the guest room and passed out."

I was about to apologize for her poor etiquette as a houseguest when I remembered being in my house and seeing her clothes on the bed.

Those clothes weren't there when I took off for Torbett's with Josh the night before. She would have come home from wherever she was drinking, seen my note and left for Torbett's house. She didn't have any clothes with her when she got there. That meant she'd gone back to the house tonight, after I told her not to. She'd come home, changed and gone out again. Anyone could have seen her and followed her. I realized she was lucky to be alive, but I wanted to howl at her for going home under the circumstances.

We turned up Lamar and west on Third, just outside the realm of downtown, where we reached an electrical substation, normally a graveled area about half a city block in size, surrounded by chain-link fence topped with razor wire. Inside the fence a small, one-story brick house and six electrical towers. Each of these had a base like a four-legged monster, roughly a ten-by-eight-foot rectangular frame, maybe twelve feet high, rising to a single column that pierced five porcelain cones and connected to cables heading out in two or three directions.

Now more fire trucks than I could count surrounded the yard, along with trucks from City of Austin Utility and maybe two dozen men in hard hats, white shirts and neckties. One of the towers looked somehow askew. Another was completely charred, splattered with white foam. The top half of it had snapped off and crashed to the ground.

Torbett said, "City of Austin knew where this happened the moment it happened. It just took us a while to get the news."

"Who'd you hear it from?" I asked. Two phones working at HQ, and neither was in Torbett's office. He ignored the question and found a fireman who looked like he knew what he was doing. The fireman was talking to a couple of civilians in hard hats, and one more with his back to us, wearing a charcoal gray suit a cut above anything he might have bought in Austin. The suit was tailored to fit his neat, military posture. When he spun to look at us, a confident, smug expression on his face, I realized that I was looking at the man who had saved me twenty-four hours before, from a burning warehouse he himself had set aflame: FBI Special Agent Alex Chu.

Torbett said, "Agent Chu."

"Lieutenant Torbett." They shook hands.

"You guys know each other?" I asked, making sure everyone realized just how clueless I was.

Chu said, "Lieutenant Torbett used to sit on the APD-FBI Task Force."

"I never got to do that," I said.

Chu said, "Why do you figure, Bugsy?"

Cops have lots of thoughts about the FBI, but you'll never see a cop refuse to work on an FBI task force. It's like a taste of Hollywood to us.

Torbett pointed to the fractured tower. "Any idea of the cause?"

The older of the civilians, a hefty guy of sixty or so, with plastic-frame glasses and a permanent pout, said, "Someone clipped the fence." He pointed to a gap in the fence. "He tossed a chain up to the transformer so it wrapped two of the cables. Must have taken a few tries. Then he did it again."

He pointed to the first tower I saw, the one that looked askew. There was a length of heavy chain wrapping two of the cables, one above the other, that led away from the transformer.

"That's it?" I asked. "That's all it takes?"

He went on. "Enough to make it short out. The transformer is like a circuit breaker. It kicks itself off automatically to protect itself from damage."

Chu asked, "Any chance they were just screwing around with the transformer and got lucky?"

"No. They knew what they were doing."

"So what happened?" Torbett asked.

"If one goes out, it's no big deal. The other transformers pick up the load. The grid compensates. If two go out, it creates too much of a load on the system. Someone at Central sees that, they shut down the area."

Torbett asked, "Is that what happened?"

"Would have," the younger of the two hard hats said. "But sometimes the transformer doesn't take itself out when it should. So instead of just flipping a circuit breaker, you've got a short, from a tower pumping twenty-seven thousand volts. Explosion, fire. That's what happened here. Probably they tossed up one chain, realized the system was compensating. They tossed another and got what they were looking for."

I asked, "How long to get the lights on again?"

"Twelve hours if we're lucky. Maybe twenty-four. And we'll have to turn them on slow."

Chu asked me, "Do we know who did this?"

Torbett shot me a questioning look.

Chu separated us from the crowd and said, "Gentlemen, we should talk."

◆ ◆ ◆

Chu sat in the driver's seat of his black Chrysler. I sat next to him, Torbett in back.

"I've read up on Zelig," Chu said. "The Elmira office faxed me the highlights. Any idea how he's involved with this?"

Torbett said, "Would Zelig know how to sabotage a power station?"

"No," I said, "but he'd find someone who would." I remembered what Zelig had told me at Magnolia about how he could hire someone to do whatever he needed. "He prides himself on it." I told Chu about the deaths of Ida and her husband, the gunman I shot and Pop's kidnapping.

"Why the blackout?"

"To show us who's in charge?" I suggested. "Bring the town to its knees."

Torbett asked, "What does the file say?"

"For one thing," Chu said, "he's bankrupt. He has four credit cards under his own name, and three are maxed out. He has nothing in the bank."

I said, "Bullshit, he's loaded. Take a closer look at the file. He has new enterprises going. Computers. Internet gambling and mobile phones. He could have all his cash in a safe."

Chu said, "You're convinced of this?"

"I've seen guys who went broke. They get desperate and they think small." I waved at the fire engines. "Is this guy thinking small?"

Chu registered a satisfied smile. He'd been testing me. He said, "The file says what you think it says and more."

I said, "Zelig brought at least three people here with him. The gunman is at Brackenridge. He's one of the gorillas from the warehouse last night. The one with two good ears. The only ID on him called him Craig Saffer."

Chu said, "Stuart Lambrecht," with an assurance that was already starting to grate.

Torbett said, "How did you know that?"

Chu waved the question off, as if he didn't have time to explain details to kids like us. "We've been to the hospital. Who else?"

I said, "The other two guys from last night. Another big one, with a ripped ear, and a smaller one."

Chu said, "Could you identify these men in a lineup?"

"Maybe," I said. I knew I could tell him what the open end of a wood chipper looked like. Chu handed me ten mug shots. I pulled two. He nodded and put them aside. "Also," I said, gesturing to the transformers, "whoever helped him with this. An electrician? An electrical engineer? Maybe it was one of those two guys."

Chu asked, "All this over your father?"

I explained how Irina was still in hiding somewhere. My father was never the prize Zelig was after, only the obstruction.

"Ah, yes," he said. He spoke like a professor quoting Bogart. "Dames. They'll get you every time."

"My father's been kidnapped," I said. "We can't put a tap on my phone because our headquarters are dark. I think maybe Zelig has a mobile phone, but we can't check that out either." I took a breath. With most people in law enforcement, the last thing that gets you help is straight-out truth. Something made me try. "My father is seventy. He's injured and needs medical attention. Do you think you can help me?"

He put the Chrysler in gear. "All you had to do was ask."

Torbett got into his car and followed us up MoPac. In the Chrysler, Chu picked up the car phone and hit two buttons. "It's Chu. Send a team over to—" He turned to me. "What's your address?" I said it into the phone. Chu said, "We have a kidnapping. Maybe a mobile phone. See what you can find." He hung up.

I said, "They'll need my key."

"Don't worry about it. The phone lines run on separate power. Not affected by the blackout. My people can run their equipment on juice from the truck and forward your calls to our office. You know that kidnapping is a federal offense, right? And that makes it the province of the FBI."

I said, "I knew but I forgot."

City cops have a suspicion of feds that sometimes borders on hostility or, in my case, jealousy. Feds tend to come from better schools, tend (at least by myth) to be raised from purebred stock in places like Connecticut and Ohio and Utah. They talk better and they dress better. Their shirts don't wrinkle. Even Chu, not an Anglo, had the sound and smell of New England about him. Naturally, city cops like to point out what they have that feds don't have, which generally comes down to street smarts. We acquire this while working patrol, so the trauma-laden first years a cop spends on the street are referred to as his "street degree." Say a young cop wants to work administration and he manages to dodge patrol. He may work his way up, may gain rank fast. But cops will never consider him a real cop.

Feds don't have such a thing as patrol. The most streetwise of feds—unless he's an ex-cop—probably knows less about the streets than someone who spent one year on patrol. Cops look at feds the way war veterans look at politicians.

So city cops don't ask feds for help if they can avoid it. This is so ingrained that I didn't even think to call them when Zelig drove off with Pop. I was a fool to stall, especially when minutes might mean my father's life.

We pulled off MoPac at Research Boulevard, part of the newer northwest end of town, with its modern houses, beehive apartment complexes and "office parks." All the lights in the area shone, untouched by the blackout that was causing havoc a few miles south. We turned up a service road, past a forest of overgrown shrubbery, into a parking lot, relatively thin with cars. Chu parked near a security booth with a guard inside. Torbett pulled up beside us. On the lower half of the guard booth someone had stenciled the words, PLEASE DO NOT DISTURB THE GUARD.

The building stood four stories, a monolithic block with sealed dark windows rising up in pairs. We headed in through revolving doors and showed our badges. Chu waved at security and led us through to the elevator. I recognized the elevator, faintly, from the moments after the warehouse fire.

The FBI Ten Most Wanted list hung on the back wall of the elevator. As we rode up, I looked over the unfamiliar faces and said, "I don't know them."

Chu said, "They're not famous. The list was created to publicize lesser-known criminals to make them recognizable to the public. Hoover's idea."

"Smart man," Torbett commented.

Chu said, "He wasn't just a pretty face in a dress."

The doors opened. On the floor tiles, the crest of the Justice Department. Beyond that, a carpeted waiting area I didn't remember at all. On one wall a color photo of the U.S. Capitol at night. On another a two-foot-high replica of an FBI agent's gold shield.

Chu swiped a card on a panel near the inner door. Something showed up on the screen that I couldn't quite see from my angle. He punched some sequence, and the door unlocked. Inside, a man with long hair and a sweatsuit answered the phones.

"Yes, ma'am, it's possible your neighbor is a spy. But not based on what you just told me." He waved at us. If he'd been there the night before, I hadn't seen him.

Surrounding the man on the phone, a few computers, stacks of loose-leaf notebooks and a bank of security monitors showing the building's halls and entrances. Chu explained the setup as he led us through. "This office does the same things as any other Bureau office. The only difference is size. In a smaller office, one or two people will do everything. Gang violence, drugs, terrorism, counterintelligence, bank fraud. Kidnapping."

We went through another door, leading to a wide floor of cubicles and three glass-walled offices, abandoned but for a man wrestling with a printer. And a small hallway leading to another door, labeled COMMAND POST.

"What we need to do," Chu said as he strode through the door, "is track all possible leads. Where is he staying? Does he have contacts here? Who else did he bring with him? If it's not in-house talent, where did it come from? Disgruntled city electricians? Someone knew how to take out those transformers. Who's feeding him his intelligence? Dirty cops?" I thought fleetingly of Lowry. Chu may have been thinking of me.

The command post held workstations for about fifteen, but the four people moving around seemed to keep it busy enough. The left wall, mostly paired windows, was hung with white vertical blinds, four-inch-wide strips that hung down like streamers, with every third or fifth strip missing. Over one window a hand-shellacked wood panel bore five clocks, their time zones indicated by an obscure code, its key written in grease pencil on a mounted placard. SU was Salt Lake City. I knew there was something wrong with the clocks, because if it was 3:30 in Austin, it couldn't be 4:05 in New York.

In the back of the room, a glass booth. Overhead fluorescents lay dormant, but white spotlights on a steel track illuminated our movements. At the front of the room hung three rear-projection screens, each about six feet square. One showed maps of Austin, shifting every few seconds from one area to another. One screen showed CNN, no sound, and the third stood dark.

Two semicircular banks of wood-grain Formica faced the screens, each allowing for about five workstations. Each workstation consisted of the earliest generation of push-button phone, along with an office phone with access to a dozen lines; also a computer keyboard and monitor, a microphone on a twisting neck and a tiny television.

At the front of the room, the third screen lit up looking like a computer monitor, with the words STATUS BOARD, and then,

<u>Subjects.</u>
<u>Zelig, Sam</u> Whereabouts Unknown.
<u>Lambrecht, Stuart</u> Brackenridge Medical Center.

Chu handed someone the two mug shots I had picked as my other abductors. I saw he was palming a remote control. He announced, "Ladies and gentlemen, these are Lieutenants James Torbett and Daniel Reles of APD. Please make them feel welcome. Lieutenant Reles's father is being held captive, we think, by Sam Zelig. He is not above suspicion in the death of Paul Berelman."

That threw me. "You know he didn't do that."

Chu corrected me. "We *think* he didn't do it. Just like we think you're not accessory." On consideration, even I wasn't sure of that. Chu brought in the room with a wave. "The equipment isn't state of the art. But these people are the best."

In about five seconds, we were looking at a projected map of Austin with a blue light where my new house would be, and another where Ida and her husband had bought the big one, just after Ida called the police to deliver a monologue about my father's intrusion. A final light marked the Congress Avenue Bridge, where Zelig had slammed Pop and taken him captive. Chu hit some buttons on the remote and lit up a slide on the smoked glass, a recent newspaper photo of Zelig. The four agents in the room slowed down to watch his presentation.

"People, we're looking at Sam Zelig, born Shmuel Zeligman, 1923, Bronx, New York. Younger brother of Isaac Zelig, seventy-three,"—mug shot of Ike, which on first glance looked like the head of an octopus—"now serving ten to twenty, Elmira Correctional Facility. Both brothers have arrests dating back to 1940. Both have multiple convictions, imprisonments lasting as long as five years, in Sam's case, for extortion." He clicked through ten pages of rap sheets. "More recently Sam has been charged in a series of assaults, each more vicious than the last. Not surprisingly, the victims in all of these cases refused to testify."

Chu went on. "According to the Elmira office, Sam has an active staff of twenty to forty or more. An exact figure has been difficult to gauge. You've been given files of all known associates." I didn't see any files but noticed mug shots flashing on everyone's computer screens. Modern technology. "These include captains, collectors, drug runners, a very small bevy of prostitutes, a driver, bodyguards and a host of freelance consultants. How many he brought with him is anybody's guess. Lieutenant Reles has seen three. Reles, anything to add?"

I said, "Why didn't he just stay home and let someone else do the dirty work?"

"You tell us."

I followed the voice to one of the agents, who looked like he'd just washed down a raw steak with steroids. He was five-ten or so, reddish brown hair in a grown-in crew cut with a small bald spot. He was so muscled up that he couldn't drop his arms down to his sides. They hung out at an angle, as if he had a loaf of bread in each armpit. His red-striped necktie was loose, and I guessed that buttoning the collar over his thick neck was an impossibility. I would have guessed Scottish ancestry from his coloring, but the quantity of superfluous hair suggested a grandparent with a tail. Chu introduced him as Reardon.

"How would I know?" I asked.

"He's your pal. He took a personal interest in this situation. Maybe you know why."

Reardon tried to stare me down and lost. He turned to Chu. "Zelig's vehicle was a new 1995 Lincoln Town Car," he said, "found at Nueces off Fifth Street by APD. The car was rented at six-thirty P.M. at Alamo Rental at San Antonio Airport, by someone using the name Gary Petkanas. We've talked to Alamo, and the customer matched Zelig's description."

I said, "So we know he flew into San Antonio."

Reardon said, "A contribution from Lefty Rabinowitz."

Torbett coughed suddenly and when I glanced at him, he was giving me a warning look: don't take the bait. Reardon went on.

"Yes, we think he flew Elmira to Cleveland to San Antonio. We'll talk to the airlines and see who else booked that route. Maybe we can trace their credit cards and see where they've gone since. Also, we don't have any reports of cars stolen in the area after he abandoned the Lincoln."

Chu said, "Probably somebody was waiting for him with a new car. He knew anything he drove would be seen at the bridge."

Torbett chimed in. "APD found a cellular phone in the Lincoln."

Reardon said, "Possible he's got a sack of them. We fed the EIN to the Elmira office."

"EIN?"

Chu said, "It's a number unique to the phone, like a serial number."

A woman hung up a phone. A heavy flood of dark blond hair fell to her shoulders. Hazel eyes, small nose, smooth skin. She was pale and slim, the result, I guessed, of working nights for the Bureau. She had the most unremarkable features I'd ever seen.

She said, "I have a last-minute booking from Elmira to Detroit to Atlanta to Austin. Came in last night at ten. One Carol Hornby."

Torbett asked, "What does she do?"

"He."

Chu said, "Okay, what does he do besides wish he had a better name?"

Tap-tap on the computer keys. Wait, pick up the phone, dial, wait. "Hello, I'm sorry to wake you. This is the Federal Bureau of Investigation. No, please don't be alarmed. May I speak with Carol Hornby? Ah, Mr. Hornby. Sir, do you carry a Chase Visa card? No? Is your Social Security number . . ." She read him the number. "Yes? Okay, thank you." She hung up. "Identity theft," she told us. "They're using real Socials and getting credit cards in real people's names."

Chu said, "Keep track of the names. See if we get a double hit. Reles, this is Cathy Bennett," he said. "She was training to work the Russians when the Iron Curtain fell."

"Can't have everything," she said.

I didn't detect an accent of any kind on her. If Chu's speech gave away a New England education, if not a New England rearing, Bennett sounded like a language tape. I asked where she was from.

"My parents were in the foreign service," she said.

"Double agents," Chu said. If he was joking, she didn't acknowledge it.

She said, "I went to American schools."

Chu added, "But she's the best cryptographer we have, and she speaks Russian like a native."

She eyed me and said something in Russian. I was no linguist, but she'd gotten the rhythms of post–Cold War Russia to a tee.

I said, "I don't understand."

Reardon grumbled, "Try Yiddish."

Chu said, "She wants to know if you're Russian."

"Oh. Um, Galicia," I said, giving it the Eastern European pronunciation. "Poland, I guess, or maybe the Ukraine. My father never got more specific than that."

She smiled at my face a little longer before she swiveled back to her screen. Reardon seemed to notice the exchange. I realized that the other agents were making phone calls like her own. "What are they doing?"

Chu said, "Calling everyone who flew out of Elmira in the last twenty-four hours. If we can find them in Austin, we have someone to question. If they're in Elmira, we have another credit-card fraud to trace. Your friend Hayden has been running around Elmira trying to track Zelig's credit-card source. He came up with a suspect in the city jail, pending sentencing, who said he gave Zelig six cards for two thousand dollars a week ago, but he can't remember all the names. He remembers John Ayala and Randall Appelfeld. So we're waiting for a click on those." He pointed out another agent making calls. "He's just calling car-rental places."

Another phone rang. An Indian woman grabbed it. She was tall and dark, with a stiff British accent.

"Yes. Right. All right then, send it." She held the phone to her chest. "They're at his house." She saw me. "Your house. The phone's ringing now. D'you want to hear it?"

"Quiet, everyone. Play it," Chu said, and though I wouldn't have told her to, she flipped a switch, and everyone grabbed a phone. They handed me a receiver. Zelig talked to my answering machine.

"Daneel! Yingel, it's Uncle Sam. I can't believe you're not home."

Faces shifted toward me to watch my reaction. I tried to keep cool. It wasn't until Chu shoved me that I realized I had a two-way feed.

I said, "I'm home."

"He-hey! I hope you liked the picture."

Chu mouthed, "What picture?" I shook my head, not important.

Zelig said, *"Hell of a broad, your mother. What we used to call a good-time gal. Wasn't just me. Ike used to take her around, too."*

Sweat trickled down my neck. I looked to Torbett. If he was thinking anything useful, he didn't pass it my way.

Zelig spoke away from the phone. *"You wanna say something to Dan?"* Then, *"Your father wants to talk to you. Go ahead."*

Then Pop's voice, babbling, *"Get the . . . geggeh. Don't . . . don't, please."*

"Where are you?" I said.

"I can't . . . Hurts so . . . please. Beh beh beh . . . vvv . . ."

Something in my chest tried to batter its way out through my rib cage. Zelig had been working my father over, maybe since the bridge. I stood stock-still, breathing in short blasts.

Zelig said, *"Benny. You're not making any sense."* Then, into the phone, *"He don't look so good. He's all white and clammy. Shaking like a virgin. Like your mother. Ha! No, not like your mother at all. Who are we kidding? You should feel his heart. It's like an outboard motor. And blood from his nose, from his mouth . . ."*

Pop yelped.

"What do you *want*?" I pleaded. Torbett put a hand on my arm.

Zelig chuckled, then said, *"What do you think I want?"*

"I don't know where she is!" I knew that was wrong as soon as I said it.

Soft-spoken again, but with more than a little menace, Zelig said, *"Benny. You don't trust your son? That's wrong. I hate when people don't trust people."*

Now I'd told Zelig that I didn't know where the girl was, which, if he thought about it, meant either that I was lying or that only Pop knew where the real Irina was. And Pop wasn't talking. So his only option was to torture Pop, even if Zelig was the kind of guy to be squeamish about that sort of thing, which he wasn't.

"Wait, wait!" I said. "We can work something out. You can have any girl."

"I want that one!"

"But, but . . ."

He growled, low and breathy. *"You don't understand me and women. I'm not a slam-bam guy. I like to have a little time with a woman. Spend a while warming her up, loosening her, a little romance. Then I move in real slow for the kill."* Suddenly he shouted, *"YOU DON'T INTERRUPT!"*

"Sam, listen—"

"You know I once ripped a guy's throat out with one hand? One hand!" He roared in frenzy now. *"Reached in with my fingers and pulled his wires out. Stall me, Reles. I dare you."*

I sputtered, "That's . . . that's not what I'm doing!"

He hung up.

I stared at the computer screen in front of me, a panel of little icons like a phone keyboard. When I looked up, every agent in the room was gaping at me as if I'd just been sentenced to the gallows.

Torbett said, "Anything?"

Cathy Bennett shook her head as she dialed a phone. "This is the FBI. We have a mobile-phone EIN. Can you tell me who owns it?" There was a pause, and she gave them a number with ten digits or so. "Okay. Thank you." She hung up. Then she called another number and made the same request. She hung up. "Phone purchased in Elmira under the name William Thorbecke. We'll try him but I can bet that's a dead end and Zelig never uses that phone again. And he turned the phone off. We can't triangulate until he turns it back on."

Reardon said, "He *knows* how hard it is to trace a cellular phone, how many channels we have to go through. He's fucking with us by talking so long on the phone! He thinks he's dealing with the local police."

I could feel a shift in the room. These people had dealt with dangerous men before, mob bosses and child killers. And they knew that Zelig was bad news. But they hadn't heard his voice before, not until now. He was big and powerful, and they could hear it in his lungs. He was the one who would have ground them beneath his shoes in grade school, if they hadn't gone to private schools. He had resources, endless resources. And he'd do anything to get what he wanted. He didn't care about the consequences.

"What does that mean?" I asked the room in general. "The thing about my father, his heart is pounding. Blood from his nose and mouth."

Someone said, "Internal bleeding."

I followed the voice to Reardon. "Are you a doctor?" I asked.

"I'm a nurse."

Chu said, "Don't you remember? He's the one who patched you up last night?"

I knew sometimes the FBI hired people with science backgrounds—chemists, nurses, pharmacists—the same way they sometimes hired people with a second language. The nursing background didn't fit with Reardon's oozing hostility. Or maybe it fit just right.

"Internal bleeding?" I asked.

"From his stomach. That would explain the shaking, the elevated heart rate and the blood from his nose and mouth."

Chu said, "Zelig might have said something if it was a *lot* of blood. Maybe it's just a little."

I said, "Then what?"

Reardon said, "It could mean his organs weren't too badly damaged. That he might have some time."

Torbett said, "What do you think? What'll your father do?"

"What do you mean?"

Chu said, "Will he give up the girl?"

Pop. Thirty years earlier Zelig could have trusted him to drive the girl to a new pimp. Now Pop had more invested. Maybe he loved the girl. But mostly he was trying to do something right before he died. And he probably knew that might be soon.

I said, "I don't know."

Torbett: "Where could they be?"

Chu: "He'd want to stay close to town so you can drop the girl. He could have gone to a hotel, but how many hotels would let in one guy carrying another guy?"

I said I knew of a few. I mentioned their names to the people making calls. Beyond that, we could search the sleazier motels, brothels and any run-down house whose tenant could have been approached by Zelig waving a fifty and saying, "My friend is hurt. We're on the run from bad guys. Can we stay here awhile?"

Someone hung up a phone and said, "APD's generator is up."

I marveled that they knew our business so fast. Torbett got on a phone.

Chu asked, "Any chance Zelig had friends in the Austin underground?"

I said, "He's never been here before."

"Does he know anyone here who could have connected him? Helped him find local resources."

Chu, not a dope, could have read my mind by the sudden glow in my eyes and the slackness in my jaw. Of course Zelig knew someone.

"Your father," Chu said.

"Maybe," I said. "But Pop hasn't been here in years. Hardly anyone he knew turned up."

"Ida Menard did."

I couldn't argue that. I said, "I wouldn't put it past Zelig to buy some friends of his own in an hour or two." I could tell by his expression that this didn't convince Chu of Pop's innocence in his own misfortune.

Reardon turned to Chu. "How long are you gonna listen to this?"

I said, "To what?"

Chu said, "He thinks you're with Zelig."

Reardon said, "No I don't. I think we're helping one gangster against another. Rabinowitz shouldn't even be here."

Chu, Bennett and the Indian woman were all watching me, along with

Reardon. They hadn't dismissed the idea that I was cut from the same cloth as Zelig, which, in a sense, I was.

I asked Reardon if he was nursing in a hospital when he got hooked on steroids.

Torbett hung up the phone. "Generator's up, but we're an hour behind. Now *three* rapes reported. And someone died in custody."

"What does that mean?" I asked.

Torbett snapped, "I don't know what it means. That's all I heard."

Chu said, "Just what Zelig wanted."

I said, "How many patrols you think we can get?"

"Now?" Torbett asked. "None. Some of them have two or three separate arrests in their cars. It'll take over an hour to process those. Others are running around trying to create a presence. Lights are restored, but only in sections, spotty throughout the city. Charlie Sector is still dark."

Charlie Sector, East Austin, without light, would be the first place to slip into total anarchy. If Zelig knew how to find the place, he'd have felt right at home.

I waved at the glass map on the wall, one of three projection screens, shifting between various maps of Austin. "Can you fix that on a general map of Central Austin?"

Chu nodded. Reardon tapped some buttons, flicked through some screens and gave me the map I was looking for. The river cut off about the southernmost third of the image.

I said, "He's getting around with no trouble, finding everything he needs. He's got a map, or maybe one of his guys knows Austin, but not one of his regular guys. Maybe he made a connection when he got here."

"So?"

"We know he didn't bring his guns on the airplane. Where do you buy those in Austin, late at night?" Our eyes shifted to Charlie Sector, now in total darkness thanks to the blackout.

Torbett called Dispatch and got them to promise they'd send two patrols to cruise Charlie Sector as soon as they could, looking for a good place to buy a gun or hide a hostage. Then I called Mora, who by then would have had two hours' sleep—she answered on the second ring—and asked her to do the same. But it was a big sector and there had to be a better next move than just sifting through it in the dark.

Torbett said, "What do we have? In terms of personnel."

Chu said, "What you're looking at. Plus whatever men you have on the street."

I added, "And Zelig has three men that we know of."

But that wasn't right. He had two men that we knew of. The third, the one I shot after he shot up my house, was in intensive care at Brackenridge Hospital. We knew where to go next.

We made it back out into the cold night air. Chu and I headed toward downtown with Torbett following. As we rolled along MoPac, Chu started talking, driving with his left hand and fiddling with a red sponge ball with his right.

"Taylor Hayden, my colleague in Elmira, he's been on this case for a while. Granted, they're only a two-man office, so he's been on *every* case for a while. But he's familiar with the Zelig files. A few hours ago, I asked him to tell me something that would give me a sense of who we're dealing with. And believe it or not, that's what he himself was trying to find out just a few months back."

The sponge ball spun between his fingers, which didn't seem impressive after what I'd seen him do with the bronze coin.

He went on. "Naturally, in organized crime you have a lot of tough guys who don't mind knocking people around. And some guys who enjoy it. But word on Sam's penchant for extreme violence was so widespread that Hayden decided to touch base with a professional on the subject. He took his question to an Elmira dominatrix."

At this point Chu squeezed the ball in his fist. When he opened the fist, the ball had somehow changed from red to black.

"Now, you wouldn't think a dinky little town like Elmira could support a professional dominatrix, let alone two, which it turns out is how many are working there. You're talking about a town smaller than the one you left in '68. A ghost town. Empty houses, barren stores and factories. The whole region is now part of what's called the Rust Belt. Elmira is the buckle of the Rust Belt. No jobs, no money. The only new industry is methamphetamine. But there are a few people who can afford her services, the pro-dom. Same as it is with drugs. People who can't afford it will buy it anyway. The woman, her name is Mistress Circe"—he pronounced it "SIR-see"—"she says it isn't illegal to torment someone, and that's what they come to her for, that's what they pay her for. Pain and humiliation. Hayden said, 'Ma'am, look at this town. Can't they get those things for free?'"

He rolled the black sponge ball between his fingers.

"Anyway, Zelig started mixing with these people. But he always got out of hand. Took girls further than they wanted to go."

He squeezed the black sponge ball in his fist again and drove with both hands for a while.

"Word got out, even to Buffalo and other places with bigger S&M crowds. Zelig had no *boundaries.* No one would play with him, no matter how much he paid. He had no qualms about drawing blood, or even doing permanent damage. He didn't care about consent. The S&M community was too restrictive for him. He didn't belong with them."

"Where did he belong?"

Chu said, "Prison? Anyway, that was years ago. He must have been insulted. So instead of taking consenting women further than they want to go, he takes women who have no idea what they're getting into. Also, he's believed to be worse now. Each episode has to give him a greater high. That's not the point. The point is that you and I think logically and reasonably, like someone with a developed superego, someone who can keep his anger and desire in check. Zelig doesn't have that. He had enough self-discipline to stay out of jail, but maybe only for a while. His superego was his big brother, Ike. Now Ike's in prison, and Sam's had two years with no restraint."

We turned off MoPac and headed east toward downtown. I could still see dark skyscrapers against the night sky.

"When we're raised, sent to school, socialized," Chu said, "that's when we learn the rules of the game. Zelig doesn't follow them. He doesn't know how to behave, so we don't know what to expect. We don't know what the variables are. Which hand is the ball in?"

He turned up his right fist. His hands had never gone near each other. I checked his steering wheel to see if he'd hidden the ball. "The right," I said.

"You sure?"

"Yes."

"How sure?"

"Open your right hand."

He opened his right hand, palm up. And sitting on his palm was a big black sponge cube.

Stuart Lambrecht, the bargain-size gunman I'd punctured at my house after he shot out my front windows, lay on his bed in intensive care and the duty nurse told us he couldn't be disturbed, so we went in.

The hospital had its own generator and was the brightest spot in the neighborhood. There was no guard on Lambrecht. His greasy hair lay matted to his elephantine skull. His EKG beeped heartily and blood drained from his shoulder tube. He would surely live long enough to go to jail, unless Zelig bought his freedom or killed him to keep him from testifying.

Torbett walked in after us and he spoke loudly. "This the guy you shot?"

I boomed, "Yeah. He put a few holes in my house, woke the neighbors."

Lambrecht blinked and opened his eyes. He saw the three men standing around his bed and got a sense of where he was and how he'd gotten there.

Chu said, "You're lucky to be alive, Stu."

I said, "I shot you. That was me."

"Water," he choked out. I stalled, scanning the room for a waitress. Chu got a Styrofoam cup from the night table, and Lambrecht sucked water through the straw. Then he blinked and seemed to come to life. "Lawyer."

Chu said, "You're a lawyer?"

"I . . . I want a lawyer."

I asked, "Who was on the plane with you?"

"No one," he said.

"So you didn't travel with Zelig?"

No answer. Then, "I refuse to talk on the grounds"—His throat kept giving out in midsentence, forcing him to reach for the water—"that it may tend to incriminate me."

Chu said, "Do you know the other two men who were with you?"

"No."

"So you admit there were two other men?"

"I refuse to testify on the grounds . . ."

"Never mind," Chu said, and fished out the mug shots of the two men I thought had been with Lambrecht when they held me over the wood chipper. "Do you know this man?" No answer, but his eyes gave him away. "How about this one?" Same. Finally Chu showed a picture of my father. "Do you know *this* man?" Lambrecht's facial features drew closer to each other. "Tell me something," Chu said. "How long have you been working with these guys?"

"I refuse to . . ." His throat hurt him. He reached for the water, and I pulled it away.

"You mind if I look through your stuff?" I opened the night table's drawer. He shook his head violently. "Just say the word if it's a problem. I'll take silence as permission."

I found his plane ticket among the items they'd removed from his clothes, some things I hadn't found in my cursory frisk at the house. The ticket was purchased for cash and had him flying into Austin about two hours before he and his buddies dragged me off to the warehouse. With the ticket he had a credit card under the name Craig Saffer and about four hundred in cash.

Chu said to us, "That would give them time to make contacts and buy a gun before the Magnolia incident, even if they didn't know anybody in town. We could trace the gun."

Torbett said, "Working on it."

I handed Lambrecht the water and showed him the picture of my father again. "Have you ever seen this man?" He shook his head. He was lying.

Chu asked if he'd ever met an old couple named Ida Menard Thomason and Wallace Thomason.

"No," he croaked. "Why?"

"Just trying to figure out how many murders you're responsible for."

Ida was killed by hand and Wallace by screwdriver, both of which suggested Zelig's personal touch. Lambrecht may have been there.

Chu put a guard on the room, straining his already-skeletal nighttime staff. We'd need Lambrecht, and we'd need him alive, if Zelig's case got to trial.

I'd already decided it wouldn't.

The duty nurse scowled at us as we left the room, but she'd concluded earlier that our authority was greater than hers, and all without our flashing a badge. People are funny about authority. I took her aside.

"What does it mean if someone was hit by a car and he's bleeding from his nose and mouth? He's shaking and has an elevated heartbeat."

"Who?" she said. "Where?"

"Just supposing."

She said, "Internal bleeding, stomach. He needs surgery."

"How fast?"

She said, "Now."

Chu, Torbett and I stepped out of the hospital and stood under an awning. The air felt a special kind of lonely cold.

Torbett said, "Mora radioed. Nothing. She's still looking, knocking on doors, and now there are two patrols out doing the same." It sounded desperate, and it was.

Chu said, "Zelig wants the girl. Maybe she witnessed something, like Berelman's murder, and he needs her out of the way. Maybe it's some freaky S&M thing. Maybe he's just obsessed."

Torbett said, "If we at least had her, she could talk to him on the phone. We could use her as bait."

Chu stared at me. "What is it?"

I said, "I'm thinking."

Pop had looked up all his old friends, Donny and Bobby and whoever. He said everyone was gone, dead or in prison or out of town, except Ida.

Pop got drunk and told his life story to Zelig. He must have given Ida's last name and whatever else he knew, and Zelig remembered to go to her when he was looking for Pop. We already knew Zelig's operation to be effective at finding people even if they hid, and Ida wasn't hiding.

And when Pop found out that Ida was dead, that Zelig had hit Ida's house, he needed to go there right away. Guilt? Maybe. But once he got there, he looked out the window. Why?

We headed to Ida's.

We parked down the sleeping block from Ida's house. I walked alone toward the house, scoping for movement. Then I got an idea. I signaled Torbett and told him to give me ten seconds. I ran around the back of the house, where I could see the left side, though only by moonlight. Chu hid near the right side.

Torbett pounded on the front door. "Open up. Police!"

A window opened in the back of the house. Irina climbed out head-first—white-blond hair, yellow raincoat and all—and landed on her hands, rolling onto the grass. She got to her feet, slid the window shut and ran for the bushes. I headed her off, running across the darkened yard. She poured on speed, but I grabbed her around the waist. She kicked at me as we fell, spitting words in Russian that must have been curses.

"Irina, it's me!"

Chu appeared and pulled her far enough from me that her kicks couldn't reach my legs. She kicked at the air and shouted until she broke down into a sob.

In the threadbare, bloody interior of Ida's home, Torbett, Chu and I talked to Irina by candlelight.

"You send police for us!"

"What are you talking about?"

"The hotel. Police come. Shine lights. Go."

"Irina, I didn't tell anyone where you were. Not a soul."

"Fuck you!" She talked tough, but the long night had taken its toll. I was the only one who knew that Pop and Irina were at the hotel. If the patrols ran their lights over the place, they were probably making normal rounds. I kept on, figuring eventually she'd have to know I was on her side. Life hadn't made her a trusting soul.

"Irina, please. If I wanted to arrest you, someone would have come in and arrested you." A long look at her told me that wasn't it. I said, "We won't give you up to Zelig. Is that what you're worrying about? We won't."

"What you care about me?"

"That's not the point. We don't do that."

I reached to put a hand on her shoulder. She pulled away. Call it a conditioned reflex. I kept my hand where it was, about three inches from her shoulder. I needed her to know that I wasn't Zelig, even if something inside her told her that every man in the world *was* Zelig. When she saw that I wasn't coming after her, she relaxed a little. I laid the hand on her shoulder. She wiped her nose with the back of her hand, looked at me with apprehension, and nodded. I let her go.

We found her a glass of vodka and some cigarettes. Suddenly it was like she was safely home in Siberia.

"Your father bring me here. Talk to his girlfriend, Ida. Her husband. Is no place in house to hide. The *makher* come, she send me out the window. She will signal when is clear, only no signal. I come back, see them." Her eyes started tearing. "Police come, I hide in bushes again, come back when police leave."

I said, "I was here with Pop. Did he see you? Signal you to keep quiet?"

She lowered her head, not quite nodding.

I asked if she had any guess where Zelig might have stashed Pop.

"No."

"Did Zelig know anyone in Austin besides Pop?"

She didn't think so. Then she volunteered something. "I will not testify."

"Yeah, I know," I said.

"I don't know anything about his business. Only his dick."

"Well," I said, "if you can think of something, it really might help. Zelig hit my father with his car while Pop was trying to save me. Pop needs a hospital, but Zelig's keeping him tied up in some closet somewhere."

I looked around Ida's living room, grasping for just the right words.

"Listen. Pop was the only one who knew where you were, and Zelig is trying to get that information out of him right now. Pop's bleeding internally, and Zelig is working him over, and if I know my father, he still hasn't given you up. If he does, you won't be here waiting for him. You'll be safe with us. So the way I see it, you and I both owe my father *one big fuckin' favor,* and if we don't pay him back now, we might not get another chance."

I heard a little chirping sound, and Chu pulled a phone from his jacket pocket. "Yeah." Listening. "Okay." He hung up. "Zelig's phone is still off. But the fire captain found something for us."

was not making friends among my new neighbors.

Sometime after the shoot-out on my block, an ambulance had come around for Lambrecht. Between the shooting (my gun had no silencer) and the flashing lights and siren, most of my new neighbors had been roused from sleep, to discover the power outage. They could reasonably blame the general disruption on the neighborhood's sudden influx of Jews.

After the noise settled, my neighbor across the street, the one I'd introduced myself to by shooting a guy next to his house, wandered around the yard and found something near where the gunman had been standing. It was a small, silver-colored, plastic cylinder, maybe a liter's worth, like a small fire extinguisher. It had a black cap on top with a double valve.

The neighbor called 911, explained the earlier shoot-out, and 911 sent the fire department. Given the context of the shooting, the fire department alerted the Department of Public Safety. DPS, being a state department, had labs that generally outshone ours. They would know what the contents were, some undetermined type of gas. DPS figured out the contents and called APD Dispatch, who knew I was with Chu. We drove up Lamar, past traffic lights that worked and ones that didn't, past dark stores and stores with broken windows, and met at the DPS lab.

"It's acid gas. Miss, you can't smoke in here," said Charles Sackett, a lab tech who worked graveyard. Irina registered his declaration as arbitrary, rolled her eyes and put the cigarette back in the pack, dropping it into her bag.

The DPS lab had many projects going at any given moment. The alert from the fire department, Sackett said, was what gave the gas canister priority. "It's natural gas, but it has up to twenty percent hydrogen sulfide. Two downsides. The first is that once you get a good whiff of it, your olfactory nerve is paralyzed and you can't smell it anymore."

Torbett asked, "What's the second downside?"

"It's highly toxic. And highly flammable. I guess that's two more downsides."

I asked where someone would get it.

"It comes up from the ground like any other natural gas. It has to be processed for household use, remove the sulfide. So he'd have to be someone who had an 'in' at a gas company."

"Here?"

"Could be out of town."

There was no reason to think a guy couldn't fly with a one-liter plastic container in his luggage.

Chu flipped open his phone again, dialed, and left the speaker on so we could all hear the other end.

"*FBI.*"

"It's Alex. What do we know about Zelig's other two men, the little one and the one with the hurt ear?"

Some time passed, and the woman's voice came back. I recognized her as Cathy Bennett. "*Little one ID'd as Nicholas Baldo. Residence Elmira, New York. Priors include assault, burglary, possession of a weapon. Extortion charge dismissed. This is assuming Reles can positively ID him as the man who kidnapped him.*"

She went on. "*The bad-ear guy is Lawrence Sampley.*" Chu fished out the photos again. I wasn't sure of Baldo, the smaller one who reminded me of a rat. But the big guy, the one whose ear I had torn, was distinctive. He had heavy eyebrows that met in the middle. His head peaked at the rear and sloped forward, his lips perpetually pursed, and I seemed to remember a roll of fat at the back of his neck, which the photo, a front shot, showed to be possible.

Chu showed the photos to Irina. She registered them and looked away. She'd spent time with the mob. She knew the rules.

"*Sampley has a similar rap sheet, but shorter. He had a juvie record, then nothing for maybe fifteen years. Then, starting in '86, more arrests.*"

"What did he do those fifteen years?" Chu asked.

"*Just a second.*" And a minute later, "*Elmira Power and Light. General Utility Mechanic, Grade B. He was a gas man.*"

Bingo. Elmira had once been a town filled with trained and untrained labor. But the flood and the recession made them unemployed labor. So there's Sampley with skills Zelig might someday need, and a criminal youth. A job's a job, he thinks.

"When did they know your father was in Austin?"

"It was early yesterday." I realized we were well past midnight. "The day before yesterday, almost forty-eight hours ago. Maybe nine A.M., when I called Lowry."

He said, "What do you think, Cath?"

"*I'll get back to you.*" And she hung up. We thanked the DPS tech and headed out into the generator-lit parking lot. The chill sharpened us. Irina fired up a cigarette and sucked it as if she'd been holding her breath all that time.

Torbett said, "Possibilities?"

Chu said, "We should be thinking about what resources he could have stolen. Things he couldn't bring on a plane."

"A night of looting," I said. "He could have stolen the capitol."

Chu said, "This is a lot of trouble over one girl."

We all looked at Irina, who was smoking comfortably. She shifted at the sudden and unexplained attention.

Chu said, "I guess we can call this confirmation of Zelig's role in the blackout. Who's gonna tell Cronin?"

Cronin and I had been at odds for most of his tenure as APD chief, and the only reason I kept my job was that I once played to the TV cameras and made him shake my hand in front of the whole city. He wouldn't have forgotten.

Torbett said, "That's me, then."

Torbett dialed Chu's phone. "This is Torbett. I need to talk to Chief Cronin. Emergency." Silence. Then he said, "Did you hear me?" She answered, and he hung up.

"What?"

"He's in conference, not to be disturbed under any circumstances. I have to go down there."

Chu gave Torbett his card, and Torbett headed to APD to tell the chief about Zelig's involvement. Chu, Irina and I went to my house.

In my new home, the FBI trap-and-trace team—two neatly dressed agents—had hooked up a circus of equipment to my phone lines. Monitors and screens and a digital recorder. All this operated from an extension cord that ran out to their car, which idled in my driveway. Battery-powered lamps provided manageable light for each room. The agents had ransacked my closets and boxes and tacked sheets and blankets over every window. They'd patched the shot-out windows with tape and cardboard and vacuumed up the broken glass. They were polite and well dressed. They brought their own coffee. They seemed more at home in my new house than I did.

"Get anything yet?"

"We put his number into the processing center. A trap fires when the office processes that number." I didn't understand that, so I started nodding thoughtfully and continued nodding when he went on to explain something about how a cellular phone constantly looks for a tower. "If no tower in the area can find the phone, the call gets dropped. The same technology finds the phone by EIN, the number unique to the phone, like a radio station's call sign. When that number comes up, we've found them. You need three fixed towers to find someone, but then you can locate them to within ten feet. Various fixed points could be charted to find out where he was calling from, or even a route he was traveling."

"Thanks," I said, giving him one last nod. "I'm using the phone."

"Use mine," he said.

In the kitchen I punched in the number of Dispatch and had them put me through to Mora. They caught her in her car.

"Anything?"

"*I busted up a crack house and scared some squatters. I'll keep doing this till you tell me to stop.*"

I felt like an idiot for not coming up with a better order, but I couldn't. "Thanks," I said.

"Sorry about your father."

I hung up. Too early to be sorry. I hoped.

In the living room, they were playing the tape of my earlier conversation with Zelig. I heard Pop babbling, *"Get the . . . geggeh. Don't . . . don't, please."*

"Where are you?" That was me.

"I can't. . . . Hurts so . . . please. Beh beh beh . . . vvv . . ."

"Benny. You're not making any sense. He don't look so good. He's all white and clammy. Shaking like a virgin. Like your mother. Ha! No, not like your mother at all. Who are we kidding? You should feel his heart. It's like an outboard motor. And blood from his nose, from his mouth . . ."

Pop choked out a cry, like a wounded dog.

Irina's nose turned red, and she ran from the room. I found her in my bedroom, kneeling over the bed, sniffling and crying, the one privilege of womanhood. She'd known him for a week and she was allowed to cry. He was my father and all I could do was stand in the doorway. Chu joined me.

Chu spoke to Irina. "He won't give you up."

Irina held still a moment.

Chu went on. "He might hang on a few hours. But the pain. And all this time he's not telling where you are. And you're safe, and he's dying in some hole."

"Chu," I said.

"Suit yourself." He turned to go.

Irina said, "Wait." She sat up on the bed, wiped her eyes and seemed to draw up her dignity. She was an Eastern European woman. Dignity was all she had. And Zelig had taken most of that.

"Close the door," she said.

Chu and I stepped into the bedroom and closed the door.

Everything anyone said about Sam Zelig was true, Irina told us, and more. He was crazy, lived to see anyone in agony, especially women. Inflicting pain had replaced sex for him.

She'd heard rumors about his mother doing things to him. Whether these things involved sex or torture, Irina didn't know. And she didn't care. Lots of people have bad parents. They don't all turn into monsters.

What she knew for sure was that Sam was bad and, as everyone seemed to agree, he was always getting worse.

There had been a series of women before Irina. She knew that. She didn't know who any of them were. But she knew about one girl, the last girl, because Berelman told her.

Zelig charged Berelman with taking care of Irina, which meant keeping her fed and, to a degree, entertained, and making sure she had anything she needed, except access to the outside world. Berelman treated her kindly, brought her Russian foods when he could. A gentle jailer. He might have set her free, but he didn't want to die himself.

They kept Irina at the house for some time before Zelig even introduced himself to her. Irina believed that the previous girl was still there when she herself arrived. Zelig must have known he was almost done with the other girl. He had Irina lined up.

Berelman escorted her around the house, to the game room, to the dining room. There was enough space and enough comfort that she might have forgotten she wasn't allowed out alone. But she didn't.

One night she heard movement, Zelig's shouts, something being dragged and a car driving off. She wasn't sure, but she believed that was about two weeks ago.

So she'd been there close to a month, rather than a week as she'd told me earlier.

When she saw Berelman the next day, he looked pale and ghostlike. He stared at the ground, lost track of what he was saying. Once she caught his eye, and he seemed on the verge of tears. He reached to touch her cheek, then stopped himself.

The next night Zelig invited her out to dinner. He brought her to one of the better restaurants among Elmira's now-humble offerings. He wined her and dined her. Berelman stood by the entrance. There was no option of running, not like there was any place to run.

Zelig brought her home and left her by her bedroom door. The bedroom itself had no windows but otherwise was well appointed. Silk sheets and matching night tables. Antique lamps. Its own bathroom, also windowless. A TV with cable. No phone, of course.

Zelig took her out every night, each time moving closer, from a handshake to an embrace to a cordial kiss to a deep kiss. Then he sucked at her neck until she shrieked. Then he pulled down her dress and pinched her nipple.

Irina began to understand what was coming. Zelig always approached her with a level of excitement that seemed to have continued from the night before. He was always excited but never actually wanted to fuck. There was nothing that made him seem satisfied and dissipated, the way men did after sex.

He started slapping her.

It was the last night Berelman was there that he told her about Zelig, about how bad he was, especially to women. By now, of course, she'd had a sampling. But each night got worse. Once he tied her to the bed and left her there for a day. She couldn't get up to go to the bathroom.

Berelman told Irina it would get worse still. He knew he risked death by telling her this. The last girl died, Berelman said. But Zelig didn't kill her. Irina had to press him to tell her what happened.

The girl hanged herself in her room. Berelman cut the cord she dangled from, lowered her to the bed. He was supposed to get rid of the body. One reason Zelig kept him on was that Berelman still worked part-time at the crematorium and he could get in at night. He could fire up the oven, turn a body to dust and then scatter the ashes. But he didn't. He was high that night, as he usually was. The combination of drugs was such that it stifled his sense of self-preservation while inflating his normally suppressed conscience. Instead of burning the girl, he dumped her in the Chemung River. Berelman wanted someone to find the body.

Why?

He knew what Zelig had done, how he had tortured the girl, how death was easier for her than a life like that. Berelman had helped keep her captive. He felt responsible. And maybe he figured his days were numbered anyway. Like Pop, he wanted to make a last-ditch effort to impress God.

When Berelman told Irina about this, he was full of apologies. He promised to break her out, whatever it cost him. This was easier to say than to do. There were other men on guard. And they all knew that crossing Zelig could get you something worse than killed.

Berelman said that the body in the river would be found, and soon. Zelig would hear about it and know who was responsible. Maybe Berelman figured he had some time to come up with a plan.

The next day Berelman was gone.

It was a few days later that Pop showed up and filled in the gap that Berelman had left. Except for being twenty years older and a few inches taller, Pop could have *been* Berelman. They both looked too skinny and little for the hard business of organized crime. In spite of their advanced age, both seemed like the kid brother who would get knocked around and sent on errands. But Pop was less conflicted because he didn't quite know how Zelig treated women. He'd been gone almost thirty years and Zelig had grown worse in that time. And by now Zelig was moving in on Irina. She made sure to be agreeable when she could, and he gave her a longer leash. There were certain rooms into which she could go unattended. The threat of punishment was so great that she was afraid to step out of line.

If Zelig was crazy, he wasn't stupid. He knew Irina was on to him, and the longer she stayed alive, the better the chance of her talking. But there was more he wanted to do to her. It must have been difficult for him, but eventually his limited wisdom won out over his desire, and he sent her off with Pop to the foundry to be killed. In the car she laid out the situation, convincing Pop that his own life was on the line also. He listened. In spite of a lifetime of being run around by the mob, he turned away from the foundry and kept on driving.

hu called the FBI in Elmira, the police department there and the downstream communities. Yes, they had found a girl a ways down the river in Ashland on the tenth, probably two days after she was dumped. The county sheriff's office ran her prints and her teeth against missing-persons files from various upstream communities, identifying her as Connie Davies of Elmira. Her mother, a cleaning woman, single, had believed that Connie ran off to New York City to make her fortune.

The thin bruise mark circling her neck, said the Elmira PD file, arced up behind her right ear in an inverted V, suggesting hanging as opposed to strangling, and probably with an electrical cord. No, no one at EPD stopped to consider the unlikelihood of Connie's both hanging herself *and* throwing herself in the river. In my living room, one of Chu's techs suggested with a grin that "maybe she was *really* depressed," but he didn't get any points for it. Chu finished on the phone, and told me that the Davies case was now under the jurisdiction of the FBI. Technically it was suicide, but the dumping of the body put Zelig under more than a little suspicion. We'd have to connect it with Berelman's death to make a solid charge of murder.

Five minutes later Chu was coaching Irina as she stood, smoking, by the blanketed front window.

"Don't ask him where he is. You're just trying to keep the conversation going until we can find him."

By that point Chu had two cars in different parts of town. I called

Dispatch, and now I had three patrols plus Mora, all ready to converge once we gave them a location.

Chu said, "I'll talk first."

"Bullshit," I said. "I'll talk."

"This isn't about ego, Reles."

"He gets wind from your Harvard English that he's talking to a fed and his alarms will go off. This is a guy who *owns* city cops. But he doesn't want to go toe-to-toe with you, not with racketeering charges hanging over him."

Chu said, "He's not thinking rationally."

"He knows me and he knows I'm in on this personally. He'll be waiting for me to fuck up."

"Will you?" A curious silence from the staff.

We dialed the mobile phone he'd called from. He could have tossed it by then. The phone rang four times and went into voice mail, a female recording saying, "*You have reached the voice mail of . . .*" and then Zelig saying, "*Cody Jarrett,*" the name of a gangster from a James Cagney movie.

I said, "I've got what you want," and hung up.

We waited. Twenty minutes passed. The phone rang, and we all jolted. I picked up, trying to ignore the frantic spinning of dials, the clock ticking on my father's life, agents wildly pantomiming information to each other.

"Yeah?"

"*Where was she?*"

"Funny thing," I said. "Remember those two nice old people you killed? The ones off South First, I mean."

"*I'm listening.*"

"She was in their house the whole time."

"*Bullshit.*"

"I shit you not. She rolled out the window when you knocked. If you'd walked around the house, we wouldn't be having this conversation now."

"*Motherfucking goddamn shit . . .*" He went on like that for a while, then hung up.

Chu said, "Well?"

The techs said, "He turned off the phone. We lost it."

It slowly dawned on me what a mistake I'd made. By telling him he'd missed Irina, I'd also made it clear that he'd killed two people for nothing. In time he'd realize we could prove those murders. Even if he stopped Irina from testifying, we still had him. He had an out, and now he'd lost it.

"Shit. Try him again."

I said, "No. Wait."

We waited. The phone rang. The crew went back to work.

I picked up. "Yeah."

"Put that bitch on."

"Put my father on."

"He's not here."

"Where is he?"

He roared like a flamethrower. *"Keep fuckin' around, smart boy! You'll never see him again!"*

I took a breath and handed the phone to Irina. Someone passed me a set of headphones so I could listen to the conversation. It started with a click and dead air. One of the techs said, "Son of a bitch." He was gone again.

We waited again, this time for ten minutes.

Finally the phone rang, and we had Irina pick it up. "Hull-lo." There was no question mark at the end.

"Baby, it's the makher."

She looked at us like we could tell her what to say. Chu made a gesture that could have meant "Go on."

"Yes," she said.

"I know they're listening in."

I nodded at her. She said, "Yes."

"Aw, don't be like that. I lose my temper sometimes. I'll make it up to you."

Zelig could lose his temper, I'd give him that. But that's not what his torturing women was about. That was about pleasure. Was he either crazy or stupid enough to think she'd come back and we would let the whole thing go? Was he just plain obsessed, so much that anything besides getting his favorite whipping girl back, even just to kill her, was beyond his notice?

Or was he two steps ahead of us?

Chu tried to mouth a word to her. She said, "Ow."

" 'Ow' what?"

Chu puffed breath in her ear. H-ow. How.

"How will you make it up to me?"

"*Money,*" he said. "*Minks. Big nights in Manhattan.*"

One of the techs mouthed, "We got it," with a thumbs-up, grabbed his jacket and exited through the front door.

She said, "You let my friend go?"

"*Are you kiddin'? We're old pals. I wouldn't do Ben any harm.*"

Another tech scribbled something on a piece of scratch paper and handed it to Chu. I followed him into the kitchen.

"Zilker Park," he said. Very bad news. The park was big, packed with trees and small structures, and in the hours before dawn, dark. Since the park sat solid in blackout territory, if there were any lampposts they'd still be out. In general, it made an ideal spot for an ambush. Chu phoned the location to his cars on the street, and I called it to Mora and the patrols.

Back in the living room, Irina had hung up the phone and was clearly fighting back tears. They rewound the tape for us and played it.

"*You let my friend go?*"

"*Are you kiddin'? We're old pals. I wouldn't do Ben any harm.*"

Silence. Then, "*Okay.*"

"*Okay?*"

"*Okay. You let my friend go. I come back.*"

Now it was Zelig's turn to think. Finally he started to laugh. He stopped just long enough to say, "*Okay!*" and kept on laughing until he settled down to silence.

Irina said, "*Where do I find you?*"

Even Zelig at his stupidest would see through that. He did, and gave his chilling answer, the one that ended the call.

He said, "*I'll find you.*"

Irina stayed at my house with the two agents and a pack of cigarettes, while Chu's tame-looking sedan hit 120 as we sped down the barren MoPac Expressway to the park, the car's bright lights illuminating the way. We pulled off to a dark side street, circled around and headed into the starlit park along a narrow pavement not intended for street vehicles. Chu dimmed the headlights and inched along, as we scanned the path and the woods on the odd chance Zelig was there, hoping that he didn't see us first. The radio came on.

"Go right, Alex," Bennett said. "It's by the amphitheater."

He followed a path to the right. The trees opened onto a huge, sloping meadow, with a stage at the bottom. Some kind of structure, like a small house, stood at the back of the stage, along with two patrol cars.

In any closed situation, like a building, the suspect on the inside has a significant advantage over the officer on the outside. The officer doesn't know where the suspect is, which entrances he may be watching, how many allies he has, how heavily armed he is or what he may have rigged up to make the officer's entry a disaster. For this reason there are many prohibitions and guidelines regarding entering a building. In this case a patrol officer would be instructed to wait for backup such as a senior officer, someone higher ranked to give the orders and take the risk.

But add a few mitigating factors—the late hour, fatigue, inexperience, isolation, boredom broken by sudden excitement—and you have a rookie out to make a name for himself. Such was the case when Patrol Officer Elliot Siïdmarc walked into the structure at the back of the amphitheater, seconds before we drove up, his weapon drawn, took several steps in the dark, found a light switch and flipped on the light.

We saw the windows light up for a split second before the explosion shattered them.

Mora arrived shortly after the blast. She sat with Chu and me on the grassy slope leading down to the burning amphitheater, as the fire department saturated it. Rookie Patrol Officer Elliot Siidmarc had lost most of his skin by the time the firefighters hauled his water-soaked carcass out of the smouldering building. Along with him, the FD found two more gas canisters, each about the size of a household fire extinguisher, each connected to a simple pump. The fire captain guessed the tanks had contained natural gas, but it didn't take much of a leap to guess that it was probably the same acid gas we'd found a tank of earlier, more poisonous and more volatile than the household variety. The light switch, or something attached to it, had created the spark needed to ignite the gas. Lawrence Sampley, the big guy with the damaged ear, had worked for the gas company in Elmira. He would know how to rig up something that simple.

What they also found was the half-melted remains of two mobile phones wired together. Sam Z had never set foot in the shack.

Historically, Sam had dodged the cops and the feds with only a few short jail sentences over a criminal career spanning four decades. But that was with his big brother keeping a leash on him. In the past few weeks, Sam Z had tortured Connie Davies and driven her to suicide. He and his men had killed Ida and her husband almost at random. They'd sabotaged an electrical substation, creating a blackout and plunging a city into frenzy, so they were indirectly responsible for three rapes and at least one death. They'd kept Irina in captivity; Sam had tortured and beaten her. They'd hit my father with a Lincoln, kidnapped him and kept him from medical attention. And now they'd killed a patrol officer. Someone would have to wake the patrol's wife and tell her he wasn't coming home. And they'd done all this with a couple of sharp objects, some gas and a piece of chain. Entropy, as Chu had said before. Things tend to decay, fall apart, collapse. It doesn't take much to encourage them.

What was next?

Chu finished a long call on his car phone and looked pretty important doing it, which by then I'd guessed was the desired effect. He said, "Bennett got a hit on a credit card, Antonia Roque, pronounced 'ROE-kay.' "

"So Zelig's traveling with a woman?" I asked.

Mora said, "What do we do?"

On a reflex I said, "Find him and kill him." I realized that the events of the last two days had taken their toll. Thoughts that normally just crossed my mind now rolled out of my mouth.

Chu smiled, the flashing lights of the fire trucks illuminating his face. "That's very funny," he said. "I saw your expression when you heard that first tape from Zelig. I know what you were thinking, and everyone else in the room did, too."

"I wasn't thinking anything," I said, but no one was convinced.

"Watch yourself, Reles," he said.

There were a thousand things that could go wrong during an arrest or on the way to a trial, especially for a mob boss. Zelig and men like him had been evading prosecution successfully since the dawn of crime. So the temptation to kill someone "accidentally" during an arrest was great. It had to look like an accident, or it had to look justified. Otherwise it was just murder. And there would be witnesses.

When we got back into Chu's car, we got a message to call Torbett. We got him on the radio.

Torbett said, "*I saw Cronin.*"

I said, "Yeah?"

"*He wants to see you.*"

I asked Chu if his people could take care of Irina a while longer.

"Sure, buddy. We can keep her at the office till this blows over. Mind if I tag along with you?" Like anything from the Bureau, it wasn't exactly a request. Chu and I headed toward HQ. Mora went off on her own.

On the way I brainstormed for what Zelig might have in store next. Land mines? Drugs in the water? If he blasted along a fault line, he could create an earthquake. I would have dismissed the idea right off if I didn't know Zelig.

Also, he had to realize by now we had evidence of his kidnapping Pop and of his murdering Ida and her husband. Even if he managed to kill Irina, it wouldn't get him off the hook. There was something else.

I didn't know much about sadism but I knew that for some, at least for Zelig, it had a sexual component that didn't involve orgasm. Did that mean it was never quite satisfied? That he'd always be looking for a greater high, even if it meant he would go to prison for it? Even if it meant he would die?

And maybe he'd had something else planned for Irina at the foundry. Maybe he planned to show up there later, to finish her off, and Pop, too. Maybe he was setting them loose to increase the pleasure of catching them, but catching them had proven harder than it should have been.

He could have a thousand reasons for wanting Irina dead, but few that would bring him to Texas personally. My gut told me that he came here in a state of sexual frustration. That things had gotten so bad he would need to finish her off personally. That every muscle in his body was crying out for a particular release, the kind that would end with Irina dead at his hands.

As Chu drove us through a downtown spotty with light, with dark figures roaming the streets in packs, I racked my brain for a logical spot Zelig might have stashed Pop. An abandoned building would suit the purpose, or a sleazy motel, especially if Pop was tied up and maybe sedated. Mora and her patrols would go back to checking those. I grabbed the microphone and asked them to patch me through to an APD channel.

"Homicide six."

Mora answered, *"Homicide six, go ahead."*

"Think about abandoned businesses, like factories, warehouses. Plus the motels."

Long silence. *"That's it?"*

Torbett was waiting for us in the APD parking lot. The sky had turned a slightly lighter blue by the time we landed in front of the building. We saw two TV news vans parked there instead of four, and only a handful of other reporters. Chu, Torbett and I raced past them and through the doors. With the generator working and the lights back on, the activity had slowed from frenzied to hectic. We were able to take the elevator instead of the dark stairs up to the Fifth Floor. Oliphant's office door was wide open, but the other two, Macaffee's and Bueller's, were shut. Two suited administrators I didn't know by name were speaking in hurried whispers.

"Nobody would believe it."

"You'd have to prove the symptoms. Irrational behavior, extreme exertion—"

They noticed the three of us and stopped dead. A uniformed sergeant pointed us to the conference-room door, the one I'd entered earlier in the dark. I'd visited Cronin in his office in the past, but not in the conference room. Inside, I saw what I'd missed before: a massive conference table, probably carved oak, attended by a dozen brown leather swivel chairs. A minibar. Hanging overhead, a crystal chandelier, simple but elegant. In the city police headquarters. At public expense.

On the walls, useful items. Charts, maps of the city by sector. At the head of the table sat Cronin, looking like death, attended by Assistant Chief Oliphant. The table wore the signs of the earlier strategy conference, strewn with loose papers and coffee cups and envelopes bearing the red stamp CONFIDENTIAL. Cronin had a coffee cup, but there was a bottle of gin next to it. I wondered how long ago he'd opened the gin and if it had something to do with his earlier brilliant decision to impose martial law. He looked up. "Agent Chu," he said.

Chu inflated slightly. He took in Cronin's shock and dismay like a round of applause. In his tailor-made suit and stylish shoes, Chu looked like a civilian consultant, a Harvard grad, among the military.

Cronin waved Oliphant out of the room. Then he stood, more to respond to the threat of Chu's presence than out of courtesy. Chu, Torbett and I faced him from the far end of the table.

Cronin spoke. "Power outages caused by vandalism at the electrical towers. Four sectors black or browned out. Charlie Sector still in complete darkness. HQ dark for an hour until we got the generators going. No radio contact during that time. Patrols running blind. Three rapes. Lootings. One looter died in custody."

"How?" Chu asked.

Cronin faltered and went on. "Violence. Seventy-five arrests so far tonight."

Chu pushed. "How did the looter die in custody?"

Cronin didn't look inclined to answer any direct question from Chu. I realized that the hostility and jealousy city cops felt toward feds knew no rank.

Cronin had to give an answer. He stammered. "Sudden . . . in-custody death syndrome."

It probably would have been easier on Cronin if Chu hadn't laughed. We'd all received memos on sudden in-custody death syndrome and we'd all laughed, but not in Cronin's face. The signs of SICDS could include agitation, heightened heart rate, inappropriate nudity, unusual strength and other warnings that the suspect might be experiencing serious physical and psychological changes which could result in his death. The memo struck most cops as a jaded attempt by the department to cover future beating deaths of prisoners. I realized it was what the two administrators were talking about when we got off the elevator. Some dumb, vicious cop had beaten a prisoner to death, adding to the night's events.

Cronin reddened. He shifted from defense to offense. "You're here with something on your mind. What is it?"

Chu said, "We have reason to believe that the sabotage of the lights was committed by someone we know."

Cronin nodded. "Torbett told me. What's the name again?"

I considered dodging the question but couldn't figure how.

"Sam Zelig," I said. "He's an organized-crime figure from western New York State."

Cronin turned to Chu. "And how do *we* know him?"

It wouldn't have sounded better coming from someone else. I said, "My father . . . used to work for him."

Cronin's eyes showed a trace of sadism, his revenge for Chu's laughing in his face. "*Work* for him?"

I said, "My father drove for a noted crime family back in the fifties and sixties. My father is an ex-convict. This is all in my file, sir."

Cronin nodded, the muscles in his face grinding against each other like rocks. "So you're telling me that a Mafia boss followed you here from New York State. And that he's responsible for all this."

I could have said, "No, it's not me he's after. It's some girl," or "It's not my fault, it's my father's." Nothing would have taken the heat off.

I said, "More or less. Sir."

Torbett explained in a matter-of-fact way how Sam Zelig had come to town and killed Pop's old girlfriend and her husband, while looking for Pop and Irina. Then how he kidnapped Pop and made two attempts on my own life. I would have left the last item out.

Cronin nodded, looking strangely peaceful. Then he turned to me. "You're suspended. You create a threat to this department. This case is going to Organized Crime, where it belongs." He picked up the phone and dialed. I started to speak up, but Torbett cut in.

"Sir," Torbett said, "Reles knows the suspect personally. His help would be—"

Cronin said, "Reles, you're to share any information you have with the Organized Crime division."

"You just suspended me."

Chu said, "He can't work while he's suspended."

Cronin garbled a cluster of curses in a combination I'd never heard before and hung up the phone. Torbett said, "Reles grew up in this world, sir. He can make best guesses at the suspect's next actions."

Cronin fumed. He could have taken the affront better without a fed as witness. As it was for most men, I realized, Cronin's greatest fear was being humiliated. He said, "You're on borrowed time, Reles. Okay. Take all the resources you need. Chu, I expect the Bureau's cooperation. Torbett, I'm holding *you* responsible." We were out the door before he changed his mind and fired me.

We left Chu in the lobby, which still buzzed with complaints, arrests and shouting. I asked Torbett, "What's the sudden in-custody death?"

"It was a taser."

"What?"

Before he could elaborate, Halvorsen, from my squad, suddenly appeared before us, grabbing me by the arm like we were old war buddies. To make things scarier, he was smiling. His free hand held a large manila envelope.

"Reles! Torbett! You won't believe . . . ! Stay here. Stay here."

We did for the moment, and he walked toward a man he'd stationed about ten feet from us, who stood obediently. A genuine hick from the sticks, Halvorsen's man wore dirty shoes, threadbare jeans, a down vest and a cap advertising his favorite motor oil. His eyes peeked over an overgrown yellow beard and what little exposed face he had was marred by broken blood vessels and excess sun. Halvorsen buttonholed a patrol headed out to the street, gave some instructions, and the patrol escorted the hick into the building. Halvorsen leaped over to us and rushed us into a corner.

"We got a call after we put the rabbit story on the news, with the dead chick's face. Killeen PD. Some guy"—he pointed to where the rube had been standing—"that guy, called in with a missing-persons report on his wife. He said she was pregnant."

"Halvorsen—" I broke in.

"No, listen. So I go out there, I got a gut feeling, a gut feeling! He's still at the PD, they're keeping him. And I look at the report. The clothes she was wearing, they match the maternity clothes we found in the Dumpster. So I ask if he wants to come to Austin and we can do a full report. He says okay. And he comes all the way back with me, not a peep in the car."

"Why?" I asked.

"So we could get him on tape!"

Of course not. Halvorsen wanted an audience.

"Good," I said. "Take care of it, Halvorsen."

"Don't you wanna watch the interview?"

"I'm busy."

Halvorsen gawked as we turned from him. Just as I thought we'd make it out of the lobby, he shouted, "Whatta you got against me, Reles?!" Loud enough to garner attention in the crowd.

"Nothing."

"Bullshit," he said, louder than necessary. "You didn't want me to have a full squad, you didn't want me near Mora—"

In a department where ratting someone out can get you killed, listing my dubious behaviors in front of the head of Internal Affairs would be acceptable only in an excited moment, such as the middle of an argument. Halvorsen knew what he was doing.

Before I got to respond, Torbett said, "We have time."

Zelig, and my father, would wait.

The patrol set up the suspect in an interview room. A video camera rolled on him. He didn't ask why. He sat behind a table, opposite Halvorsen, Torbett and me. I shifted in my chair and checked my watch: 7:30 A.M.

Halvorsen said, "State your name."

"Bobby Joe Lemon. You the one working the found-head case?"

We looked at each other. The TV news report never suggested that the woman's head was in any way separated from her body, just that the woman had gone missing.

Halvorsen said, "Yeah, that's us." Lemon nodded. Halvorsen asked small, simple questions. When did you last see her? What was she wearing? What did you talk about? Lemon told us the names of some of her friends. He told us the name of the family dentist, whose services Lemon himself had apparently avoided.

Then Halvorsen opened the manila envelope. He pulled from it the ID photo the department had manufactured from the victim's head, made up and cropped and doctored to look like she was still alive. Just a woman who took a bad picture.

"Is that your wife?"

Lemon said, "No."

"She fits the description."

"That ain't her." Lemon's cheek twitched.

Halvorsen said, "You know her dentist has her records. When we talk to him in the morning, the teeth won't match?"

Both his cheeks twitched. "N-no."

Halvorsen nodded and pulled out another photo. It was similar to the first photo, but large enough to show that the head had no body attached. The eyes gaped, the mouth hung open, and the cut that severed the neck was sloppy with blood.

"Is *that* your wife?"

Lemon's whole face twitched. He tried to say something, lost breath and tried again. "If it is my wife, what does that mean?"

"You tell me."

"You won't be mad at me?" Lemon scanned all our faces.

"No," we agreed.

"Absolutely not."

Lemon talked at length. She got pregnant. She said it was another guy, Anthony Debaudry. Lemon knew Debaudry enough to know that he lived in Austin and worked at a 7-Eleven. She left Lemon with their first kid, a boy two years old. She wrote him a nasty letter from Austin, told him how she was glad he wasn't the father, what a piece of shit he was, what a rotten lover.

Men don't like to be humiliated.

One day last week, he ran over a rabbit, or so he said. Brought it home. He was in the house cleaning it with a kitchen knife. She came in. She's about nine months pregnant now, he said, and "fixin' to domino." She said she was broke, she needed money. Then she started abusing him again and wouldn't let up. He cut her throat with the knife.

This would have gotten him some leeway with a jury. He had the knife when she walked in. He wasn't planning the murder in advance. But the story didn't end there.

He wanted to see if the unborn child was his. So with the same knife still in his hand, he cut it out of her and held it up to his screaming two-year-old, to see if they looked alike.

Then he freaked out. He saw what he had done. He cut up the woman's body, brought Junior to Grandpa Lemon's house, left parts of the body outside the house and brought parts of it to Austin. He wanted to plant it where the lover worked, so he dumped it at a 7-Eleven, but he got the wrong 7-Eleven. Then he went back to Grandpa's and stayed for a week.

He saw the report on TV. He had some drinks and felt guilty. So he called in the missing-persons report.

Halvorsen turned to me with a smug grin like I'd just witnessed him bedding a couple of Hollywood starlets. I pushed my chair back and got up to leave the room. As I headed into the hall, Torbett following, Halvorsen shouted after us, "That's it? That's it?!"

I said, "What do you want?"

Torbett stood quietly. Halvorsen said, "You had it in for me from the start."

"File the case, Halvorsen. I'll put in for your medal in the morning."

"I know what this is about. It's about Mora."

I said, "What are you talking about?" It sounded like I was acting.

He stood close enough for me to hit him, but not so close that it would look like he was angling for it. "You don't like that I'm sleeping with her."

Better wisdom kicked in between the moment my jaw dropped and the second later when I would have said, "You're sleeping with *Mora*?!" I turned to Torbett. "Are we done here?"

As we stepped down the hall, I glanced back and saw Halvorsen's face turn from angry to satisfied. I'd given him what he wanted.

The sky had lightened while we were inside, another day beginning without a night's sleep in front of it. I fought a wave of fatigue. For all the struggle, I'd assumed that Torbett would have some brilliant plan when we left HQ. But when we got into his car, he headed east on Seventh Street and I realized we were going to his house, where our wives and children were sleeping. Or at least his wife. In the absence of traffic lights, cars sped down the street.

I said, "Clock's ticking, Torbett. My father's tied up somewhere. He's hurt."

Torbett said, "Chu's people are working on that, along with Mora and her patrols. They have your phone wired. There's nothing we can do now. Nothing."

"But my father—"

"Your father thought he could outrun the Mafia. You know how those stories end, and so does he."

"But—"

"What's the difference between Bobby Joe Lemon and Sam Zelig?"

I put aside the obvious—money, ethnicity, culture. What did Lemon have that Zelig didn't?

"Remorse?"

Torbett nodded. "Lemon didn't even think about what he did until his rage wore off. If he had a pillow in his hand instead of a knife, he would have hit her with the pillow. When he realized what he'd done, he felt guilty. Zelig is different. Your father is old, and I'm sorry to say it, but he's a dead man."

I saw a patrol car on the side of the road, with its lights flashing. I saw the patrol working a guy over with a nightstick. I figured it was fifty-fifty the guy had actually done something, so I let it go.

We passed a church and a cemetery, then turned down Torbett's block, Walnut Avenue.

He said, "You know why there's two empty rooms at my house, why there was a room for your wife and another for your son? One is a guest room. The other belongs to my son, Guy. He won't come home for Christmas. Says I screwed up his life."

He pulled over in front of the dark house.

"Talk to your wife, Reles. Talk to your son."

Inside Torbett's home he pointed to two doors, then continued on down the hall. One door would open to the guest room where Rachel was staying. I turned the knob of the other, gently pushing it open.

Josh lay under a light blanket pulled up to his chin. He wore his plaid flannel pajamas. His face angled to one side and I noticed his head jerk slightly, in a way that made me wonder if I'd woken him. Then his feet moved. I couldn't tell if he was having a nightmare, and whether I should interrupt his stormy last few minutes of sleep. His life so far hadn't trained him to sleep restfully. He always felt like he had to be ready for the next disaster, as if he had to sleep with his sneakers on, just in case. I'd promised to put an end to that. I'd promised to give him a stable home. I'd screwed up already.

I thought about the kind of father Pop was. He raised me in a gym, brought me along on minor heists, taught me to live in fear of his murdering bosses. I wanted to be different. But being a cop was practically the same, a gangster's life in reverse. There were always threats from the outside, and from within. Stress, anxiety, alcoholism. Divorce. The family pays and pays. They were paying for my decision to join the force. Fifty years ago Pop decided to join the mob. And we were all paying for that still. I had to free us.

I closed the door and slipped into the guest room, where Rachel slept on her side, breathing thickly. A glass of wine sat on the night table in lieu of water, just in case she started to sober up in the middle of the night. I lifted the blanket and slid in next to her. She shifted to accommodate me, raising her arm to let mine wrap around her midsection.

"What's going on?" she asked.

I told her. Then I said, "Were you out of the house earlier?"

"Why?"

"I just want to know. Were you at home?"

Long silence. She said, "I can't take much more of this."

I glanced at the wine on the night table and thought, Neither can I.

I closed my eyes. I don't know if I was out for a second or an hour, but suddenly Torbett was knocking on the door, saying, "Reles!"

I followed him through the house and out the front door, which he dead-bolted behind us. Chu's Chrysler idled out front. I got in, Torbett following in his own car. Chu put it in gear and headed north. He said, "Tell me again about Berelman."

I said, "He worked for Zelig. He wound up dead in his hotel. We think he was witness to Zelig's torture of Connie Davies."

Chu said, "So what are the chances he charged a room at the new Ambassador Hotel up on Parmer Lane?"

He flipped on the flashing light on his dashboard, but the streets were mostly quiet. Sunday morning, Christmas eve. Traffic would cook up in an hour when the stores opened.

I could tell that Chu was giddy. He spoke double time. "We tried everything," he chattered. "Zelig's whole file, known associates back to 1960. All the names we had, all the names from the flight lists. Finally someone said, 'What about the guy in the hotel in Elmira?' We thought no, he's not that stupid. He wouldn't go around using a murdered man's credit card. A *freshly* murdered man." He laughed. "This doesn't quite clear your father for Berelman's murder, but close."

I hoped I'd get the chance to tell Pop that.

In spite of being out in the middle of nowhere (convenient only to the smaller Austin Executive Airport), the Ambassador Hotel rose eight stories high, a monument to hope that the town would keep growing big, keep growing north. By the time we got to the hotel-room door, another agent, Reardon, was already positioned there, his weapon drawn. He was talking into a shoulder-mounted microphone when Chu approached. Other hotel guests appeared from their rooms. Torbett and I quickly waved our badges, and they retreated like mice.

Reardon whispered, "We have men on the balconies of both adjoining rooms, in case he makes a run. Ready?" He addressed the last word to me, like he still wasn't sure which side I was on.

He had the key card from the front desk. We drew our weapons. I felt myself hoping that Zelig would fire on us, just to give me the excuse to shoot him. I didn't want anyone else to die, and if he knew we were there, someone would. I positioned myself in front. Reardon slipped the card into the lock, which flashed green, and the four of us rushed in.

Lying on the bed, fully dressed and snoring, was a fat, tall, balding man in a blue sweatshirt and baggy black suit pants that pulled without pity at his bulging gut. His lips pursed in what looked like a whisper, and I could see the roll of fat at the back of his neck. What's more, his right ear was wrapped in gauze and all but taped in place. He hadn't seen a doctor since I tried to yank it off.

On the nightstand stood a fifth of cheap vodka he'd put a considerable dent in. With it, a glass and two more one-liter gas tanks like the ones we'd seen earlier. Lawrence Sampley, Zelig's gas man.

Reardon checked the bathroom and the balcony, behind a vast sliding glass door that opened onto the sleepy downtown. All clear. Torbett reached a wallet out of the gas man's pocket without waking him, found credit cards under three different names, including Berelman's, and a driver's license naming him Lawrence Sampley. I slapped Sampley's face just enough to wake him up. When that didn't work, I slapped him again.

Chu said, "Reles, please." He took out a small tube from his pocket, smaller than a ChapStick, opened it and waved it under Sampley's nose. Sampley snorted, gasped, coughed and opened his eyes wide. Then he looked around the room, saw us and said, "I'm cooked, right?"

Chu said, "That depends."

He nodded. "I'm cooked."

"You want to tell us what you're doing here?"

Sampley opened his mouth, tried to work up some moisture. He reached for the vodka and stopped himself. "You mind?" he asked. We didn't. We settled in around him.

After a drink his vocal cords loosened up. He told us a bit of what we already knew, about the plane flights and the credit cards. Chu asked how he hooked up with Zelig.

"I had a job with the city. Elmira Power and Light. I was a GUMBY. General Utility Mechanic, grade B, on the gas system. Everybody in town is losing their jobs, I figured I work for the city, I'm safe. Then the city laid me off." He sipped vodka. "So I put an ad in the paper. Household repairs, pipes, heating, electricity. I fixed Sam Z's stove."

I said, "So he brought you in."

He nodded. "I was tough when I was a kid. Time in juvie. But people change. Anyway, I knew who he was. I didn't wanna come back to this. What was I gonna do? It was real money."

I said, "Real money? Wow. He practically forced you."

Torbett said, "Who else was traveling with you?"

Sampley didn't seem to get the question. "I'm gonna die now."

"The blackout," I said. "Did you do that?"

"What?" He seemed not to know the words.

"Did you throw a chain over the electrical towers to make the lights go out?

He dropped his gaze. "Sorry."

I showed him the picture of my father. "Have you seen this man?" No recognition.

Sampley said, "I been up for two days. Since we came in. I was supposed to go do something, I don't even remember what it was. And I saw this place, and all I could think was 'bed.' He'll be pissed."

We'd been holding off on the big question to warm him up. I finally dropped it. "Where is he?"

Sampley closed his eyes. Chu leaned over him and said, "We're wondering if he has something big planned."

Sampley shook his head and looked up. "There are things you can't undo. This stuff." He reached for a canister. Reardon tried to yank it from his reach. "No," Sampley said, "it's okay." And for some reason we took his word. Something about authority. Sampley said, "Very bad. Toxic. See?"

And before we could think, he popped the valve, put his mouth half over it and sucked it deep. Torbett grabbed it from him and tried to replace the valve while Chu hoisted a chair and smashed the picture window, but it was too late. Sampley coughed once, then vomited. His eyes rolled back, and he started to convulse, his body jerking, head swinging back. We held him down, turned his head to the side, but for nothing. By the time we called for a doctor, he was dead.

Chu left Reardon to deal with the aftermath, and Torbett and I got back into his car with him when we heard Cathy Bennett's voice on the radio.

"Alex, pick up."

"Go ahead."

"Call from APD Ballistics. Remember that gun from the shooting at Re-les's house? The Ruger automatic with the mounted scope."

We remembered.

"Well, they found the owner."

When they couldn't get me or Torbett on the radio, Ballistics called Mora, who followed up fast on the gun owner, Barney Rostro, whom Mora described as "a hapless G.I. Joe fan in an efficiency apartment he moved to when his parents threw him out." Rostro let Mora search the place, which didn't take long. He said he'd sold the gun two months back to a "collector" named Billy Hawk, who lived just east of town near the wastewater-treatment plant. We made a few calls to APD until we found someone who knew Hawk's address. Ballistics told us that Hawk was a gun nut, that he was heavily lawyered though he himself did not believe in the concept of law and that, beyond all that, he was a gun dealer we hadn't quite nailed yet.

The sky was bright by the time we all reached Hawk's home outside the edge of town. The sun hurt my eyes and made my head pound. Mora and Torbett slipped around the back of the house. There was no screen door, only a steel front door like Torbett's but unpainted, giving it a more industrial look. It was fair to guess that the walls were lined with steel also. Chu and I approached the front door and knocked, not expecting any response, so we were that much more off guard when the door swung open as if moved by a hidden third party. Both of Hawk's hands gripped the Uzi semiautomatic machine gun he pointed at us.

To turn a semiautomatic gun into a fully automatic one, one you can fire continuously by just holding the trigger, is a skill that many people possess. Hawk was a likely candidate to be among them. I'd seldom seen such a weapon, owing to its high expense and consequent rarity on the street. I'd certainly never seen one from that angle.

Hawk must have been about sixty, Caucasian, ruddy complexion. A heavy drinker, he had an angry scowl imprinted on his features. He wore motorcycle boots, a red T-shirt and a black vest, gut protruding over black denim jeans. His long, reddish hair and beard were fading to white, and if he'd been more involved in marijuana than guns, he could have stood in for Willie Nelson. In what might have been the seconds before my death, I noted the tattoos coating both arms. I didn't stop to read them, but I supposed they extolled the virtues of killing 'em all and letting God sort 'em out.

"Git off my property," he said.

We showed him our empty hands. I said, "I'm Lieutenant Reles with APD. This is—"

Chu cut me off: "Lieutenant Chu." I flinched but realized if there's one thing gun nuts hate more than a cop, it's a federal agent. "We just have some questions."

"I don't gotta answer nothin'."

Chu said, "You had a weapon we're interested in. A Ruger automatic with a mounted scope? You bought it from a . . ."

I said, "Barney Rostro," like that name was going to help me.

Hawk's eyes pinched closer together. I hoped for Mora and Torbett to try something. The front of the house was steel, so I could guess the same about the back. If they followed us around front, they'd be as vulnerable as we were. I wanted them to survive, but not just so they could tell my family how bravely I'd died.

I regretted how deeply my automatic was buried in my shoulder holster, but if I'd been holding it when the door opened, I might be dead already. I waited for brilliant words to come to me, but they didn't. I opened my mouth anyway, hoping something useful would roll out.

"You're trying to protect your home and your family."

Chu added, "We're no threat to you."

I said, "There's a man who got hold of that gun who used it against an innocent couple in their home." I couldn't tell him that the gun had been used against me in my home. He'd like that. I was starting to take heart in the fact that I wasn't dead yet when he raised his Uzi slightly and pointed it in the direction of my face.

Suddenly we heard glass break inside the house, probably a window. In the second I took to register what was going on, Hawk spun to look into the house and Chu and I jumped him, knocking him to the ground. Chu managed to throw most of his weight on the Uzi, which left Hawk free to pummel me with what must have been an anvil. Torbett appeared and, not figuring Hawk for someone who would respond to the word "freeze," pistol-whipped him, drawing a trickle of blood and just enough attention to let Mora try to cuff his wrists, a difficult maneuver under easier circumstances. Hawk grabbed for Torbett's leg and yanked it from under him, Torbett going down hard on the cold grass. Chu pointed the Uzi at Hawk, and I foolishly kicked at Hawk's head, allowing him to grab my shoe and twist. I would spin under my own power or watch my leg spin without me.

Chu shouted "Freeze!"—which had as much effect as I thought it would. In the blur I saw Torbett on his back, arm around Hawk's neck, as Hawk reached out a butterfly knife from nowhere and flipped it open in time for Mora to grab his knife hand and twist it, sending the blade into the flesh between Hawk's pectoral muscle and his shoulder.

Inside, Hawk lay on his woolen sofa. The blade hadn't gone too deep, and he insisted on treating it himself. When the knife pierced him, he conceded defeat, though he claimed we'd only caught him because of the goodness of his heart.

Usually when four cops have trouble taking down one man, he's psychotic. Given the instantaneous calm he showed when he let go of the blade, this one wasn't even angry. He was protecting his home, he said, on principle.

Mora said, "You should probably see a doctor."

"Been stabbed lots of times," said Hawk, and the scars on his torso bore him out. "Didn't see no doctor then."

His house was ordered in its clutter. Stacks of pamphlets, crates of ammunition and canned food. Lit bright by battery-powered lamps and gas lanterns, evidence of a man ready and waiting for society to fall. The walls formed a museum of right-wing literature, Confederate flags, blown-up photos of lynchings and the odd spiritual aphorism. My favorite was "Guns cause crime like flies cause garbage." He offered us whiskey and seemed oddly friendly considering he was hosting his least likely guests: a Jew, an African American, a Latin woman and a federal agent of Asian parentage. From his point of view, he might as well have been pouring drinks for Karl Marx and Malcolm X.

Yes, he'd sold Zelig the gun, he said. Zelig found him by way of a tip from a bartender. He'd sold Zelig the ammo, too. No, there was no license, and what were we gonna do about it? No, he hadn't sold Zelig anything else.

I explained my father's situation and Irina's, an innocent young woman. I asked, nicely, if there was anything else he could tell us before we left.

Hawk thought hard. He wanted to live undisturbed in his fortress, sell guns and, if the wall decorations were any indication, string up minorities. But on some level he saw himself as good.

"On William Cannon Drive, 'bout a mile west of 35."

"Yes?"

"Behind the Rent-to-Own, there's a warehouse. Well, it ain't no warehouse, it's a chop shop. He said he needed a car."

That the chop shop really operated where Hawk said it would was a gift from God. Through the slats of rickety garage doors, we could see the small auto shop that took stolen cars apart piece by piece, for convenient sale. I suggested we enter without knocking.

Both Chu and Torbett tried to veto this plan. Torbett said, "We have to check it out, make sure we're not interfering with an ongoing investigation."

I said, "We're not arresting anyone. Just asking questions."

Chu said, and I heard it coming, "Fruit of the poisoned tree." He didn't have to explain. Anything they told us was sullied information if we got it outside of standard legal procedure. If we pinpointed Zelig's car and that helped us catch him, the arrest could be thrown out.

"Okay," I said. "Fuck it. We go get some coffee and wait to see what he does next. How bad could it be?"

Chu and Torbett exchanged looks. Surely there were ways of doing things. But not this time. There were a million things we weren't supposed to do and only a few that we could. Torbett and Chu were human. They got caught up in the flow, and now they wanted Zelig almost as much as I did. And it was full morning already, the rest of the world starting up without us having more than a few winks of sleep. People who have been up most of the night make decisions they'd never make on a night's rest.

Chu said, "Ideas?"

Not far from us, a trailer truck started its engine. It had just completed a delivery to the Rent-to-Own. I eyeballed the garage doors of warped wood and ran for the truck, climbing up on the running board and waving my badge.

"God dang it!" the driver shouted. "I didn't do nothin'!"

"Of course not."

In exchange for two twenties from my wallet, the driver backed up to a series of evenly spaced beeps, and woe to those who got behind him, then slowly moved into the door, finally ramming through with a satisfying *c-c-c-crrrrrunnnchhh.* Then he pulled out and disappeared for Dallas and points north, and we followed through the ample entrance, unnecessarily waving guns as we intruded into what could have been any auto shop in town, except that it seemed more focused on taking cars apart than putting them together. We talked to the one man who wasn't holding a blowtorch, asked him if he was in charge. When he didn't say no, Chu waved Zelig's picture.

"I won't talk until I see my lawyer."

I said, "Tell us if you've seen this guy and you may not have to."

He considered that, then said, "He was here around eleven." Zelig must have planned on changing cars after the bridge meeting.

The car they gave him, for a reasonable price, was a '93 Ford LTD Crown Victoria in bronze, freshly painted, with a bogus license plate the guy didn't have record of, but he knew it was from Tennessee. I called Dispatch and put out a search for the car. We left the chop shop alone and exposed to the elements.

In the meantime we had something to keep us busy. Sam Z had called.

"Dano, it's Sammy Z. I knew you were having phone trouble at home, so I decided to call you at the office."

Doing that, he'd managed to dodge the trace. The feds took the liberty of checking my office voice mail for me, a neat trick considering I hadn't given them my password, but their abilities no longer surprised me. I stood with Torbett, Mora, Chu and Bennett in the FBI command post among the reduced crew. Some of the other agents were running around town in my interest. I watched the flashing maps on their projection screens and the helicopter shot, with a spotlight scanning the streets for a bronze LTD with Tennessee plates, and I tried to stay moving just fast enough to keep from thinking too rationally about my father's chances.

"*Benny, say hi*," the recording went on.

My father's weak voice muttered something. I finally made it out: "*I'm good, I'm good. . . .*" It sounded almost like a question. Did he know he was talking into a phone? Was he trying to convince me, or God, that he had repented after a lifetime of bad deeds? Or maybe just that he was, at his core, a good person.

"*Your old man, he's not doing so hot. His belly is all swolled, tight like a drum. Listen to what happens when I kick it.*"

I heard a dull thump and my father crying out, his cry fading to a weak whimper. And Zelig's laughter.

"*I figure he's got about an hour at this rate, depending on how much I kick him. I gotta respect it, him standing up for a girl like this.*" Then he roared, "*BUT SHE WAS MY GIRL! MINE! And I want her back!*"

I could feel everyone's eyes on me as I sweated, whispering, "Please. Please, hang on, Pop."

"*I never seen him like this. First time he didn't roll over. People surprise you. So I blacked out your town. That was a warning. See what I can do. See my POWER! And get ready for something bigger, way bigger. You have an hour. Give me my fuckin' GIRL!*"

The tape ended. "When?" I said.

"Fifteen minutes ago," Cathy Bennett said.

Torbett said, "So we have forty-five minutes to find out what he's planning."

"Where is he?" Mora asked.

"Fair question," Bennett said. "He used a calling card, so the call was routed through the calling-card company in Pennsylvania. Then we tracked it to a pay phone on Airport Boulevard, but by then he was long gone. Here, I'll play it again."

"Don't," I said. I lost some of their respect for it, but I couldn't hear my father take another kick to the gut. His life under Zelig had been full of them.

Bennett said, "Okay, the call came from the street. But the part with your father getting kicked, the static was twice as heavy. It took us two listens to figure that out. Zelig did it on purpose, calling from the street like that."

"What do you mean?"

"He kicked your father and got that on tape. He wasn't kicking him out on the street. He left your father someplace, maybe tied up, maybe with someone else. Remember, he's got one guy still with him, at least. Or a woman."

I looked down at Bennett's fake-credit-card list. She was pointing to a name, Antonia Roque, the only female name on the list.

I said, "Maybe my father is dead already." No one argued.

She said, "Which only addresses part of the threat. This man." She held up the photo that looked like the smallest of the three men who abducted me, the skinny one with the nasal rasp. "Nicholas Baldo. Is he the man you saw?"

"I think so. I'm not sure."

Bennett said, "Well, we know he's associated with Zelig, so we'll say probably. Besides him, we know Zelig brought Lambrecht, the gunman, and Sampley, the gas mechanic. We don't know who else he brought or what other calamity he has planned. If he was ever afraid of getting caught, he's given that up. And it isn't like he has a conscience to get in his way."

Bennett and Chu stared at me, as if they were setting me up for something. Finally I blurted, "What is it? What? What?"

They exchanged a look before she sighed and said, "The only way out of this is to—"

A heavier female voice said, "To give him what he wants." And we realized that Irina had entered the room.

"Listen," Torbett said, breaking the silence that followed. "There's only one way to do this." As we listened to his plan, I thought of my father trying to undo a lifetime of illegal and immoral acts through one ill-conceived good deed. I thought of the deaths that had resulted from it and the ones that might still result. But those deaths weren't his fault. He pissed off a murderer. The murderer was the guilty one.

I saw the eyes of Mora and the feds as they listened to Torbett, then one by one checked on me to see what I was thinking, what I was planning, how I might try to undermine their plan to catch Zelig and bring him to trial, a long, painful trial that might result in his freedom.

And I thought of my father's joke, the Jew in front of the firing squad who says, "Meyer, please! Don't make trouble."

Don't make trouble.

And I got an idea.

When you approach the place of battle, the priest shall step forward and speak to the people. He shall say to them, "Listen, Israel, today you are about to wage war against your enemies. Do not be faint-hearted, do not be afraid, do not panic, and do not break ranks before them."

—Deuteronomy 20:2–3

The city would be awake by now, including those who'd overslept. They'd be mopping up the puddles from the defrosting freezers, sorting through the perishables to see what was damaged of the food they'd planned for breakfast and lunch and Christmas dinner. They'd be hitting the road for Pflugerville and Killeen and Houston, if they hadn't already, to slug out generation-old fights with family members they loved or loathed, in celebration of the holiday.

At FBI headquarters, Chu, Bennett, Mora, Torbett and I ate bologna sandwiches and sipped coffee, though I could have popped two Valium and it wouldn't have quieted my jitters. Mora watched. Torbett listened. People scanned screens. In the glass booth, Reardon and another man played with sound levels. When the phone rang, if it rang, everyone would snap into action. I was to go into the booth while they tried to triangulate the signal.

The clocks ticked against each other, providing irritating counterpoint in the otherwise-hushed space, the eye of the hurricane. I thought about Pop, taking a kick, or several, in a stomach bloated from internal bleeding, all to protect a woman he'd just met. I thought of his careers as a boxer, leg breaker and thief. I wondered if, in the great scheme of things, his one noble action would make up for all that. One decent action, not counting how he'd taken care of me, when I was a kid and when he faced down Zelig's charging Lincoln on the bridge.

I felt like talking to Rachel, hangover or no. But if she was awake, she'd be trying to pull herself together and eat breakfast. She wouldn't want to talk to me as much as I wanted to talk to her. I'd talk to her in an hour or two, once everything was over.

I walked the hall. In a break room, under a sign reading NO SMOKING, Irina puffed a cigarette with great focus, as if it were the most important thing she would ever do. I sat upwind of her.

Chu had promised to make calls to the Justice Department about getting her a green card, in exchange for her cooperation. But she had something bigger at stake.

There are questions you don't ask. When you know that someone's suffering has been so great that for her to speak of it would be to relive it. But the question hangs in the air. And sometimes, when you're forced together, when you're suddenly and briefly a community, someone has a thing to say and she's afraid she won't get another chance. She needs to talk as much as you need to listen.

"When I am first go to Istanbul," she says, "I worry about police, customs. Today I think, if they only deport me, I would be in Russia now. What they do to me is worst thing"—and here, finally, she dropped tears for herself—"is worst thing someone could . . . do.

"Your father, he see me. I see in his face what I have not seen. Pity. What is word? Compassion. Second day we make telephone call to Russia. My mother dead. Is no home to go back to. I have no one. But one friend. In my whole time, he is first to show kindness, first person to stand up, to help me."

I thought of my father's life of buckling under, of not making trouble. Maybe his running away with her was motivated by pure self-interest. But he'd done plenty for her since then. I said, "It's kind of a first for him, too."

Irina shook her head. "You do not understand."

And Chu was swinging the door open, hissing, "Now!"

I walked into the sound booth, picking up the phone. Irina followed me in. Reardon and another agent spinning dials in front of us, both with headsets. Beyond the glass, Torbett, also with a headset. On one screen a projected map of Austin, something that looked like radar. Sun shone in the windows to rattle my skull.

I said, "This is Reles."

Zelig laughed. "*Yingeleh, I know who it is.*"

"How's my father?"

"*He's a rock, God bless him.*"

Chu leaned over someone's shoulder. He was pointing and giving directions and getting more and more agitated. Something was going wrong. He scribbled a note, passed it to another agent, who ran for the booth and held it up to the glass. It read "SPOOFING TECHNOLOGY. ROUTING CALL THRU INDIA, THAILAND, ENGLAND, ETC. STRETCH OUT CALL."

"Can I talk to him?" I asked.

"*He's not where he can talk right now. Where's my girl?*"

"She's right here."

"*Well, put her on!*"

"She can't talk now either."

He boomed, "*Put her on, you motherless fuck!*"

I handed her the receiver and took a set of headphones.

Irina said, "I am here."

"*Rini. Baby. What have they done to you?*"

I sensed her stiffen at the words, his suggestion that he would save her from someone else.

"I am fine," she said. "I am coming back."

He didn't answer. Irina looked scared, and I motioned her to wait. Beyond the glass, Chu had started to pace. Not much, only four steps in each direction. He spotted Irina and made the "stre-e-e-etch" motion.

Irina was the first to break the silence. "You are going to be good to me."

Zelig said, "*Of course I am. You know me.*" I sensed he was grinning. Good. Irina handed back the phone.

"*Show me my father and I'll give you the girl,*" I said. My whole job was to keep him on the line.

"*Bullshit,*" he said. "*Give me the girl, and if I feel like it, I'll tell you where your father is.*"

Chu was beside himself. Zelig knew we couldn't find him, and he was having fun. He went on.

"*Some fuckin' gratitude after all I did for him. Hey, you guys find me yet?*"

Chu looked suddenly hopeful. He motioned me to wait, looked at a screen, then motioned me "two" and pointed to his watch. Two more minutes. Stretch. He scribbled another note and passed it on.

"GOING THRU CELLULAR SWITCHING POINT. ALMOST THERE."

Torbett had written something on a notepad, and he held it up to the window: "ASK HIM SOMETHING HARD." There was only one question left to ask, and it was harder for me than for Zelig.

"What about my mother?"

"Ah," he said, "your mother. Hot little piece. Classy." He tried a new word, and it sounded uncomfortable in his mouth. "Elegant. Too good for your father by twice."

"But not too good for you."

"I'm a big man!" he yelled, annoyed. "What's your father? GOR-NISHT!" He almost sang the word. "Nothing!"

"You stay in touch with her?"

Silence. "I'll be damned. You never knew where she was!"

I choked on that. To Zelig, the drama between him and my parents happened over twenty years ago. I was just a footnote. For his money he was talking to the servant's kid. I tried to keep my voice level. "Do you know what happened to her?"

I knew they'd had an affair. I didn't know the circumstances, and I didn't know where she disappeared to. But I could bet he'd tortured her.

"Tell ya something, kid. You guys with your badges and whistles, you think you're so fuckin' smart. Maybe I'm not so smart. But I can hire people who are."

He'd said that before. He liked saying it. He'd probably heard it in a movie. I thought of the female name on Bennett's credit-card list, and I said, "Like your girlfriend?"

"What?"

"The woman you came down here with."

Zelig let loose with a violent string of invective. I counted four straightforward curses, two allusions to inappropriate sexual pairings within my immediate family and one reference to rape.

The FBI crew gaped at me. I'd nailed it. Zelig's fourth man was a woman.

I said, "Suppose you get away with Irina. You can't get her out of the state. You can't go home to Elmira. The feds have you on kidnapping charges and two murders."

I wondered if that was too much information to give him, enough to make him know just how desperate his situation really was.

I shouldn't have worried. He said, *"But I'll HAVE her."* And I realized that he was completely out of his mind.

"Okay," I said. "Where?"

"Gee, I don't know the town so good. You tell me where."

"South mall at the university. MLK just east of Guadalupe. You'll see a big fountain with horses. North of that, a lawn with statues all around it. Wide open so you'll feel safe." We had discussed all this, Chu and Torbett and I. We'd already set the trap, and, if necessary, we could move it to a new location. We would ambush him from behind a dozen statues and buildings. We would shoot low and wound him, question him, get what we needed. I would give him a chance to attack me. Then I'd shoot him high.

"Neat idea," he said. *"But I thought of something better. You had what I want. Now I have what you want."* Then he hung up.

Chu was motioning to me. I ran out of the booth. Lights moved on the projected map.

I said, "You got that we're looking for a woman? He's got a woman."

Reardon held his hand over a receiver. "We got it, we got it. I'm talking to Hayden."

Cathy Bennett said, "Okay, 240, 220 . . . east of I-35, south of MLK . . ."

I heard Torbett whisper something. "Jesus. Jesus . . ." It seemed out of character, and it took me a moment to realize that he was praying.

"Chestnut," she said. "Pleasant Valley. No. Here. This is it." And she pointed to a spot on the projected map like it was the best news we'd ever heard. "Twelfth and Walnut. That's it!"

The intersection by Torbett's house.

I turned to Torbett. He was already running for the door.

A convoy raced down MoPac Expressway in the morning chill. Three Bureau sedans, a van and Torbett's car raced between last-minute shoppers. The helicopter was ahead of us. I called Dispatch and shouted at them.

"This is Reles! We have a hostage situation, repeat, hostage situation at 1205 Walnut Avenue—"

The operator said, *"That's Lieutenant Torbett's house!"*

"Are you listening? Four hostages . . ." Torbett's wife and daughter. Rachel. Josh. Four. "Four hostages—two women, two children. Subject armed, dangerous. Mentally ill. Put . . . put . . ." Wrong time to lose my cool. "Put all the p-patrols you have. Block all the adjacent streets. No unofficial vehicle in or out of those blocks. You hear me?"

"Yes," she said. *"Yes."*

I didn't ask for a SWAT team, but I knew there'd be one. And once they showed, it was their game to win or lose.

I wondered how Zelig had found them. Maybe he'd followed Torbett and me when we traveled to and from the house. But cops check for tails almost unconsciously. And we'd hit the house in minimal traffic.

But Rachel left the Torbetts' and went home, got clothes, probably had a few drinks and headed back. If Zelig or his minions were watching my house, they would know where Rachel was hiding. And Sam Z held that information and waited for the right time.

In Torbett's car, muttering something to herself in Russian, with ghostly blond hair and discount-store clothes, sat the image of the Eastern

European laborer turned sex slave. I hoped she could keep it cool. And I'd told everyone to aim low. We had to keep Zelig alive long enough to tell us where my father was. Just long enough.

We turned off MoPac at Enfield, shot across town and reached the end of Walnut, barricaded by two patrol cars. They cleared the street and let us in, all five vehicles. The bronze LTD Zelig had picked up at the chop shop was nowhere to be found. Torbett jumped out of his car and headed for the house. Chu and I gave chase and had to drag him back to the car.

"Get the fuck off me!" Torbett shouted.

I said, "Rachel's in there too, man."

"You don't know," he said. "You don't know," and in spite of the rage, I could see tears in his eyes. Sure I knew. We could lose everything, more than everything.

Four agents crawled around the house. We crouched behind the Bureau's cars. Chu handed Torbett his phone. Torbett dialed, listened. "Nothing," he said, and we heard the dead line.

Chu dialed Zelig's most recent phone number and handed me the receiver. Why not? I was Zelig's best pal.

He picked up on the fourth ring. *"Boychik!"* he said, with what might have passed for fondness. *"You came!"*

"Sam, this is over," I said. "The house is surrounded. You'll never make it to your car. Throw the hostages out. It'll look better to the jury."

He said, *"You know I'll never see a jury."*

That chilled me. He had Rachel and Josh, as well as Nan and Jule, and he knew he'd be dead in ten minutes. What's more, he didn't care.

Training films tell you that guys in these situations want to die. They want you to pull the trigger, and they want to take as many of you out with them as possible. Maybe Rachel and Josh were already dead.

But I knew Zelig. He wanted to see someone in pain, maybe the hostages, maybe me. But mostly there was Irina. Irina wouldn't do him any good, but he needed her anyway. Maybe he needed one final shot at her before he died: he needed to see her die. It wasn't that he wanted to die himself. He just needed what he needed, to finish the act, the prolonged sadistic act that had begun with her abduction, had increased the first time he hit her and would climax with her death. If the climax resulted in his death too, that was a secondary issue, maybe even a plus. He took our families hostage because it was the only way to get what he needed. And if we killed him first . . . well, he wouldn't need her anymore.

I had more to lose than he did.

Torbett broke for the door. I said, "We're coming in."

"*Suit yourself.*"

I chased Torbett to the door. We drew our weapons. He turned the knob. Unlocked. He pushed the door open and we ran in, separating.

No one in the living room, the dining room. The kitchen. We shoved the guest-room door open. I expected either a shot fired at me or the sight of Rachel and Josh dead. Nothing. The bedrooms, the bathroom. The house was empty.

We ran outside.

"Gone. They're gone."

Chu called his office. Zelig's cellular phone signal was gone. We were fools to think he would give up his location, then sit there waiting for us.

"Where would he go?" someone asked.

"He left town," I said, without thinking why. "He's not gonna stay, not with hostages. He doesn't want to be cornered. He took them and ran."

"Which way?" Torbett asked.

I thought of the options. Torbett's house was a stone's throw from I-35. I said, "He could take I-35 north to Dallas or south to San Antonio."

Reardon said, "That would have him driving right through town either way. Maybe he'd take 290 or 71."

Highway 290 led, with few obstructions, to Houston, a pretty good destination if you were trying to disappear. Highway 71 led to Bastrop.

Chu radioed his helicopter and sent it ahead over 290, looking for a bronze sedan. We piled back into the cars, me in with Chu, Torbett on his own, the others following. I radioed Dispatch and had them call the county sheriff and the police in the town of Manor, the next stop east of Austin on 290.

"*Should they set up a roadblock?*"

"Negative!" I barked. "We have a hostage situation. Keep a tail on him. Keep someone in front of him, too, if you can."

Chu's sedan hit 100 as we roared down the open road.

Five minutes later, the helicopter radioed us. They'd spotted him, about ten miles ahead of us. Chu gunned his Chrysler up to 120. The car shook.

I muttered, "PleaseGodPleaseGod*Please* God . . ."

Torbett passed us, lights flashing. The patrols came up behind. The few cars on 290 cleared the way. I borrowed Chu's phone and dialed Zelig's number. No answer.

The car vibrated like it was going to break apart. The helicopter pilot came on the radio.

"*He's right ahead,*" the pilot told us.

Zelig would see the helicopter and know he was tailed. I dialed his mobile again. He answered. "*Call 'em off or I kill everyone.*"

I had Chu radio the helicopter to back off. We knew where Zelig was.

"Sam!" I said, shouting over the engine. "Let's talk this over!"

"*Nothing to talk about!*" he shouted back. "*Give me the girl, I give you your family. Now.*"

"Listen—"

"*I used to do this funny thing to your mother. I'd tie her to the bed—she hated that—and I'd light a match and touch it to her. Just touch. If she flinched, then she'd get it bad. I'd hold the match against her while it was lit. I started easy, maybe on her arm or her leg. But if she was bad, then I moved in for the big money.*"

It was what Pop had told me about. Piss your opponent off so he won't think straight. Maybe it was bullshit. Maybe Zelig wasn't that bad in those days. Or maybe he did do that to my mother, and more.

I said, "Let me hear their voices so I know they're okay."

"*Fuck you,*" he replied.

Torbett, less than a hundred feet ahead of us, inched up on Zelig's bronze LTD, close enough to pounce.

We came to a crest in the road, and as we climbed and cleared it, I could see the flashing lights of a dozen patrol cars, Manor's finest, creating the roadblock we had told them not to make. I spun channels on the radio. "This is Lieutenant Reles, APD Homicide. Back up. Stand down." It was no use.

Zelig's car might have tried a fast U-turn and headed back toward the city, but there was a deep ravine between the east- and westbound lanes. He cut to the right, into a field. The local cops gave chase, roaring into the weeds, and we had no choice but to follow. Two patrols raced ahead of him and cut off his path. He stopped the car. A few locals by the pavement climbed out of their vehicles and took cover. I jumped out, waving my badge. Torbett climbed out of his car and stood beside me.

"There are hostages in that vehicle. BACK THE FUCK UP!" After some uncertainty the patrols backed up as far as the highway. The ones farther into the weeds gave Zelig more room.

"Get back," I said to Torbett. "He wants me."

Torbett said, "Gonna let him get you?"

Zelig's car had plunged as deeply as it could into waist-high weeds or, for all I knew, corn. He couldn't go forward and he couldn't back out. We had him on multiple charges of kidnapping, plenty for a federal case with or without any other charges. He wanted Irina dead, and now it was for no good reason. He just had his heart set on it.

And he was cornered, with hostages. Chu's phone rang in my hand.

Zelig could see me, standing at a respectful distance, with Torbett about ten feet to my right. Torbett held his weapon at his side. If Zelig shot me, maybe Torbett could get a shot at him, without hitting our families. Maybe. Zelig could have taken me down right there, but he needed someone to talk to. I flipped open the phone.

"Yeah."

"*Send her over.*"

"No. You come out."

And a shot exploded over the field. Before I could figure out that I wasn't hit, I spun to see a figure behind me, in a yellow raincoat and blond hair, a crimson hole in her raincoat as she slid to her knees and fell over.

Torbett and I grabbed her and dragged her back. We scrambled for cover in the weeds while Zelig fired off shots. His bullets cracked windows and ricocheted off cars. An agent got hit. Someone fired off two shots toward the car.

I hollered, "Hold your fire! Hold your fire!" I still had the phone clutched in my left hand as we struggled to get the girl to the other side of Chu's car, where Reardon and Mora could tend to her. I heard something in the phone, someone screaming. It was Josh. "Josh!" I yelled into the phone. "It's your daddy. Josh, can you hear me?"

The shots echoed over the field and settled. I tried the phone. "Zelig?"

"How's my girl?" he asked, with an amusement that bordered on warmth.

"How do you think?!"

"I want to see her."

"Throw the kids out first."

"You still don't get it. I'm a Zelig. You're a Reles. I call the shots. Get those pigs away from the road or I kill your son."

I said, "Do that and you won't have anything."

"So?"

I waved at the Manor cops. "Everybody back a hundred feet. Everybody!"

They looked to their captain and he must have nodded, because they backed up a hundred feet down the highway. Zelig's engine started again and, with a lot of screeching and grinding, pushed deeper into the weeds and stalled out again. I could see enough rustling of the reeds to figure that a car door had opened.

I said, "I'm coming in."

"No weapons."

Mora said, "Don't do it, Reles. It's a trap."

Torbett said, "We'll both go."

I said, "He wants me."

Zelig liked me. I knew that now. Here he was stuck among a bunch of Texas crackers. His only company was the employee or two he had left. I was a New Yorker and a Jew, like him. He thought I had potential when I was a kid. And he probably still thought so. He might want to kill me. But in the few minutes before he did, he'd be glad for the company.

I lifted my automatic out of the shoulder holster, held it high in case he could see me at that distance, and threw it down. Then I walked into the grass. The weeds were high and I couldn't make out details. I couldn't spot any faces in the car's windows, just the car half hidden in the greenery ahead.

I went blind for the second that Zelig's bejeweled right fist slammed into my jaw, tearing my already-damaged cheek as it went. I was down on my haunches, and before I bothered to get my bearings, I punched his knee with all my might. It made him scream and back up but didn't create the crippling break I was hoping for. I pushed down with my legs till I found myself standing opposite him as he lunged for me. I ducked his punch, slammed a right-left-right combo I learned in my teens. The second right hit him square on the jaw, and it felt like I'd punched a Sherman tank. Zelig grabbed at my face and dug his nails in, but I got my arms straight up between his and twisted out of his grip, elbowing him in the mouth as I went. He wrapped his arm around my throat, squeezing hard enough that I couldn't get blood to my head, let alone air. I reached up with my left and grabbed his face, then yanked his right leg from under him. He fell, but he pulled me down with him. One powerful old hand went for my eyes. No time to think.

I punched at his groin, and when he didn't let up, I punched again. And when that finally loosened his hold on my neck, I saw the chance I'd been waiting for since I was a kid. I swung with all my weight. And I cracked Sam Zelig's rotten teeth.

I could feel them giving way, some cracking, others pulling loose from his jaw. He buckled at the waist, covered his bleeding face with his hands and cried out.

He lay on the ground, wheezing, spitting blood and enamel. Suddenly toothless, like an old man. Like a baby. He was seventy-two. And it was all I could do to get the better of him. But it felt good.

I rolled him onto his face and yelled, "Torbett! Mora!"

Mora cuffed Zelig, and I told her to watch him. Torbett made for the car. I went after him and found him holding Nan, with her kid and mine crying at her legs. They were fine as long as you don't understand the concept of trauma. Rachel wasn't there.

"Where is she? Where is she?!"

Nan said, "She's gone. She left after you did. I don't know where she is."

She left. Rachel went out first thing in the morning to get another drink. If there was a place in Austin, Texas, where you could get plastered at 8:00 A.M. on a Sunday, she'd know it. But Zelig could have gotten her. Nan said, "There's another man."

I blinked before I realized what she meant. Both car doors were open. Zelig's other man had fled into the weeds. I yelled something about this to the feds. Then I moved Mora away from Zelig and rolled him onto his back, on his cuffed hands. His mouth was a bloody mess.

"Where's my father?" I asked. "Where's my wife?"

"Fuck you," he said. Talking hurt him. But not as much as when my shoe hit his face.

He spit blood at me.

I started sweating. What did I have that he wanted? I said, "Think about it. Life in the Joint. Not so bad for a guy like you. Sneak in good food, dope. The S&M thing, you'd fit right in. You'd be in charge in a week."

He whispered, "Reles. Reles."

"I'm listening."

He kicked at my legs hard enough to knock me down. I landed hard on my side. Sam Z rolled at me, trying to catch me in his broken teeth or head-butt me. Mora pounded him on the side of the skull with her handgun, then grabbed the loose skin at the back of his neck and pulled him away. I made it to my feet.

"All right!" I shouted. "Let's go, let's go!"

We each took one of Zelig's arms and hauled him up, then led him, staggering, toward the road.

The feds faced us, weapons drawn. They broke formation, giving us a view of the fallen figure in the yellow raincoat, a bloody hole near her heart.

And she rose. In her raincoat and her supermarket sneakers. And she walked. Toward us, into Zelig's line of view. He opened his eyes wide. "No. No."

And she peeled off the wig. *"Zhopu lizhi mnye, yevreichik,"* she said— Lick my ass, little Jew—in what sounded like native Russian but wasn't. Special Agent Cathy Bennett made a better Irina than Mora did. Almost better than Irina herself.

Mechanics. Misdirection. Showmanship.

She unbuttoned the sweater to reveal a bulletproof vest and a plastic bladder, ruptured by Zelig's bullet. Fake blood soaked the vest and the clothes she'd borrowed from Irina.

"No," Zelig muttered.

Chu opened the door of another sedan, and the real Irina stepped out, wearing a bulletproof vest over Bennett's office clothes. They were just the same size. Irina stood, gathering the dignity she was just beginning to remember. And she walked with all she had, each step pushing against her fear, toward Zelig.

He gulped and choked and whimpered. But he didn't tell us where Pop was.

"You lock me in," Irina said, almost close enough to touch him. "You used your men to keep me inside. You cut me. When you could not rape me with your limp old dick, you beat me. I will tell people what a pathetic man you are."

It was just chance that I was looking at Zelig, and not at Irina, the moment she said, "limp old dick." He winced. He crumpled at the words. That was the other reason he needed to kill her. He didn't mind hurting her and a hundred others. He could take being cursed by them. But he was afraid to have people know he couldn't get it up. You never know where someone's fear lies.

"Hey, Sammy," I said. "Is this true? You can't get it up anymore?"

"Shut up," he spat. "Shut up!" And he groaned.

I leaned close to him. "Last chance," I said, talking low. "I won't tell the press about your limp dick if you tell me where my father and Rachel are."

It was just by chance, again, that I was looking at Zelig and not at Irina, that I didn't think to follow his gaze when his eyes widened with electricity and glee and he shouted out, "Top o' the world, Ma!" as a shot fired close by, the blast nearly knocking out my eardrum as Mora and I dove for cover and Irina's second shot hit Zelig in the groin.

Nick Baldo, Zelig's confederate, escaped into the weeds but the Manor cops raced out to find him. They dragged him back, much the worse for wear. He had apparently fallen on his face several times, the cold soil causing multiple contusions. He seemed also to have accidentally cracked his ribs. He insisted he didn't know where Pop was, even on the threat of the cops taking him back into the weeds for a few more falls.

We knew that Zelig had other confederates. It was possible he kept them apart from each other. I was pretty sure Baldo wasn't holding anything back.

The two agents at my house radioed Chu that Rachel had come home drunk, commented on their presence and promptly passed out in the bedroom.

That I'd tossed my gun out of Zelig's reach instead of handing it to another officer was a fact that would bite me in the ass just about immediately.

"You gave her the gun," Chu said as Reardon and another agent hauled Zelig into the back of a sedan at the edge of the highway, figuring they could get him to a hospital before an ambulance would find us out here on the edge of nowhere. Torbett had found some bandages, and I tried to patch my bleeding cheek.

"You should be questioning him," I said. "He's the only one who knows where my father is."

"He's out cold," Chu said. "And no, you can't talk to him. You tossed down the gun so Irina could get it."

Mora countered. "He tossed it out of Zelig's reach."

"You set it up," Chu said. "I walked in on you talking in the break room."

"Why would I want to shoot him before he said where my father was?"

"You didn't plan it that way," Chu said. "She was supposed to wait for something, maybe a signal. Admit you wanted to kill him."

"I—"

Torbett said, "Don't admit anything, Reles." I wasn't sure that Torbett thought I was innocent, only that he wanted to know for real before he handed me over to the feds.

Cathy Bennett, half out of costume, said, "What did that mean, 'Top of the world'?"

"It's from a movie," I said. "He loved movies. James Cagney gets blown up on top of a gas tank."

And we looked at each other, Torbett, Chu, Bennett, Mora and I.

Top of the world.

had only my instinct and a knowledge of the workings of Sam Zelig's diseased mind to tell me that he had set up some disaster at a gas facility, something to replicate the end of a particular James Cagney film. But we had nothing else to go on.

Labeled CITY OF AUSTIN in deco lettering that must have seemed clever and modern when they built the thing in 1920, the Lakeview Gas Facility on Town Lake featured a visual spectacle that was magnificent, yet so slow-moving as to relegate it to near invisibility.

Imagine a steel cylinder, a hundred feet in diameter and fifty feet high, rusted to a deep, earthen orange-brown. Then imagine another cylinder fitting just inside it, interlocked like the rings of a collapsible cup. When the cylinder is empty, it's collapsed at its shortest. But as gas is pumped into it from the pipeline, the smaller cylinder goes up, raising the structure to its impressive full height of a hundred feet. A framework of girders around the structure guides the top cylinder evenly up and down on tracks. Then, once the tank is full, the weight of the upper cylinder forces the gas out through pipes, gravity maintaining pressure in the gas lines that lead to the city's homes, factories and schools.

Now imagine a second holding tank by its side, a twin of the first. As the tower on the right is filling and rising, the one on the left is lowering, pumping gas out to the city. This seesaw spectacle happens at a rate imperceptible to the naked eye, like watching flowers grow. Because the other machinery—pipes and valves—is minimal and underground and because of the lack of action, the facility is unmanned, unguarded and unlit. These qualities make it uninteresting even to stoned teenagers. I know this from experience.

A bulbous fifty-year-old man in white shirt, nylon jacket and baseball hat, introduced himself as Henry Skinner, the acting plant supervisor. His emergency people, he said, were on the way. We split up—Chu, Torbett, Mora and I—and scanned the area.

"Reles!" Mora shouted. I chased her voice. On the farthest side, in the recesses of gas unit two, amid a tangle of weeds, lay my father under a black blanket of heavy wool with leaves shoveled on top. Mora had pulled the blanket down from his pale, sweating face. I dropped to my knees.

"Pop?" He didn't answer. "It's me. Dan."

His lips quivered. Blood reddened the areas around his nose and mouth. The air held a harsh chill, but sweat soaked his shirt. He was in shock.

"Reles." It was Torbett, standing over me. He peeled Pop's blanket away, and my stomach dropped. A web of wires coiled around Pop just tight enough that he couldn't be moved. We didn't have to draw back much more of the blanket to see that these wires attached to a timing device, a unit the size of a small radio. Red and blue wires coiled from the device into a metal box just over a cubic foot in size—a file box you'd buy in an office-supply store, welded to the base of the tank and leaking some kind of goo.

A digital readout counted down. It crossed sixty minutes—59:59:99 and counting. The hundredths of a second raced by.

"Bomb Squad," I said. "Now. And an ambulance."

"On their way," Chu said.

"And get him some water."

The rest of them dropped back to confer. I knelt close to Pop, pulling the blanket up over his shoulders. Zelig had left the wool to hide him, not to keep him comfortable.

"We're gonna get you out of here," I told him. I put my palm to his forehead, something he'd never done when I was a child. I'd learned the gesture from my mother. I didn't know what a forehead was supposed to feel like, but I knew it wasn't supposed to be that cold unless the subject was dead. And Pop was still shaking. I took off my jacket and laid it over his blanket.

Mora came over with a bottle of water. I tipped some into the cap so I could pour drops of water into his mouth. These he took, lapping his tongue against the roof of his mouth. One went too far, and he coughed. I poured some water on my hands and wiped his forehead.

The EMTs arrived first, two of them, hauling air tanks and bandages and a stretcher. They took his pulse and temperature and prodded him and gave him a shot of something, laid another blanket over him and handed me my jacket back. Then one of them whispered something to Torbett—not to me—and they all rose and moved back toward their vehicle. I got in their way.

"Wait a minute. Where are you going?"

Torbett said, "Reles . . ."

"Get back there," I said. "He's sick. Take care of him."

The leader of the medics, the one who'd been giving orders to the other, looked to Torbett.

Torbett said, "They have to leave."

"For what?" I asked. "What's more important than this?" But they kept going until I went after the head medic and grabbed him by the arm. "Let's go!"

"Reles!" Torbett pushed in between us and shoved me away. The medics ran for the ambulance.

I shouted after them. "What are you doing?!"

Torbett lowered his voice, a counter to my desperate plea. "Nothing they can do, Reles. Not here. It's not their job to . . ."

He trailed off. I finished the sentence. "To die?"

I watched the clock. Forty-nine minutes. Forty-eight.

It was another lifetime before the Bomb Squad showed. I sat beside Pop and held my hand on his forehead and talked.

I talked about how brave it was that he'd stood up to Zelig, how it saved my life when he danced in front of Zelig's car. I couldn't think of anything else to give him, so I tried to tell him how good my life was, how I loved Rachel, how we had a son and a beautiful new house. And I kept talking even though it seemed like he couldn't hear, just because it was all I could do. I told him about Rachel's drinking problem, how good things had been before she started drinking again, how I thought it was bad for Josh, how I didn't know what would happen.

And I told him how grateful I was that he'd stuck by me when I was a kid.

I felt something crashing down. All my life I'd hated him for driving my mother away. To me she was an angel. But she left and he stayed. It never crossed my mind until now. She said she loved me, and he never said much of anything. But he didn't leave, no matter what. And she got into a cab and disappeared.

Thirty-seven minutes, and counting.

Finally I heard voices, and the grassy terrain shifted in the presence of the Bomb Squad. They cordoned off the area and warned away the crowd of joggers that had begun to gather. Two fire trucks pulled up on the grass, lights flashing, and stood by, ready for anything. Skinner came over and asked me to move away. I told Pop I wasn't going far.

The rest of the Bomb Squad, shielded in padding and steel armor, moved in on Pop and took away his blankets. They measured, calibrated, deliberated. I stood back with Chu and Torbett and Mora. My knees rattled under me. The officer in charge of the Bomb Squad, nametagged Lieutenant Burke, left the others working. He conferred with Skinner, and the two walked over to us.

Burke, looking something like a Nazi storm trooper, said, "The gelatin leaking out of the box, it's dynamite."

I said, "I thought that came in sticks."

Burke said, "You get it in sticks. Inside is a gel. It's made of nitroglycerine, diatomaceous earth, a few other things. Probably they stole it from a quarry or a construction site, maybe seventy-five pounds' worth, and tore the cardboard sticks open. What's worse is, the hull of the gas tank is rusted and only about five-eighths of an inch thick anyway. The blast would cut enough of a hole in the tank to ignite it."

"What does that mean?"

Skinner looked up at the tower. "Eight hundred thousand cubic feet of natural gas? Figure an explosion seven hundred feet in the air. Shatter any window within a mile or two. Level any building in proximity. You'd want to get some distance."

Downtown wasn't a mile away, and thousands of houses weren't either. I said, "We can evacuate the area."

"No time," Burke said. "We can put it on the radio and TV, but no guarantee people will hear it. We can't go knocking on doors, not with only half an hour."

I said, "Can you let some gas out, dissipate the explosion?"

Skinner said, "Gas weighs more than air."

"So?"

"Think of a tidal wave moving faster than the speed of sound. Only instead of water, it's a wave of fire."

I could picture it, and I knew that the reality was minutes away. About thirty minutes.

Torbett asked, "What are you going to do?"

Burke said, "We're going to try to defuse the bomb. But the wiring is redundant. We could clip ten wires and still get a blast. We can't see where the wires are leading, because they all feed into the sealed box. Any one could be attached to a trip or trigger mechanism. We saw ten pins around your father's body that might set it off if we jarred them. If we find the pins first, we might be okay. But if not . . ." The rest of the sentence wasn't necessary.

He went on. "One of those wires, or more, probably leads to a blasting cap, like a metal-encased firecracker. The electric current will cause the cap to explode, setting off the dynamite."

"You could pull the wire," I suggested.

"If we knew which one to pull. But if the guy who set this is as good as I think, he's created enough fail-safe devices to maintain a state of neutrality."

Torbett said, "Meaning?"

"You cut one wire, you could cause an increase or decrease in voltage and set off the blasting cap."

Zelig was unconscious, laid out in an operating room. And he was still killing people.

"You have a plan?" Mora asked.

He looked at his watch. We all followed suit. Then he took a deep breath and let it out. "We have twenty-seven minutes. If we can take the device apart before it detonates, we'll call the medics in and they can take him."

Twenty-seven minutes. Twenty-six.

Torbett said, "What if you cut away the panel around the bomb? We can lift the old man and the bomb away from the gas."

I gawked at Torbett. He was suggesting that we sacrifice my father.

Burke shook his head. "If we go at it with a saw, there'll be sparks. Any gas escaping will be ignited."

I listened, nodded, turned away. And that would have been the right moment to leave, as I've replayed it in my head many times. But the worry and the sleep deprivation and the fatigue of almost three days of nonstop frenzy all added up to the one act that I had to be crazy and stupid enough for just one second in order to commit, the act that couldn't possibly have made my life or anyone's better. As if it were the only possible action, I reached for my shoulder holster.

I said, "Burke, you get my father out of there!"

I heard Torbett's voice. "Reles." That he happened to be watching me at that moment, that he seemed to have figured out exactly what I was thinking, was enough to freeze my hand in my jacket where it was.

Chu must have been watching us by then, but I couldn't break my gaze from Burke. Torbett said, "Reles, you can't do anything for your father. Anything. You can get yourself thrown in jail. Are you listening? You have a wife and a kid. *That's* your job. You can stay here and die with your father. But if you really want to be a hero, then go home and take care of your wife and kid."

Burke was frozen under my gaze.

The whole thing—everything Torbett said, Mora's familiar grip on my arm, Rachel and Josh waiting for me to come home and protect them, feed them, make sure they got what they needed, just like my father did for me—it all made sense. But it came to me like words in a dream, like an idea remembered from years back. I'm responsible? I have a wife? A son? They're waiting for me?

And here was my father, who hadn't said a word to me in fifteen years, who showed up to put me and my family and my whole town at mortal risk. He needed me, too. And there wasn't a thing I could do for him.

I spun at the sound of an approaching siren, another black sedan rolling up onto the grass. Mora took my hand gently from the inside of my jacket.

The car pulled up to us. Reardon climbed out of the driver's seat, opened the back door and helped out a dark woman of about thirty, short hair, athletic. She wore a blue down coat, black pants and handcuffs. Another agent climbed out of the back seat after her, weapon drawn.

Reardon said, "This is Beth Oren, formerly of the U.S. Army Corps of Engineers. We found her at the airport with Antonia Roque's credit card. Ms. Oren has confessed to setting that explosive. And Zelig's dead."

It caught me off guard. "What?"

Reardon glared at me. "Sorry you weren't there? He died in the operating room. Heart failure. We got word on the way to the airport."

Zelig's death didn't get us out of trouble. Beth Oren's eyes were puffed up. She'd been crying. We escorted her to the squad, who gave way when she appeared. She burst out crying again when she saw Pop wrapped in wires. "I didn't mean to!" she sobbed.

Chu said, "Defuse that bomb and things will go better for you in court."

The clock hit twenty-two minutes and counted down fast. They unlocked her cuffs, and she joined the Bomb Squad.

"Dan?" I heard a choked little voice. Everyone turned.

"Pop?" I couldn't even remember the last time my father had used my name.

The Bomb Squad cleared the way for me to kneel by Pop's head, but they kept working, Oren now among them. His eyes were open now, but he was still stark white and shaking.

"How are you, Pop?"

The injection the EMTs gave him addressed the shock, I guessed. His forehead felt a more normal temperature. I checked his pulse, and that felt something like normal too. He blinked, looked at me, scanned the Bomb Squad, the gas tank, what he could see of his body. He'd been hit by a Lincoln, kicked in the stomach and confined for over a day. Now he was coiled in the wires of a time bomb at the bottom of a natural-gas storage unit. How was he?

"Truth is," he whispered, "not so great."

"Can I get you something?"

"How's the—" Pain gripped him for a moment before he said, ". . . girl?"

I realized that he might not even remember her name. He wasn't in it for love. He was in it for redemption. "She's fine, Pop. She's safe. You did good."

He laid his head back and closed his eyes. I could see a sense of satisfaction.

Burke and Oren muttered between them. Burke said something technical that sounded like he was asking if she could open the box.

"Latching system," she said, as if she'd told him before. "I made it to close once. It can't be opened!"

"Which wire goes to the blasting cap?"

She cried, "I don't know!"

I spoke softly to Pop. "I found out about Mom and Zelig," I said. In his weakness I could see suspicion rise, apprehension. He'd gone to great lengths to keep me from learning that. "You looked out for me."

He closed his eyes a moment, then opened them. "That's *two* good deeds."

"Yeah."

"And I'm only . . . seventy."

I put my hand on his forehead. He felt warmer.

Burke and Oren had another exchange. I missed the details, but Burke was laying out some possibility and she was nixing it. She'd boobytrapped the bomb four different ways. He asked her why.

She said, "Do you think this was my idea?!"

Zelig wanted us dead. But he wanted to drive us crazy first.

I said, "Pop. Zelig is dead."

His jaw dropped. "You're kiddin'."

"No. Dead and gone."

I could see Pop relax as an unseen force lifted his burden. Irina had walked free, and Zelig was dead. He got another idea. I saw it light up in his eyes.

"I outlived Zelig."

"Yeah."

"I'm the last *makher*."

I'd never seen him look happy with himself before.

"Yeah, Pop."

He scanned the area. He wanted to see how far his fame had spread. Then he dropped his head from the exertion.

I squeezed his hand. He looked up at me, and his eyes almost sparkled. Then he closed them, looking very restful, squeezed my hand and pushed it away.

The clock reached fourteen minutes.

Burke rose. Torbett, Mora and Chu grabbed me and started to pull me back. The five of us stood in a tight circle.

Burke said, "We can't drill the box for fear we'll create sparks. We can't bend it open and draw out the explosive with a tube because it's welded quarter-inch steel and the wires are motion-sensitive. We can't pull them because she doesn't know which is which, and any wire could set it off."

Torbett said, "What *can* we do?"

There was a deadly silence among us, even in the presence of the fire trucks and the soft movements of the Bomb Squad.

Pop had sacrificed himself for me, and for a woman he barely knew. It was hard not to be grateful.

I could spend what little time we had to work with by trying to save his life. But half the town hung in the balance. I had a job to do, and a family also. What was more important? Or, more to the point, who could I save?

My mouth opened and I heard the words, "Can you break the bomb away from the gas tank?"

The rest of the circle—Chu, Torbett, Mora, Burke—shifted. "What?" Burke asked.

"The box is welded onto the gas tank. Can you get a blowtorch and burn it loose?"

Burke didn't pause. He ran over to talk to Oren and the squad.

Torbett said, "You know what this means?"

"Of course I know what it means!" I spat. "You think I'm stupid?"

One of the bomb techs ran over to the fire truck, and they started uncoiling hoses. Another ran back to the Bomb Squad van and unloaded some equipment. Burke walked back to us.

"One of the fail-safe devices these people like to use is a magnetic switch. You pull the box away from the tank, the current changes, and you set off the device. She didn't use one."

"So?" Mora said.

"We do Reles's idea."

I could see one of the Bomb Squad flick a flint and set off the roaring flame of a blowtorch. The firefighters stood by with a hose. The welder worked on the box of dynamite.

Burke said, "We'll keep the tank as cool as we can. Heat could ignite it, but only in the presence of oxygen. We just need to get that box loose without setting it off or cracking a hole in the tank."

I watched the burst of sparks from the blowtorch. Mora took me by the shoulders and turned me away. "Don't go blind," she said.

Chu said, "Let's go, Reles."

I broke free from both of them. "Get away from me."

Mora said, "There's nothing you can do here."

"Go home," I said. "I'm staying."

Torbett and Chu exchanged a glance.

Torbett said, "There's nothing any of us can do, not here."

I shook my head. I wasn't going anywhere. Torbett and Chu headed across the grass without another word.

"Look, boss," Mora said. "I'm with you. You know that by now." I looked over her face. She meant it. She went on. "I'll take a chance if it'll make a difference. But that motherfucker's gonna go off in"—she checked her watch—"eight minutes. And I don't want to be here when it does."

"No one's asking you to."

She was quiet a moment. Then she pointed to where Torbett and Chu had disappeared. "I'm parked just across that grass. I'm leaving the engine running and the door open, for seven minutes. Then I'm gone."

I nodded.

She added, "Am I a coward?"

"No. No. Go on."

She put a hand on my shoulder and squeezed hard. She turned away. Then she stepped close and put her mouth near my cheek.

I felt her warm breath as she whispered, "If you stay here and die with him, you're a fucking idiot." She ran across the grass.

The firefighters held the hose, trickling a steady stream of water against the tank. Then they turned it off and retreated. I walked close as two Bomb Squad workers took hold of the box, held it steady and, with a single movement, cracked it away from the tank.

The digits counted down past four minutes.

Two firefighters showed up with an army-style stretcher, sheets stripped to reveal a smooth black vinyl pad, and laid it flat on the grass next to Pop. A bomb tech and Oren slipped in between Pop and the tank, gently laying the box next to him.

"We need hands," Burke said.

There must have been nine of us kneeling around Pop—five bomb techs, two firefighters, Oren and me. Oren held the bomb against Pop's side.

Burke said, "Without moving the old man, slip your hands under him. Now."

I knelt, reached over the stretcher and slid a hand under Pop's head, another under his shoulders. Four other people held similar positions.

Burke said, "When I say 'ready,' we're gonna lift him and set him down gently on the stretcher."

Tears dropped from Oren's eyes. Pop lay still with his eyes shut, opening and closing his mouth.

Burke said, "Ready? Lift!"

We raised Pop's small body just an inch off the grass—he seemed to weigh nothing—and slid him onto the vinyl pad of the stretcher. Oren had kept the bomb pressed against him. She set it on the stretcher by his side.

"That's it," Burke said, and one of his techs rolled out a length of silver duct tape, wrapping it around the stretcher, the device and my father.

That's when it hit me what we were doing, what I'd suggested. They had taped the bomb to Pop. They would never peel the tape off.

"Clear out," Burke ordered, and everyone gave him a wide berth. Oren, the firefighters, even his own team, made for the hills. "You wanna help?" Burke said. "Grab the other end. Keep it level. Don't trip."

We crouched and gently hoisted the stretcher, Burke in the front by Pop's feet, me in the rear. We headed away from the tank, closer to the river.

The counter read two minutes. "Burke . . ." I said.

"I know. Here."

We climbed over a slight incline, maybe a hundred feet from the tank, and then laid the stretcher and Pop down on a piece of level mud at the river's shore. Burke wasted no time running for cover.

I leaned close to my father and tried to take his hand. "Pop . . ."

He waved me off. Go. Don't worry. Take care of your things.

There are decisions you make that, no matter how right they seem, are wrong. You reach for your Browning automatic to threaten the Bomb Squad leader, as if that'll help him save your father's life. You run around trying to protect your father, while your wife and kid hide out at someone else's home, defenseless.

And there are decisions you make that, no matter how wrong they feel, are right. Your wife and kid need you, even if she needs a drink more, even if he doesn't seem to like you. And there isn't a thing in the world you can do for your dying father, except die with him, and that wouldn't help him any. So you turn your back on him. You're so weak you can barely walk. You stumble up the incline at the river's shore and find your friend, in her idling car, shouting, "Run! For God's sake! Run!" And behind you your father shakes and sweats and waits.

And as you jump into the car and it screeches away, with you still reaching to pull the door shut behind you, you think how God called Abraham to sacrifice his son, how this time Abraham refused, told God to fuck off, danced in front of God's limo. And the kid turns around and sacrifices his father.

The sun shone bright as we tore off onto Lake Austin Boulevard, then east on Cesar Chavez Street toward downtown. We got about a mile away before we heard the blast.

After the death of Moses the servant of the Lord, the Lord said to Joshua son of Nun, Moses' attendant:

"My servant Moses is dead. Prepare to cross the Jordan, together with all this people. . . . I charge you: Be strong and resolute. Do not be terrified or dismayed. . . ."

—Joshua 1:1–9

I sat outside the conference room on the Fifth Floor in my rumpled jacket and tie, politely ignored by Mrs. Heron, a civilian secretary in her sixties, as I awaited my time with the chief, like a kid called to the principal's office. Mrs. Heron answered the phone five times in as many minutes, each time saying, "No, he's not in. . . . No, *he's* not in either. . . . Let me transfer you to Public Information." She seemed flustered, but I didn't give it any thought. The events of that morning still shook me, marked by the fresh stitches in my cheek following Zelig's punch.

After the emergency room released me with some pain pills and antibiotics, I managed to find Zelig in the hospital. The conversation was a touch one-sided.

They'd left him in a private room for a requisite two hours before moving him to the morgue, on the chance any loved ones wanted to say goodbye. But he didn't have any loved ones. He'd spent his seven decades making enemies, taking everything they had and, often, killing them. Now he lay with a sheet pulled up to his chest, his arms above it and at his sides, palms curled upward. He wore a delicate white hospital gown with short sleeves. His huge, hairy arms looked pale and green under the lights. His lips caved in where his front teeth had been. He wasn't Sam Zelig anymore. And still I had to shove him to make sure he was dead.

Zelig, his surgeon told me, had lost his balls, something he'd feared all his life. Even in their absence, he might have lived to torture more innocent girls, or to create a new fortune in Internet gambling and cellular phones, as he'd planned. But his heart, never as strong as he thought it was, gave out on the operating table. The doctors failed to bring him back. The postmortem showed that he had blocked arteries, high blood pressure and astronomical cholesterol. It was amazing he'd lived to be that old, a nurse commented.

His life spanned seventy-two years. He'd survived prison terms, rival gangsters, a decades-long FBI investigation and a shot in the balls from a wronged woman. But it was the steak-and-eggs breakfasts that killed him. Life is funny.

After I left the hospital, a call on the radio brought me straight to HQ. I waited for Chief Cronin to call me in for my hanging. My cheek hurt from the stitches. I'd taken several punches and blows to the head and body over the last three days, and a few to the gut. I couldn't remember the last time I'd strung eight hours of sleep together, or even five. In a half-dream state, I imagined what was in store for me.

They would blame me for raiding the chop shop with no warrant. Chu would testify against me for tossing the gun to Irina. Torbett would get me for withholding evidence and for using my office to protect my father. Halvorsen would kick in his testimony about my prejudices against him. And Mora would toss in something about our affair of eight months earlier, adding sexual harassment to the fire.

Cronin would blame me for bringing Zelig to Austin and, by extension, for the blackout and the blast at the gas facility. I would lose my job and my pension. I'd need a new job. It would have to be something related to my background, so whatever it was, Rachel would hate it. Maybe I'd become a security consultant. I'd design the system that protected the mall from shoplifters and weenie waggers. Or I'd talk to Miles, my old CO, about getting me work at the DA's office, the last bastion of fallen cops. Worse came to worst, I could hang out a shingle and become a private investigator. I knew a few in town, but they tended to work white-collar and financial crimes, and they tended to turn up dead.

The few people situated to see the explosion at the crack of brunch on Christmas Eve would say, variously, that it looked like a burst of flame, a car fire or a grenade. But not a mushroom cloud. And not seven hundred feet high.

Considering the shape Pop was in, the noise alone would have killed him. As it stood, the detonation was so thorough as to render burial unnecessary.

Top of the world, Pop.

I'd been cooling my heels for a solid twenty minutes when the secretary's phone rang again and she answered it. "Administration." She listened. "Oh, my. . . . Oh. . . . Okay." She hit two buttons, and a voice came from the intercom.

"Yes?"

She looked at me, then talked close to the intercom. "Never mind. I'll be right in."

She got up as fast as her arthritic legs would allow and made quick, tiny steps toward the office door of Assistant Chief Oliphant, disappearing inside and closing the door behind her.

Something possessed me to get up and tap on the conference-room door. No answer. I opened the door. Empty.

I knocked on Chief Cronin's door. Also empty. No one at Cronin's desk. I closed the door just before Mrs. Heron and Assistant Chief Oliphant stepped from his office, Oliphant striding with authority toward the elevator, tapping the DOWN button with a strangely peaceful expression on his face. Mrs. Heron returned to her desk.

The elevator opened and Oliphant stepped in, the doors closing behind him

"What's going on?" I asked.

Mrs. Heron said, "Nothing. Nothing." I stood by the elevator and watched the numbers. It went down to the first floor.

"Mrs. Heron," I said, staring hard at her, and she looked up from her desk, fearing attack. "What's going on?"

She didn't come up with another answer, and I took to the stairs, two at a time, until I reached the main floor. I followed the flow of traffic in the lobby out the front entrance, out to the bricked steps.

The press had gathered again, along with a crowd of civilians and a crowd of cops. I was too far from the center to hear what anybody was saying or even figure out who the principals were, but I knew that one of them was Assistant Chief Oliphant. I worked my way around the periphery and stopped dead when I came to a familiar face. Slim, graying, bespectacled. A reporter with no camera. I'd seen him the night of the blackout.

"*Statesman?*" I asked.

"That's me." He grinned. He had a pen and pad, but he wasn't working too hard to take notes.

I asked, "What's going on?"

"That's funny," he said. "You asking me that. It's almost like the press has some kind of responsibility to tell people what's going on."

"You're not taking notes," I said.

"I got my story. In today's paper."

"Do I have to go pick it up?"

He pulled me away from the crowd. "You must know about that guy who died in custody."

"Sudden in-custody—"

"Yeah," he said, laughing. "Donald Ray Penner. Police stopped him with a bag of something, called him a looter, said they wanted to search him. Donald Ray spoke up. Refused to be searched. And they shot him with a taser. It's funny me telling you this stuff. You really owe me."

"I'll remember. What happened?"

"Well, you're not supposed to taser anyone in the chest, especially if he has a history of heart trouble, which they couldn't have known, except that he was in his late fifties and overweight. Maybe they were just lousy shots. One of those new tasers that shoots a barb from a few feet away. Naturally, Donald Ray goes down flat, muscles seizing, and by the time they figure out he's had a heart attack, it's too late to get him to the hospital. And they look in his bag, and there's a pack of flashlight batteries and a gallon of water. He was holing up for the blackout."

"Shit."

"Did I mention who the two cops were? I'll give you a hint. Both their names start with the words 'Assistant Chief.'"

"Oh, Christ." The two white assistant chiefs, Macaffee and Bueller. They went out during the blackout, armed with guns and batons and tasers and no street skills to speak of. They came back with a corpse.

"Yep. Two dumb white office jockeys find a black man coming home from the bodega and taser him to death. That's not the hook, what makes my article the award-winning epic it is. The hook is that less than an hour before the tasing, Cronin sent his administrators onto the street with a 'take no prisoners' order."

I'd witnessed this, when Cronin said, "No arrests." But I wondered who leaked it. "Where'd you hear that?" I asked.

"I protect my sources." He winked. "You may be one of them one day."

I pushed through the outer layers of the crowd, the reporter at my heels. I got close enough to see Assistant Chief Oliphant as he shook hands with a mature black man in a dark suit. A community leader. Cameras flashed.

And Oliphant looked pleased and calm, as if nothing about the situation had ever worried him.

As I drove away from the building, I couldn't stop thinking about how serene and happy Oliphant looked approaching the press, as if he knew what was going to happen before it happened, in spite of the fact that his two colleagues and his boss were about to be roasted on a spit. It was hours later when, in the absence of an available alternative, Oliphant was named acting chief.

I made it to Torbett's house to get Josh. I knew he didn't see me as a father, but he'd gotten used to me. He knew I was the most likely and regular source of breakfast and dinner and whatever else he needed. And I had been gone God-knows-where for over a day, a long time to a little kid, all while he got shuffled around and kidnapped, a living nightmare. I entered Torbett's living room to see Josh sitting on the couch. He looked up at me, his face sad, pained, hopeless. But he didn't fight when I scooped him up.

Come September he'd be starting kindergarten, spending half a day with other kids and no Mommy. This business of being with other kids was hard work for him. Whatever skills a kid needs to go out in the world, we hadn't given him yet. We had about nine months to get him ready. It seemed like a tall order.

I got him home, made soup and a sandwich and put him down for a nap before I went into the bedroom to check on Rachel.

Sun filtered through an orange sheet the FBI had tacked over the window. She lay still, with her hair half across her face. I almost lost her features in the haze. I sat on the bed. She groaned at the motion.

"How are you?" I said.

"Sick."

"Sick sick or hungover sick?"

"Does it matter?"

"Where'd you go."

"For a drink," she said. Then, "Shut up."

"I didn't say anything."

"I went for more than one drink. I went for a lot of drinks. But I didn't do coke."

"You could have been killed."

Her voice cracked in a rough whisper. "You're never home."

"That's not true," I said, but I knew it was true once, years ago, and the unpredictability had taken its toll. I felt like I owed her for all those times I'd answered calls in the middle of the night, all those broken dates. But Josh didn't.

She groaned, "It's your fault I'm like this."

I took that one on the chin. She'd had a pretty good run of not drinking before I came along, something like ten years. And while the event that got her drinking again four years back wasn't my fault directly, I'd dragged her into it. There was no question that she would have been better off without me back then. I hoped to make up for that.

But she'd ditched Josh twice to go drinking. That couldn't happen again.

She went on. "Dan, I have no idea where I went. Give me a rest."

It sounded meaner than I meant it when I said, "How much rest do you need?"

"I'm *tired*!"

"No!" I shouted. "You're always tired. You're always sick. You have a son. He needs you."

Her face crumpled up like a baby's. "I try to stop."

"Well, *stop.* Just fuckin' *stop!*"

"I hate myself for this!"

I said, "Take a shower. Get dressed. You'll feel better."

She nodded and settled back onto the pillow. "Soon," she said.

I kissed her on the cheek and very gently said, "Now." Then I pulled off the blanket.

"No," she groaned, pulling her knees up.

"You're not the kid here."

"I just want to feel normal."

"I've met lots of normal people," I said. "They always turn out to be child molesters. Look, I'm sorry for everything I did. I'm sorry for what your father did. If I was there, I'd have killed him. But it was a hundred years ago!" And I shouted, *"Grow the fuck up!"*

Rachel and I had come to a crossroads. She couldn't take much more of the cop life. I couldn't take much more of her drinking.

She offered a solution. I jumped at it.

There's James Torbett standing in the front row with Nan Torbett and their daughter, Jule. There's Medical Examiner Margaret Hay. There's my old CO, Miles Niederwald, now an investigator for the DA's office, looking nearly sober himself. There's my buddy Jake Lund and his wife, Lynn, Jake here on unofficial business and not even doing me a favor. And there's Josh.

The carpet and walls swirl with various shades of burgundy and maroon, except for the stage set behind the rabbi. There's the Ten Commandments in Hebrew, eight feet high. I can't imagine Moses carrying one of these tablets, no less both. There's two stained-glass windows reaching up to the sky.

There's my father standing beside Josh, one hand on Josh's shoulder. This looks perfectly natural to me. I blink and it's not Pop. It's Jake. Of course it's Jake.

There's a canopy over our heads. And there's Rachel, sober as a Christian.

Naturally, a synagogue in central Texas isn't the hardest room in the world to book on Christmas day. Rachel insisted on it. She didn't want to be affiliated with her parents' religion, whatever that was. She didn't want to be married by a judge or have anything to do with a judge or with any part of the legal system. And she wanted Josh to be part of something.

Rachel wore a dress of blue silk. I wore a blue suit. It wasn't a maiden voyage for either of us. We'd aged ten years since we met, when she was married to my best friend. We'd been through a lot, together and apart. She'd gone through a pregnancy and five years of drinking. I'd been shot at, stabbed, bitten, burned and dumped in a river. She knew what she was getting, and so did I. And I felt lucky.

The wedding ceremony, if we thought about it, was more of a break from our life than a way out. I thought of Rachel as my wife already.

The rabbi said something in Hebrew and something in English and I didn't get a word of any of it. What I did get was that he placed a crystal wineglass in a soft velvet sack and put it on the floor in front of me. Considering the circumstances, it seemed more like Rachel should be the one to break the glass. Rachel must have read my thought because when I looked up her eyes locked with mine. We still understood each other.

I raised my eyebrows, a question. Do we crush the wineglass, for good?

She closed her eyes, then nodded.

I stamped on the glass.

There were cheers and a sweet kiss from Rachel, and Josh broke from the front row and ran for us, shouting "Daddeeeee!" I reached down, and he jumped up into my arms, hugged me and reached for Rachel.

It was the first time he'd called me Daddy. It turned out that he had a unique understanding of the day's ritual. He'd been told for months that I was his father, but he'd never bought it. It had something to do with a scientific process that was no concern of his. As far as he knew, a daddy was the man married to Mommy. Glad to hear it, kid. Thanks for having me aboard.

I took two weeks' vacation, a fraction of what I had coming to me. Whatever disciplinary measures might have been heading my way disappeared with Chief Cronin's sudden retirement. I'd return to the work that Rachel hated, but that wasn't today's problem. We'd work it out when we got to it.

We took no trips over the holidays as a couple or a family. Rachel didn't drink, and I didn't arrest anybody. We unpacked our boxes and bought drapes and decorated the new house. Rachel still refused to allow a Christmas tree but authorized Josh to buy whatever lights he wanted. He wrapped them around the TV and the lamps and the living-room chairs and gazed at their blinking splendor. He had fun.

Looking back, I should have guessed that a few magic words from a rabbi in a language none of us understood weren't going to fix anything between me and Rachel. She'd still have a drinking problem, and I'd still have to make a living. The week after Christmas was her longest dry stretch, she said, since before Josh was born. It seemed to hurt. I should have seen that it wouldn't last, that she had a bad binge coming on, made more severe by the thirst she'd worked up over the week. Hoping for the best, I saw the signs, but I ignored them.

I wish I hadn't.

New Year's Eve we went to bed early. I dreamed I was in the boxing ring with my father. He was young, the age he was when I was in high school, but I was grown up. He was teaching me to duck and weave, to keep moving constantly. Then I was outside the ring watching Pop and me, only it wasn't me in the ring, it was Josh. Josh padded around the canvas, moving, dodging right and left, throwing fake jabs at Pop.

Then we're in a mobile home, a trailer, propped up on blocks somewhere in the mountains of western New York. There's a bunch of people, a party, then there's just me and Pop. I say, "Wow, it feels like we're moving."

He says, "We *are* moving!"

The walls are gone and replaced with chain-link fence, which we grab onto, each holding one side, as the trailer barrels down a winding dirt path in the wind, somehow following the twists in the road, past ravines, along a cliff and a fifty-foot drop, across a bridge that spans a river.

The wind is whipping past us, and Pop glances at me, making eye contact, a goofy grin on his face. Then he turns his face into the wind, and I can tell that he's enjoying the ride.

Dirty Sally

Michael Simon presents the first in a series of ferociously paced crime novels set in Austin, Texas. The time is the oil-bust year of 1988. The detective is Dan Reles, a New York–born Jew marooned among good ol' boys and unhinged by the violent death of his partner. His career depends on solving the case of a murdered prostitute whose body is arriving in grisly installments at inconvenient locations. As he tries to find out who killed "Dirty Sally," Reles starts crossing the lines between his town's crack-ridden ghettos and the watering holes of its moneyed elite.

ISBN 978-0-14-303531-2

Body Scissors

The year is 1991. Operation Desert Storm is raging and Texas has war fever. But Detective Dan Reles has battles of his own to fight, not least the attempted assassination of a prominent black activist. A stray bullet, a chase across Texas, and a strange disease cutting a path through college campuses all add up to Reles finding himself up to his eyeballs in a miasma of murder, sex, and drugs—and up against a killer who might just get him first.

ISBN 978-0-14-303805-4

Little Faith

In this pulse-quickening thriller, Michael Simon continues to do for Austin what James Ellroy has done for L.A. It's 1995 and Texas has a new governor, the heir to a political dynasty. As pols and lobbyists converge on the capital, a former child star and recent porn actress is found murdered and a thirteen-year-old boy is sent out to make a treacherous living on the streets. This is just some of what Dan Reles—Austin Homicide's leading loose cannon—has to deal with in this gritty mystery from Simon.

ISBN 978-0-14-311231-0